8 E 25-9. 0?

CW00373500

Gwen Madoc lives in Swansea with her husband, Harry. She worked as a medical secretary and managed a medical clinic before joining the Civil Service. She studied for five years with the Open University. She loves Swansea and its people, and has a keen interest in local history.

Daughter of Shame

Gwen Madoc

CORONET BOOKS

Hodder & Stoughton

First published in Great Britain in 2000
by Hodder and Stoughton
First published in paperback in 2001
by Hodder and Stoughton
A division of Hodder Headline

A Coronet Paperback

10 9 8 7 6 5 4 3

A catalogue record of this book
is available from the British Library

ISBN 0 340 79278 7

Printed and bound in Great Britain by
Mackays of Chatham PLC, Chatham, Kent

Hodder and Stoughton
A division of Hodder Headline
338 Euston Road
London NW1 3BH

For my dearest husband, Harry.
Thank you for your patience, love and support.

Chapter One

THE RHONDDA VALLEY, SUMMER 1920

Jenni trudged on, leaning forward against the steep incline, the thick leather soles of her boots striking the tarred surface of the road with a satisfying clatter. She'd miss that when she'd saved up enough of her wages to buy a pair of real shoes. Patent leather ones, if she could afford it. Saving the money would take a long time but there was no hurry, was there?

She was tempted to pause and pick a few daisies and buttercups from the grass verge. Mam loved the little posies she brought home sometimes, even if the flowers were often dusty and coal-specked.

But today was Saturday, her half day off, and she wouldn't waste a minute of it. She hurried because her belly was rumbling with hunger, and also because her father was home for the first time in many months; since last September, in fact. He hadn't come home for Christmas last year, hadn't even written. Now, suddenly, he was back.

Jenni persevered up the steep mountain road, feeling the midday sun on her shoulders through her white cotton blouse. She was hot in her narrow navy blue serge skirt with its hem that almost touched the tops of her button-sided boots.

She didn't know whether she was glad her father was home or not. Seeing so little of him in her life, she couldn't help viewing him as a stranger — one who periodically interrupted the cosiness of her relationship with her mother.

Yet she owed him a debt of gratitude, didn't she? He'd given up his savings so that she could have her dressmaking apprenticeship. He must think something of her, after all.

She *was* grateful, yet a feeling of resentment lingered, too. Why couldn't her father work in the mines around here like other men in Trehafod, she wondered not for the first time, instead of going off to the Forest of Dean, leaving her and Mam for months on end? He'd been born in Gloucestershire, but Trehafod was his home now. Why wasn't he content to earn his living where his family dwelled, like other men? It was a question she'd never dared ask him.

In the brightness of midday, Jenni squinted up the road ahead of her. A few more steps and she'd be able to see the first house in the village. The sight always cheered her, especially when glimpsed through drizzling rain.

And there it was! Dappled with sunshine today. Not much further to go now. She'd soon be home, tucking into one of Mam's beef suet puddings, with jam roly-poly to follow. And Mam sitting at the table with her, wanting to know how she'd got on with her training that day, and what the Misses Jukes had said and done. Then they'd have a good old giggle together, because the Misses Jukes were so comical and didn't even know it.

At the thought of the meal waiting for her, Jenni wanted to break into a run. Before she could take the next step, however, the hedgerow just a yard or so in front of her was forced aside and a burly figure jumped out on to the road.

'Hey you — Jenni! Jenni Goodenough. Ha, ha! Or maybe that's Jenni Not Goodenough!'

With a suppressed groan of annoyance she recognised

Ogmore James, one of the wilder village youths and the bane of her life.

She glared at him, unafraid, even though he was a year or two older and much larger than herself.

'Out of my way, Oggie, or I'll kick your shins black and blue!'

'Oh, there's scared I am! Look, I'm trembling.'

He grinned broadly at her, standing square in her path, gaitered legs apart and fists on his hips, like a prize fighter.

Jenni tried to dodge past him but he intercepted her move, planting himself in her path again.

'Warning you, I am, Oggie!'

His face creased in a frown.

'Don't be like that, mun, Jenni. Been waiting for you, haven't I?' He grinned again and chanted, 'I know something you don't know.'

Jenni could feel her temper rising. Oggie James was loud and uncouth and vulgar, just like the rest of his family. She didn't need her mother's warnings to keep away from him. But Oggie wouldn't leave her alone, that was the trouble. He was always following her, mocking her, trying to snatch the bow from her plait; jumping out at her from hidden places. Why her? She couldn't understand it.

'Like a big kid, you are, Oggie,' she said scathingly. 'I'm not playing silly games. I'm going home for my dinner.'

For some reason Oggie thought this hilarious. He hooted with laughter, doubling over in glee. Jenni took the opportunity to slip past him, breaking into a run as best she could up the steep hill.

He whirled round in a flash, lunging after her, gripping her arm and bringing her to an abrupt standstill.

'Let go!'

She snatched her arm from his grasp, kicking out savagely at his ankles. He laughed as her flying boot went wide of its mark.

'Jenni redhead! Pretty Jenni with her nose in the air! Jenni

Not Goodenough anymore. You're just like me now, Jenni. Just like me.'

She was about to take another angry kick at his ankles but paused, perplexed by his words and his expression of barely suppressed excitement.

'*Twp*, you are, Oggie. Stupid idiot, that's what you are!' Jenni exclaimed cuttingly. 'What are you on about anyway?'

Something was on his mind, Jenni could see. He acted like an idiot, but she knew from past experience he was as cunning and crafty as any vixen with cubs.

'Haven't told you what I know yet, have I?'

He was grinning again in a way that set her teeth on edge.

'If you don't stop pestering me,' she said in a threatening tone, 'I'll tell Dai Book and Pencil about you. Then you'll be in clink, like your da.'

Everyone knew Oggie's father was in prison for trying to rob the Post Office at Penybryn. Oggie's four older brothers were just as worthless, and the tales Jenni's friends had told her about Oggie's mother had made her blush, even though she thought herself almost grown up at fifteen.

Still, she might have felt sorry for him if he hadn't elected himself her tormentor. Now she despised him, lumping him together with the rest of his no-good family.

Oggie scowled.

'Dai Book's got a lot more on his mind today than me,' he said. 'Like I was trying to tell you, Jenni, he's at *your* house. He's come for *your* da.'

She curled her lip in disdain. Oggie was a liar as well as a pest. What would the police want with her da, anyway?

'You're a fibber, Oggie James,' Jenni yelled. 'I'm going to tell Dai Book about you as soon as I've had my dinner.'

Oggie reached out and gripped her wrist tightly, yanking her forward so that she almost lost her balance. His expression was triumphant.

'Don't you get on your high horse no more, Jenni Not Goodenough,' he said harshly. 'You're no better than me. Your da's going to clink, too, see.'

Jenni was struck dumb for a moment by his awful words. Then suddenly she was in a rage with him for trying to frighten her.

'You dirty liar!' she screamed. 'You're horrible, you are, Oggie James, telling lies about my da. And I've had enough of you.'

She sprang forward and savagely raked her fingernails across his cheek. Yelping with pain, he let her go and jumped back out of reach.

'Get you for this one day, I will, Jenni.' He glared at her in impotent fury, pressing a hand against his injured face. 'Bad blood,' he muttered darkly. 'There's bad blood in you, Jenni. That's what my mam says.'

'Your mam!' Jenni's tone rang with contempt. 'She'd know all about bad blood, wouldn't she? From what I've heard!'

'How d'you mean?' He looked genuinely puzzled.

Jenni raised a hand threateningly, fingers curled in a claw.

'Stay away from me in future,' she panted, anger hot on her tongue. 'Or I'll scratch your eyes out next time.'

Oggie took a few steps back, his face reddening even more.

'Dai Book's got your da in handcuffs, so there!' he shouted belligerently. 'So *you* got nothing to be stuck up about. They've sent down to Merthyr for the Black Maria – your da'll rot in prison. And serves you right, Jenni Not Goodenough!'

She turned and raced up the hill as fast as her legs would carry her, Oggie's continued taunts resounding in her ears.

She whimpered as she ran, in between gasping for breath. He was a barefaced liar and God would strike him dead. He was trying to frighten her, just for a joke.

All the same, she couldn't move fast enough now. She had to get home to reassure herself that her father was safe.

When she reached the corner of Ysgol Street, she saw a crowd of people hanging about on the pavement near her home;

neighbours and strangers, too. A black van stood at the curb, the big chestnut horse between the shafts pawing at the road as though its feet hurt.

In terrible dread Jenni moved slowly forward. Someone in the crowd turned and saw her. There was a general murmur and fingers pointed in her direction. She advanced slowly and the crowd gave way as if she was royalty or else a leper.

The tall figure of Dai Book and Pencil emerged from the doorway of her home and came towards her. Silence settled on the crowd.

'Jenni, *bach*, there's been . . . an accident.'

'Where's my mam?' she wailed.

She tried to rush forward into the house, but Dai's hand was firm on her shoulder. She struggled furiously, angered that he was keeping her from her beloved mam.

'Jenni, *cariad*, you must go with Mrs Bevan by here. She'll take care of you until . . . until arrangements can be made.'

'I want my mam!' Jenni screamed. 'Mam! Mam! Where are you, Mam?'

Someone came and put warm arms around her, hugging her tightly. Jenni looked up hopefully into her face, but it wasn't her mam. It was only Mrs Bevan from next door.

A tall man, wearing a black bowler hat, appeared from inside the house, followed by two uniformed policemen. They were strangers, but the man who walked between them was very familiar. It was her da!

George Goodenough was in shirtsleeves, wrists handcuffed in front of him. His face was chalky white, eyes staring straight ahead as if sightless.

'Da!' Jenni screamed, struggling against Mrs Bevan's restraining arms.

George Goodenough turned his gaze in her direction and stared at her fixedly for a moment, as if he didn't recognise her. Then his eyes widened.

6

'Jenni!' he exclaimed desperately. 'I didn't mean it. As God is my witness, I didn't mean it.'

He tried to move towards her but the policemen's hands tightened on his shoulders and he was bundled forward into the waiting van, lost to Jenni's sight.

Chapter Two

TREHAFOD, THE RHONDDA, EARLY AUTUMN 1919

Sarah Goodenough placed the coins on the scrubbed kitchen table, one after another, in two separate piles, counting as she did so. Eleven shillings for the rent and nine shillings and sixpence for food and housekeeping. Not quite a guinea. The value of the postal orders George sent her each week never varied.

Never once did he ask her if she needed a little extra; something for herself. She hated asking him for anything more, and might wait an hour for his answer when she did. While he mulled it over she felt like a beggar.

He was due home tonight on his usual monthly visit to them. The homecoming was always tinged with anxiety on her part. Would the visit be different this time? Could she please him? Would there be one glimmer of warmth in his greeting?

Distracted, she ran nervous fingers through her hair, then remembered she must fix it in a tight bun at the nape of her neck before he came home. She was proud of her abundant auburn locks and loved to wear them loose around her shoulders, but George would frown if he saw her like that. Just frown; nothing more.

Sometimes she wished he would shout at her, even strike

her perhaps — anything to show how he felt; to show he *had* feelings. But he never touched her now, not in any way.

Tonight, though, she had to make a beggar of herself. She'd wait until his belly was full of mutton, suet dumplings and vegetable broth. Maybe that would mellow him enough to favour her plea. She wasn't asking for herself. It was for Jenni.

Sarah absentmindedly twisted the wedding ring on her finger. Jenni *must* have what her mother couldn't have. Independence. Freedom to choose her way of life. Sarah's mind had been made up years ago: her daughter would have a trade, a livelihood at the back of her that would make her independent. She need never be trapped in a loveless marriage; never be beholden to any man.

She'd drummed that into Jenni, and knew her young daughter understood. Being your own woman was of the utmost importance. It could be done; the war had proved it. Women were doing extraordinary things these days. There was no hope for Sarah herself but Jenni *must* have the chance to live her own life, be her own woman.

Sarah glanced in the big mirror over the mantelpiece framing the kitchen range, lifting her hands ready to twist her hair into a bun. Then she let it fall back over her shoulders again.

She'd wait until after Bert Herbert came for the rent. It always gave her a lift nowadays to see the open admiration in his eyes. At one time she'd dreaded their weekly encounter; now she eagerly anticipated his call, in no doubt about Bert's feelings. It made her blush sometimes, the way his gaze devoured her. George had never looked at her like that, not even when they were first married.

Sarah avoided her own gaze in the mirror. She shouldn't be thinking about Bert at all, much less about the desire she read in his glances. It was disgraceful, and her a married woman. And Bert was disgraceful, too. But he was a man, and men were like that. That is, most men. But not George.

Sometimes she wondered if he had another life, unknown to her, in the Forest of Dean. Some other woman whom he really loved? She almost wished he had. At least it would explain his disinterest. But if he loved another woman, why would he come home to Trehafod at all? For Jenni? He took hardly any notice of his daughter; never encouraged or questioned her about her future. Jenni was as neglected as Sarah herself.

Sarah was proud her daughter had inherited her stature and colouring; average height, auburn hair, green eyes. At fourteen, Jenni was already pretty and growing into a beautiful young woman. That beauty must not be wasted on an uncaring man, to wither away through his indifference. She didn't care what she had to do to ensure her daughter's escape to a better life; to real love.

Sarah set her jaw in determination. Tonight George would be made to see that he had to provide for Jenni's future. Otherwise . . .

She turned and met her own reflection with a steady gaze.

Otherwise, she might be forced to do something desperate.

Bert Herbert rapped on the door and lifted the latch before Sarah had time to answer.

For a long time she'd met him on the doorstep with the money ready in her hand. Somehow, though, he'd insinuated himself inside her home. A glass of water. Use of the lavvy in the yard. She couldn't remember his excuse. Now he gave only a perfunctory tap on the door before stepping into the passage and straight through to the kitchen.

People might notice his interest. She should choke him off, be firm with him about it and get things back on a less personal footing. But again today she let it slide.

"Morning, gorgeous!"

'Now stop that, Bert.' Sarah flicked back her hair, always

embarrassed by the warmth of his tone. 'There's your money on the table.'

'Oh, aye. No rush, is there?'

'Yes, there is. My man's coming home today.'

She always referred to George as her man. It was pathetic really, wasn't it? George was the man whose name she used; the man who paid the rent; the man with no love to give her. And she needed, wanted, love. She needed the kind of glances Bert was giving her now. She really felt like a woman when Bert was around. He made her feel . . .

Sarah pushed those thoughts aside. They were dangerous and just thinking them made her feel dizzy.

'Your man must be *twp*,' Bert said softly. 'How can he stay away from you, *cariad*?'

Sarah tilted her head.

'Don't you be familiar with me, Bert Herbert. I'm no sweetheart of yours.'

Bert's eyes glinted, and his smile was one-sided.

'But if you *were* mine and I worked away, I'd go barmy wondering who you were with and what you were getting up to . . .'

Sarah tossed her head, pretending to take offence.

'Don't know what you mean, Bert Herbert. I don't get up to anything when George is away.'

His smile was sly now, his gaze steady on her face.

'But you could, though, Sarah. You could get up to anything you like with me – any time you like.'

He was going too far. He was insulting her, wasn't he? She should order him out. Why didn't she?

Sarah stiffened, confused by her own feelings. Her legs trembling, she moved quickly so that the table stood between them.

'I don't like that kind of talk,' she said primly. 'You'd better take your money and go.'

Unabashed, Bert sat down at the table.

'How about a cup of tea, lovely?'

Sarah bit her lip. She had given him tea on a couple of occasions when she was feeling very down, and very lonely; when she'd ached for a bit of comfort and warmth. It had been a mistake, a bad mistake. Bert obviously thought there was more to be had. He was becoming bolder each week. She must put a stop to it before . . .

'No, Bert. Jenni'll be back any minute.' Suddenly she felt rattled. 'Anyway, you've got a blooming cheek! Anyone would think we were . . . friends.'

'We could be,' he said, softly. 'Real friendly, like. You must be lonely, *cariad*, on your own so much.'

Bert had a soft voice for such a big man. He was quite good-looking, she decided. She remembered, back in wartime, seeing him home on leave, an impressive figure in his uniform. A real Tommy Atkins: brave, dashing and nobly romantic. She wondered why he wasn't married.

As he looked at her now, with that ill-concealed fire in his eyes, she knew. One woman would never be enough for him. At least, she pondered, none of the women he'd previously known.

Sarah shook her head to clear those thoughts. They would lead her along a perilous path if she paid heed to them.

'Lonely and . . . hungry,' he went on. There was a breathless quality to his voice.

Sarah felt her face flame. She snatched up the rent from the table and held it out to him.

'Not going to listen, am I?' she answered tartly, refusing to look at him. 'Do you say such awful things to other wives?'

He grasped her fingers tightly around the money.

'Only you, Sarah, *cariad*. I swear to God!'

His grasp was so tight he was hurting her, but perhaps he didn't realise it. His gaze was intense, inflamed, and Sarah's heart began to thump even harder in fright.

'Bert! Don't . . .'

She snatched her hand away and the coins fell on the mat, some spinning away across the linoleum.

He took a rasping breath.

'It's all right,' he said thickly. 'I'll get them.'

She watched him on his hands and knees, stretching under the Welsh dresser to retrieve the last one. George would never do that. It was undignified.

She had retreated to the door of the scullery by the time Bert was on his feet again.

'Sarah . . .'

'Go on! Go!' she cried out. 'You've been in here too long already. Her next door will notice.'

He took a step forward.

'I don't have to take the rent this week, mind, Sarah. We could come to some . . . arrangement.'

'How dare you?' She felt outraged and close to tears.

He shook his head, as though denying he'd said anything wrong, taking another step forward. She retreated further into the scullery.

'Sarah, *cariad*, I can see it in your eyes, mun. I can *feel* it when I stand near you. Your man — what does he really mean to you?'

'Get out, Bert Herbert! Get out and never speak to me again.'

She slammed the scullery door in his face then leaned against it, her heart pounding, her cheeks already wet with tears.

She was humiliated, shamed. To think that she was so transparent, her need so painfully obvious. Who else realised it, saw what Bert saw?

Sarah's hand flew to her throat in anguished shame. She must be the talk of Trehafod! Gossiped about in the sewing circle at Soar Chapel; sniggered over in the pubs on a Saturday night.

What would George say if he ever found out?

*

At teatime Jenni came home. Sarah bustled about, trying not to think too much about the episode with Bert Herbert. She'd concentrate on the coming evening with George, instead. Silently, she rehearsed what she'd say, and how she'd say it.

'Is Da home yet?' Jenni asked.

Sarah glanced at her daughter sharply. Jenni didn't sound her usual cheerful self. It was boredom, Sarah decided. At fourteen she wanted to take a job, like some of the other girls, but Sarah wouldn't allow it. Jenni was meant for bigger and better things. There'd be no tuppenny-ha'penny job for Sarah Goodenough's daughter.

'Not yet,' she answered. 'What have you been doing all afternoon?'

'Me and Dilys climbed to the top of Bryn Coch. There's wild ponies up there, Mam.'

Jenni was absentmindedly pushing bread and cheese around her plate.

'Dilys's da is taking her and her brother Hughie down the funfair over in Llanbedws this evening. She said I could go with them if I liked but . . .'

Sarah seized on the opportunity.

'Oh, that's a good idea, love.'

It would be better if her talk with George was in private. With Jenni out of the way she could speak freely, tell him exactly how she felt for once.

Jenni looked up, concern in her wide green eyes.

'Mam, why is it my da never takes *me* anywhere? Doesn't he like me?'

Sarah moistened her lips, her heart suddenly aching.

'Da works hard down the mines, Jen,' she answered with difficulty. 'When he comes home he needs to rest, especially after travelling from Gloucester.'

It was awful to have to make excuses for his negligence as a father. How much longer must this go on?

Jenni pushed her chair back from the table suddenly and jumped to her feet.

'Well, why can't he work round here, then? I hardly ever see him. When I was still in school he never once came to see me in the St David's Day concert. All my friends' fathers were there. Some of the kids used to tease me that I didn't have a da.'

Sarah's lips thinned.

'Which kids?'

Jenni pouted.

'Well, Oggie James for one.'

'Oggie James!' Sarah was appalled. 'You keep away from him, Jenni. His family are the next down from tinkers. They're a disgrace to Trehafod. I don't want you associating with him in any way.'

Jenni wrinkled her nose.

'I wouldn't anyway. He smells!'

Sarah wasn't surprised. Only yesterday down at the Co-op she'd heard some women gossiping about Peggy James, Oggie's mother. The things they said about her were enough to make your hair curl.

Sarah paused for thought as an idea turned her blood cold. Were those same women gossiping about her, too, behind her back? Had they noticed Bert Herbert's partiality for her? People always blamed the woman, and it was so unfair!

Sarah pulled herself together. She wouldn't think about that right now. There was something more important to consider. Jenni's future. If she trained as a dressmaker she could go anywhere to work, maybe to one of the big towns: Cardiff or Swansea. There'd be decent, respectable men to meet there, and she'd be her own woman.

'You must go with Dilys this evening,' Sarah said firmly. 'It'll cheer you up. Maybe I'll have a nice surprise for you when you come back.'

'What, Mam? What?'

'Wait and see.' Sarah indicated Jenni's plate. 'Now you finish your bread and cheese, and be off up to Dilys's. And here's thruppence to spend at the fair.'

Jenni's face lit up.

'Oh, Mam, thanks!'

Jenni had been gone half an hour when George arrived. Sarah helped him out of his coat and hung up his haversack behind the kitchen door, while he sat down in front of the range and removed his boots.

'Is everything all right?' he asked.

Sarah nodded. No arms open for her; no eager kiss for the wife he'd not seen, let alone touched, for a month.

She looked at him closely, consciously comparing him with Bert Herbert. George was of medium height and build. His sandy hair was thinning a bit, she noticed. His skin was as white as ever, except here and there where coal dust had stained the pores with unearthly blue markings. No amount of scrubbing would remove those, the miner's trademark.

'Where's the child?' he asked as he placed his boots neatly to one side.

Sarah felt a spurt of anger. What a strange way to talk about his own daughter.

'Jenni,' she exclaimed with emphasis. 'Her name's Jenni. Is that so hard to remember, George?'

He glanced up at her in mild surprise but remained silent.

'She's gone to the funfair over in Llanbedws,' Sarah went on, half surprised herself that she'd been so forthright for once.

'A funfair?' He frowned. 'Bit young, isn't she, to be traipsing about on her own?'

'She's with Tom Lewis and his children. Quite safe.'

If he really cared, Sarah thought angrily, he'd be here day in, day out to see that she was safe. But he didn't care. That was becoming more and more obvious to her.

She put a basin of broth on the table in front of him, with a thick wedge of crusty bread. He ate slowly while she sat, impatient for him to finish.

Sarah rehearsed her words again. There were no interruptions to her thoughts. George apparently had no questions to ask about the intervening weeks when she and Jenni had been here alone. What did he think she did with herself throughout those lonely hours and days . . . those lonely nights?

Suddenly she wanted to tell him about Bert Herbert. To say: 'George, a man tried to make love to me today in your home, in this kitchen, right where you're sitting. He wanted me, George, the way a real man wants a woman. What are you going to do about it?'

But of course she kept silent. She could never tell anyone about what she saw in Bert's eyes. It was too . . . Sarah searched for the word . . . precious.

George pushed the empty basin away eventually, left the table and went to sit in the old rocking chair near the range.

'That was very nice, Sarah,' he said. 'You're a good cook.'

She was partly mollified. He appeared to be in a good mood. Now was the time to ask for Jenni's premium. But suddenly she felt curious about the quality of the food he ate when away. She knew absolutely nothing about the other life he led.

'You miss my cooking, then?' she asked slyly.

He leaned back in the chair, rocking gently.

'I've been well provided for up until now,' he said. 'When I go back, I'll have to change digs.'

'Oh?' Sarah's curiosity mounted.

'My landlady died.'

'Died?' Sarah was startled. She'd had visions of a youngish landlady, attentive and willing; the right sort of company for a man separated from his family.

'She *was* seventy-six,' said George. 'A good age. I'm not looking forward to starting in a new place. I've lodged with Mrs Pomford for quite a few years. I don't like change. I won't go back until Thursday, I think.'

A week! He hadn't stayed home that long for years. Suddenly Sarah felt elated. This week could change the rest of her life if she was clever and used the days, and maybe nights, to her advantage.

She sat on the wooden chair opposite him and picked up her basket of darning.

'What do you do with yourself, George, in your spare time?'

She'd never considered asking him before, half afraid he'd reveal a satisfying other life in which she played no part. But now he'd told her about his aged landlady, she wanted to know more.

'I mean,' she went on, 'you're not working all the time, are you? The pub, is it? With your workmates?'

He looked at her for a moment, his face expressionless.

'I read.'

'What, all the time?'

'Most of the time. I'm not much of a one for company.'

Sarah wanted to laugh outright at the absurdity of it. She'd been his wife for fifteen years yet it was still necessary for him to tell her of his likes and dislikes. They were no better than strangers. Didn't he see that? Or maybe he did!

She swallowed down her sudden resentment, not wanting to seem riled. He'd be here for a week. Plenty of time for her to work on him, for Jenni's sake . . . and her own.

'George, there's something important I want to talk about,' she began. 'Jenni's future.'

'How is she doing at school?'

Sarah tried hard not to feel vexed.

'She's fourteen, George. She's left school.'

He looked mildly surprised again.

'I suppose she's looking for work? Nothing much in Trehafod for a girl, is there?'

'Exactly! And Jenni's set her heart on dressmaking,' Sarah blurted eagerly. 'Took her over to Llawr-y-bryn last week to see the Jukes sisters, didn't I? They're willing to take her on as an apprentice straight away.'

She glanced down at the hole she was darning in the elbow of her daughter's navy cardigan, one Jenni had knitted herself. And fine work it was, too.

'The apprenticeship is for three years, and there's a small weekly wage. But . . .' Sarah swallowed hard before continuing '. . . there's a premium to pay. Twenty-five pounds.'

She knew it was a lot of money, but she was sure her husband had it. After all, he gave her the same amount each week for the housekeeping, even though prices had continued to rise since the war. He lived a steady life, according to him. So there must be some money saved. Surely he could spare it for Jenni? It was her birthright after all.

'George?'

He leaned forward to pick up the poker, thrusting it into the hot coals, lifting them slightly so that the flames flared up, renewed.

'Don't want much, do they?' He sounded amused rather than sarcastic.

'I want her to have it, George,' Sarah said firmly. 'She must have the security of a trade. I don't want her to be . . . beholden.'

He pursed his lips as though considering, then shook his head.

'No, I don't think so, Sarah.'

'What?'

'It's not worth it for a girl. She'll be marrying within a few years, I expect, then have babbies. It'll be all wasted.'

'But it'd be security for her, George!' Sarah stood up suddenly, letting the basket slip from her lap. 'She must have something to fall back on.' A way out, she wanted to add.

'She'll have a husband,' he said, calmly. 'That's all the security she needs.'

'But suppose she's left . . .'

'Suppose! Suppose!' George was frowning up at her from the rocking chair. 'I've said no, Sarah. I see no need for it.'

She was furious.

'*You* see no need!' She stood over him, shaking. 'You see nothing George Goodenough! You don't want to see. You're not interested in your daughter, and you're not interested in me either. Why do you come home at all?'

He stood up and Sarah stepped back, suddenly conscious she'd gone too far. Yet his face was expressionless still, though a tiny nerve flickered near his right eye.

'You're overwrought,' he said.

'Oh, I'm that all right!' she gasped. 'You're a neglectful husband, George, and a negligent father.'

With trembling hands, she released the pins holding her hair in place, letting it fall over her shoulders like a plush red curtain. Her hair was beautiful, she knew it was. It sent Bert Herbert crazy. Why didn't George see what Bert saw?

'Why are you never curious about how I spend my time, George? Tell me that! Aren't you jealous about who I see? Other men would be.'

There was a fleeting reaction visible on his face, but it passed too swiftly for Sarah to read it. She felt she'd scored a point just the same.

'I always believe you to be a respectable, moral woman, Sarah,' he said stiffly. 'I wouldn't dream of doubting you.'

'Yes, of course!' she sneered. 'I have a husband. What else could I possibly need? Only, I *don't* have a husband, do I? You're never here. I'm alone. Alone, lonely and . . . hungry.'

Why couldn't he see the need in her as Bert did? But now she'd confessed it to him she felt vindicated by her outburst. Whatever happened next would be his fault.

'I can tell you, that isn't going to happen to my Jenni,' Sarah rushed on. 'She'll have a better life. I'll do anything I can to make sure of that. So think again, George, and think carefully. Will you give me the money for Jenni's premium?'

Without a word he moved past her to the foot of the stair-case in the far corner of the room.

'George!' she screeched at him. 'Don't walk away from me as if I'm of no consequence! I demand an answer.'

He paused with his foot on the first stair, but didn't look back at her.

'I've changed my plans,' he said flatly. 'I'm going back to Gloucestershire tomorrow.'

George was up early the next morning and didn't even answer when Sarah asked him if he wanted laverbread and bacon for breakfast. She made a pot of tea. He drank it in silence.

Then he was reaching for his cap, jacket and haversack and starting his long walk, a good five miles, down the mountain to the railway station in Cwmgelligors.

He went without a word or a look. She might have been invisible. Sarah was glad Jenni wasn't up to see him go like this. She wondered if she would ever see him again, and suddenly didn't care. She had no husband, just a name. All she wanted from him now were his postal orders each week.

When Jenni got up Sarah busied about, a plan already in her mind.

'Where's my da?' the girl asked.

'Gone.'

'Gone!' Jenni stared at her, uncomprehending. 'But he hasn't been home a day yet, Mam. Is he angry with me? Did I do something?'

Sarah bit her lip in consternation. It was hard on Jenni, being virtually fatherless. She'd been on the point of telling her daughter the truth, but suddenly realised, at Jenni's words, that the girl might blame herself for her father's reaction.

Sarah could understand such feelings. She'd hardly slept herself for wondering whether the rift between George and herself was all her own fault. She'd come to the inescapable conclusion that the fault lay with George alone. There was something lacking in him; some deadness within that couldn't be reached or remedied, and there was nothing she could do about it.

'Not at all, love!' Sarah tried to sound brisk and untroubled. 'He had to go. Some kind of problem with his lodgings. I expect he'll try and come back next week.'

Jenni didn't look convinced.

'How did you enjoy the funfair, then?' Sarah asked jovially, trying to distract her.

Jenni cheered up immediately.

'Oh, it was great, Mam. I had a go at the coconut shy, and rolling-the-penny. I won sixpence! Spent it on having my fortune told by a gypsy, didn't I?'

Sarah tutted.

'What a waste!' But she was curious. 'What did she say?'

Jenni looked excited.

'She said I'll never want for anything all through my life.'

It was fanciful but suddenly Sarah felt gratified. That would indeed be the case if Jenni could get the apprenticeship. And Sarah would set about that this very morning.

'What else?' she teased. 'A tall, dark, handsome stranger?'

Jenni tilted her head shyly.

'She said the man I will love will use a needle and thread to make his living.'

Sarah gasped and stared then studied Jenni closely. Was her daughter teasing her in return?

'Don't tell me your fibs, you little monkey!'

'Honest, Mam!' Jenni nodded emphatically. 'She said the man I marry will be good but not perfect. What did she mean, Mam?'

Sarah couldn't help smiling at the gypsy's crafty prophecy.

She was on safe ground there. Some men were good, but what man *could* be perfect?

'Is that all she said?'

Jenni frowned.

'There was something else but . . .'

'Well? Go on, Jen!'

'She wouldn't tell me. Said there were some things best left unknown.'

Sarah sniffed disparagingly.

'Gypsies can't tell you the future anymore than I can. A waste of sixpence!'

Jenni tossed her head.

'Well, I think I got my money's worth anyway, Mam.'

Sarah relented.

'So long as you're happy, my lovely girl, that's all right. But hurry up now and put on your best Sunday dress. We're going down to Llawr-y-bryn this morning to see my cousin Blodwen.'

'Oh, why, Mam?' Jenni wailed. 'Blod Thomas is horrible!'

'Hey, now!' Sarah's tone held a caution. 'She's Auntie Blodwen to you, my good girl, and don't you forget it.'

Jenni looked sulky. 'She's not my auntie, though, is she?'

'Never mind,' Sarah returned firmly. 'There's a bit of business I want to talk over with Blodwen. So you be nice to her, right?'

Sarah didn't add that Jenni's future might depend on it.

'Don't like her, I don't,' the girl cried. 'And she don't like me. She hates children.'

'Being a spinster, she's just not used to them, that's all,' Sarah said. 'Now, best behaviour, mind, Jenni.'

She knew just how her daughter felt, though. Blodwen Thomas was a difficult woman and Sarah wasn't looking forward to the coming meeting either.

Blodwen was the only child of Sarah's mother's eldest brother, and a lot older than Sarah herself. Spinsterhood was Blodwen's lot, though not from choice, Sarah was certain.

Blodwen's father had been the local undertaker in Llawr-y-bryn, and had also owned the dairy. Although Blodwen didn't have a husband, she'd never needed to go out to work. So there was money there, bound to be, and plenty of it. It was surprising some enterprising man hadn't snapped it up, despite Blodwen's vinegary disposition.

Since her cousin would never have a child of her own, she might well take an interest in Jenni. Sarah had to admit the possibility was remote but it was worth a try. If Blodwen would give, or even lend, the premium money, Jenni's future would be secure.

The only trouble was, Sarah had to acknowledge, she and Blodwen had never really got on. Still, she was determined that nothing, nothing at all, would stand in her daughter's way, least of all family animosity.

She wasn't looking forward to asking, begging even, a favour from Blodwen, but looking at her pretty daughter across the table, Sarah knew she would go to any lengths, suffer any humiliation, to secure Jenni's happiness.

Chapter Three

Terrace after terrace of small, dark stone houses clung precariously to the steep foothills around the village of Llawr-y-bryn. Blodwen lived in the last house in a street high above the main road, the imposing majesty of Zion Chapel right next door. As Sarah climbed the front steps from the pavement she wondered how Blodwen managed in winter when ice and snow were thick and dangerous.

The brass knocker was polished so thoroughly Sarah could see her reflection in it and took advantage of the fact to adjust her hat. Like Jenni she was wearing her Sunday best, keen to make a good impression on her cousin.

Sarah lifted the knocker and gave it a resounding tattoo, then waited.

'She must be out,' Jenni said, obviously hopeful.

She was restless and shuffling her feet. Sarah knew she was already bored with the visit. She herself half-hoped Blodwen was out. But that would mean returning another day and it was no good putting it off. She might weaken and then Jenni's future would sink without trace. Blodwen was their last hope.

As she was about to knock again the door opened, just a little, and Blodwen peered round the edge at them. She stared at them blankly, apparently not recognising her relatives. Well, it was over a year since they'd met, perhaps nearer two.

'Yes?'

'Hello, Blodwen,' Sarah began, trying to smile serenely. 'Brought my Jenni to see you, haven't I?'

Recognition glimmered in Blodwen's small dark eyes, and her mouth tightened.

Oh, dear! Sarah thought, with sinking spirits. She's going to be difficult. After a few seconds' hesitation Blodwen opened the door wider, looking at them questioningly. No invitation to step inside, but Sarah was determined.

'Long walk down from Trehafod, it is, Blodwen,' she said meaningfully. 'Took us near an hour. Jenni here is thirsty.'

Anyone else would have welcomed them in with open arms, Sarah reflected bitterly, with true Welsh warmth and generosity. Obviously reluctant, Blodwen stepped back to allow them into the passage.

'Only water I got, mind,' she said with a sniff. 'You'd best come in the kitchen. Just cleaned the parlour, I have.'

Anywhere else they'd be shown into the best room; offered a share in whatever was on the table.

Keeping her feelings tightly under control, Sarah followed her cousin down a passage pungent with odours of carbolic and furniture polish.

In the kitchen a cup of water was provided for Jenni who drank it dutifully, her green eyes fixed on her mother in protest, while Blodwen stood by silently, not inviting them to take off their coats.

Without being asked, Sarah pulled out a kitchen chair and sat down. She would have liked to remove her coat, and her hat, too. It was hot in the kitchen, with the fire in the range well stoked up. A copper kettle was already steaming gently there.

Sarah eyed it ruefully, running her tongue over her lips. A cup of tea would go down a treat now.

'How are you, Blodwen?' she began, her gaze searching her cousin's face for some sign of warmth but finding none.

She looked much older than when they'd last met. Her thin hair was scraped upwards and secured in a meagre bun on the top of her head. It was an unattractive style, and made her large nose look more prominent than ever. Her figure, dressed in black as always, seemed squarer and dumpier. But Blodwen had never made any effort with her appearance.

'Why d'you ask?' Her glance was steely. 'It'll be a long time before I'm a customer of Teifi the Box, if that's what you're hoping.'

Sarah was nonplussed for a moment, and then piqued at the suspicious nature of her cousin's thoughts. Death had never even crossed her mind. But, mindful of her mission, she replied carefully: 'I'm asking because we haven't seen each other in a while, have we?'

'You was down in Llawr-y-bryn last week,' Blodwen returned accusingly. 'Saw you going into the Jukes' shop, I did. Didn't bother to call here, though, did you?'

Sarah couldn't have planned a better opening to the reason for her visit.

'Oh, yes.' She smiled, eagerly, ignoring the tartness in her cousin's voice. 'Seeing about an apprenticeship for Jenni, I was, with the Jukes sisters. They'd be delighted to take her. She's such a bright girl, you know, Blodwen. She deserves a good chance in life.'

She pulled at Jenni's arm.

'Sit down by here, Jen, *cariad*.'

Jenni sat obediently, but her face was screwed up in protest.

'The thing is, though, Blodwen,' Sarah went on, a confiding tone in her voice, 'they want a premium, you know. Twenty-five pounds.'

Blodwen looked down her large nose.

'What you telling me for?'

Sarah swallowed, a little nervous now.

'Well, I was wondering . . .'

'Oh, wondering if you could squeeze it out of me, was you?' Blodwen exclaimed sharply. 'Well, you've got some neck, you have, Sarah. Why don't you ask that husband of yours?'

Sarah felt her cheeks flush but hung on to her temper determinedly. Blodwen was deliberately trying to get her goat. They'd never been friendly, not even as girls. She was well aware that her cousin's jealousy of her went very deep. Sarah had been popular in her girlhood with many friends and suitors, too, while Blodwen, sour and plain, had watched from the sidelines. Her cousin obviously couldn't forgive.

Maybe she should have made an effort to be friendly years ago, Sarah speculated now, but remembered that Blodwen's very unattractiveness had put her off. Now she regretted her own carelessness.

Sarah bit down on her lip before answering, reluctant to admit her failure to persuade George.

'Her father won't hear of it,' she said quietly. 'Because she's just a girl.' She gazed up at Blodwen appealingly. 'That's not fair, is it? You and I never had the chances we should have had, did we?'

Blodwen sniffed.

'I didn't need chances or anything else. My father provided well for me.'

Sarah couldn't help running an appraising glance over Blodwen herself, seeing her drabness; and although spotless, how bleak the kitchen was, with its bottle green and brown walls and the rag mat on the floor in front of the range. The rest of the house would be as clean as a new pin, but equally dark and spiritless.

'And where's it got you, Blodwen?' she couldn't stop herself from asking bitterly. 'Stuck by here, never been anywhere or done anything worthwhile. That's because you were never given a chance, see.'

'Got my chapel, I have,' Blodwen said defensively. 'Staunch Baptist, I am, through hail and snow; never miss a service. And respected as well. You ask anybody round here.'

'Doesn't stop you being lonely, does it?' Sarah said quickly, feeling sure she was making headway.

'Don't you look down on me, Sarah Goodenough,' retorted Blodwen, suddenly angry. 'For all your fast and fancy looks, you're not doing so well, are you? Can't even persuade your own husband to give you the money. Seen through you, has he?'

Sarah got hastily to her feet, her heart beating a little faster.

'What d'you mean?'

Blodwen's thin lips were pursed in disapproval.

'Coming here, trying to get money out of me! It's sinful, that's what it is. But I'm not *twp*, you know.'

'What do you mean — "seen through me"? What are you implying, Blodwen?'

Her cousin sniffed disdainfully, looking Sarah up and down. The clothes she was wearing were not new by a long chalk but they were good, and she knew how to look after them and make them last. Sarah was smart, something Blodwen would never be, and wouldn't understand either. Her jealousy was never more obvious.

'All dressed up, like a . . . well, a loose woman!'

Sarah gaped, appalled.

'*What!* How dare you?'

'Oh, don't get high and mighty with me!' Blodwen's lip curled derisively. 'You've always been full of fancy ways and frivolous notions, Sarah. It's sinful the way you carry on. And you're teaching your child bad habits as well.'

Sarah lifted her chin angrily.

'You're so eaten up with jealousy, Blodwen Thomas, you don't know what you're talking about. You can't help being plain,' she said cuttingly. 'But you could at last try cultivating a bit of charm. No wonder you could never get a husband.'

'Oh, you spiteful hussy!'

'And you're a drab and dried up old prune!' Sarah flared, suddenly losing control.

'Mam!' Jenni cried out. 'I want to go home.'

'Be quiet, Jenni!'

Sarah was quivering with anger, and couldn't help snapping at her daughter. She'd made a complete hash of her mission, but it wasn't all her fault.

'Get out of my house!' Blodwen stormed.

'Gladly!' Sarah snapped. She glanced around her with disdain. 'It's more like a hothouse than a home anyway. Feel the walls closing in on me already, I can, and we haven't been here five minutes.'

Blodwen tossed her head.

'Well, at least it's not a sinful house.'

'What?'

Blodwen gave a tight, sly smile.

'I know what goes on up in Trehafod. Got friends up there, I have, mind. They tell me the rent man always leaves your house until last. There's funny, isn't it?'

In panic Sarah glanced around at Jenni to see if she was taking anything in. But her daughter was already in the passage, her hand on the door knob.

'What are you getting at, Blodwen?'

Her cousin's mouth stretched into a sneer.

'Bert Herbert is well known around here. There's a piece living at the top of Megan Street . . . takes him a long time to collect the rent from her, too. Well, we all know it's more than the rent he's picking up, don't we, Sarah?'

She stared at her cousin for a moment, feeling the heat rise in her cheeks but unable to control it.

'Your house is spotless, Blodwen,' she said at last through clenched teeth. 'Pity you don't keep your mind just as clean. It's filthy! You're a frustrated old spinster, that's your problem. No man will look at you, let alone touch you. You're so repressed, you see . . . *sex* everywhere.'

Blodwen gaped.

'Don't you utter that disgusting word in my house,' she cried. 'A clean-living, respectable woman, I am. Staunch Baptist. I have Pastor Williams here to tea every Sunday. Now then!'

Sarah felt her lips twitch at the irony.

'Oh, right! Hoping one day he'll pick up more than a Welsh cake, is it?'

Blodwen's eyes opened wide, and she seemed to rock back on her heels.

'Get out, you brazen hussy!' she screeched. 'And take your brat with you.'

Walking down the steep street towards the main road, Sarah's legs felt stiff and heavy. She was still trembling with rage, and shock, too. So people in Trehafod were already talking about her? It made her face burn to hear that, especially as she'd done nothing to deserve their gossip.

She thought back to the previous evening with George. He'd left this morning without a word, and somehow she'd felt this had set her free. She didn't owe him anything so why should she worry about his good name? Perhaps if he hears talk, she reflected, it might bring him to his senses.

'Are you all right, Mam?'

Jenni clutched at her hand, squeezing gently.

Sarah tried to smile brightly.

'Of course I am, lovely girl,' she said. She wanted to sound cheerful, but she realised her voice was strained. Jenni was young, but no fool.

'She upset you, Mam. The old battle-axe! I hate her.'

Sarah couldn't help smiling at the passion in Jenni's voice.

'She's inhibited, that's what it is,' she said. 'You should feel sorry for her.'

'What's inhibited, Mam?'

Sarah bit her lip, regretting her careless talk.

'It's when someone's so . . . shy, she doesn't even take her vest off to have a bath.'

Jenni's peals of laughter were a tonic.

Feeling a little better, Sarah linked arms with her daughter as they walked home. Jenni was all she had. Sarah had failed with George and with Blodwen, but she was determined she wouldn't fail Jenni. Somehow, some way, she'd get the money for the premium.

Unbidden, an image of Bert Herbert's face came into her mind's eye. He'd made some suggestion about the rent, hadn't he? Of course, it was unthinkable. Out of the question. She wouldn't stoop that low. Yet people were already talking about her – for nothing.

A wicked little thought crossed her mind. Maybe she *should* give them something to gossip about? What had she to lose now? Whatever she'd had with George was over, if it had ever really existed. He'd proved that neither his wife nor child were any consequence to him. He'd shown her exactly where she stood. It was enough.

Sarah felt her footsteps lighten. She needed to change her life, and she would. Her visit to Blodwen wasn't a complete loss. It had been an eye-opener really. She suddenly realised that if she wasn't careful, she'd end her days like her cousin: dried up and frustrated. Why not live a little?

Sarah shivered slightly at the notion. It frightened her. Bert frightened her in a different way; not for himself, but for the way he could make her feel.

She sensed that for a long time a force had been building up inside her, increasing in intensity with every passing, lonely year. With George, the force had been tightly, safely, capped. Instinct told her Bert Herbert had the power to let that force loose. The danger was, she knew implicitly, that, once free, it would carry her away. She'd never be able to control it again.

Then God knows to what heights, or depths, it would take her.

Sarah felt a cloying heat engulf her body at the sudden knowledge of what she was unconsciously planning. She was very aware of Jenni, innocent and untouched, walking beside her. Whatever was to happen in the future, her daughter must be protected against what Sarah might have to do; needed to do.

She would set herself free, and set Jenni free, too.

To salve her conscience, she could pretend it was a sacrifice, the ultimate sacrifice for her child. But that would be self-deception, and wouldn't be fair to Jenni either. What she intended to do was as much for herself as it was for her daughter's future. There was no reason to hold back on her natural inclinations now, was there? George didn't care.

And Bert Herbert would make it easy for her.

Chapter Four

Sarah scrubbed the front step with more vigour than usual on Friday morning, rent day. By half-past nine she'd cleaned the house from top to bottom although it really didn't need doing again.

She had to keep on the move; work off as much energy as possible. Not that her exertions were doing any good. She still felt like a coiled spring; like a boiler about to burst under pressure; like a volcano about to erupt.

Oh, God! She didn't know how she felt!

Her thoughts – her life, even – were topsy-turvy since visiting Blodwen. When she'd gone down to the butcher's to get some scrag-end of lamb for stew yesterday, she'd felt sure he was smirking at her in a very suggestive way.

And in the Co-op, when buying soda, she couldn't help noticing how Mrs Prosser and her next door, Mrs Bevan, stopped talking abruptly when they saw her. It was plain they could hardly bring themselves to nod in her direction. It was true what Blodwen had said. She was the talk of Trehafod. And she'd done nothing wrong!

And she wasn't likely to do anything wrong, either, she told herself, despite all her longings. She didn't have the nerve. It was all very well to want to break free; to long to satisfy the hunger;

to plan it. But carrying out those plans was beyond her, wasn't it? Her upbringing wouldn't allow it. She was too respectable, and momentarily she regretted it. She felt the hunger gnaw at her; felt the force grow, and realised respectability was a cage. Look at poor Blodwen.

Sarah smiled ruefully as she wrung out the floor cloth.

Never mind Blodwen! What about herself? What about poor, frustrated Sarah? She'd found a silver hair amongst the red yesterday. Soon it would be too late. Just as well, perhaps.

When Bert came for the rent later on she'd have it ready as usual; fend off his banter; shoo him out of the house as quickly as possible; put temptation firmly out of her way.

She thought she might wait for him, meet him on the doorstep with the rent, but she dismissed the idea. People were bound to notice and misinterpret it as eagerness. She'd do nothing unusual, she decided. Just wait.

But although she was waiting, expecting him every moment, when she heard the front door open – when he called her name in that familiar way and strode into the living-room – Sarah almost dropped the flat iron she was just placing on the hob. It nearly went straight into the fire instead.

She whirled round as he came in, feeling more unnerved than ever. He mustn't stay long. She had to get rid of him.

'You didn't close the front door, did you?' she blurted.

He looked bemused.

'No, *cariad*. I'm not *twp*, mind.'

Distracted, Sarah brushed a stray strand of hair away from her eyes.

'That's all right, then.' She sniffed, trying to regain her composure. 'There's your money by there on the sideboard, Bert. I'm busy. Haven't got time to talk.'

To prove her point, she turned her back to rearrange the old folded flannelette sheet she used as a base for ironing on the table, and lifted out another pillowcase from the basket. She gave it a vigorous shake, then scooping up water from a basin nearby, sprinkled it on the creased cotton.

To her consternation, Bert pulled out a chair nearby and sat facing her. She could feel his gaze and wanted to squirm. Without even touching her, he could make her tingle. She felt ashamed.

'Bert! I said, I'm busy.'

'What's the matter, Sarah?'

His gaze was searching, penetrating, seeing too much; understanding too much, perhaps. Sarah turned abruptly away to reach for the flat iron heating on the hob, holding the handle with a pad of stitched flannel.

'Nothing! Now take your money and go, will you?'

'You're upset, *cariad.*'

'Don't call me that!' she flared. 'I'm nothing to you and don't want to be. Why don't you go and visit your piece of fluff in Megan Street. She's always ready to entertain you, so I've heard.'

'Megan Street?'

She stared at him, embarrassed by the sharp interest in his voice and the almost hysterical pitch of her own. She hadn't meant to mention that. She wasn't jealous, but she could understand he might think so by her tone.

It wasn't jealousy. It was disappointment that, by the things he said to her and by the knowing glances he gave her, he was lumping her together with the tart from Megan Street. Sisters under the skin, so to speak.

But were she and this unknown woman so very different? Sarah hated the inner voice that asked her that question because she didn't want to face the answer.

'In Llawr-y-bryn,' she went on lamely.

'Don't know what you're talking about, *cariad.*'

'Liar!' Sarah caught her breath, trying to steady herself.

This was getting out of hand. And why was she getting so het up? What he did was nothing to her. Except, she reminded herself, when people gossiped about them.

Bert leaned back in the chair, crossing his legs with one ankle resting on his other knee. He looked relaxed and in no way put out by her accusation.

'Someone's been talking, is it?'

Sarah swallowed hard, struggling to regain her composure. She was ashamed of her outburst, conscious that every word she uttered seemed to give substance to their association. She must guard her tongue.

'My cousin from Llawr-y-bryn — Blodwen Thomas,' she said in a calmer tone. 'She's got friends around here. They've been telling her things . . . like how you leave my house until last to collect the rent. It's not right, and I don't like it!'

Bert looked down at his hands as though contemplating what he should say next. His hands were smooth and well-formed, not calloused like George's, and Sarah experienced a quiver as she imagined . . .

'It's true,' he said. 'I do see her in Megan Street.' He looked steadily at Sarah. 'Why shouldn't I? Not married, am I? And she hands it to me on a plate, mun.' He gave a laugh. 'What right man would say no, eh?'

'Oh!' Sarah turned her back, disconcerted at the rawness of his words and meaning.

'You're not like her, though, Sarah.' His voice was suddenly soft and caressing. 'And I'd give her up tomorrow if . . .'

'I should think not!' Sarah exclaimed, interrupting quickly. She couldn't bear to hear what he was about to say. 'Respectable married woman, I am. You remember that, Bert Herbert.'

He frowned at her sharpness.

'Yet people are gossiping.'

'That's your fault!'

'Is it? Your husband is never here, and people aren't fools, *cariad*. The men are curious about you; the women jealous.'

'Stop talking like that!' she flared. 'I just want to be left alone in peace and quiet.'

'No, you don't.'

'Get out, Bert!'

He rose and scooped up the money from the sideboard. But he didn't go. Sarah turned back to the ironing. The flat iron had gone cool, but not before it had left a brown scorch mark on the pristine white pillowcase.

'Why didn't you tell me you need money?' he asked.

Astounded, Sarah whirled round to stare at him.

'*What?*'

'Blod Thomas has been doing some gossiping herself.'

'Oh, no!'

Sarah felt betrayed, and appalled, too, by her cousin's malice.

'Look, I can lend you whatever you need, Sarah.'

She shook her head vehemently.

'No!'

'No strings, kid, honest. Not unless you wanted . . .'

'Where would *you* get twenty-five pounds?' The disdainful words were spoken as soon as thought.

'I can get it easy, don't worry.' Bert was eager. 'Listen, kid. Trust me, right? I can let you have it tomorrow, if you like.'

Sarah reached for a chair and sat. Her legs were trembling so much she felt they couldn't hold her upright any longer. It was madness even to pay attention. Of course she couldn't borrow money from him. It was an outrageous idea. She was a fool to listen.

'It's such a lot to owe,' she murmured.

If she skimped on food, maybe took in washing or did a bit of cleaning, she could pay him back a few shillings a week.

'It would take me years to pay it off . . .'

Bert was silent for a moment.

'Don't worry about paying it back for now,' he said, reassuringly.

'Don't worry?' She stared in disbelief. She'd be beholden to a man again. He'd have power over her. It was unthinkable.

Yet this was just the very chance she'd wanted for Jenni, an inner voice told her. Hadn't she already made up her mind she'd go to any lengths for her daughter's future? If she took the opportunity, no one but Bert would know. Could she trust him, though?

'How do I know you wouldn't boast about it down the Mountain Dew on a Saturday night, when you'd had a couple?'

'I'm teetotal, kid.' He grinned. 'Beer can spoil a man's – er – performance, and I pride myself on that. You ask her in Megan Street.'

Sarah turned her face away at his vulgarity. This was all so belittling. She was cheapening herself by even listening to his crude talk. She should tell him to go; tell him his familiarity was unwelcome; tell him to keep away in future.

After a moment's silence she said: 'It would be purely business, Bert.' She glanced up at him. His presence seemed to fill the living-room. 'Lending me money won't give you any ... privileges, mind. I'm not handing you anything on a plate.' She flushed at her own choice of words.

'I know that. I respect you, Sarah, honest.' He rubbed his thumb against his jaw. 'Look, I won't see her from Megan Street anymore.'

Abruptly, Sarah got to her feet, tossing her head.

'Why should I care? Do as you like. Your private life has nothing to do with me or our arrangement.'

Sarah paused. Was she agreeing to the loan? Was she out of her mind?

'All the same,' Bert said carefully, 'drop her, I will, just for you to know I'm being straight with you. Getting tired of her, I am, anyway. She's a widow and keeps hinting about marriage ...'

'I don't want to know!' cried Sarah. 'I'm not interested in your sordid affairs.'

'Right! Of course.' Now he seemed embarrassed and she glanced at him in curiosity. Did he really have feelings to hurt?

'I'll get the money by tomorrow. I'll come round about dinnertime.'

'No.' Sarah shook her head. She felt calmer now and was able to think more clearly. 'I don't want you coming here twice in one week. Leave it until next rent day. Jenni's waited long enough. One more week won't matter.'

He shuffled his feet.

'I'll be going now, then. See you next week, Sarah.'

She didn't answer but turned her back to lift the flat iron on to the hob again. She heard him walk down the passage and the door closing gently.

She flopped down on to a chair, feeling suddenly exhausted. What had she done? What had she agreed to? This was all madness.

Bert was just bragging, though, she told herself, reassuringly. He stood no chance of laying his hands on that kind of money. He'd only said it to impress her and she'd fallen for it, like a *llelo*.

But, suppose he did, and she accepted it? He might be keeping his distance now, but once she was indebted to him, he might want a return on his money. Don't worry about paying it back, he'd said. But knowing the kind of man he was, he must have an ulterior motive.

Sarah felt a tremor go through her. What did Bert Herbert really have at the back of his mind? What did he want from her? And did she really want to find out?

By rent day the following week Sarah had half-convinced herself that Bert was all talk and nothing more would be said on the matter of the loan. At the same time she had a strong urge to bolt the front door and pretend she was out when he called for the rent. That was impractical, though. So she waited in trepidation.

He was later than usual. She was in the scullery peeling potatoes for dinner when he strode into the living-room, calling her name as usual. Sarah hastily wiped her hands on a towel before going to face him, her heart fluttering in anxiety.

He threw a small brown paper parcel tied up with string on to the table.

'There you are, *cariad*. Good as my word, I am, see. Don't let nobody tell you different.'

Sarah stood still, regarding the parcel with awe.

'Well, go on, then,' he urged. 'Twenty-five quid, and it's all yours, Sarah.'

With a trembling hand, she pulled at the string bow, releasing the stiff brown paper. A bundle of notes sprayed out like a pack of cards; one pound notes and ten shilling notes. Sarah couldn't help staring. She'd never seen so many notes together in one place before.

She looked up at him.

'How . . . ?'

He shook his head.

'You don't need to know, *cariad*, except that I didn't steal it.'

Sarah fingered the notes, biting her lip. She could make the future safe and secure for Jenni by just accepting. Did it matter what happened to herself? Whatever that was, it would be between her and Bert Herbert. No one need ever know. She could explain it away by saying George had relented and sent her the money. If he ever returned, she could tell *him* the money was a loan from Blodwen.

Sarah paused for a moment, wondering at the complex web she was spinning. She must be careful not to get caught in it herself.

She pushed the open parcel across the table towards Bert, shaking her head.

'Can't take it. It wouldn't be right.'

'Don't be afraid of me, Sarah,' he said quietly. 'I mean you no harm, honest.'

She lifted her head, giving him a bold stare.

'Then why have you gone to all this trouble, Bert? It's not Christian charity, I'm sure.'

He met her stare candidly, and she felt suddenly breathless at the look in his eyes.

'I want to be your friend, Sarah.'

'Is that what you told *her* from Megan Street?' said Sarah waspishly. Was he taking her for a fool?

'I respect you and I want to help you.' He lifted the palms of both hands as though to check any retort she might make. 'All right! Attracted to you, I am. You're a beautiful woman, but a lonely one, too.' He shook his head. 'I'm not trying to take advantage of you, Sarah, honest to God!'

He pushed the money towards her again.

'Take it. No strings attached. I want nothing in return ... only ... only what you're prepared to give me.'

'What?'

'Friendship, I mean, kid ... only friendship.'

Sarah's lips thinned purposefully.

'If I take the loan it's business only, nothing more, so don't get any ideas. And you're to keep your mouth shut, Bert.'

He put his hand over his heart.

'Swear to God!'

With trembling fingers she gathered the notes together and slipped them into the pocket of her apron. For a moment she felt as though she'd stepped through a doorway into an unknown land, but suppressed the sensation promptly. This was for Jenni, she must remember that.

Bert pulled up a chair and sat down.

'Cup of tea going, is there?'

Sarah was immediately on the defensive.

'No, there isn't.' She took the money out of her pocket and held it towards him. 'This doesn't get your feet under my table, Bert.'

He rose to his feet hastily, lifting a hand to pacify her.

'Didn't mean anything, mun.'

Satisfied by the repentant expression on his face, Sarah replaced the money in her pocket.

'There's the rent by there,' she said stiffly, pointing to the sideboard. 'You'd best take it now, and go.'

He stood for a moment, looking at her intently.

'Just done you a good turn, I have, Sarah,' he said. 'You could at least say thank you.'

She flushed, annoyed at his reprimand. She'd wanted to thank him, but was afraid he'd see it as weakness. Instinct told her she must tread carefully where Bert Herbert was concerned.

'I am grateful, Bert. Thank you. But . . . don't expect any favours, mind.'

His smile was slow and relaxed.

'As if you'd ever let me take advantage, eh?' Then his eyes seemed to glow with a compelling warmth that made Sarah's heart flutter. 'But if ever you did, there are things I could teach you . . . things you've never even dreamed about . . .'

'Stop it!'

He paused and the warmth subsided, but Sarah was left breathless.

'I'm all talk, kid,' he said jocularly. 'You should be used to me by now.'

He scooped up the rent money.

'Well, Sarah, see you next week, eh?'

One teatime, two weeks after she'd accepted the loan, Sarah fondly watched Jenni tuck into a dish of jam roly-poly.

'Oh, Mam! The Misses Jukes are very nice,' she enthused. 'They're funny but kind. I'm so glad my da changed his mind.'

Pushing down a twinge of guilt for her own lie, Sarah felt happiness swell in her breast at the excited expression on her daughter's face. It was a full week since Jenni had started her apprenticeship and she was so enthusiastic. Of course it was early days yet and everything was new to her, especially the fact that she was earning a living now, but Sarah was certain it wouldn't pall.

Jenni was clever with her hands, artistic, and patient and meticulous over anything she worked on, whether it was embroidery or making a doll's dress for a neighbour's child.

And she was always drawing on bits of paper – her dress designs, as she called them. Sarah viewed them with admiration, wondering where her daughter's talent came from. And they weren't mere drawings, either. Jenni knew instinctively how such garments could be constructed.

Sarah congratulated herself on her own courage and foresight in ensuring her daughter had her chance at last at a trade to which she was admirably suited.

'Saw Auntie Blodwen this morning, I did,' Jenni announced suddenly, making Sarah's blood run cold. 'When I was on my way to the dairy for the Misses. Her face went all red when I told her I was apprenticed at Jukes'. She never even said goodbye, the old battle-axe!'

Sarah moved away from the table.

'Did she ask any questions?'

'Told her straight, I did. My da thinks the world of me. That's why he gave up his savings for me. That's right, isn't it, Mam?'

'Quite right, lovely girl,' Sarah said absentmindedly.

She must be prepared for people's curiosity, she told herself sternly. No one could possibly be allowed to know the truth.

Bert had collected the rent as usual over these last couple of weeks without once mentioning their arrangement, and Sarah felt reassured.

Jenni pushed her empty dish away.

'When I've helped with the washing up, Mam, can I go down Dilys's?'

'Only for half an hour, mind,' Sarah warned. 'Bed early. You don't want to be late for work, do you?'

'No fear!' Jenni grinned as she picked up the tea towel and began polishing a wet plate. 'We're making a wedding dress at the moment. Oh, Mam! You should see it. White satin with a train of pure white lace. The Misses Jukes are making rosebuds out of satin to decorate the neck. It's wonderful! They're going to teach me how to do it.' Jenni lowered her voice. 'But don't tell anyone. The dress is for a mine-owner's daughter in Merthyr.'

Sarah was sceptical.

'If I was a mine-owner's daughter,' she said, laughing, 'I'd be off to Paris for my wedding dress, not Llawr-y-bryn.'

Jenni lifted her chin loyally.

'Not if you wanted it perfect.'

Jenni came back from Dilys's in good time and went obediently to bed. Sarah lingered a little, wound up the old gramophone and sat listening to music while darning stockings. But after a while, on impulse, she lifted the needle off the record. Tonight the music was unsettling. It made her feel lonely, and even empty.

With a sigh, she gathered up her darning, pushing it into the basket. She turned off the gas mantle, leaving the room in warm darkness. It was still reasonably early but it was better to find oblivion in sleep than sit alone in the crowding silence.

Her foot was on the bottom stair when she heard the sound – a soft tapping. In the gloom she looked towards the scullery. Someone was knocking on the back door.

Startled, Sarah glanced at the clock on the mantelpiece. Half-past nine. Who could it be at this time? And at the back door, too. Any neighbour would call at the front.

Sarah moved apprehensively through the gloom into the scullery, pulling back the curtain a little to peer into the small backyard. In the dusk she could see a tall broad-shouldered outline and recognised Bert Herbert immediately.

Sarah pulled back with a gasp, her heart almost in her mouth. She was thankful she'd extinguished the gas light. She would wait quietly and he would go away, believing she'd gone to bed.

But the knocking came again, louder this time, more insistent. What did he want?

To her dismay he spoke her name, whispering at first then louder.

Dear God! Jenni might hear and come down. And worse! The Bevans' back door was just beyond the wall. She could see the glow of their gaslight reflected on the roof of the lavatory.

A man's voice calling her name at this time of night . . . the scandal of it would finish her.

With a little moan of despair Sarah hastened to unbolt the door but held it only partially open.

'What in God's name do you want?' she hissed.

'Let me in, Sarah.'

'No, go away!'

'I won't go. I want to talk. Let me come in.'

'Have you no decency?'

'Sarah, please? Patient I've been, mind. Stay here all night, I will, if you don't talk to me.'

Sarah hesitated. A warning bell was ringing in her head but Bert was very capable of making good his threat. She couldn't go to bed with him out there, knocking, calling her name. It was easier to let him in. Let him say his piece, then maybe he would go.

She opened the door wider.

'It's just for a minute, Bert. You understand?'

He stepped over the threshold, removing his cap. Sarah retreated into the living-room. The matches were on the mantelpiece and she quickly re-lit the gas-mantle.

The glow springing to life revealed Bert standing close by. He was looking at her intently. Instinctively, although she was fully dressed, Sarah wrapped her arms around herself as though for protection.

'Well, what do you want to say?'

He hesitated, flicking his tongue across his lips as if they were dry.

'Had to see you, I did.'

'Keep your voice down! My daughter's upstairs.' She peered at him closely. 'Have you been drinking?'

He was suddenly impatient.

'I don't drink, I told you.'

'Then you must be mad, coming here this time of night,' cried Sarah, moving away to stand on the other side of the table. 'What do you mean by it?'

A muscle moved spasmodically in his jaw.

'I've been patient, Sarah. I've waited.'

She felt her throat close. She couldn't mistake his meaning, not when his eyes were revealing his thoughts. He'd come for his payment. But she could pretend she didn't understand.

'Waited for what?'

He took a step closer, breathing deeply, his gaze eager.

'Don't play games, Sarah,' he said quietly. 'You took the money. You knew what you were doing.'

'I was doing business,' she retorted swiftly. 'No strings, you said, Bert. Remember?'

He gave a short, humourless laugh.

'You didn't believe that no more than I did.'

'I did! I thought you were a gentleman, Bert Herbert.'

His smile was sly.

'You *know* I'm not. That's why you're interested in me, isn't it? Fascinated by thoughts of what I can do for you . . . what we can do for each other.'

Sarah straightened her spine.

'Stop! How dare you? I'm a respectable . . .'

50

He lowered his head, staring at her through his lashes, his eyes glowing.

'No, you're not, Sarah.' There was a huskiness in his voice. 'Not deep down, not right inside. You're just like me. Hungry . . .'

She caught her breath. How could he know her pain and anguish? How could he know what it was that drove her to the point of despair? How could he, a virtual stranger, understand her so well?

'You insult me,' she cried desperately. 'Get out of my house.'

He took another step closer.

'Listen!' he said tensely. 'I got that money for you, and it could cost me dearly. My job. Maybe even my freedom. So, you see, Sarah, I didn't do it for nothing.'

Aghast, she stared at him for a moment.

'You *stole* the money?'

'Fiddled the rent collection records, didn't I? Bit here, bit there. Old man Meredith trusts me. Bloody fool!'

Sarah clapped her hand to her mouth in dismay.

'You did that for me? Why?'

His laughter sounded hollow.

'Now, why d'you think, *cariad*?'

Sarah could only stare. What had she done? And how could it be undone now? The money was spent. Jenni was so happy. She couldn't destroy that. She wouldn't!

'Bert?'

The glow was in his eyes again; that searing heat that set her skin tingling, and her heart beating like a drum.

'I want you, Sarah.'

She was quivering as though she'd never stop.

'Bert, what do you mean? You don't know what you're saying!'

'I *want* you. You want me. You want what I can give you. Don't trouble to deny it. I can see it in your eyes. Face up to it, Sarah. I want my reward, and you want to give it to me.'

She shook her head vehemently.

'No! Bert, it's wrong.'

In a moment he was close to her, gripping her upper arms.

Sarah gasped at his touch, hot even through the serge of her dress. She wanted to struggle. Her conscience commanded her to fight, but her body wouldn't obey her mind. It was in rebellion, glorious rebellion, feeling sensations she'd never known before. There was terror yet there was exaltation, too.

'You wouldn't force me against my will, Bert?'

His breath was warm on her face, and his voice soft.

'I won't need to, *cariad*.'

His arms were around her, his mouth a breath away from hers. His voice was no more than a sigh now.

'You're mine already, aren't you, my lovely Sarah?'

Chapter Five

SUMMER 1920

'There's your money, *Mr Herbert*. Now be off with you!'

Sarah smiled at him, knowing her cheeks were flushed with eagerness; feeling her heart bursting with excitement at the sight of him; longing for his touch.

He grinned widely, taking the rent from the sideboard, and came a step towards her, his eyes shining.

With a little breathless laugh, Sarah turned her back, quivering with anticipation. They loved to play games which were an important part of their ardour. She lived for these moments now, and for the hours they would spend together at night when Jenni was in bed and darkness hid their passion; a passion that lifted her to heights she'd once only dreamed about.

He came close behind her, slipping his arms around her, cupping her breasts, holding her tightly against his body. Sarah moaned quietly as the wonderful sensation of his lips on her throat sent ripples of ecstasy through her.

'Sarah, *cariad*, you drive me crazy.'

'Call me darling, Bert,' she breathed. 'I've always longed for a man to call me darling when he's loving me.'

Bert laughed softly.

'You're *twp*, you are.'

'Please, Bert. Please say it.'

His lips were against the pulse in her throat again.

'I want you, Sarah darling. My beautiful darling, I want you now.'

Sarah reluctantly eased away a little and turned to face him.

'Not now, Bert. There isn't time. We've got to be careful, haven't we? You'll come back tonight, won't you? Won't you?'

'Nothing could keep me away from you, *cariad*,' he replied huskily. 'Neither flood nor flames.'

'Kiss me, then, and go,' she whispered, feeling the scorching fire of her need about to consume her. 'Before I give in.'

His kiss was demanding and hungry, and Sarah felt both intoxicated and reassured. Her one fear was that he'd grow tired of her. She couldn't live without his lovemaking now. She needed it more and more. Her hunger was insatiable, but she wasn't ashamed of it. It was the way God had made her.

She gave him a little push, just to show him she was in control. Her need of him was greater than he could ever guess, but he must never know. Instinct told her the way to hold on to Bert Herbert was to keep him a little off balance if she could; mystify him, and never be clinging. She wouldn't look further than their next love-making. It was enough for her.

'See you tonight, then,' she said. 'And don't keep me waiting too long, will you?' She smiled provocatively. 'Or I might find somebody else.'

'You do and I'll kill him,' Bert growled convincingly.

It was all part of their game.

Jenni was slow in going up to bed that night, and Sarah was consumed with impatience. She knew Bert would watch for candlelight in the back bedroom before he would venture to open the door from the backyard, which she'd left unlatched for him.

'You'll be late for work in the morning, my girl,' Sarah said impatiently. 'What're you hanging about for?'

'It's this magazine the Misses Jukes loaned me,' Jenni said eagerly. 'Pictures of lovely clothes in it. They said I should study it. Then they'll look at some of my dress designs.'

'Don't try to run before you can walk,' her mother responded sharply. 'You're there to learn the dressmaking trade, not design dresses. There's no bread and butter to be earned from that.'

Sarah prised the magazine from her daughter's fingers.

'Now, up you go.'

'Oh, Mam!'

'Go on!'

Reluctantly, Jenni went. It was a good ten minutes before Sarah heard the latch being lifted softly, and her heart lurched with excitement. Anticipation was already burning her up. As soon as Bert appeared in the scullery doorway she flew to him, flinging herself into his arms.

'Oh, God, Bert! I couldn't have waited another minute. Let's hurry.'

She tried to push the coat from his shoulders but he gripped her hands, preventing it.

'Sarah, *cariad*, something's happened.'

A note in his voice made her stand still, her heated blood suddenly cooling. It was a tone she'd never heard from him before. It sounded like panic.

'Bert, what's wrong?'

'It's old man Meredith,' he said shakily. 'The bugger suspects something. He's getting the auditors in. My fiddle was clever enough to fool him, but the auditors will spot it in a minute. They'll be here in three days, then I'll be in deep trouble.'

She clung to his lapels, suddenly terrified.

'What're you going to do, Bert?'

'Getting out, Sarah.' He pushed his fingers through his hair nervously. 'Early tomorrow. Lose myself in Cardiff, perhaps. Got to get away, I have.'

'Oh, Bert, don't leave me! You can't leave me alone here.'

He tugged her hands away from his coat, shaking his head.

'I can't stay, Sarah. I can't face prison. And that's what'll happen.'

'Take me with you, Bert,' she cried frantically. 'Please!'

He stared at her.

'What about Jenni?'

Sarah swallowed hard.

'She could come with us.'

Bert shook his head emphatically.

'No, I'll be on the dodge. Can't have a kid holding me back.'

'Then let Jenni stay here!' Sarah was desperate. She couldn't lose what she'd found. Life wouldn't be worth living without him. 'But, please, take *me* with you, Bert.'

He continued to stare at her.

'You'd leave Jenni here alone?'

She felt rebellious. She couldn't live without her new life, the fire and warmth he'd brought to her. And why shouldn't she think of herself for once? She deserved to live, too.

Sarah lifted her chin defiantly.

'I've set her up for life. Done all I can for her. She's pretty and clever — she'll survive. I won't. I'll die without you, Bert.'

She clutched at his lapels again.

'I *won't* be parted from you. I can't be alone again. God knows I need you.'

She was clinging, she knew, but out of despair. She'd be finished if she lost Bert. Anxiously she watched his face as he made up his mind.

'All right, *cariad*. I'll be waiting in the back lane early. Don't bring too much with you. A small bag. We've got to travel light. We'll walk down to Cwmgelligors, get the early train to Cardiff.'

He took her hands in his, looking keenly into her face.

'You *are* sure about this, *cariad*?'

She reached up and briefly touched his lips with hers.

'Very sure. But I must wait until Jenni's left for work. I can't go before. She'll raise the alarm if I'm missing. She usually leaves for Llawr-y-bryn about seven o' clock.'

He nodded.

'Pack tonight. Meet me straight after she leaves.'

He seized her suddenly, holding her to him and kissing her deeply.

'A new life, my lovely girl. Together.'

From the cupboard under the stairs Sarah pulled out a battered old suitcase. It was hardly bigger than an attaché case but it would be enough to carry the few pieces of clothing she planned to take. Nothing else. Nothing that belonged to George.

She wouldn't let herself think about Jenni. Her daughter was fifteen, almost a woman now. She'd have her wages from the Jukeses and there were the postal orders her father sent each week. Of course she'd be upset, at first, but she'd get over it. Her whole life was before her.

And, Sarah thought belligerently, let George take care of his daughter from now on.

She crept upstairs quietly. Lighting a candle, she began filling the case from the chest-of-drawers.

Jenni's life hadn't yet started but Sarah's was already half over. Bert was her last chance, and she deserved to have someone better than George. She couldn't go back to being neglected and empty.

She'd never known such freedom as when in Bert's arms, sharing their hours of pleasure. He made her feel alive, and vital, and real. Yes, that was it. With Bert she was a real person, a real woman. Jenni would understand. She *must* understand.

When she and Bert were settled and safe, Sarah would write to her daughter and explain everything.

'She must write a short note to Jenni now, and leave it for her to find tomorrow when she came home from work. Quietly Sarah went downstairs again.

She'd found an old envelope and was just searching for the stub of a pencil when there was a knock on the front door.

Sarah held her breath, startled and confused. It was very late. Who could it be? Had Bert returned? Or had someone come looking for him here? She didn't move until the knocking sounded again.

With a thumping heart Sarah put her hand on the bolt of the door, then hesitated. Her throat felt dry, but she managed to find her voice.

'Who is it?'

'It's me, Sarah, your husband. Open the door.'

'George!'

Astounded, Sarah's hand flew to unbolt the door and opened it wide. George stood there on the doorstep, the light from the gas mantle casting shadows across his face.

'George!' She could only stare at him aghast, agitated at his sudden appearance.

He stepped across the threshold and Sarah retreated, still staring as though he were an intruder.

'What are you doing here?' she asked. 'You never wrote to say you were coming.'

'Last-minute decision,' he said. 'Where's Jenni?'

'In bed, of course. Do you realise what time it is? It's almost midnight.'

'Took the last train. Walked up from Cwmgelligors.'

He took off his cap and jacket and hung them behind the door as if it were the most ordinary thing in the world to arrive home at midnight. Sarah just stood there, clasping her hands together tightly. Her escape to a new life was threatened. How could she get away now?

He looked at her expectantly.

'I could do with a cup of tea.'

Without a word Sarah went into the scullery, filled the copper kettle and lit the gas ring. Her mind was in a whirl. She'd convinced herself she'd never have to see George again. Or was that wishful thinking? Now here he was. Sarah clenched her teeth stubbornly. She be damned if she'd let him interfere with her plans.

She thought of Bert. If he hadn't left earlier tonight George would have caught them together. She shuddered at the idea. Maybe that's why he'd arrived so late – to catch her out. Had he heard something?

He stood in the scullery doorway, rolling up his shirt sleeves.

'I'm hungry,' he said.

His voice was matter-of-fact. He didn't sound as though he suspected infidelity. But would he even care?

Sarah pulled herself together.

'There's some broth left,' she said dully. 'I'll warm it.'

She brought him the tea and then the hot broth. He sat at the table, pulling pieces of bread apart to drop into the steaming liquid, stirring them with a spoon.

He glanced up at her as she stood there, staring at him.

'Something wrong, Sarah? Anything you have to tell me?'

She hurriedly shook her head.

'No, why ever do you ask that?'

'You're up very late.'

'Darning, I was,' she lied. 'Fell asleep in the chair. Just going up when you knocked.'

She suddenly remembered the open suitcase on their bed. She'd packed all she needed. Now she must hide it. She took off her wraparound pinny and laid it over the back of a chair.

'I'll go up now, George, if you don't mind.'

He nodded, finishing off the last of the broth.

'All right. I'll be up shortly. I'm pretty tired now after that walk. I'll probably lie in tomorrow.'

He could lie in all he wanted, Sarah thought grimly, climbing the narrow staircase. She'd meet Bert as soon as she'd seen Jenni off. It would be the last time she'd see her daughter, for a while anyway.

In the bedroom Sarah pushed the suitcase under the bed on her side. It would be quite easy to slip that out unnoticed in the morning while George was still asleep. In a way, she was glad he'd come home. Now Jenni wouldn't be alone when she read her mother's goodbye note.

At six o'clock the next morning Sarah slid gently out of bed. She wanted to get the suitcase downstairs and in the cupboard under the stairs until she was ready to leave. But Jenni was already up. Sarah heard her padding down the stairs. The suitcase would have to stay where it was for the moment.

Jenni was washing herself in the scullery sink when Sarah came in to put the kettle on the gas ring.

'Your da came home last night,' she said.

'My da!' Jenni looked as astonished as Sarah had felt last night.

Sarah got out the frying pan and put a knife-length of lard into it, then fetched bacon and eggs from the larder. As soon as the kettle boiled she made a pot of tea then put the frying pan on the gas ring, conscious that this was the last time she'd make her daughter's breakfast.

'He's having a lie in,' Sarah said carefully. 'I don't want you disturbing him. You can see him when you come home this dinnertime.'

The last thing she wanted was Jenni and George talking together this morning before she could get away. Jenni would be sure to thank her father for his generosity in giving up all his savings for her apprenticeship, while George wouldn't have the least idea what she was talking about. Then Sarah's lies and deceit would be exposed. She didn't care what happened after she'd escaped with Bert.

'Will he think me ungrateful scooting off before saying thanks for giving me the apprenticeship?'

'It can wait,' Sarah insisted sharply, her nerves in disarray.

Then she was sorry she'd been sharp. She was parting from Jenni, perhaps for years. She wanted to say goodbye but knew she couldn't. Jenni must have good memories of her mother, Sarah thought sadly. She wouldn't dwell on the thought that her daughter would be left feeling deserted. It had to be this way. Sarah couldn't live without love's pleasure and warmth now. When Jenni was a woman she'd understand.

Jenni settled down to eat her breakfast to Sarah's relief. Later, as the girl prepared to leave, Sarah put her arms around her impulsively, hugging her tightly.

'You're a good girl, Jen,' she said. 'Your da knows you're grateful.'

She held Jenni away from her for a moment, looking into her face and her clear green eyes.

'You're beautiful, my lovely girl. And men will try to take advantage of you.'

Sarah smiled as Jenni blushed and looked away.

'Never let them, though. Know your worth, my girl. Know what you want in life and in love, and never take less. Always remember you are your own woman, and then you'll never be beholden to any man.'

'There's serious you are this morning, Mam,' Jenni said, her cheeks still pink. 'What's the matter?'

'Nothing, chick. In fact, for once, everything's going my way.'

She kissed Jenni's cheek quickly, then gave her a little push.

'Go on, now, or you'll be late for work.'

Sarah's heart gave a painful lurch as Jenni stepped through the front door with a cheerful wave. She had an impulse to call her back, tell her everything, take her with her when she went to meet

Bert. But he might be angry and refuse to take either of them. She just couldn't risk it. It was her daughter or love's pleasure. She'd made her choice last night.

Sarah had a hasty wash in the scullery then went quietly upstairs to dress. George was breathing evenly and deeply, and Sarah felt confident enough to slide the suitcase out from under the bed and place it on the narrow landing outside.

She dressed and was reaching for her coat from the wardrobe when George stirred. Sarah hastily flung the coat out into the landing as her husband sat up in bed.

'Is there a cup of tea going?' he asked, rubbing a hand over his face.

Sarah swallowed her fright.

'I'll fetch you one up.'

She felt her anxiety mounting. She intended to go right now, as soon as she was out of George's sight. She thought of Bert in the back lane. Would he have the patience to wait for her? Would he go without her if she didn't appear soon?

Please, God, let him wait?

George threw back the bedclothes.

'I'll come down.'

'No, no. You stay there, George. Still tired, you must be, from travelling yesterday.'

He hesitated, looking at her. She was wearing her best dress. Would he notice? He glanced at the alarm clock on the side table.

'You're dressed to go out? It's still early.'

Sarah swallowed.

'Going down to the butcher's, I am, to get you a pork chop for your dinner.'

'He won't be open yet.'

'I'm going down to Owens' in Llawr-y-bryn. His meat's cheaper, see.'

'Sarah . . .'

She stepped towards the door.

'I've got to go, George. It's a long walk, isn't it? I'll fetch your tea.'

She didn't give him a chance to argue further but hurried out, snatching up her coat and case and almost running down the stairs. She pulled on her hat, viewing herself in the mirror over the mantelpiece, then slipped into her coat. She picked up the case then suddenly remembered the note to Jenni.

The bed springs creaked. Was he getting back into bed? She prayed he was. But perhaps he was coming down?

She was torn between running while she had the chance and delaying long enough to write the note. With a little cry of despair, Sarah put down the case again. She couldn't leave Jenni without a word of explanation.

She found the old envelope from last night and a pencil. The note must be brief. She didn't have time for anything else. Bert was waiting; Bert, and the pleasure she'd lived without for so long.

The bed creaked as George lifted his weight from it. He'd slept poorly, and felt stiff and bone weary. He pulled on his trousers over his flannel vest, securing the buckle of his wide leather belt. The envelope in one pocket rustled, reminding him again that it was there and why he'd decided to come home so suddenly.

He took the envelope out and stared at it. He'd already read the letter it contained so many times in the last twenty-four hours, he knew every word. He wouldn't read it again. It could tell him nothing new. Only Sarah could do that.

There was something about her this morning which disturbed him. Her high colour; and agitation; the way her gaze would look anywhere except directly at him. There were questions to be asked; accusations to be refuted.

George padded across to the door, wincing as his bare feet came in contact with the cold linoleum. He went silently down the stairs, aware that there were no sounds coming from the scullery to indicate Sarah was preparing a pot of tea for him.

At the bottom of the stairs leading directly into the living-room, George stopped and stared. Sarah had her hat and coat on, and was bending over the table scribbling on a piece of paper. His gaze fell on a small suitcase at her feet.

'Sarah, what are you doing?'

She whirled round, her mouth gaping open, obviously aghast at the sight of him.

'I . . . I . . .'

'Don't tell me another lie,' he said flatly. 'So it's true?'

'What?'

'You've been carrying on behind my back.'

'George!' Her face flamed red and she dropped the pencil. 'How dare you say that!'

He took the letter out of his pocket and held it out.

'That's what it says here anyway,' he said. 'This is from Blodwen Thomas, your own cousin. She makes an accusation, Sarah. Will you deny it?'

'She's a liar!' his wife cried out, agitated. 'She's always been jealous of me, George. She's a shrivelled up old spinster who can't bear the thought of me having what she can't have . . .'

Sarah paused, biting her lip, then glanced towards the scullery. There was expectancy in her glance and George felt tension swell in the pit of his stomach. What was she expecting? Who was she expecting?

Yesterday he'd been half ready to dismiss Blodwen's charge. He'd never liked her and Sarah's estimate of her was pretty accurate, he reckoned. But now, looking at his wife, he barely recognised her, and suddenly realised he hardly knew her at all. With a flash of insight he realised, too, how strange that was after so many years of marriage.

'What's the suitcase for, Sarah?' he asked harshly. 'Where are you going? And where's Jenni?'

'She's in work.'

'Work?'

Sarah looked at him boldly.

'She's apprenticed to the Jukes sisters.'

'But I forbade it,' he said. 'Where did you get the money for the premium?'

'From Blodwen.'

'Another lie, Sarah.' He held out the envelope again. 'In this letter she says you got the money from your . . . lover.'

Sarah stepped back with a gasp, as though he'd slapped her.

'Where are you going with the suitcase, Sarah. Answer me!'

Her mouth tightened, and suddenly her expression darkened with resentment so intense, he was startled by it.

'All right, then!' she cried out savagely. 'I'm leaving you. I'm running away with my lover.'

Now it was confirmed, he didn't want to believe it.

'You don't know what you're saying, Sarah.'

'Oh, yes, I do!' Her laughter was bitter. 'And I know what I'm doing, as well. Bert is a real man. He's not like you, George, with water in your veins and ice in your heart. He knows how to treat me. He knows what I want.'

'Sarah!'

'Oh, what's the matter, George? Shocked, are you? Or perhaps your feelings are hurt? Do you have any feelings? I don't think so, George. You're a cold fish.'

Angered, he took the letter out of its envelope and waved it at her.

'*Everyone* must know about this. Blodwen will have seen to that.' He stared at her in painful realisation. 'You've made me a laughing stock in this village.'

'You've done that yourself,' Sarah retorted heatedly. 'Neglecting your own wife and child. There was gossip long before I started seeing Bert.' She gave a slow, unabashed smile. 'How long did you think I could go on without a man in my bed?'

'You slut!' He crashed his fist down on to the table nearby.

'You've dragged my good name though the mud, and Jenni's too, that's what you've done, Sarah.'

'*Your* good name!' Her eyes flared bright with triumph. 'That's all there is to you, George, a name. You're not a man, you're a . . . a . . . nothingness. And I'm sick of it – sick to death of it. But no more.'

She reached down, grasped the suitcase and straightened up.

'As a husband, George, you're a joke. A washout!'

She stared at him with defiance and arrogance so fierce it made the skin on his face tingle with outrage.

'How you ever managed to produce a child, I don't know,' she said, her tone scathing. 'Now Bert . . . *he* knows what a woman is for. Oh, there's a real man for you. And he makes me feel like a real woman. He makes me feel wonderful. Shall I tell you how he does it, George? Shall I paint pictures for you?'

At her jeering words images flashed into his mind; images so disgusting he felt his stomach heave and nausea rise in his throat. And with it a terrible anger.

'You whore!'

As though of their own volition his hands reached out for her, seizing her by the throat and shaking her violently. Her scream was drowned out by the terrible pounding in his head and suddenly he could hardly see her face. He was glad of that. Her look of disdain and contempt was too much. He'd squeeze them out of her.

Her fists were pounding at him but he hardly felt them. She was trying to speak. He didn't want to hear her words; couldn't bear to learn of the unspeakable things she had done. He *must* make her stop!

Her fists stopped pounding and she sagged against him. But he held on. She was his wife and he must subdue her to earn her respect again. Then they could go back to being the way they were.

'Christ Almighty! What are you doing, man?'

Another voice, a man's, pierced the red mist in his mind.

Startled, he let go her throat. She sagged at the knees, toppling over sideways. There was a sickening crack as her head smashed against the corner of the brass fender. She lay still, making no sound.

He stared down at her in disbelief.

'Sarah, get up.'

There was a ghastly silence in the room, and suddenly George felt very afraid.

'Sarah, you shouldn't have said those terrible things to me. Get up now. I forgive you.'

Her stillness intensified his fear. He dropped to his knees at her side and lifted her head. There was blood all over his hands.

'Sarah! I didn't mean it. Sarah!'

He looked questioningly towards the scullery door.

'Why won't she get up?'

The tall broad-shouldered man standing there, with a khaki duffel bag on his shoulder, stared at him, horror in his eyes.

'You bloody maniac, you've killed her!'

George shook his head.

'No!'

But the man turned on his heel and ran.

George looked down at the pale face of his wife.

'Sarah? Sarah, I didn't mean it . . .'

Chapter Six

Jenni wiped the last dinner plate and put it with the others in the wall cupboard over the sink. There were always so many dishes to wash at the Bevans'. She didn't mind, though. Keeping busy stopped her thinking about Mam's funeral yesterday, and the terrible days before it. Keeping busy didn't allow her any time to cry. She'd cried too much already.

The lump of grief and misery started to rise in her throat again but she forced it down. Crying wouldn't bring Mam back.

She still couldn't believe any of it had happened, mostly because she didn't understand *why* it had happened. All she knew was that her beloved mother was gone and now she was alone.

Jenni tried not to think of her father. There was only hatred in her heart for him now, though that didn't seem right. It was best not to think about him at all. She didn't know where he was, or what had happened to him, or what would happen to him.

She remembered Oggie's jeering words: 'They're going to string him up,' and could only shudder at the horror of it. Yet it all seemed so unreal. Looking on it as a horrific nightmare was the only way to deal with it and get through each day.

She didn't look to the future. Tomorrow was an unknown land, shrouded in mists. Yet she had to get away from the Bevans, that much was clear. Mam had never liked Mrs Bevan, said she was a snooper, and she talked incessantly about the tragedy next door until Jenni felt like screaming. No, she couldn't stay here much longer. But where could she go?

Leaden with misery, Jenni went listlessly into the living-room. Someone had knocked on the front door earlier and Mrs Bevan had taken them into the front parlour, so it must be someone she respected.

Perhaps it was the Reverend Geraint ap Hywel. Jenni closed her eyes in despair. She couldn't stand to see his solemn, pitying face again, regarding her like a lost soul.

The parlour door was ajar, and creeping into the passage and listening a moment, Jenni could hear the conversation clearly. Mrs Bevan was prattling on as usual. When the other person spoke Jenni recognised the voice of Miss Emily Jukes.

Her heart lifted a little. She hadn't been to work since the tragedy; hadn't even been outside the Bevans' door. People would only stare and whisper. She was thankful she hadn't been expected to go to the funeral.

People like the Reverend ap Hywel called, stared at her, but never spoke to her personally, as though she'd suddenly gone soft in the head. Mrs Bevan seemed to have appointed herself Jenni's spokeswoman. But now here was Miss Jukes, her employer, come to call. Why hadn't Mrs Bevan summoned her to come and see her visitor?

Jenni was about to tap on the door and walk in when she realised Mrs Bevan was in the middle of yet another recital of her part in the drama, and felt hot blood rise to her face in humiliation and anger.

'A screaming match, it was, Miss Jukes, next door. About eight o'clock in the morning, I suppose,' Mrs Bevan was saying. 'These walls are paper thin, you know.'

Miss Jukes gave a loud sniff.

'Really?'

There was an uncertain titter from Mrs Bevan.

'Well, anyway, quarrelling they were, full pelt,' she went on doggedly. 'Then, suddenly, everything went quiet. My husband's on nights. I wanted him to go and look but he wouldn't get up again. So I went.'

Mrs Bevan took the deep, dramatic breath she always did at this point in her story and Jenni clenched her hands in consternation, knowing what was coming.

Mrs Bevan had described the scene in her presence so many times, it was now firmly etched into Jenni's brain. It was only force of will which prevented her from living the horror of it over and over again. She had an urge to put her fingers into her ears now to avoid having to listen, but at the same time she was curious about Miss Jukes's reaction.

'Next door I went, through the back entrance,' Mrs Bevan was saying breathlessly. 'And there he was in the living-room, kneeling by the body of his poor wife. I could see the blood on the mat from where I stood by the scullery door. Oh, Miss Jukes, it gave me such a turn!'

'I don't doubt.' Miss Jukes's tone was dry.

Mrs Bevan cleared her throat.

'Well, anyway, I ran home, told my husband and he went and got Dai Book and Pencil. After that it was like a funfair by here, I can tell you. My nerves haven't been right since.'

'How's young Jenni?'

'Well – down, you know, very down.'

'Poor child.'

'Yes,' Mrs Bevan said inattentively. 'It was a big funeral, mind, very big. Crowds! Hundreds! Sightseers, most of them. Disgusting, isn't it?'

'Hoi-polloi!' Miss Jukes agreed. 'Tell me, Mrs Bevan, what was the quarrel about?'

Jenni was suddenly alert. No one had asked this question in her hearing before. She was longing to know the answer; to know the whys and wherefores and to make some sense of it all. What had made her father do such a terrible thing? She had to know. She held her breath, waiting for Mrs Bevan's reply.

'Well . . .' Mrs Bevan sounded cautious. 'Jenni's name was shouted a couple of times, see.'

'Oh, no! Tsk, tsk!'

Jenni felt a sudden coldness engulf her. Her parents had quarrelled over *her*? Her mother had been killed because of *her*? She felt nausea rise in her throat. What had she done to make her father so angry?

Jenni pushed her fist into her mouth to stop herself from crying out in despair and remorse. It was her fault. She was responsible! How could she go on, knowing that?

She was about to rush away, to look for a place to hide and cry in private, when Miss Jukes's next question made her pause.

'What will happen to Jenni now?'

'Orphanage, I suppose,' Mrs Bevan said in an offhand tone.

Jenni stifled a sob. Orphanage! She'd rather run away.

'I can't take her in for good, see,' Mrs Bevan went on. 'Not with four strapping sons in the house. It wouldn't do, would it? You know what I mean, Miss Jukes?'

'Jenni's not going to any orphanage,' Miss Jukes said firmly. 'My sister and I will take her. She's already apprenticed to us.'

'Oh, that's very good of you, I'm sure.' Mrs Bevan sounded surprised yet at the same time sceptical. 'But it all depends on the Authorities, isn't it? Can't go against the Authorities, Miss Jukes.'

Miss Emily sniffed again disdainfully.

'My sister and I aren't without influence, mind, Mrs Bevan,' she said sharply. 'Very friendly with Councillor Taylor and his lady wife, we are. Pastor Williams as well. Oh, no, I don't think the Authorities will quibble.'

Jenni swallowed her sobs. The Misses Jukes! They'd save her from the orphanage. She felt so grateful, she rushed into the room without thinking or knocking first.

'Ah, Jenni, my poor dear girl!'

Miss Emily Jukes' pale, rather gaunt face was unsmiling, not in the least welcoming as she'd expected. Jenni waited for the invitation to be repeated. Instead Miss Jukes looked so sombre and silent, Jenni's momentary relief was stifled.

'Come to see how you are, I have,' Miss Jukes said at last. 'You can come back to work whenever you're ready, my girl. But there's no rush, mind.'

For some reason Jenni felt crushed. She wanted to say, yes, yes, without being asked; yes, she'd be glad to come and live with the sisters. She'd come tomorrow, if they wanted.

But the invitation still wasn't extended and suddenly Jenni felt contrary.

'I don't know whether I want to go on with my apprenticeship, Miss Jukes,' she said sulkily.

Perhaps her father had changed his mind and wanted his savings back, and that's why her parents had quarrelled.

'Oh, tut-tut!' Mrs Bevan had to put in her fourpennorth.

'Yes, you do, Jenni,' Miss Jukes said, quickly and firmly. 'Besides, if you give up now, it means your mother died for nothing.'

Open-mouthed, Jenni could only stare at her, speechless. Even Miss Jukes believed she was the cause of her mother's terrible death. With a sharp cry, Jenni fled from the room, and the awful truth.

A few days later Blodwen Thomas called at the Bevans'. Jenni deliberately went out into the backyard to avoid her. Mrs Bevan took the visitor into the parlour as usual. Jenni didn't bother to go and eavesdrop. She'd had enough of that! Her head ached from crying and her heart was sore from the knowledge that she had caused the tragedy. She didn't want to hear anyone else say it again. It was unbearable.

Since learning the truth about the cause of the tragedy, she'd thought long and hard about the last time she'd spoken with her mother. Looking back, the things Sarah had said that fateful morning now seemed meaningful and poignant, almost as if she'd had a premonition they'd never see each other again. Jenni shivered at the very thought of it.

She was putting the broom around the backyard when Mrs Bevan came looking for her.

'Miss Thomas is here, Jenni,' Mrs Bevan told her. 'Your mother's cousin – your next-of-kin.'

'I don't want to see or talk to her, the old battle-axe!'

Mrs Bevan looked startled.

'I think you'd better Jenni, because she's got some news about your father.'

Jenni looked apprehensively into Mrs Bevan's face. No one had mentioned her father to her since the day he'd been taken away in the Black Maria. Through the intervening weeks she'd hated him for what he'd done, but knowing now that she was the cause of her parents' quarrel, hating him seemed unfair.

'Where is he?'

'Miss Thomas will tell you, Jenni. And she's got some other news as well.'

Reluctantly, Jenni followed Mrs Bevan into the front parlour. Blodwen sat, like a large spider, on the edge of a chair by the lifeless fireplace. Dressed in black as ever, a small shapeless hat concealed her thin hair. Her skin looked pasty, Jenni thought, while her nose pointed forward as though determined to dominate every other feature in her plain face.

Jenni stuck out her lower lip belligerently, remembering the last time they'd met at Llawr-y-bryn, when Blodwen had humiliated her mother. She'd never forgive her for that.

'Jenni?' Blodwen said.

Her glance slid away from the girl's truculent stare.

She's ashamed, Jenni thought; ashamed of the way she treated my mother that day. So she ought to be, the ugly old harridan!

'You've got news of my father, then,' she said pertly. 'So spit it out!'

Both women gasped, but Jenni didn't care that she'd been rude. She'd hear what her mother's cousin had to say, then she'd get out of the room and away. She wanted nothing more to do with Blodwen Thomas.

Blodwen sat up straighter, though Jenni could see it took an effort for her mother's cousin to look her straight in the eye, and at the back of her mind, Jenni wondered at it.

'You watch your tongue, my girl!' Blodwen said, with an energy that startled Jenni. 'With your elders and betters.'

'Under a strain, she is, Miss Thomas, see,' Mrs Bevan butted in, her tone conciliatory.

Blodwen sniffed.

'No more than me,' she said, obviously piqued. 'I can hardly hold my head up in chapel anymore.'

'Say what you've come to say,' Jenni exclaimed heatedly. 'Then leave me be.'

'Your mother never taught you any manners, did she?' Blodwen pulled in her chin, her mouth set in a hard line. 'Your father's in prison, waiting for the case to be heard in the Cardiff Assizes in two months' time. He's pleading guilty so mercifully the hearing will be short.' She sniffed. 'Well, it's the least he could do under the circumstances, isn't it?'

She might have thought that herself, Jenni decided, but she didn't like Blodwen saying it in that nasty tone of voice.

'What business is it of yours anyway?'

Blodwen's small dark eyes sparked angrily.

'The awful disgrace to our family is my business,' she said, huffily. 'But the hearing won't be the worst of it. He'll almost certainly be convicted of murder, and that's a hanging charge.' She placed a hand on her bosom. 'Oh, to think such a scandal could happen in *my* family.'

Jenni glared at her. Blodwen *was* like a fat old black spider, and Jenni, wanting to take revenge for her callousness, longed to stamp on her.

'You're only my mother's cousin,' she said belligerently. 'And she never liked you. I'm no part of your family.'

'Oh, yes, you are!' Blodwen declared with a venomous gleam in her eyes. 'I'm your next-of-kin – your blood relation. And I know my Christian duty, too. That's why I've been to see the Authorities.'

'*What?*' Jenni's eyes opened wide with a sudden premonition of a new disaster in her life.

'You're coming into *my* care.' Blodwen nodded as she spoke. Her tone brooked no contradiction. 'The Authorities have made me your guardian, so to speak.'

'No!'

Jenni was aghast. She'd rather go to an orphanage, sleep on a slag heap, even remain with the Bevans, than live with a miserable, sanctimonious old woman like Blodwen.

'The Misses Jukes want to take me,' she said desperately. 'I'm going with them.'

'They've got no claim,' Blodwen said, with a narrow smile of triumph. 'I'm your kith and kin, Jenni Goodenough, and you'll do as I say from now on.'

Jenni was furious.

'I won't go with you, so there!'

'Well, we'll see what Dai Book has to say about that, my girl.'

Jenni hesitated, suddenly apprehensive. Dai Book had terrible power. She'd seen that the day he'd taken her father away in hand-cuffs, without letting her say one word to him; without giving her the chance to ask her father why he'd done such a horrible thing to them all. But, of course, she knew why now, didn't she?

Jenni swallowed hard.

'Nobody asked me where I want to live. Nobody asked my opinion,' she said sullenly.

'You're a minor,' Blodwen said dismissively. 'Your opinion is of no consequence. I know what's best for you. So do the Authorities.'

'They don't even *know* me,' Jenni flared. 'Who are they anyway, these *Authorities*?'

'People who make the laws about orphans like you,' Mrs Bevan put in hastily. 'It's no good arguing about it, Jenni, *cariad*. It's the law.'

'What you need badly is a good, clean, Christian upbringing,' Blodwen said sharply. 'When I think of the way you've been dragged up . . .'

'That's not true!' Jenni stormed, outraged at the slur against her mother. 'My mother was the best in the world. How dare you blacken her memory, you big-nosed old hypocrite!'

'Ooh!' As though stung, Blodwen bobbed up from her chair, the faint smell of carbolic rising with her. 'May God forgive you, biting the hand of Christian charity like that.'

'Jenni, for shame!' Mrs Bevan looked scandalised.

'I don't care!' she shouted. 'I'm not having her call my mother names.'

'Nobody's doing that, *cariad*.' Mrs Bevan's tone was soothing. 'Nobody speaks ill of the dead, do they, Miss Thomas?'

'She does!' Jenni pointed an accusing finger at Blodwen. 'You don't like me, and I don't like you, so why are you doing this, Blodwen?'

Jenni was astonished to see Blodwen's cheeks turn pink, and her glance slid away again. It looked almost furtive, she thought.

'We're family,' Blodwen said, though there was no real conviction in her voice. 'It's for your own good.'

She straightened up, regaining her composure before stepping towards the parlour door where she paused, glancing back at Jenni, eyes gleaming again.

'And from now on, miss, I'm *Auntie* Blodwen to you, remember that. I'll come for you and your things early tomorrow.'

She gave Jenni another piercing glance.

'Remember, I've got the law on my side.'

Jenni fumed, but had no answer to give. The law was implacable. She'd seen that for herself.

'Oh, by the way,' Blodwen went on haughtily. 'Your father has written to me. In the event of his . . .' her tongue stumbled over the word '. . . death, he has left you his life's savings – seventy-five pounds. I'm to open an account for you at the Post Office.' She sniffed. 'Not much, but think yourself lucky, my girl.'

'I don't *want* his money,' screamed Jenni, almost beside herself with grief and rage. 'I want nothing of his. I hate him!'

Bursting into tears, Jenni rushed from the room, jostling Blodwen in the parlour doorway, making her tut-tut in disgust.

She took refuge in the lavvy in the backyard, her only place of privacy from Mrs Bevan's prying eyes.

She didn't care if it *was* wicked, she hated her father. His money could rot in the Post Office. It was stained with her mother's blood and never, never would she touch a penny of it. She'd starve first!

Chapter Seven

Jenni sat in the pew, trying to concentrate on the words of the sermon, but it was no good. Her jumbled thoughts, her sheer unhappiness, kept getting in the way.

She couldn't resist glancing across at the opposite pew where Dilys sat with her family. Why was her friend being so distant? They always sat together but today Dilys had had only a brief, wan smile for her when she'd come into her old chapel in Trehafod, and now was pointedly ignoring her. In fact, everyone was ignoring her.

Jenni glanced along the pew where she sat. It was empty except for herself and, at the far end of the highly polished wooden bench, the tall, straight-backed figure of the local undertaker, Davies the Death. Jenni glanced away quickly. Looking at him always gave her the horrors.

Perhaps she shouldn't keep coming back to Trehafod like this. But it was only here in the village, in this chapel, that she felt close to her mother. And she missed her so much; ached to see Sarah's smiling, lovely face one more time.

The weeks since she'd gone to live with Blodwen in Llawr-y-bryn had crept by slowly and painfully. There was no love in her life now; no comfort; no support. Well, except for the Misses Jukes.

They were good to her. They didn't ignore her or treat her any differently. Jenni still wished she could have gone to live with them instead of Blodwen, but they'd never again mentioned their willingness to take her. Perhaps Miss Emily hadn't really meant it, Jenni reflected sadly.

She suddenly realised the sermon was over. Everyone was joining in the pastor's prayers. Jenni bowed her head, too, but today she just couldn't pray. Her life had been turned upside down, her heart broken by the terrible loss of her mother, and she couldn't help wondering why – why had it happened to her and her family? Why?

There was a rustle throughout the chapel as everyone reached for their hymn books, and the pastor was calling out the number of the last hymn.

Jenni fumbled with her hymn book, struggling against tears. She wouldn't make a fool of herself in chapel. She wouldn't!

She found the right page at last and stood as the small organ struck up the first notes. The voices of the congregation swelled as one, and the chapel was filled with music and praise, yet Jenni found she had no voice. Her throat was parched, and no sound would come. Suddenly, she felt ashamed and didn't know why.

Why? That question still haunted her. Would she ever get an answer?

The hymn was over and then came the blessing. Jenni felt she wanted to stand up again, open her arms to receive it. Of all the people in the congregation that day, she felt she needed a blessing the most.

The final Amen. Then clothes rustled and feet shuffled as people prepared to leave. The pastor was at the chapel door ready to shake hands as they left.

Jenni rose too and left the chapel hurriedly, being amongst the first to go. The pastor smiled at her kindly and squeezed her hand. She *was* grateful for his kindness but she wanted to get outside as quickly as she could. She was determined to corner Dilys and demand an explanation.

Jenni knew from past experience that groups of people would loiter outside the chapel talking, or rather gossiping. Tom Lewis and his wife always chatted to the pastor for ages after. Normally Jenni and Dilys would wander off, preoccupied with their own entertainments.

Jenni stood on the pavement, concealed behind a gate pillar, waiting. People spilled out of the chapel into the morning sunlight. Most of them paused, forming into groups and cliques; hatted heads nodding in conversation, gloved hands gesticulating. Impatient children ran and jumped up and down the steps to the chapel.

Peeking round the pillar, Jenni saw Tom Lewis in deep discussion with the pastor. Mr Lewis knew his Bible inside out and fancied himself a bit of a lay theologian. He'd be at that half an hour or more.

Mrs Lewis was with her cronies nearby, probably deciding who would provide the flowers for next Sunday while at the same time tearing somebody's reputation to shreds. That's what Mam had always said anyway.

Jenni drew back as Dilys, obviously bored to death, began to saunter towards the gates. As she came through them, Jenni grabbed at her arm and, ignoring her protests, dragged her along the pavement and away from the chapel.

'Jenni. Stop it!'

'I won't,' she gasped, hanging on like grim death and forcing her friend further along until they rounded the street corner.

'Now then, Dilys,' she said, panting a little. 'Why wouldn't you sit with me today? What's the matter?'

Avoiding Jenni's gaze, Dilys glanced down, scuffing the heel of her white shiny patent leather shoe on the pavement.

'My mam and dad say I can't be friends with you anymore.'

'What?' Jenni was astonished. 'Why?'

Dilys shrugged.

'It's because of the scandal and what it says in the papers, Jenni.'

'Papers?'

'Newspaper, mun. You know, Jen, about your da. He's been had up, hasn't he? For what he did to your mam, like.'

'What do the newspapers say?' Jenni was suddenly eager to find out.

She'd seen the placards outside the newsagent's, headlines screaming out her father's awful deed, but had not been able to find the courage to buy a paper; unwilling to revive all the horror she'd known in those first terrible days. But perhaps Dilys could tell her all she needed to know.

But her so-called friend looked pained.

'Not supposed to read newspapers, am I?'

'Oh, come on now, Dilys,' Jenni said impatiently. 'I know you. When do you ever take any notice of what your mam and dad say?'

'Well . . .' Dilys gave a wicked grin. 'There was a picture of your da in the *Cambrian Leader*. My dad bought a copy when he was down in Swansea last market day. My mam's having a new three-piece suite . . .'

'Never mind your mam's suite. Who cares?' Jenni cried, crossly. 'Tell me about my da.'

She wasn't jealous, but it cut her to the quick that other people's lives were going on as though nothing had happened, while hers had fallen apart.

'Your da has pleaded guilty, hasn't he?' Dilys went on archly. 'But he won't explain what happened exactly. The papers mention a mysterious letter . . .'

'A letter?' Jenni pounced on the new information. 'Who from? What was in the letter?'

Dilys shrugged again.

'They don't say. My dad says they're making it up just to sell papers. My dad says . . .'

'Oh, shut up about your dad!' Jenni snapped, annoyed by her

friend's prattling when she wanted to think.

Dilys looked annoyed.

'Dai Book told my dad that the story has got into the London papers, as well.' She looked defiantly at Jenni. '*My dad says* he wouldn't give two duck eggs for your da's chances, now.'

Jenni was startled.

'What d'you mean?'

Dilys lifted her nose, her expression arch again.

'He's a murderer, isn't he? He'll be hanged.'

'No!' Jenni screamed the word. The sound seemed to echo along the terraced street. 'No! Don't you say that.'

'Well, everybody's saying it, Jen. Why d'you think they're all keeping out of your way? My mam says I mustn't associate with a murderer's daughter. Bad blood, you know.'

'Ooh!' Jenni thought she'd choke on her anger and hurt.

Dilys suddenly looked abashed.

'Sorry, Jen. Honest, I am. It's not me that says it, is it? We can still be friends in secret, though. I'll write to you sometimes but . . .'

Dilys took a step back, and half turned away.

'But I can't talk to you anymore. You do understand, don't you, Jen?'

'No, I don't!' she cried out furiously. 'What kind of a friend are you? False, that's what you are. False, like it says in the Bible. Don't bother to write to me, Dilys. You're no friend of mine. I'll find new friends. You just wait and see!'

Jenni turned on her heel and rushed away. This was the last time she'd visit Trehafod. There was nothing left here for her now. No home; no friendship. Just lies, bad feelings and bad memories. But she'd wipe them from her mind and start again. There were plenty of chapels in Llawr-y-bryn and friends to be made there, truer than Dilys had ever been.

*

Jenni woke with a start, suddenly aware of knocking on the bedroom door. She glanced guiltily at the alarm clock. A quarter to six!

'Jenni!' Blodwen, out on the landing, sounded furious. 'Get up this instant. There's work to do.'

'All right, I'm up!'

She scrambled out of bed and opened the door, rubbing her eyes. She still felt tired.

'The alarm didn't go off, Auntie Blodwen,' she said defensively.

Blodwen's lips thinned.

'Same old excuse, isn't it?' She pulled in her chin, looking aggrieved. 'Now,' she went on, 'the fire wants lighting for starters. But clean out the ashes and blacklead the grate first.'

She turned to go back to her own room while Jenni leaned on the doorknob for support.

'I always do.'

Blodwen ignored her words.

'Scrub the scullery floor. Oh, and the parlour needs dusting in case Pastor Williams calls.' She glanced back over her shoulder. 'You'd better hurry to get it all done before breakfast. You don't want to be late for work, do you?'

Cleaning the grate later, Jenni found her thoughts were as black as the blacklead she was vigorously brushing on the iron bars.

Blodwen was taking advantage of her, getting far more out of her than the worth of her keep. Jenni fumed at the unfairness of it. But what could she do? Nothing, she reminded herself firmly. But just wait a few more years! When she came of age, she'd be free to go where she pleased.

The one advantage of living in Llawr-y-bryn was that she didn't have to face the long walk up and down the mountain road each morning and evening. At a run she could get from Blodwen's house to the shop on the main road in ten minutes, and still be on time.

Jenni was just finishing her breakfast porridge when Blodwen came down.

'Don't let me have to get you up again,' she began harshly, spooning oats into the saucepan which Jenni had just washed. 'Out of the Christian kindness of my heart I let you live here scot-free. Are you grateful? Oh, no. You take advantage of me at every turn. A bit of help is all I'm asking.'

Bit of help! Jenni pressed her lips closed, trying to keep a rein on her temper. She didn't trust herself to answer civilly right this minute. She felt too weary and the day had hardly begun.

'Five-thirty is your time, my girl,' Blodwen said.

She poured a cup of cold water on to the oats and dumped the saucepan on the gas ring which stood on the draining board next to the sink.

'Your mother let you run wild but this is a Christian house, this is. Early to bed, early to rise. Work and more work, that's what keeps a girl out of temptation's way. Pity your mother didn't follow that . . .'

Jenni jumped up from the table, unable to keep silent a second longer.

'You leave my mother's memory alone,' she shouted furiously. 'She loved me and took care of me. She was a wonderful woman. *She* knew what love is.'

Blodwen's small eyes squinted in anger.

'Yes, and look where it got her,' she snapped. 'You'd better listen to me or you'll come to a bad end as well.'

Jenni gaped. It wasn't Blodwen's first snide remark about Sarah, but it was her first direct reference to the tragedy since Jenni had moved in. She recalled Dilys's revelation about the newspaper stories. Blodwen must be aware of them and know more than she was saying.

Jenni felt resentful. Why was she being kept in the dark? And why were people shunning her, as though she herself had done something wrong? Did they all know she was to blame for the terrible quarrel? She felt sick at the thought.

'Is everyone saying it's my fault?' she asked tentatively. 'Are the newspapers saying that?'

'Newspapers?' Blodwen was stirring her porridge. She paused, looking startled.

Jenni felt suddenly angry, remembering how people in her own home village had turned their backs on her; how even Dilys, her one-time friend, wanted nothing more to do with her.

'Christian charity!' she spluttered. 'You're as bad as that lot at Trehafod. I'm never going back there again, not after the way they treated me last Sunday. I'll find a new chapel round here.'

Blodwen took the saucepan off the gas ring and put it to one side. Her expression was one of intense interest.

'Who's been talking in Trehafod?'

'No one,' Jenni exclaimed impatiently. 'That's the trouble. You know what's going on with my father and the hearing, Auntie Blodwen. Why don't you tell me?'

Blodwen immediately turned back to the preparation of her breakfast, lips clamped together tightly.

But Jenni wasn't going to be put off. She had a right to know what was happening to her father. She could never think of Blodwen as an ally, but her mother's cousin was the only person who could help her now.

'People are saying my father will hang,' Jenni went on desperately. 'Everyone knows what's going on except me. What are you hiding, Auntie Blodwen? Who sent the letter?'

'Letter!' Blodwen jumped back from the gas ring as though she'd been burned. The saucepan toppled sideways, spilling steaming porridge on to the draining board.

'A mysterious letter the newspapers are talking about. What does it mean, Auntie Blodwen?'

Not that the letter could have had anything to do with the tragedy, Jenni thought miserably. She already knew who was to blame, and wondered if she'd ever be able to forgive herself.

Blodwen was staring at her, pink spots high on her cheeks.
'Why should I know anything of a letter?'

'I ought to be told what's going on,' Jenni insisted.

Blodwen ran her tongue quickly over her lips. She looked
puffed out for a moment, as if she had difficulty breathing.

'You're just a child, Jenni,' she said. 'These matters are for
adults who understand them.'

She frowned absentmindedly at the spilt porridge, her
thoughts obviously elsewhere.

'As for Sunday worship,' she said, her tone vague, 'you
couldn't do better than join my chapel.' She rallied, eyes sharp
and challenging. 'I'm going to the Bible meeting tonight. You can
come with me.'

She sounded as though she was doing the girl a great favour.

'No, thanks!' Jenni jumped up from the table. 'I've had enough
of hypocrites.'

Miss Emily was showing her how to finish off a buttonhole. Jenni
watched the older woman's fingers, so nimble and sure. She'd
taken scraps of material home to practise on, but couldn't yet
match Miss Emily's skill, though one day soon she would.

'Right,' Miss Emily said. 'You do the next one, Jenni.'

'Me?' She was astonished. 'But this is Mrs Councillor Taylor's
new suit. What if I make a mistake?'

'Then you'll unpick it, my girl,' Miss Emily said dryly. 'And
do it again. Go on with you, Jenni. You'll do fine.'

Finding more confidence from her employer's warm tone,
Jenni set to. She was concentrating so hard she soon forgot the
important personage for whom the garment was being made. She
loved sewing and felt it was more than a craft. It was an art in itself.

'Well, now!' Miss Emily examined her work closely. 'That's
fine work, Jenni. Fine work. You're doing well. Your mam would
be proud of you.'

Jenni was elated at the praise, yet felt sad, too, at the mention of her mother. Of course, she must be in everyone's mind, with the stories in the newspapers and everything, Jenni mused. You couldn't blame people for being curious.

She felt very grateful to the Misses Jukes. The sisters' attitude to her had not changed one iota from the day they'd first agreed to take her as their apprentice. How different her life would be now if only they'd taken her in after her mother's death. But it was no good dwelling on what might have been. Thanks to them she still had her work, and that was all in all to her now.

While they continued sewing the buttonholes, Jenni spoke about her quarrel with Dilys the previous Sunday, and the scandal in the papers.

'Have you seen them, Miss Emily?' Jenni asked. 'Can you tell me anything?'

She knew she'd get a straight and honest answer from the older woman.

Miss Emily was silent for a moment.

'Jenni, take some advice,' she said at last. 'Don't delve. I suggest you distance yourself from the whole thing.'

The girl was astonished.

'But how can I when it's my own father!'

'Jenni, listen.' Miss Emily put down her piece of sewing and touched Jenni's arm kindly. 'You have a future, a life of your own to live. It's cruel, I know, but you can't afford to associate yourself with this scandal, or even with your own family name.'

'But that would make me no better than the people who've turned their backs on me,' Jenni cried passionately. 'I'd be doing the same thing to my father.'

'You can't help him now,' Miss Emily said firmly, squeezing her hand at the same time. 'I believe he pleaded guilty to save your name being dragged through the courts; to save you from the shame and humiliation.'

A sob caught in Jenni's throat. Everyone believed the tragedy was her fault. Now her father was trying to save her from the consequences. She shouldn't hate him for what he'd done.

Jenni couldn't help bursting into tears.

'Oh, don't drip all over Mrs Councillor Taylor's new cashmere suit, Jenni, for goodness' sake!' Miss Emily said, snatching the garment from her fingers.

Tears flooded her eyes yet she wanted to smile at the same time. Quaint and funny though the Misses Jukes were, their hearts were true and in the right place. She should listen to their advice.

'Sorry, Miss Emily,' Jenni said, wiping the tears away with the heel of her hand.

She mustn't give in like this. Miss Emily was right. She had to make a new life. But how would she live through the years before she came of age? How could she manage to survive without her mother's love?

'I'll try to be more grown up in future,' she murmured.

Miss Emily inclined her head, looking at Jenni kindly.

'That old witch Blodwen Thomas is making life difficult, is she?'

Jenni nodded. She trusted the sisters but she wouldn't tell them everything about her relationship with her mother's cousin. People knew too much about her already.

'Well, look, Jenni,' Miss Emily said cheerfully. 'Why don't you start taking in bits of sewing? You know, to make an extra shilling or two.'

Jenni stared at her in astonishment.

'You'd let me do that? You wouldn't mind?'

Blodwen had warned her that her employers wouldn't stand for her doing sewing privately.

'You wouldn't think I was taking bread from your mouths?' Miss Emily smiled broadly.

'Well, we wouldn't expect you to start making two-piece suits wholesale, mind. But I see no harm in your running up a skirt or two. Taking up hems.'

Jenni was overwhelmed. It was the last thing she'd expected. But she couldn't work at home anyway. It was out of the question. Her shoulders dropped.

'Haven't got a sewing machine, have I? And besides, Auntie Blodwen would never stand for it.'

Sewing made too much mess, she had declared, but Jenni suspected it was just perversity.

'You can use the machines here. After hours, of course.'

'What?'

'Put a postcard in the window at the Post Office,' Miss Emily suggested. 'Or the newsagent.'

'Oh, Miss Emily!' Jenni felt a lump rise in her throat at their kindness. 'This is very generous of you.'

'One thing, though, Jenni, my dear.' Miss Emily looked serious and somewhat sad. 'Don't advertise under your own name. I suggest you start calling yourself Jenni Thomas from now on.'

It was Miss Emily who told Jenni the date of the impending execution a few weeks later. Her mind had been less anxious of late. She'd found a new chapel, and though she'd made no friends as yet, people did not seem so unfriendly as they were at Trehafod.

She heard nothing more of newspaper stories or any talk about the terrible event that had changed her life forever. She'd almost believed it might all be quietly forgotten. Miss Emily's revelation came as a severe shock.

When Jenni came into the workroom at nine that morning the Jukes sisters were already there, bent over a newspaper spread out on the workbench.

Miss Emily snatched it up as Jenni appeared, folding it roughly and holding it behind her back. Miss Lucy was looking at Jenni, bespectacled eyes wide and somewhat frightened while her sister's face was white and more gaunt than usual.

'Jenni!' Miss Emily sounded as though she was the last person in the world they'd expected to see at nine o'clock of a Friday morning.

Jenni felt apprehension in her chest, cold as stone.

'What's happened?'

'Sit down by here, my dear,' Miss Emily said. There was a tremor in her voice, and Jenni felt her legs begin to tremble, too.

'What is it?'

Miss Lucy gave a short stifled sob which made her sister glance at her sharply.

'Lucy, go and make a pot of tea for us all,' she said swiftly.

Apprehension growing, Jenni watched Miss Lucy waddle from the room.

One so stout and one so thin, she pondered absentmindedly, the sisters did make a curious pair. They'd been so very kind to her over these last terrible months, though, her only friends. She loved them both dearly. But what had they to tell her?

Jenni turned her gaze back to Miss Emily and could tell by the older woman's expression that worse was yet to come.

'Jenni, you have to be brave.'

She felt her courage shrink.

'Sentence has been passed on your father, my dear,' Miss Emily went on solemnly. 'It's in the paper here. No! Don't look at it,' she cried as Jenni reached out a hand.

'I *must* see!'

'No!'

She pushed Jenni down on to a work-stool.

'Your father has been sentenced to death.'

The bald statement made her heart lurch painfully and she opened her mouth to gulp in air, feeling she was suffocating.

'Jenni, are you all right?'

She nodded dumbly, though she was far from all right. Everyone had been telling her for months that her father would hang for what he'd done. Some, like Oggie James, who'd made it his business to seek her out, had been more graphic and cruel, obviously delighting in the pain they caused her.

Her own commonsense had told her that her father must pay for what he'd done, yet she'd never really believed it *would* happen. Now her worst nightmare was coming true. Would the aftermath of her mother's terrible death ever be over?

'What is to happen?'

Miss Emily ran her tongue quickly over lips that were obviously dry.

'The execution is set for next Monday morning at eight o'clock.' She paused then went on: 'I'm so sorry.'

Jenni was silent and still. A coldness was creeping over her; it felt like the coldness of death. She stared at Miss Emily dumbly and was aware of tears glistening in the woman's eyes.

'They can't do it,' Jenni whispered, as much in defiance as anything else. She could hardly form the words, her lips were so cold and stiff. 'They can't hang him.'

It was already the middle of September and she had lived with the pain and misery of the terrible events all summer. Now the Authorities were planning to wreck her life further. How could she bear it?

'Jenni, my dear, it's inevitable. Your father pleaded guilty, and what's more, offered no defence or explanation of his awful deed. I really think he was full of remorse and *wanted* the ultimate punishment.'

'But what about me?' Jenni cried out. 'Am I to live with this shame all my life?'

'No, you don't deserve that,' Miss Emily said firmly. 'Drop your family name of Goodenough. It can only bring you notoriety and disgrace from now on. In a few years you'll finish your apprenticeship. Leave the Rhondda then. Get away to some big town where no one knows you. You'll find happiness, Jenni, and success, I know you will, if you leave the past behind.'

She put a hand gently on Jenni's shoulder.

'Sunday night you'll sleep here. We're your friends, Lucy and me. And you'll need friends to comfort you, my dear, at eight o'clock next Monday morning.'

Chapter Eight

LLAWR-Y-BRYN, FEBRUARY 1924

Jenni shivered, the chill of the workroom striking through to her bones. In fairness to her employers she'd put out the oil heater two hours before, unable in all good conscience to use their sewing machines free of charge and burn their paraffin at the same time. They'd been so good to her over these last four years and she didn't want to take advantage now that her apprenticeship would soon be over.

With a sigh, Jenni put the garment she was working on to one side, folding it carefully. She had no idea what to do once her apprenticeship was over. She and Blodwen had become used to each other over the years, but it was never easy living together; never comfortable or companionable. There was no warmth in their relationship, and her only comfort was derived from the Jukes sisters. She dreaded parting from them, but part she must. They were already looking for a new apprentice.

Jenni wrapped the garment in a piece of brown paper and tied it around with string. She'd spend the rest of the evening in her bedroom, working on the buttonholes. She had to be careful because Blodwen was still being awkward about her bringing sewing into the house.

She slipped into the warm coat of navy wool with a big wing collar which she'd designed and made herself. Her employers had been full of praise for it, and Jenni was proud. She'd offered to make a similar coat for Blodwen but she'd turned up her nose at the offer, saying the coat was showy and sinfully extravagant. Jenni had long since given up trying to please her.

Pulling on her hat and gloves and slipping her parcel under her arm, Jenni reached up to put out the gas then went down into the shop where bales of material were stacked on the shelves.

As usual, on the counter was a daily newspaper. Always keep up with the world, was Miss Emily's motto, and she encouraged Jenni to do the same, leaving the newspaper there each day.

Jenni picked it up and glanced at the front page.

Crowds waited in the sweltering heat of Luxor, she read, while the sarcophagus of some long-dead Egyptian king was opened for the first time in thousands of years. Tutankhamun. Jenni wasn't even sure how to pronounce the name.

Sweltering heat! That seemed like another world.

She glanced through the window of the shop. Several days' snow covered the road and pavement, hardened into ice by the bitter cold of the nights.

She was reminded of yesterday when a tradesman's horse had slipped on the ice and fallen between the shafts, right in front of the shop. Her ears still rang with the awful sound of the gunshot as the veterinary surgeon had come to put the poor animal out of its pain. The snow outside was still stained with its blood and she couldn't bear to look at it.

A movement across the street caught her eye. A figure was standing in the doorway of Owens the Meat. A male figure. She'd seen the same figure yesterday evening, too.

Jenni felt her hackles rise. Oggie James! She was sure it was him. He still came down the mountain from Trehafod periodically to harass her. She couldn't retaliate by kicking his shins now. It wasn't dignified for a young woman of her age, and she intended to keep her dignity at all costs.

Even after four years, the disgrace of her father's execution for murder still hung over her like a dark, ominous cloud. Some people would never let her forget it, Oggie for one. She felt sometimes that she'd never be rid of it. The memory always brought pain and an aching longing for her mother.

Jenni peered across the road in the dim light of the street lamps. The figure had faded away now, but she knew he was out there somewhere.

Calling up the stairs to let the sisters know she was leaving, Jenni pulled the shop door closed behind her.

On the pavement, she glanced around carefully. No sign of Oggie James. There were few people about to brave the icy streets, despite its being Saturday evening. Light blazed from the pub on the corner. She could hear singing already although it had only just turned seven-thirty.

Averting her gaze from the bloodstained snow in the gutter, black now in the lamplight, she walked gingerly along the pavement, feeling the coldness strike up through the thin soles of her shoes, and resolved to get them re-tapped the following day.

As she turned the corner into the steep incline beside Ebenezer Chapel, he stepped out from the darkened recess of the doorway, a cloth cap pulled down around his ears against the cold and a muffler swathing his neck, the wool faded and thickened.

Startled, Jenni jumped aside, stifling a cry; almost losing her balance on the ice. A deep anger assailed her as she remembered another day and another time when Oggie James had been the harbinger of the worst event of her life. She hated him for reviving that awful memory.

But she was a different person now, older and hopefully wiser. Oggie had changed, too, was now a grown man, but she was no more afraid of him today than she'd been years ago, and still felt nothing but contempt for him.

'Get away from me, Oggie!'

'You're late,' he said, surprising her. 'Been hanging about by here for ages, haven't I?'

Jenni tossed her head, her surprise turning to deep irritation.

'More fool you then, because no one asked you to. No one wants you to.'

Pushing her parcel more firmly under her arm, Jenni decided to ignore him and started walking again. To her consternation, he fell into step beside her.

'Them old women work you hard, don't they?' he said conversationally. 'They wants to be told off, keeping you late on a Saturday. I'll have a word with them, if you like.'

Jenni frowned in displeasure at his presence and his words.

'What are you blabbering about, Oggie?'

'Them old scrags you work for,' he said. 'Got their needles into you, haven't they?' He guffawed at his own pathetic joke.

Jenni stopped and glared at him.

'You mind your own business, Oggie,' she snapped. 'Keep away from the shop, and keep away from me, too.'

He shrugged.

'Only trying to help you, wasn't I?'

He tried to take her arm as he spoke.

Jenni shrugged it away roughly.

'Don't you dare lay a hand on me!' she cried, outraged. 'Push off! Go on. I don't want help or anything else from you, Oggie James.'

His step seemed to falter but he recovered, pushing his hands into his pockets.

'Don't be so touchy, will you?' he retorted gruffly. 'I just want to ask you something.'

Jenni was silent, hurrying on up the slope. Row after row of terraced houses intersected the road she climbed, higgledy-piggledy streets clinging to the side of the mountain, their drabness barely disguised by winter whiteness.

Her feet slithered in her haste to outpace him. She couldn't wait to reach Blodwen's house tonight.

'The funfair will be in Cwmgelligors Monday,' he said. 'I saw the posters.'

'What? In this weather?'

'The thaw's set in down there. The roads are almost clear,' he said. 'Wondering, I was, if you'd like to come with me Monday night? It'd be a bit of fun, like.'

Astonished, Jenni stopped in her tracks.

'Go with you?' She didn't bother to keep the deep contempt she felt out of her voice. 'Not likely! Don't want anything to do with you, Oggie. Why can't you get that through your thick head? Too dim, is it?'

The nearby street lamp caught the expression on his face. He was scowling at her.

'Just trying to be friendly, that's all. You won't get no other blokes after you, if that's what you're thinking,' he said harshly. 'Everybody knows about your da – and your mam, as well.'

'Perhaps you're right,' Jenni snapped. 'But if you were the last man on earth, I wouldn't be interested. So there.'

She started to move off again but he grabbed at her arm.

'Hey! Who are you to look down on me?' he snarled savagely, and Jenni's heart gave a lurch.

She tried to shrug free but his grip was tight and painful.

'Let go!' she cried out.

'No, I won't, see.'

He pulled her towards him and, resisting, her feet slithered dangerously on the paving stones.

'What makes you so toffee-nosed, eh?' he went on, his voice thick with rage. 'You're only the daughter of a dirty whore and a murderer. You're trash, you are, Jenni Goodenough. No better than a tart.'

'*What?*'

Shock hit her like a physical blow and she was stunned for a moment. What did he mean? Suddenly furious at the insult, and forgetting she wore gloves, she raised one hand to strike his face but he caught it brutally, then with a quick flick of his wrist, twisted her arm behind her back.

Helpless in his grip, Jenni was appalled at his sudden attack. Her parcel fell on to the frozen paving stones and he kicked at it, sending it spinning out on to the road.

'Anybody'd think you was better than me,' he said harshly. 'Teach you a lesson, I will, though.'

Pulling her round to face him, he tried to draw her even closer. Guessing his intention, Jenni struggled wildly, turning her face away.

'Let go of me, you pig!' she screamed. 'I'll have you up for this, Oggie James.'

'Shut your face!' he snarled. 'A tart like your mother, that's all you are.'

Terrified, Jenni struggled like one possessed, unable to believe this was really happening. She smelled beer on his breath, and felt sick to her stomach. The pressure on her arms was agonising. She had to bite on her lower lip to stop herself crying out in pain.

Suddenly there was a shout behind them.

'Hoi!'

A man's voice.

Forcing her head back so that she could look past Oggie's shoulder, Jenni saw a man hurrying towards them from further down the road. She felt Oggie tense but he didn't release his grip on her.

'Hoi! You!' The man slipped and nearly fell but regained his balance quickly. He had almost reached them and came to a slithering stop a few feet away.

'Let her go, sonny,' the man said evenly.

Jenni felt a wave of relief go through her. This man was tall and broad-shouldered, a match for Oggie any day. She thanked God he was passing by. Her guardian angel, perhaps?

'Bugger off, old man,' Oggie snarled. 'This tart and me's got business, and it's none of yours, see.'

'I said, take your hands off her.'

There was menace in the older man's tone, but Oggie didn't seem disturbed by it and was openly scornful.

'Or what, old man?'

'Or else, Sonny Jim, I'll smash you into the ground, like I did to *your* old man once.' The man pushed back his cap, and the lamplight fell on his face. 'Remember me?'

Oggie gave a start, and Jenni could almost smell his sudden fear.

'You!'

'Yes, you know me, Oggie. And you know I can do it. Now let her go.'

Oggie released her immediately and stepped back.

Amazed and grateful, Jenni rubbed at her arms, sore and numbed where his fingers had bitten into her flesh, even through the wool of her coat.

'Thank you,' she said gratefully to her rescuer.

'That's all right, *cariad.*'

Oggie looked from Jenni to the man and back again. Illuminated by the lamplight, his pugnacious features were contorted with impotent fury. Jenni remembered seeing that expression once before.

'Oh, I see the way things are now,' he said slowly.

'Hope you do, Oggie,' the man said harshly. 'Because if I find out you've been bothering this young woman again, I'll put you on crutches — permanently. Right?'

Oggie glowered at both of them.

'Get you for this, I will,' he said through clenched teeth. 'And you'll never see it coming.'

She stared at him nervously. There was such hatred in the eyes glaring at her. They weren't youngsters anymore; she couldn't deal with him as easily as she'd once done, and suddenly she found his words and expression deeply menacing, and was afraid.

'Be even with you one day, I will, you little tart,' Oggie rasped. 'You can bank on it.'

The man took a step forward.

'Bugger off now!'

Oggie side-stepped into the road then, turning on his heel, began to walk swiftly back down the slope, slithering and sliding in his haste.

Jenni gave a long sigh of relief.

'Thank you so very much,' she said to her companion.

'No need to thank me, Jenni.'

She was startled by his use of her name. Oggie hadn't mentioned it, she was certain, so how did this stranger know it?

'You know me?' She tried to peer more closely at him. 'Do I know you?'

He removed his cap.

'You might remember me, Jenni. I used to collect the rents for old Meredith some years ago. Bert Herbert's the name.'

Jenni shook her head. There might be something vaguely familiar about him, but she couldn't be certain. Still, she was surprised he remembered her name.

It was getting colder. Her feet felt like blocks of ice and she shivered violently. She was more than grateful to him for his rescue but she couldn't stand around any longer. She held out her hand to shake his, and to show their chance meeting was over.

'Well, thank you again, Mr Herbert. I really am obliged to you.'

He didn't attempt to take her hand.

'Jenni, we've got to talk. I want to tell you about your mother.'

She stared.

'What?'

'At the house, I was, that morning. The morning she . . . died. If I'd got there a minute or two earlier . . .'

'What are you talking about?'

'I don't know what you've been told or what you've read or heard, but I want to tell you the truth. How it really was.'

She shook her head in bewilderment.

'Mr Herbert, you're not making any sense.'

He looked about them, then down the slope to the main road. 'We can't hang about here. It's too cold. I must talk to you. Look, let's walk back to the Brynmawr Arms. It'll be warm in there.'

Jenni was aghast at the suggestion, and indignant, too.

'A pub! Certainly not!' She half turned away from him, anxious now to be on her way. 'Just because Oggie called me a bad name, don't think I'm one of those loose girls who goes into pubs with men, Mr Herbert. I'm respectable.'

She caught the righteous tone in her own voice and was disturbed despite her indignation. She was beginning to sound like Auntie Blodwen.

'I know that, Jenni.' He sounded sincere. He shook his head slowly. 'I want to tell you about Sarah, that's all. Been hanging around for days trying to get a chance to speak with you.'

Jenni remembered the man in the butcher's doorway. She hadn't been mistaken in thinking she'd seen him there more than once.

'The café won't be open this time of night,' she said thoughtfully.

Now that she'd got over the shock of his words, she desperately wanted to learn all he could tell her about her mother. The fact that he'd been at her home on the morning of the tragedy was certainly something she wanted, needed, to know more about.

Suddenly her mind was made up. She stepped into the road to retrieve her parcel.

'Come with me, Mr Herbert,' she said. 'We can talk at my Auntie Blodwen's house. She'll have gone to bed by this time.'

Blodwen was usually in bed by half-past eight. She thought it sinful to stay up any later. It suited Jenni very well. Often she'd sneak back downstairs to sit in the living-room and read or do some illicit sewing. Blodwen's bedroom was in the front so she couldn't see the flicker of the re-lit gas mantle.

This evening, climbing the steep steps to the house, Jenni was dismayed to see light reflected through the small fanlight over the front door. Blodwen was still up!

She thought swiftly. She wouldn't send Mr Herbert away now. They would wait Blodwen out if necessary. Something warned her that what she learned tonight would be of great importance to her. She'd been in ignorance of the tragedy for too long.

'This way. And be very quiet, Mr Herbert,' Jenni warned softly.

She led the way to the back door through the narrow alley between the side of the house and the towering wall of Zion Chapel. Blodwen insisted she use this entrance as the front door was opened only for privileged persons such as Pastor Williams.

'Please stay out here for a while, Mr Herbert,' Jenni requested. 'Sorry to ask you to wait in the cold.'

Bert Herbert gave a low laugh.

'Don't fancy running into Blodwen Thomas, thanks!' he said grimly. 'Rather tackle Oggie James any day.'

'I'm sure she'll go up soon,' Jenni said. 'Then I'll make us some tea.'

Squaring her shoulders, she opened the back door and went in.

Immediately, Blodwen called to her from the living-room.

'Jenni! Is that you?'

'Yes, of course, Auntie Blodwen.'

With a deep sigh of resignation, Jenni went to see her, pulling off her hat and gloves and removing her coat as she went.

Blodwen was in nightie and dressing gown; thin, straggly hair hanging limply around her ears. Her glare was fierce as she looked at Jenni, her mouth set in a prudish pout.

'Where've you been?' She pointed to the clock on the mantelpiece. 'Do you know what time it is? It's gone half-past eight. No respectable girl stays out until this time.'

'I was late leaving the shop,' Jenni said, defensively.

She had no intention of relating her unpleasant encounter with Oggie James. Blodwen would deliberately see the worst side of that.

'So you say!' Blodwen peered at her keenly. 'Have you been with a man?'

Jenni's mouth dropped open in astonishment, then shock and anger.

'How dare you ask me that?' she flared. 'What are you suggesting?'

Blodwen sniffed disparagingly.

'Blood will out, that's what I say,' she answered darkly. 'You was brought up on bad habits. It's bound to show one day. I've been expecting it, but I won't have any looseness around my house.'

She jerked her head towards the stairs.

'Now get to bed, will you?' She walked towards the stairs herself. 'Keeping decent people up until all hours,' she muttered. 'It's disgusting!'

'Not had a cup of tea yet, have I?' Jenni answered defiantly. 'Cold, I am. I'll go up when I'm ready.'

Blodwen paused at the foot of the stairs, staring at her suspiciously.

'If you're going to turn out like your mother you'll have to leave. You're old enough now. My debt is paid.'

'What do you mean?'

'Kinship has its limits, my girl. Won't have you bringing trouble to my door, I won't.'

With one last suspicious look, she disappeared up the stairs and Jenni let out a sigh of relief. For years she'd put up with Blodwen's snide remarks about her mother. Perhaps tonight she'd find out what lay behind it all. Then there were Oggie's uncalled-for insults earlier. What did it all mean?

Jenni hurried to open the back door. Bert Herbert was standing huddled in the doorway of the outside lavatory. He hurried forward when she beckoned, finger pressed against her lips in a warning to him to be silent.

'Go in the living-room by there,' she said in a hushed voice. 'But for heaven's sake, Mr Herbert, keep your voice down.'

She made a pot of tea and put a few buttered scones on a plate.

He was warming himself in front of the range. In the small room he looked enormous and overpowering, and suddenly she had doubts about the wisdom of inviting a comparative stranger into Blodwen's home, especially at this hour.

'Mr Herbert, it's late, and I have to get up early in the morning. Perhaps you'll drink your tea and go.'

He sat on the chair near the fire and accepted the cup of tea she offered him. He took one of the scones and bit into it hungrily.

'No need to fear me, Jenni, *cariad*,' he said, his mouth full. 'Old enough to be your father, I am.'

'You're a stranger to me, Mr Herbert.'

He took a sip of tea then looked at her keenly, the directness of his gaze making her cheeks flush.

'I wasn't a stranger to your mother, Jenni. Sarah and I were . . . close.'

'What are you talking about?' she responded tetchily, not wanting to understand what he was implying. 'You were just the rent man.'

'No, Jenni.' He shook his head. 'It was me who gave Sarah the money for your apprenticeship at Jukes. I stole the money from old Meredith. I did it for Sarah.'

'No!' Jenni jumped up, almost spilling her tea.

She spoke louder than she'd meant to and then stood paralysed, afraid Blodwen had heard. But silence reigned as she and Bert Herbert stared at each other.

'No,' she said in a hushed voice, subsiding on to her chair again. 'No, it's not true. My father gave his savings for my premium. My mother said so.'

'She lied, *cariad*,' Bert Herbert said quietly. 'Me and your mother planned to run away together. We were going that morning.'

Jenni put down her tea cup with a rattle, her hands shaking with anger.

'Now I know you're lying,' she hissed fiercely. 'My mother would never have left me. She loved me too much.'

Bert Herbert put down his cup too, wiping crumbs from his mouth with the back of his hand.

'Jenni, I'm not going to treat you like a child,' he said. 'You're a woman now, and I feel I can speak frankly.'

There was a rawness in his tone. Jenni knew instinctively that he was telling the truth.

'Your mother and me . . . well, we were lovers. Do you understand what that means?'

Jenni felt her cheeks flame.

'Of course I do!' She bit her lip. 'But I can't believe it of her. Not my mother.'

'Your mother loved you, Jenni, but she also wanted to live a little. Your father, God rest his soul, couldn't give her the life she wanted. She was coming away with me.'

'She wouldn't leave me!' Jenni whispered miserably.

She'd never believe that of her mother, no matter what he said. But even as she thought that, memories returned of that last morning. Her mother had said some strange things. In premonition of her own death? No, Jenni realised, because Sarah *knew* she was going away and leaving Jenni behind. This man had become more important to Sarah than her own daughter.

Jenni bit down on her lip in an effort to quell the hurt in her heart at the thought. Why had that happened? What power had Bert Herbert wielded over her mother? Jenni didn't understand it.

She watched him covertly as he held out his hands towards the grate and the waning warmth of the fire.

'When she didn't meet me in the lane, I came to the house looking for her.' He clasped his big hands together suddenly, as though wincing from a hurt. 'If only I'd been a few minutes sooner, I could have stopped him. But Sarah was already dead . . .'

Jenni couldn't bear to hear more.

'Don't, please!'

'Sorry, *cariad*.'

He was silent for a moment while Jenni forced back tears. Why was he telling her all this? What had he to gain from it?

'Your father kept his mouth shut,' Bert said at last. 'He was a fool! He might've saved himself from the rope if he'd told the truth. An unfaithful wife; an outraged husband. He'd have got plenty of sympathy.'

He glanced across at her and Jenni quickly blinked tears away.

'He did it to save you from the scandal, I reckon. Huh! It was a useless sacrifice. People talk, malicious people, and the papers soon got wind of it. The scandal erupted anyway, and your mother's name was dragged through the mud.'

'Why are you telling me this now?' she whispered.

'Couldn't before. Old Meredith found out about the money I'd stolen. Had to disappear, didn't I?'

He reached for another scone.

'Been knocking about down London, I have. Heard from a friend about Meredith dying. Risked coming back for a few days, but I can't stay.'

He looked at her earnestly.

'Wanted you to know the truth about your mother, Jenni. She wasn't a tart, and she wasn't bad, like you might've heard. She was a woman with plenty of love to give. And she gave it to me. And I . . . I loved her.'

But Jenni was hardly listening, too busy with her thoughts. So this was what people had been hiding from her. Auntie Blodwen, despite all her faults, had made a good job of protecting her from the truth these last years. But it didn't prevent people from calling her bad names. People like Oggie James. The stink of the scandal still clung to her, even though she hadn't even been aware of it. She realised it would always cling as long as she remained in the Valley.

Jenni swallowed hard. It was time for her visitor to go. She had a lot to think about and to plan.

'Thank you, Mr Herbert.' She rose to her feet. 'I know now what I must do. I've got to get away from the Rhondda.'

'Perhaps I can help you there . . .'

'No!' Jenni answered quickly.

Suddenly she felt angry.

'I think you've done enough, Mr Herbert. My mother died because of you.'

He stood up, towering above her. There was a roughness about him that made her wonder why her mother had associated herself with him. It wasn't only that he'd fallen on hard times as could clearly be seen from the well-worn look of his clothes. He was in every way the opposite of Jenni's father.

He picked up his cap and held it against his chest.

'Don't blame me. No one's to blame. Not even your father for that matter,' he said gruffly.

'I don't blame him anymore,' Jenni said. 'Now I understand why he did it.'

'If there *is* any blame,' he went on, 'it lies with whoever wrote that bloody letter.'

'Letter?'

Jenni was suddenly alert. She remembered mention of a mysterious letter years ago. No one had ever explained that to her, either.

'Tell me about the letter.'

'Sarah's head must have hit the brass fender,' he said slowly. 'Your father was kneeling beside her. I saw a letter, open, on the mat beside them. They were quarrelling over it, I reckon. The police never disclosed exactly what it said or who wrote it because it might have saved his neck. But I've a good idea who sent it.'

Jenni felt breathless.

'Who?'

Bert Herbert put his cap on and wound his muffler more tightly around his neck.

'Ask Blodwen Thomas.'

Chapter Nine

Jenni could hardly contain herself next morning. She'd slept badly, her mind filled with disturbing thoughts and images conjured up by Bert Herbert's story.

She still didn't want to accept that her mother had planned to desert her, but at the same time she knew for certain that when Bert had confessed to being her mother's lover, he'd spoken the truth. The memory of Sarah's last words to her and the look in Bert's eyes were enough to convince her. He had the look of a man with a weight on his conscience and despair in his heart.

Just as he'd been about to leave, he'd given her a searching glance.

'You're so like your mother, Jenni,' he'd said quietly. 'So beautiful. It's uncanny. You were just a gawky kid when I last saw you.'

Then, with an assurance she would never see him again, he was gone.

Jenni had pondered on his words in the sleepless small hours. She was well aware she had inherited her mother's striking looks, but that was as far as the likeness went. She would never be as foolish as Sarah. That foolishness had ended in a tragedy which had wrecked three lives, maybe four. Jenni would never let her feelings overrule her sense of rightness. Her mother had been too emotional; too easily led. Jenni resolved that no man would do that to her. And when she married, as she hoped she would, she'd be very careful in her choice of husband.

She was glad when the alarm clock sounded at six-thirty. There'd be no cleaning or other chores required of her today, the Sabbath, so she could get up an hour later than usual. Auntie Blodwen would attend the morning service at her chapel. She was probably up already, washing herself in the sink in the scullery.

Then there was the Sunday School class Auntie Blodwen took in the afternoon. Jenni always pitied the pupils. Finally, tea for Pastor Williams in the front parlour, before the evening service.

Today, though, Jenni was determined to confront Auntie Blodwen before she left for chapel. She had to learn the truth about that mysterious letter. Bert Herbert had hinted Blodwen was responsible. Jenni knew she wouldn't be able to rest until she had uncovered the whole truth.

Blodwen was running cold water into the saucepan she'd used for making porridge, to let it soak. She was in her flannel dressing-gown, her hair still hanging loose. Jenni could tell by the shiny, scrubbed look of her face that she'd already washed.

'Auntie Blodwen, I want to talk to you.'

'To apologise, I expect,' she said with a sniff. 'I should think so, too.'

'No,' Jenni said quickly. 'It's about a letter.'

She caught Blodwen's startled blink.

'What letter?' She bustled away from the sink. 'Haven't got time to talk now, have I? The service starts at eight, and I've still got to dress myself.'

She pushed past Jenni in the scullery doorway and headed for the stairs. Jenni hesitated, then let her go. She'd have her break-fast first, wait for Blodwen to come down again. She was determined to have this mystery solved before the day was much older.

She'd made her own porridge and eaten it before Blodwen

reappeared, wearing a black hat and coat. Why did she always look as though she were in mourning? Jenni often wondered, watching her mother's cousin fussily pulling on a pair of black kid gloves.

It was obvious Blodwen had never known what it was to be happy. She was more to be pitied than anything else. Jenni's life had been spoiled by a bitter tragedy, but at least she had known the joy of warmth and love from her mother. And she had plenty to give herself. Blodwen, on the other hand, seemed to have nothing to give anyone.

With a sigh, Jenni looked at the clock on the mantelpiece.

'You're leaving very early this morning, Auntie Blodwen,' she said. 'Are you trying to avoid talking to me?'

'Certainly not!' Blodwen's eyes glinted in annoyance. 'I've got to instruct Mrs Parry about the flower rota,' she said as she picked up her black patent handbag. 'There's too much backsliding at the chapel. Only saying as much to Pastor Williams, I was . . .'

'You can spare me five minutes, then,' Jenni interrupted quickly. 'I've been speaking to Bert Herbert.'

Blodwen's jaw dropped and her face turned a shade paler.

'What?'

'He told me something about the day my mother died that no one else knows, not even the police,' Jenni went on, encouraged by Blodwen's stunned expression.

'What?' She seemed incapable of saying anything else.

'He was there, in the house, that morning. He saw what happened but was too late . . .' Jenni felt the words catch in her throat. 'Too late to stop it. There was an open letter lying on the mat. He said it was obvious Mam and Dad had been quarrelling over it. Do you know anything about that letter, Auntie Blodwen?'

She clutched at the back of a chair for support.

'Me? How should I know?'

'The police kept that letter quiet to secure a conviction,' Jenni said breathlessly. 'It must have been pretty damaging to someone. It was a malicious act, and whoever sent it is responsible for what happened as much as my poor father, because whatever it said, it drove him into uncontrollable fury.'

'No!' Blodwen clutched at her throat. 'I mean, I don't know what you're talking about, Jenni. I don't know why you're telling me this.'

Jenni's lips thinned in sudden anger.

'I think you do, Auntie Blodwen. You hated my mother. You were jealous of her. I saw it myself the day we called here to ask you to lend us the premium money. I believe it was you who sent that letter.'

'That's a lie!' Blodwen turned on her heel. 'I'm not standing by here listening to this wickedness.'

She marched off along the passage to the front door. Jenni hurriedly followed her, determined that Blodwen shouldn't wriggle out of accepting responsibility.

'It *was* you, wasn't it?' Jenni cried out after her. 'You've got guilt written all over you. How could you do such a terrible thing to my mother? How could you deliberately cause trouble?'

Blodwen pulled open the front door, hesitating on the step. Bitterly cold morning air rushed into the passage, making Jenni shiver. The air was tinged with the smell of snow that had lain on the ground too long. It made her feel nauseous.

Blodwen seemed unaffected by the chill. She looked back over her shoulder at Jenni, fury in her face.

'Accusing me . . . wickedness! You're a sinful person, Jenni Goodenough, just like your mother. I won't have sinful people in my house. I don't want you here anymore. Pack your things and go.'

'What? Auntie Blodwen!' Jenni stepped back, appalled. 'You don't mean that? You can't!'

'Yes, I do!'

'But where can I go?'

'The Jukes sisters were always keen to have you. Go to them.'

Jenni rushed forward, grasping her arm.

'You don't mean it, surely? You can't put me out, Auntie Blodwen. I've always done everything asked of me. I've worked hard for you . . .'

Blodwen pulled her arm away.

'Huh! You just admitted you've been associating with that Bert Herbert. It was him that caused your mother's downfall, did you know that? Now you're going the same way as her.' She shook her head furiously. 'But not in my house, you're not.'

With another withering glance at Jenni, Blodwen hurried towards the steps that led down to the pavement. Wearing only her nightdress, Jenni couldn't follow. She stared after her, suddenly alarmed at Blodwen's undue haste to get away. The path was dangerously icy, and as Jenni watched apprehensively, Blodwen slithered a little.

'Be careful, Auntie Blodwen!' she called out anxiously. 'Those steps are treacherous.'

'Treacherous, yes, that's what you are all right.' Blodwen paused on the top step, turning her face towards Jenni. 'Going behind my back. Immoral, that's what it is.'

She took a step down, her face still turned to Jenni.

'You'll come to no good end, my girl, just like your mother. In the dirty gutter, you'll end up. Mark my words.'

Jenni clutched at the neck of her nightdress in apprehension.

'Watch what you're doing, Auntie Blodwen, for goodness' sake!'

But Jenni's warning came too late.

Blodwen's foot slid from under her and she went tumbling down the steps, screeching as she went, to land with a sickening thud on the pavement below, where she lay spread-eagle, unmoving and silent.

Jenni let out a scream.

'Auntie Blodwen!'

Horrified, and heedless of the icy air striking through her thin cotton nightdress, she hurried down the steps, treading carefully herself.

When Jenni reached her, Blodwen's eyes were closed but she was moaning a little. Jenni breathed a sigh of intense relief. For an awful moment she'd thought Blodwen was dead. Yet, Jenni realised with renewed concern, there might still be serious injuries.

She looked about desperately. Someone must help them. But the street was deserted at that time on a Sunday morning.

'Help!' Jenni called out loudly as she knelt on the frozen pavement. 'Help, someone, please!'

Like an answer to a prayer Blodwen's next-door neighbour, Mrs Gethin, appeared on the pavement at the bottom of her own steps.

'Oh, *bach*! What's happened?'

'Help me!' Jenni cried out, in tears now. 'Please! Auntie Blodwen's had an accident.'

In no time there was a crowd of helpers on hand, including Mrs Gethin's husband and two strapping sons. They carried Blodwen back into her home while someone hurried off to fetch the panel doctor.

It was a hard task getting Blodwen up the narrow staircase because, as one of the Gethin boys pointed out, unnecessarily Jenni thought, Miss Thomas was no featherweight.

Blodwen was still moaning faintly but hadn't opened her eyes yet. She was obviously in shock.

'Put her on the bed,' Mrs Gethin instructed. 'We won't try to undress her until the doctor's looked at her. She could have umpteen things broken.'

Jenni was shaking with fright more than cold, and too shocked herself to think straight. She was relieved that Mrs Gethin had put herself in charge.

She turned to Jenni, giving her a sharp, appraising stare.

'The doctor'll be here in a minute. Go and put some warm clothes on, *bach*, while I make some tea. You'll get pneumonia standing by there in the cold.'

Jenni hurried to her own bedroom and dressed with difficulty, her hands shaking so much she could hardly slip into her clothes. Why was it that tragedy dogged the people around her? First her parents, now Blodwen. Jenni shivered again with dread, and a shaft of guilt pierced her. If Blodwen died, she'd be completely to blame. The truth of it appalled her. She felt as guilty as if she'd actually pushed Blodwen down the steps.

Another thought struck her and she was immediately ashamed of the selfishness of it. If Blodwen died, she'd be alone, homeless, without kith or kin. That prospect really frightened her.

It seemed an endless wait for the doctor to arrive. Blodwen opened her eyes once to stare at them both, obviously without recognition.

'Cracked her skull, she has, I shouldn't wonder,' Mrs Gethin observed bluntly, making Jenni wring her hands with distress.

She'd expected to see old Dr Frasier, Blodwen's panel doctor, but instead an unknown fresh-faced young man arrived at last, saying he was the locum. His manner was so cheerful and bright, Jenni's teeth were set on edge.

His examination was very thorough, she'd give him that. She watched anxiously as he washed his hands in the china basin on the stand by the window.

'She's got a broken wrist. A shoulder is dislocated, and there's swelling of a knee and ankle. She should go into the cottage hospital at Cwmgelligors for X-rays, though.'

Mrs Gethin looked dubious.

'Is that necessary, Doctor?' She glanced at Jenni. 'I mean, think of the expense!'

The doctor shrugged his shoulders.

'I'm worried about her head.' He looked around. 'She can pay, can't she?'

Jenni nodded eagerly, deciding to take charge.

'Yes, she can pay.'

After all, Blodwen was always boasting how well off her father had left her. It was time his money did her some real good.

'Is she in any danger, Doctor?' Jenni went on. Her heart was in her mouth as she waited for his reply.

'I don't think so, but we'll have to wait for the hospital's assessment.' He broke into a cheerful smile again. 'Not to worry, though, Miss . . . er . . .'

It was all very well for him to say that, Jenni thought with irritation, but it didn't allay her fears. Blodwen wasn't young anymore and the fall had been a heavy one. Some older people never got over the shock. Homeless and alone. The thoughts haunted her.

Blodwen stayed in the cottage hospital almost a fortnight. Luckily, the snow had largely cleared so that Jenni could walk down to Cwmgelligors each evening for the visiting hour, then walk back. It was still bitterly cold, though, but she put up with the discomfort of spending her evenings tramping the mountain road, rather than sitting before the warm range at Blodwen's house, because she still couldn't help blaming herself for her cousin's awful predicament. It she hadn't upset poor Blodwen that morning, carping on about the letter, the accident would never have happened.

Blodwen was very subdued during the visits. Jenni hadn't moved out of the house, and wondered if Blodwen still wanted her to. She didn't mention it, however, thinking that such matters could be settled when Blodwen finally came home and was more herself.

Fortunately, the X-rays had shown no serious head injuries, and Jenni began to feel a measure of relief. The dislocated shoulder had been attended to, and the swelling of her ankle had gone down though her knee remained troublesome. The only outward sign of the accident now was her right wrist and arm in plaster.

When Jenni entered the ward on the Thursday evening a young nurse came forward to tell her Sister wished to see her in her office. Jenni felt a tremor of nervousness, fearing a new complication had arisen overnight.

The door to Sister's office was standing open and Jenni knocked gently, waiting to be invited in. She could see Sister sitting at her desk, writing busily in a patient's notes, her starched white apron stiff and pristine, cap in sharp folds fixed squarely on her head.

Jenni waited patiently, afraid to knock again. After a long moment, Sister looked up.

'Oh, yes, come in, Miss . . .'

Without thinking Jenni almost gave her real name. She knew it was still associated with horror and scandal in people's minds. Too often in the beginning she'd seen the flicker of recognition, together with open curiosity, but more often revulsion and fear. The tragedy in her family would haunt her forever. It might yet destroy her future if she wasn't careful.

'Thomas,' she said at last. 'Miss Jenni Thomas.'

'Well, Miss Thomas,' Sister went on briskly, 'your cousin can go home tomorrow.'

Jenni was delighted.

'Oh, that's wonderful.'

'Yes. Er . . . you live with her, I believe?'

Jenni nodded.

'Well, you understand, don't you, that she'll need care and bed rest for quite a while? Doctor is not altogether happy about her, but there's no physical reason for her to remain in hospital. Tell me, is your cousin inclined to depressive moods?'

Jenni was alarmed. Blodwen might be abrasive at times, often difficult to live with, but she'd always been too full of herself to suffer from depression.

'Oh, no. Very active in her chapel, she is, and has a social life as well.'

Jenni wondered if this was an exaggeration. Entertaining Pastor Williams on a Sunday afternoon wasn't exactly a heady social whirl.

'Perhaps it's just the aftermath of the accident,' Sister went on. 'I want you to understand our concern.' She elevated her nose in a haughty gesture of dismissal. 'You may visit the patient now.'

'Thank you,' Jenni said meekly. She wasn't sure whether she ought to curtsey.

In the long ward, Jenni sat down at Blodwen's bedside.

'Thought you weren't coming,' she said querulously, a gruffness in her voice. There was a touch of the old bullying in her tone, Jenni decided, but wondered if perhaps Blodwen was also near to tears. That was totally unlike her.

'Spoke to Sister,' Jenni explained. 'You're coming home tomorrow. Isn't that good news?'

There was a fleeting, wintry smile on Blodwen's face, followed almost immediately by a frown.

Jenni put her brown paper parcel on the bed.

'Look, Auntie Blodwen, I've made this for you.'

She undid the string to reveal folded pink satin that gleamed in the light of the ward.

'There was a remnant of satin in the shop, left over from bridesmaids' dresses, and I thought to myself, that'll make a lovely bed jacket for Auntie Blodwen.'

Jenni held up the garment. It was so pretty, with its deep frilled bell sleeves and scalloped collar and edges, tied at the neck with pink ribbon. She was proud of the style which she'd designed herself. Miss Emily had commented wryly that it was fit for any bride but would be wasted on the likes of Blodwen Thomas.

There was a brief acquisitive gleam in Blodwen's eyes as she looked at it, then the interest disappeared as though a candle had been snuffed out.

'It's too fancy for me,' she murmured flatly. 'It's almost . . .'

Sinful! Jenni knew what she was about to say but wasn't annoyed. She'd seen that gleam. Blodwen only needed persuading.

'It's just the thing to cheer you up. When you're home, I expect you'll get visitors from the chapel. You'll want to look your best when Pastor Williams calls.'

Blodwen looked appalled.

'Receive Pastor Williams in my nightclothes! Oh, the shame of it. I won't see anyone.'

She was beginning to look upset. Jenni patted her arm comfortingly.

'You don't have to do anything you don't want to, Auntie Blodwen. And you mustn't worry otherwise you'll make a slow recovery.'

Blodwen's blunt fingers plucked at the bedclothes.

'If I don't worry, who will? How am I going to manage with my arm in plaster? And my knee's not right, you know. Can't put my weight on it. I have to ask for the . . .' her face turned scarlet with embarrassment '. . . bedpan all the time.'

'Everything's going to be all right, Auntie Blodwen,' Jenni assured her cheerfully. 'We'll manage somehow.'

'We?'

Jenni bit her lip. Surely Blodwen wouldn't continue to insist that she left the house? She didn't want to leave, and now there was more reason than ever why she should stay. But would Blodwen be contrary even in the face of her own dire straits? Or was it just bravado?

'You need me now, Auntie Blodwen,' Jenni said, gently but firmly. 'You know you do.'

An emotion that Jenni couldn't read flitted across Blodwen's pale face and she began to pluck at the bedclothes again.

'Well, just until I get better, mind,' she said, eyes averted from Jenni's gaze. 'Then we'll have to see.'

On the surface her words seemed grudging, but Jenni detected a tremor of relief in her voice, and suspected Blodwen wasn't far from tears again.

To her own astonishment, Jenni felt a rush of tenderness towards her mother's cousin. After all, as far as she knew, Blodwen was her only living blood relative. In the four years since her mother had died, Jenni had missed the warmth of loving and being loved, and there was a void in her life because of it. She had so much warmth and love of her own to give. Perhaps she could lavish it now on Blodwen, who suddenly needed her.

'I'm packing in my training,' Jenni said quickly. 'Until you get on your feet, you'll need full-time care.'

Blodwen looked genuinely astonished.

'But what about finishing your apprenticeship? The Jukeses may not give you your indentures. Without those you won't get a decent job as a dressmaker.'

'I've only got a few months to go anyway,' Jenni assured her cheerfully.

She tried to sound confident but knew she was taking an awful risk with her future. She had worked so hard and diligently over the last four years. The Jukes sisters were pleased with her, she had no doubt, but how would they react to her giving up early?

But what else could she do? She couldn't callously desert Blodwen now. Besides, Jenni didn't want to be out there in the world alone. Perhaps she needed Blodwen as much as her cousin needed her. And surely the Jukes sisters would understand?

A small, bitter voice reminded her that Blodwen might have been the cause of the tragedy that had wrecked her life, but Jenni firmly subdued it. She couldn't turn her back on Blodwen now, and she couldn't take revenge. It just wasn't in her nature.

'It's a pity,' Miss Emily said. She shook her head. 'That woman doesn't deserve you, Jenni. Don't let her make a slave out of you, mind. She'll run you off your feet if she can.'

Jenni also shook her head sadly.

'I'm worried. Auntie Blodwen is a changed woman. There's no go in her anymore, and she seems to be getting smaller, sort of fading away. That fall was a terrible shock, you know. It'll take her a long time to get over it.'

'Cats don't change their stripes,' Miss Lucy commented wryly. 'And Blodwen Thomas is the cattiest woman I know. We're going to miss you, Jenni, *bach*.'

'My indentures . . .' she began hesitantly.

Miss Emily put her hand on Jenni's arm.

'Don't you worry, my girl. You've more than earned those. You're the most talented apprentice we've ever trained. Don't let that talent go to waste, will you?'

Jenni felt the tears start and couldn't hold them back. She looked from one sister to the other, her heart full of affection and gratitude. On impulse, she put an arm round each of them and hugged them to her, kissing each on the cheek.

'Thank you so much for all you've done for me,' she said, her voice faltering with emotion. 'You were both brave to keep me on in spite of everything. I'll always be grateful.'

Miss Emily gave a loud sniff and quickly brushed her fingers across her cheek.

'You're like the daughter I never had,' she said gruffly. 'You'll always be welcome here.'

Jenni missed the shop and the sisters. She missed the work that satisfied a creative longing in her, but couldn't give up altogether. She had to earn a living as Blodwen had made it clear she would not pay for Jenni's keep.

Looking after her cousin took a great deal of Jenni's time, but a card in the Post Office brought in some work, enough to keep herself in the essentials of life.

It was a lonely life, though, Jenni found; just she and Blodwen, days and evenings, too. She'd expected Blodwen's friends from the chapel to rally round, visiting, showing their support for her, but hardly anyone called, not even Pastor Williams. Jenni's only contact with the outside world was when she called in on the Jukes sisters or did some shopping.

The weeks went by while Jenni waited for Blodwen to get back on her feet. It was worrying when her cousin developed a persistent cough. Jenni blamed it on the weather and looked forward to the spring when, surely, Blodwen would rally and get some of her old strength back.

Inwardly worried, Jenni tried to appear cheerful. She fussed over her charge, ignoring her grumpiness, and made nourishing meals which Blodwen hardly touched.

'Got a pain, I have,' she complained. 'In my chest. It catches me when I breathe.'

Jenni wanted to call the panel doctor, but Blodwen was scornful.

'Listen, I'm not made of money, mind. There's a bottle of opening medicine in the cupboard. A dose of that'll put me right.'

Helping her to the commode the next day, Jenni noticed how short of breath Blodwen was, and her worry increased. She was tempted to call the doctor anyway, and risk Blodwen's wrath. Her cousin appeared to read her mind.

'No doctor, mind,' she said breathlessly, when back in bed. 'Right as rain, I'll be, in a week or two.'

One morning in mid-April Jenni was up early and made a pot of tea as usual. Going into Blodwen's bedroom, she saw her cousin still lying amongst the pillows, eyes closed. Her face was paler than usual, and her breathing laboured and wheezy.

Jenni put the tray on the bedside table, and bent closer to look at her cousin.

'Auntie Blodwen, I've brought some tea, look,' she began hopefully, though her concern was growing.

Blodwen was always ready for her early-morning tea, and

fussed if it was late. Now it seemed she hadn't heard a word Jenni said.

She'd banked the fire up in the little bedroom grate the night before, so the room wasn't cold, yet when she touched Blodwen's hand it was icy.

'Auntie Blodwen, are you all right?'

Apprehensive, she put her hand on Blodwen's brow. It felt unnaturally hot, Jenni thought, and there was a clamminess to her skin that was at odds with the coldness of her hands.

Blodwen had a high fever, there was no doubt about it, and Jenni realised something was very wrong.

She rushed out of the room and down the stairs, feeling panic rising in her breast. She must get Mrs Gethin. Their neighbour would know what to do.

Mrs Gethin followed her up the narrow staircase and into the bedroom. She gazed at Blodwen in the bed for a moment, then shook her head solemnly.

'Oh, *Duw!* Don't like the look of her at all, I don't, *bach*. No, indeed! My husband's old mother was just like that, see, before she died.'

Jenni was appalled, lifting her hands to her head in distress.

'Hush, Mrs Gethin, please!' she whispered. 'Don't say that in front of her.'

'Oh, she can't hear me, *bach*,' Mrs Gethin replied confidently, folding her arms across her chest. 'Love you, no. She's out of this world, she is. Pneumonia it'll be, no doubt. Better get the doctor, though, just in case. I'll stay by here while you go.'

Jenni shrugged on her coat and pulled on her hat. She hurriedly made her way to the other side of the village where the doctor's surgery was.

Pneumonia. Jenni shuddered at the idea. Blodwen wasn't really old but she'd had an awful shock with that fall and was weakened.

Jenni said a little prayer, asking that Blodwen be spared. If

Blodwen died there'd be no one at all who cared what happened to her. Over the last four years Blodwen had never shown outward signs of affection for her, yet Jenni felt there had been a bond growing between them; a bond of fellowship, perhaps. Two women alone and lonely were bound to feel an affinity. They were used to each other at the very least.

Now Blodwen was seriously ill and Jenni feared for her own future, alone again.

The bedroom seemed hushed as though waiting for the doctor's verdict, the silence broken only by the harsh sound of Blodwen's breathing. Jenni watched as the doctor's hands rearranged her cousin's nightdress. She found she was holding her breath, fearful of hearing the worst.

He straightened up, pushing his stethoscope back into his bag which stood on the bedside table.

'I'm afraid it's not good, Miss . . . er . . .'

'Thomas,' Jenni said absentmindedly. 'Will she have to go back into hospital?'

It was the same young doctor as before. Now he inclined his head, looking solemn.

'She's very ill. I can't advise that she make the journey to the hospital at Cwmgelligors in her present condition. She'd do better to remain in her own bed just now. But she'll need nursing for as long as . . .'

He looked keenly at Jenni.

'You're alone here?'

'Yes, but I can take care of her,' Jenni assured him hastily.

He shook his head.

'She'll need medicines and professional nursing, Miss Thomas. Her condition is too serious. Can she pay?'

Jenni was sure that Blodwen could afford it, but her cousin was unconscious, and if what the doctor believed was true, how long would it be before she could attend to her own financial affairs? Looking at Blodwen's pale face amongst the pillows, she was beset with a deep foreboding. Jenni had no idea where her cousin's money was kept, or how it could be used to pay for nursing care.

Then suddenly Jenni thought of the money her father had left her. Seventy-five pounds it was, still untouched after four years. She had vowed never to touch it. But this was different. She could use it to take care of Blodwen. It seemed fitting that she should, too. This way the money would be cleansed of her mother's blood. Jenni had hounded Blodwen over that mysterious letter so wasn't she in fact responsible for the accident? It was the least she could do.

'The nurse will be paid for, Dr Saunders,' Jenni said confidently. 'The medicines, too.'

He nodded.

'I'll arrange it as soon as I get back to the surgery. Nurse will be along some time today, definitely before evening. In the meantime, please make sure the following is taken care of.'

He took a small notebook from his pocket and tore a page from it, beginning to scribble instructions.

Jenni's hand trembled as she took the paper from him.

'Do you have any relatives nearby who could help you?' he asked as he prepared to leave the bedroom.

She shook her head.

'I'm sorry,' he said gently.

Jenni felt sorry, too. She hadn't felt so miserable since the tragedy of her mother's death.

The nurse came just after midday and Jenni was thankful to see her, though outwardly she looked stern and unapproachable with her straight back and starched apron that crackled as she marched up and down stairs. Although she had a quick, competent way about her, which encouraged confidence, Jenni felt very uneasy having a stranger in the small house, and couldn't help wondering what Blodwen would have to say about it all, if only she were conscious.

Jenni went to bed early that evening, feeling exhausted herself with all that had happened.

Just as dawn was breaking, she woke with a start, realising someone was in her bedroom, calling her name softly. She threw back the bedclothes and sat up. By the faint light filtering in through the window, she saw the nurse standing at the foot of the bed and was instantly alarmed.

'Miss Thomas,' the nurse said quietly, 'I'm sorry to wake you so early but I thought you ought to know that your cousin passed away in her sleep an hour ago.'

'Oh, no!' Jenni felt stunned. 'Poor Blodwen.'

All along she'd known it was a very real possibility yet she couldn't believe it now that it had happened. She and Blodwen had rarely seen eye to eye, and the matter of the mysterious letter still hung unanswered in the air, but her cousin had been a last link with the past, her happy childhood.

Blodwen had also been an anchor in a troubled time, solid and unchanging, or so it had seemed. That anchor was suddenly gone, and now Jenni was adrift in unknown waters.

She rose from the bed and reached for her old dressing gown, feeling a stinging sensation at the back of her eyes as hot tears began to well. She had to admit to herself, the tears were as much for herself as Blodwen.

Nurse reached out a hand to her.

'Why don't you stay in bed a little longer, Miss Thomas?' she suggested, and Jenni was surprised at the tenderness in her tone. 'It's still very early and there is nothing you can do, my dear.'

'No, I must be up. I can't rest now,' Jenni replied.

She had a lot of hard thinking ahead of her. Up to now she'd only speculated on what she'd do in the event of Blodwen's death. Now it was a reality, and she must face the bleak facts of her situation. She needed advice, and the only friends she could think of who might help her were the Jukes sisters. In a way they were the only family she had.

All her old school friends and acquaintances were secure within the warmth and safety of their own families. How she envied them. At nineteen she was on her own again, and very probably homeless, too. It seemed to her at that moment that fate was determined she would never be happy, that she was doomed to be alone. But would it always be that way?

One day she might meet someone, she told herself hopefully. She'd fall in love, perhaps, and have a family of her own; a husband and children to love her and care what happened to her. At this sad time it was a thought to comfort herself with, however improbable and remote the prospect.

The Jukes sisters proved their friendship once again. They took it upon themselves to make all the arrangements, registering the death and engaging the services of the undertaker, Teifi the Box.

'What about the funeral expenses?' Miss Emily asked. 'How will you manage? If you like, we can lend you something.'

Overcome with emotion, Jenni reached out and kissed the older woman's cheek, tears welling in her eyes at the thought of the kindness the sisters had always shown her. They were the salt of the earth, and she knew she'd never find their like again.

'I have some money my . . . my father left me,' she said hesitantly. 'I was going to use it to pay for Blodwen's nursing care. Now it'll pay for the funeral.'

In a way she'd be glad to be rid of the money without spending it on her own needs.

Miss Emily clasped Jenni's hand warmly.

'You can always rely on us, you know that, don't you, my girl?'

Jenni nodded, her feelings too near the surface to speak.

'Now, what about something laid on for the mourners?' Miss

Emily went on in a practical tone. 'A bit of ham would be the thing.'

Jenni gulped down her tears.

'Mrs Gethin will help me with that,' she said. 'She's been good to me, too.'

'You deserve it, Jenni, *bach*,' Miss Lucy said, placing a plump arm around Jenni's shoulders. 'You've had nothing but grief in your young life. It breaks my heart to think of it.'

Jenni thanked her lucky stars. She didn't have a family anymore, but at least she had true friends, and they were worth the world.

Chapter Ten

The funeral was over. Jenni was thankful that womenfolk were not expected to attend the burial. She could not have borne it. Mr Gethin had attended together with his sons, but apparently there were few other mourners present to see Blodwen buried in the cemetery of her beloved Baptist chapel, Pastor Williams presiding. Only two or three of the mourners came back to the spread Jenni had provided in Blodwen's house, and didn't stay long. Neither did Pastor Williams, which she wondered at.

The following day Jenni rose early. She'd hardly slept again and it was beginning to tell on her. Over a week had passed since Blodwen's passing but it was still strange sleeping in the house alone.

She didn't have to worry about getting used to it, she told herself. Soon the landlord would be in touch to ask her to leave. She wondered what the chances were of taking over the tenancy, but doubted the landlord, whoever he was, would agree. She was a single girl of nineteen, without a job.

She didn't even know how much the weekly rent was. Blodwen had never mentioned such matters to her. The rent man never called and Jenni assumed it was Blodwen's practice to take the rent directly to the agent's office. That would be very like her, Jenni thought, wryly. Blodwen had needed to feel important.

It was no good thinking about the tenancy, she decided, trying to be practical. The rent was probably more than she could afford, anyway. The best thing would be to look for reasonable rooms as soon as possible.

As ever, her thoughts turned to the Jukes sisters who would help. They knew everything that went on in Llawr-y-bryn. They'd know if there were any decent rooms going, somewhere respectable.

After breakfast Jenni walked down to the shop on Llawr-y-bryn's main road. It was still quite early and the sisters were in the workshop with their new apprentice, a tall gawky girl with thick brown hair in a plait which hung down her back. She looked very young; as young as Jenni had been when she was first apprenticed. Suddenly Jenni envied her, and the years to come in the company of the sisters.

They were delighted to see her but looked dubious when she told them of her plans.

'Wouldn't be in too much of a hurry to move, *bach*,' Miss Emily said. 'You're snug where you are.'

Jenni had to smile.

'Haven't got much choice,' she said. 'The landlord will want me out soon. I was wondering if you know of good lodgings nearby.'

Miss Emily looked crestfallen.

'We'd put you up in a minute, my dear girl,' she explained. 'But young Menna here is lodging with us now.' She indicated the tall gawky girl. 'Her mam's got a houseful, see, all boys but Menna.'

Jenni was embarrassed.

'I wasn't hinting, Miss Emily,' she said hastily. 'I thought you might know of somewhere. But don't worry, I'll find something.'

Miss Emily looked thoughtful, her finger to her lips considering.

'Hold on! Think I might know someone . . .'

At that moment the counter bell sounded in the shop. They had a customer. Miss Lucy hurried out to deal with the new-comer.

Miss Emily and Jenni strolled into the passage after her.

'There's an old lady living down the end of Cwm Road,' Miss Emily said. 'Her son's just got married, so she's got room. And I expect she's lonely, too. Have a word, shall I?'

Jenni nodded eagerly. It sounded ideal. She needed some-where homely. She was just going to voice her thanks when Miss Lucy came bustling back.

'It's Mrs Parry, Emily. Can you come and deal with her?' she said, her tone agitated. 'She wants to know why her skirt isn't ready. Wants it for a wedding tomorrow, she does.'

Miss Emily clicked her tongue angrily.

'Only brought it in yesterday,' she said curtly, striding purposefully into the shop. 'What does she think we are? One of those new mass production places?'

Jenni stood in the passage, just out of sight of the shop inter-ior. She recognised the name. Blodwen had spoken of Mrs Parry many times, denouncing her as a backslider, especially where the chapel flower rota was concerned. Jenni had expected Mrs Parry's husband to attend the funeral, but he hadn't. Neither had the Parrys sent their condolences.

Jenni could hear Miss Emily's sharp words and Mrs Parry's contrite tones now that her bullying tactics had failed; the way she'd failed to bully Blodwen Thomas.

'It's my niece's wedding tomorrow, Miss Jukes. Posh it's going to be, see,' Mrs Parry said in a smarmy voice, then went on hurriedly. 'She hasn't *got* to, mind you. Oh, no, nothing like that! Top hats and all, it is. She's marrying the eldest son of Davies the Legal, Cwmgelligors, you know. In for a partnership with his father, he is, next year. Money!' She gave a loud sniff. 'Rolling in it, mind. That's why I want to look my best, see. Mustn't let the family down.' Her voice took on a hard rasp. 'Not like *some* people around here.'

'Really?' Miss Emily's tone was wry.

'Well, I mean! Take Blodwen Thomas's funeral yesterday. Fiasco it was, by all accounts.'

Jenni drew in a sharp breath on hearing Blodwen's name spoken with such disdain. Should she show her face, she wondered, before more was said? She was about to take a step forward when Miss Emily retorted sharply: 'Your family weren't there, Mrs Parry, so how do you know?'

'Talk of Llawr-y-bryn, it is,' she declared loudly. 'Always making herself out to be more than she was, that Blodwen Thomas. Thinking herself a cut above everybody else, and smarming up to Pastor Williams.'

Jenni was furious. Again she had the urge to rush out and confront Mrs Parry, but hesitated this time. She'd probably say something she'd regret. Upsetting a customer and making a scene in the shop wouldn't do the Jukes sisters much good. It would only create more gossip. Jenni bit down on her lip and tried to hold on to her temper.

'Speaking ill of the dead is unlucky,' Miss Emily said tightly.

Mrs Parry was scornful.

'Plenty spoke ill of her alive, never mind dead,' she retorted disdainfully. 'Threw her weight about on the chapel committee, she did, bossing everybody about. She thought she was the only one who could arrange the chapel flowers properly. I tell you, she was an embarrassment to Pastor Williams.'

That did it! Jenni could hold back no longer. She rushed head-long into the shop and stood glaring at Mrs Parry, almost too angry to speak.

'Don't you talk about Blodwen like that,' Jenni spluttered in anger. 'You . . . you backslider, you!'

Mrs Parry looked startled for a moment, her eyes as round as saucers, then they narrowed to slits as, in sudden fury, she glared at Jenni.

'*You* can shut up for a start,' she said belligerently. 'The daughter of a murderer! Ooh!' Mrs Parry drew back as if confronted by an abomination. 'I don't know how you've got the nerve to stay around here, contaminating us all. Brass neck, that's what you've got.'

Jenni took a step back herself, feeling as though she'd been struck a physical blow, the heat of her anger dissipating with shock at the other woman's unexpected words. And suddenly she was dumbfounded, the wind taken out of her sails.

Mrs Parry, obviously scenting an advantage, rushed on.

'The likes of you mixing with decent, respectable people, it's disgraceful. Shouldn't be allowed.' She shook her head. 'Blodwen Thomas needed her head seen to, taking you in. I don't know what possessed her.' She turned to the sisters. 'And that goes for you two, as well. It's a wonder you've got any trade left with *her* here.'

She looked back at Jenni with a certain triumph.

'You should be ashamed!' she went on, her tone righteous. 'A murderer for a father, and a mother no better than a common tart, by all accounts. Comes out in the blood, it does, that kind of wickedness. Tainted, bound to be.' She sniffed loudly, elevating her nose. 'Us respectable people with innocent children don't want the likes of *you* around here. Get out of Llawr-y-bryn! Get back to the gutter, where you belong.'

Jenni's mouth dropped open in shock. She was vaguely aware of an angry growl coming from Miss Emily but Jenni herself could only stare into Mrs Parry's hostile eyes, feeling a deep and penetrating coldness descend on her.

Unable to speak to defend herself, she did feel ashamed. Her presence was tainting everything for her few remaining friends. She was causing bad feelings between the Jukes sisters and some of their best customers. How many others in Llawr-y-bryn felt the same as Mrs Parry? Suddenly, she wanted to crawl away and hide herself.

Mrs Parry continued to glare, and Jenni, mesmerised, began to edge towards the shop door. She had to get away from that accusing glare, from the terrible words.

Out of the corner of her eye she saw Miss Emily come out from behind the counter and move quickly towards her.

'Jenni, *bach*, don't look like that! Don't go, girl. Stay a minute. Don't listen to her! She's an ignorant *llelo*.'

But Jenni couldn't bear it. She turned on her heel and rushed out into the street. Mrs Parry shouted something after her. Jenni didn't hear the words clearly, but it sounded like . . . leper, and her heart felt as if it would burst with anguish.

It was true. She was treated like a leper. She had stubbornly refused to acknowledge that before today. Now Mrs Parry had made her face it. If she stayed in Llawr-y-bryn she'd always be treated that way. She had no friends here, except for the Jukeses.

Jenni couldn't prevent a little sob of misery escaping her cold lips as she hurried along the main road, feeling hostile eyes upon her from every window and doorway.

She had no friends in Trehafod, either, or anywhere in the Valley. Wherever she went her shame would go with her. There was no escaping it.

Jenni stumbled on back to Blodwen's house, heavy with misery and unhappiness. She was an outcast. There was no place for her in the Valley anymore. She must leave as soon as possible. But where should she go? She had hardly any money and her little bit of sewing work hadn't brought much in. Paying for the nurse and Blodwen's funeral had eaten right into her father's legacy.

Trying to think clearly through her anguish, Jenni mused on her immediate needs. To leave the Valley she'd need the train fare. And lodgings didn't come cheap, either. How long would her bit of money last if she couldn't find work? Everything looked so hopeless.

But it was no good going to pieces, Jenni thought, setting her jaw resolutely. She was an indentured dressmaker, and didn't need Miss Emily's praise to tell her she had a skill and flair that were above average. But if there was no work in her own trade, she'd scrub floors if need be. With her family background she couldn't afford to be proud or finicky.

Jenni climbed the steps to Blodwen's front door and saw Mrs Gethin standing on her own doorstep. Jenni glanced at her fearfully, expecting a fresh rebuke, but her neighbour looked very much as always.

'Jenni, *bach*, there's been a man here looking for you,' she said. 'All dressed up he was, black overcoat and bowler. Wanted to know if you were still living here.'

Jenni's heart gave a lurch. He must be the landlord's agent! She'd been expecting it. It looked as though fate had struck again, forcing her hand. He'd probably want her out by the end of the week.

She clutched at the collar of her coat, feeling sick with apprehension.

'Did he say he'd be back, Mrs Gethin?'

Her neighbour nodded.

'Said he had a bit of business in the High Street, then he'd call again.' Mrs Gethin gave her a piercing look. 'Are you all right, *bach*?'

Jenni nodded, trying to smile through her wretchedness.

'Thanks, Mrs Gethin.'

Although she liked her neighbour and was relieved not to see the hostility in her that she was beginning to expect from people, Jenni was glad to escape indoors.

Wearily she took off her hat and coat, and flopped into Blodwen's chair before the range, feeling too drained to put the kettle on the fire to boil, though she longed for a cheering cup of tea.

So she was to be evicted. A decision had been made for her, and now there was no choice but to get out of Llawr-y-bryn as Mrs Parry had demanded.

With an effort, Jenni went upstairs and took down her small suitcase from the top of the wardrobe. She'd better start packing now. There was no point in hanging on.

She packed her few bits and pieces into the case, and filled a brown carrier bag with odds and ends, then took them downstairs, leaving them in the passage near the front door. When the landlord's agent came he'd see she was ready for his pronouncement.

Jenni opened the parlour door. She'd better take him into the best room. It was what Blodwen would expect of her. She wondered then what would happen to the furniture and china, so precious to Blodwen, and which she, and Jenni, too, had tended so lovingly.

Jenni looked around the room and had to appreciate the irony. Poor Blodwen! In the end she'd had to leave it all behind.

She had just drained the last of her cup of tea when there was a knock on the front door. Jenni had no doubt who it was. Even the knock sounded official.

In trepidation, she opened the door. A tall man stood there, wearing a very black bowler and long overcoat as Mrs Gethin had described. He was in his late-forties, Jenni judged, and had a luxuriant moustache and gilt-rimmed spectacles.

She ran a professional eye over the coat. The material was of the very best quality and extremely well-cut. She wondered fleetingly how a landlord's agent could afford such high style.

'Miss Jenni Goodenough?'

When he spoke her name Jenni felt a shock of fear go through her. Suddenly she wasn't so sure he was a messenger from the landlord after all. His eyes were sharp and intelligent, and there was an educated tone to his voice. She was reminded of the man who had supervised her father's arrest on that awful day four years ago. Was this man a policeman, too? And what did he want with her?

He put a hand to the rim of his bowler, as though to doff it. 'Miss Goodenough?'

Jenni rallied, gathering up her courage, realising she must seem vacant and stupid.

'Yes, I'm Jenni Goodenough.'

He smiled and she felt reassured. He didn't look so forbidding now.

'May I come inside?' he asked politely, removing his bowler this time.

Jenni stood aside and allowed him to walk into the passage. She indicated the open door of the parlour, followed him in, then stood in the doorway for a moment uncertainly, realising that she should have asked him his business first.

'I see a suitcase in the passage,' he said, taking her by surprise. 'Are you planning to go away?'

Jenni decided to be frank.

'I expect to be evicted,' she said evenly, lifting her chin. Instinct told her it was no good beating about the bush with a man such as this. 'I don't suppose the landlord would let me have the tenancy, I'm too young, and besides, I have no income . . . at the moment.'

But she had to leave the Valley anyway. She'd never be able to work as a dressmaker in this area again; could never live amongst these people now.

'I see.' He smiled at her.

Jenni suddenly remembered her manners.

'Please take a seat,' she said.

'Do you mind if I remove my overcoat?' he asked. 'April is still nippy but it's warmer indoors.'

She took the coat from him, marvelling at its weight, and laid it carefully over the back of a straight-backed chair near the door. She hadn't been mistaken about its quality or that of the dark suit he wore.

Gold cufflinks glinted as he sat down and reached for something on the floor near his chair. For the first time Jenni noticed the small black valise which he placed on his knees and then opened, taking out some very legal-looking documents.

'Sit down, Miss Goodenough. I have something to tell you.'

Eyeing the documents nervously, Jenni drew forward another straight-backed chair and sat down, wondering what further trouble fate was about to throw at her.

'My name is John Davies, of Davies, Davies and Pritchard, solicitors, Cwmgelligors,' he announced. 'I am Miss Blodwen Thomas's solicitor and the executor of her will.'

Jenni stared open-mouthed. Davies the Legal! She'd heard his name that very day on the lips of her enemy, Mrs Parry.

'Blodwen's solicitor?' Jenni gasped. 'I . . . I've done nothing wrong!'

'Good gracious me, no!' He smiled reassuringly. 'It's good news I bring, Miss Goodenough. You've packed your bags prematurely.'

Jenni was flummoxed.

'I . . . I don't understand?'

'I'll explain,' he said, his tone becoming very businesslike. 'Last year, Miss Thomas came to see me. She wanted to change her will. In the previous will the whole of her estate was left to her chapel. However, in the new will, while the bulk of her money still goes to the chapel, she has made you a beneficiary also.'

'What?' Jenni could only stare at him, hardly able to believe her ears.

'According to the terms of her new will,' John Davies went on, 'Miss Thomas has left this house to you and the sum of one hundred pounds.'

In total surprise Jenni exhaled loudly, feeling as though someone had punched her in her midriff. She couldn't believe it. She and Blodwen had never got on at all, and yet her cousin had remembered her in her will. Nothing could have surprised Jenni more.

'I thought this house was rented,' she managed to say breathlessly. 'Blodwen never said otherwise.'

'Miss Thomas always struck me as a very private person,' John Davies said.

Jenni nodded distractedly, still unable to take in the news. She couldn't yet begin to appreciate what it would mean for her.

'There is a condition, Miss Goodenough.'

Jenni glanced up at the solicitor sharply. A condition? Well, of course there would be a catch, knowing Blodwen, Jenni thought, suddenly coming to earth with a bump.

'What is it?'

'Miss Thomas insists that you change your name by deed poll to Jenni Thomas. I can arrange that for you, but do you have any objection?'

Jenni was astonished for the second time. She'd been using that name for the last four years, but now she knew she'd been fooling no one. Everyone knew her for the daughter of a convicted murderer.

She shook her head.

'I have no objection.'

'Good.' John Davies seemed pleased. 'As I've said, I'll see to all necessary legal matters regarding the estate, the transfer of the property to you, and also the change of name.' He reached into the valise again. 'I have a cheque here for the money coming to you. I believe you should have this now.'

He held out a slip of paper but Jenni made no move to accept it. Instead she fiddled nervously with the collar of her dress. She'd never even seen a cheque let alone knew how to deal with it.

'A cheque?'

'I suggest you open a bank account in Cwmgelligors. That's the safest thing.'

'Oh, but I don't plan to stay in the Valley,' she burst out.

John Davies looked taken aback.

Jenni rushed on to explain.

'My name must be familiar to you, Mr Davies,' she said. 'You must know my family history. Changing my name won't change the way people around here feel about me. I must get away!'

She swallowed hard, suddenly making up her mind what she intended to do.

'I'm going to Swansea to live and work. It's a big town.' She really couldn't imagine what a big town was like. 'I can . . .' She paused. She'd almost said 'hide there'. 'I can build a new life, a better future for myself where no one knows I'm the daughter of a man hanged for the murder of his wife.'

She felt wretched saying those awful words aloud and glanced at John Davies, expecting to see disdain in his eyes. But his gaze held compassion instead.

He held the cheque out to her again and this time she took it, staring at it in confusion.

'I believe you are wise, Jenni,' he said. 'So, you wish to sell this property?' He gazed around. 'It might fetch a hundred pounds, maybe a hundred and fifty. I'll arrange for it to be put on the market. When do you intend to leave Llawr-y-bryn?'

Jenni wanted to say 'tomorrow' but she knew that was unrealistic.

'Within the week.' She indicated the cheque. She was familiar with postal orders but cheques were a mystery. 'I don't understand how to use this.'

'As soon as you get settled in Swansea, take it to a bank and say you want to open an account. The bank will help you.'

He stood and reached for his overcoat and bowler. Jenni stood, too, conscious that she had made a momentous decision. Now she'd voiced her intentions to leave the place of her birth there was no going back, and she was glad of it.

'Here's my card, Jenni,' he said. 'As soon as you find suitable lodgings in Swansea, write to me. When the house is sold I'll send the proceeds to you by cheque. Add them to your bank account.'

He stood smiling down at her, the valise under one arm, his bowler hat held respectfully against his chest.

'You're now financially secure. It's a good feeling, isn't it?'

Jenni couldn't say. She still hadn't taken it in. All she knew was that, unexpectedly, her life had taken a new path. She prayed it would be the right one. And suddenly she felt lost and saddened at having no one to guide her along it.

John Davies paused at the open door, ready to don his bowler. He held out a hand to her. Shyly Jenni took it and they shook hands. She felt important then, and very grown up.

'Jenni, I hope you won't mind my saying this.' He regarded her solemnly. 'My further advice is, don't talk about your money to anyone. You're young and there'll be many unscrupulous men out there ready to take advantage of your innocence. Be on your guard, Jenni. Be on your guard.'

Chapter Eleven

SWANSEA APRIL 1924

Jenni stepped down gingerly from the crowded train compartment on to the platform, then hesitated uncertainly. Fellow passengers were hurrying by her, walking purposefully, knowing they had somewhere to go – home. Heavy-hearted and with something like panic rising in her breast, she fell into step, blindly following the crowd. It was already mid-afternoon and she had nowhere to go.

It had been nerve-racking enough changing trains in Cardiff. Now she had finally arrived at her destination, she felt lost; abandoned even. And, more frightening still, she had no idea what to do next.

Nervously, she handed her ticket to the ticket-collector then followed the other passengers out into the sunshine, her steps dragging reluctantly.

Once outside she stopped and stared. Nothing had prepared her for it, not even a day at Cwmgelligors. The noise and bustle of the Swansea streets took her completely by surprise. Like quarrelsome terriers, numerous tram cars growled past each other through the wide crossroads right outside the station.

Dray horses hauled wagons stacked high with coal sacks or

barrels of beer. Push-bikes dodged between the wagons and humble handcarts. And the people!

So many people, Jenni thought, with a renewed rush of apprehension. She was struck by the contrasts. A woman wearing a silver fox stole around her shoulders strode past a group of grubby, shoeless children sitting on the pavement outside the station, playing conkers.

Sitting close to them on a low wooden stool was an enormously fat woman wrapped in a shabby coat, bundles of newspapers stacked around her feet. From time to time she bellowed words which Jenni couldn't understand. Her mysterious cry added to the cacophony that was the life of the town, and over it all Jenni could hear the raucous call of hungry seagulls, swooping continually over the low station building.

Visible above and beyond the town was a hill, green, lush and tranquil. Not a coal tip in sight!

Jenni caught her breath at a new sensation of excitement. She'd wanted the anonymity of a big town, and certainly had it here. No one would ever find her. The shame and scandal of her family's tragedy could be buried forever. She'd make a new life.

On the cobbled yard in front of the station were parked two or three motorcars — horseless carriages, as her mother used to call them. A few passengers were being greeted by relatives, no doubt, and helped into the waiting vehicles.

Jenni glanced curiously at the motor car nearest to her, big and shiny black. A man was leaning against it nonchalantly, a cigarette dangling from his lip. He wore a grey uniform, gaiters and a peaked cap.

He watched her with a lopsided smile and Jenni averted her eyes quickly, suddenly wary of the insolent expression on his face, his smile suggesting they were well acquainted. When he made a clicking sound out of the side of his mouth, she flashed him a startled glance.

'Hello, darling,' he said, grinning insinuatingly. 'Looking for me, are you, then?'

He winked at her and pushed himself away from the side of the vehicle, taking a step in her direction.

She was suddenly reminded of Oggie James, and that was enough for Jenni.

'Keep away from me!' she cried, frightened. 'Or I'll call a bobby!'

Taking to her heels, she hurried away towards the street and the traffic, feeling her cheeks flame with humiliation at the sound of his loud mocking laughter drifting after her.

As she stood uncertainly on the edge of the pavement, still confused and frightened, a tram car drew to a stop and passengers alighted. Jenni noticed a girl among them, around her own age, wearing a smart low-waisted dress in cornflower blue and a tight-fitting little hat over bobbed hair.

Jenni's hand strayed to her own hair. She was going on for twenty yet still wore her hair in a thick plait, not having the courage to put it up, let alone have it bobbed.

Living in Llawr-y-bryn she'd been reluctant to make any drastic changes to her appearance, always wishing to remain in the background and unnoticed. Too many people had been eager to point the finger at her. But now she was to live in a big town, a change of appearance might be a good thing.

But first she must find the safety of decent lodgings.

The smart girl paused on the pavement in front of the fat woman, searching in her handbag. Jenni hurried forward and touched her arm.

'Excuse me . . . er . . . Miss.'

The girl turned and looked her up and down, her expression disdainful, Jenni thought. She felt suddenly dowdy by comparison.

'What d'you want?' the girl asked sharply.

Jenni attempted a smile.

'Wondering, I was, if you knew of any reasonable and respectable lodgings in town.'

The girl smirked.

'Oh, just down from the Valleys, is it, love?'

Jenni was taken aback.

'How can you tell?'

The smirk widened to a broad grin.

'Just a wild guess, like.' She looked Jenni up and down again, then indicated the newspaper seller. 'Buy a copy of the *Cambrian Leader* from Fat Nancy, by here, and look at the rooms for rent.'

Jenni was startled, and glanced fearfully at the fat woman's face, expecting outrage, but her expression was unchanged.

'It's all right, love,' the girl said. 'Fat Nancy's as deaf as a post.'

She handed the fat woman a coin and received a paper in return, then turned to Jenni again.

'Best of luck, kid. Don't take any wooden nickels, will you?'

'Wooden what?'

The girl laughed and turned to move away but Jenni caught at her arm again.

'Just a minute! Could you help me again? Please! Can you recommend a place to eat around here? Somewhere reasonable.'

The girl looked irritated at being detained. She pointed across the road.

'You can get faggots and peas over by there,' she said, then pulled away and was gone, heels clipping on the paving stones in a hurry to get wherever she was going.

Jenni gazed after her wistfully, feeling so alone; more lonely than ever before. That seemed absurd in her present situation, surrounded by people and activity.

At the same time, the future *did* look brighter than it had. With a new life and a new name she'd make friends, but must be patient. It would all happen soon.

In the meantime she was ravenously hungry. It wasn't

surprising. Since leaving Auntie Blodwen's house just after five-thirty she'd had only home-made sandwiches midday on the train. Now she felt she could easily eat one of the dray horses that clumped by, hooves and all.

The fat woman's raucous call rang in her ears again, reminding her about the newspaper. Jenni exchanged a coin for one, then took her life in her hands to cross the road.

The faggots and peas shop had a dingy exterior; the small-paned window was dirty and steamed up. Jenni hesitated before going in. The place didn't look too inviting but that smart girl had recommended it. Jenni was very hungry and couldn't do anything more without some food inside her.

She took the plunge and opened the door. Inside, above a sawdust-strewn floor, a narrow shelf ran around two walls. A couple of men in overalls sat on stools, plates of steaming food in front of them. On the right-hand side was a wide counter behind which a short dumpy woman stood in a grubby wraparound pinny.

'Three faggots, is it, love?' she asked Jenni.

'Yes, please.' Jenni nodded, putting down her small suitcase and sniffing the steamy air.

A plate was dumped unceremoniously on the counter in front of her, and the woman ladled out three faggots, some mushy peas, potatoes and gravy.

'Bread?'

Jenni nodded. 'Please.'

The woman put a thick wedge of bread on the plate, dropped a knife and fork on the counter, then held out her hand.

'That's ninepence, love.'

Jenni paid her, then carried her plate and suitcase over to one of the stools. No one took any notice as she perched herself on it and tentatively explored her plate with the fork. The food smelled good, and tasted even better.

Jenni finished off the lot, then bought a mug of strong tea. Well satisfied with her meal, she scanned the newspaper, finding the rooms for rent and reading them eagerly. There were so many! It was getting late. How could she choose with no idea of the areas in this town?

One caught her eye. Hafod, it said, room to suit single lady in respectable family home. She was reminded of Trehafod where she'd lived so happily with her mother until tragedy struck.

Convinced it was a sign, she made up her mind immediately to view it. She must be settled in before evening. With a shiver, she thought of the man in the chauffeur's uniform outside the railway station. It wouldn't do to be wandering around the streets at night in a strange town.

But how could she get to Hafod?

Jenni picked up her suitcase, pushed her handbag more firmly under her arm and approached the counter again.

'How do I get to Hafod?' she asked the stout woman.

'A number eleven tram, love. That takes you to the Hafod.' She jerked her thumb over her shoulder. 'You'll catch one up by the church.'

Jenni asked the tram conductor to let her know when they were approaching Hafod Row, where the lodgings were.

The tram rattled and swayed alarmingly as it rounded bends in the road. As it crossed a bridge, she held on tightly to the edge of her slatted wooden seat.

Jenni knew the Welsh name Hafod translated into 'summer pastures', and all the while the tram car clattered its way along the Neath Road she expected to reach the outskirts of the town; expected the small grimy shops, the endless streets and row upon row of dusty terraced houses to give way, if not to open country, then at least to fields, trees and meadows. But the griminess of the town stretched on, relentlessly.

Although she was waiting for the conductor's signal, she was startled when he touched her shoulder.

'Here's the stop for Hafod Row, Miss,' he said. 'Just a bit further up the road.'

Jenni stepped of the tram and almost into the path of a speeding delivery bicycle, but managed to hop to safety on the pavement.

'Sorry, Missus!' the delivery boy yelled.

She was outside a barber's shop, a striped pole advertising its business. Jenni walked on, past some narrow terraced houses, a sweet shop, then an ice-cream parlour squeezed between a baker's and a pawnbroker's.

Next door to that was a double-fronted shop of some magnificence. The black paintwork was fresh and the windows very clean and shiny, in sharp contrast to some of the surrounding businesses. The sign above the doorway read 'Samuel Tregevny & Sons, Bespoke Tailors'.

Jenni paused to look in the windows which were all well stocked with items of apparel for men: flannel vests and other underwear; boxes of handkerchiefs, socks, shirts, celluloid collars and cuffs; flat caps, mufflers, trilbys and even a bowler hat, resplendent on a bronze bust.

Suddenly very interested in her find, Jenni passed to the other window where a dressmaker's dummy sported a gentleman's three-piece suit, well-cut and of quality material. There was also a lady's two-piece which Jenni viewed with a professional eye.

What wouldn't she give to get a job here? She paused a moment more, tempted to go straight in and make enquiries, but hesitated as commonsense warned that the moment wasn't right. After travelling all day she must look somewhat dishevelled. It would be sensible to find lodgings first, settle in, and prepare herself for the battle of finding a job.

Jenni walked on. The shops gave way to long terraces of narrow, poll-stone houses whose front doors opened directly on to the pavement. In many ways they were very much like the house she and her mother had lived in at Trehafod, though the poll-stone here was blacked by industry rather than coal.

Jenni felt suddenly very tired. Surely it couldn't be much further? Her suitcase was getting heavier by the minute and her shoes were beginning to pinch painfully. She was really flagging when she noticed a street sign affixed to the wall of a nearby house and realised she'd found her destination at last.

Finding the house number she wanted, Jenni saw that like most of the other houses, the front door was standing open. She knocked, and waited hopefully.

'Come in! Come in!' a woman's high-pitched voice floated out to her from down the passage. 'In the back room, I am, by here.'

Bemused, Jenni stepped into the passage and walked cautiously towards the voice. She couldn't help making an assessment as she went.

A faint smell of boiled cabbage wafted to her, making her nose wrinkle a little, but on the other hand, the linoleum in the passage, though faded, looked clean, and the mats were well-beaten.

On her right at the end of the passage, next to the stairs, was an open door, Jenni peered in cautiously. In the centre of the smallish room, dominating everything else, stood a large round table covered by a dark green chenille tablecloth. A tall mantelpiece, on which stood two white china cats, was set over a range where a fire burned brightly.

To one side of the range in a wooden chair with armrests sat a woman who was round and plump and obviously short in stature. Her face was round, too, with cheeks as bright as ripe red apples, and she was smiling at Jenni.

'Well! Hello, then!' the woman said cheerfully. 'What can I do for you, *bach*? I don't know you, do I?'

Jenni came further into the room, losing her nervousness at the warmth of the woman's tone. Her smile was glowing and her eyes welcoming, and Jenni felt immediately drawn to her.

She held up the newspaper.

'No, you don't know me. Come about the room to rent, I have,' she began. 'Wonder if I could see it?'

'Well! Bless you, dear, of course you can,' the woman replied. 'But you'll have to help yourself, *bach*,' she went on. 'My Renee's not home from work yet, and I can't manage the stairs anymore.'

It was then Jenni noticed the heavy calliper on the woman's leg.

'Oh, I'm sorry, Mrs . . . er . . .'

The woman laughed, a warm throaty sound.

'Morris, my name is,' she said. 'Meg Morris. Meg the Peg some call me behind my back. And there's no need for *you* to be sorry, *bach*.' She rapped the calliper with her knuckles. 'I've had this old thing for many a year. Wasting disease in the leg as a child, you know. But it's getting a bit too much for me now so I sleep in the parlour.'

There was cheerfulness in Meg's tone and Jenni recognised her as a woman who'd never let her circumstances get her down, and liked her immediately. She was tempted to say she'd take the room without even viewing it, but commonsense got the better of impulse again.

'I *would* like to see the room,' she ventured.

'Right you are!' Meg agreed cheerfully. 'Top of the stairs and it's the back bedroom, my Renee's old room. She sleeps in the front now. You can leave your case by here, love.'

With a laugh, Jenni realised she was still gripping her suitcase like grim death which wasn't surprising as it held all her worldly goods. Well, almost. Even though she owned the house in Llawr-y-bryn, that seemed like a daydream now. Her whole real existence was in that suitcase.

Upstairs, Jenni pushed open the door of the small back bedroom. There was a narrow iron bedstead, a chest of drawers and an ancient wardrobe. On top of the chest of drawers stood an oval mirror in a polished wooden frame, and on a small table under the window was a white china bowl and jug. It was spartan but clean and Jenni knew immediately she would take it, provided the rent wasn't too much for her.

Meg hadn't moved from her chair at the fireside.

'Well, what do you think, *bach?*'

'I'll take it,' Jenni said eagerly. 'Just what I'm looking for, it is.' She hesitated. 'But, of course, it depends on the rent.'

Meg regarded her, head on one side.

'Where are you from, love?'

'From the Valleys, I am.'

Meg smiled.

'Oh, I guessed as much.'

Jenni felt her cheeks flush. What was so obvious about her that everyone guessed her origins? Did she look like someone who'd just come down from the wild mountains?

Meg was looking expectantly at her, obviously waiting for Jenni to explain further, but she hesitated uncertainly.

No one could possibly guess who she was yet she was loath to name her village. She hated the web of prevarication she was creating around herself but fear of exposure made her go on spinning it.

'I come from Cwmgelligors,' she said boldly. 'Jenni Thomas, my name is. Both my parents are dead.'

'Tsk! Oh, bless you, dear, and you so young as well,' Meg said sympathetically. 'I worry about my Renee. Don't want her left in the world all alone.'

Jenni made a sympathetic noise in return, congratulating herself that a dangerous moment had passed.

'Got a cousin living in Cwmgelligors, I have,' Meg said unexpectedly. 'Married to the school's headmaster, she is. Megan, Megan Prosser. Lived there years. Perhaps you know her?'

Jenni swallowed hard, feeling a flush creep into her cheeks again.

'The name sounds familiar,' she fibbed, ashamed of herself.

'But I can't put a face to it,' She tried to excuse her ignorance. 'Quite a big village Cwmgelligors is, mind.'

Jenni clamped her lips together, consciously preventing herself from saying anything further. The more she said, the deeper she dug herself into a pit.

'Oh, bless you, dear, I'm like that myself,' Meg confessed. 'A memory on me like a sieve. That's what my Renee says anyway.'

She laughed again, that lovely throaty laugh. It was infectious, and despite her guilty discomfort, Jenni laughed, too.

'Well, Jenni, love, as to rent,' Meg said, 'could you manage four and six a week? I'm sorry it's so much,' she rushed on. 'But we've only my Renee's wages to manage on.'

Jenni nodded eagerly.

'I think four and six is fair.'

'The kitchen's in by there.' Meg pointed to a door in the corner of the room, obviously relieved that Jenni was agreeable. 'You're welcome to use that,' she went on. 'It's a tanner in the meter for the stove, love. And the lavvy's outside in the backyard.'

She held out a hand.

'Welcome to the Morrises, then, *bach*. Hope you'll be comfy here with us. I've got a feeling you and my Renee will get on a treat.'

Taking Meg's hand, Jenni felt a wave of relief wash through her. It was so powerful it made her feel weak. She suddenly longed to rest. She'd found a place! And so soon! Looking at the welcoming smile on Meg's face, Jenni felt good fortune was smiling on her. Well, it was about time, after all she'd been through these last years. For once things were going right.

'When would you like to move in?' Meg asked.

Jenni swallowed hard, suddenly startled. She had nowhere else to go.

'Right now, Mrs Morris, please,' she answered eagerly.

'Oh, good! Call me Meg, *bach*. Nobody calls me Mrs Morris

around here. Except the rent man, of course.' Meg's features straightened. 'I demand respect from *him*. After all, I've never been in arrears with my rent in my life, and never will be.'

At the mention of the rent man Jenni was reminded of Bert Herbert and felt a twinge of pain around her heart, suddenly missing her own mother. Meg meant no harm, she knew that, and warned herself not to be so sensitive in future. No one could possibly know her secret.

'Take your case up to your room, Jenni, *bach*,' Meg went on. 'Then you can make us a pot of tea, and tell me the story of your life.'

Jenni dawdled over making the tea, dreading the moment when she'd have to account for her past. The lies and deceits were piling up; the web she was spinning becoming more and more complicated. If she wasn't careful, she'd be trapped in it herself.

It was true what they said: a good liar must have a good memory. Her memories were best forgotten. But how could she ever forget?

No, she mustn't let herself be trapped in her own lies. It would be better to decide on a simple story about her past and stick to that from now on. Lying was despicable. It went right against the grain for Jenni. Yet she must protect herself and her new start in life, not go back to being a pariah, shunned by everyone. She needed friends — and love. Oh, how she needed some love in her life!

With reluctance Jenni carried the tea-tray into the living-room and had just set it on the big round table when a loud call from the passage startled her.

'Yoohoo, Mam! Here I am!'

'There's my Renee now,' Meg exclaimed, a beaming smile on her face.

A girl two or three years older than Jenni tumbled into the

room. She was tall and angular, all arms and legs. Her brown hair was piled up in a haphazard fashion underneath a skimpy hat. Her face, rather long and not particularly pretty, was animated with laughter and her eyes gleamed with fun. Although Renee Morris was the opposite physically of her mother Meg, the beaming smile was the same. Jenni was instantly drawn to the girl.

'Oh, hello!' Renee said, looking at her with keen interest and that ready smile. 'Who's this then, Mam?'

'This is Jenni,' Meg told her eagerly. 'She's our new lodger.' To Jenni she said: 'This is my lovely daughter, Irene, but everyone calls her Renee, don't they, love?'

Renee nodded, pulling off her hat and shrugging out of her coat to flop on to a nearby chair.

'Our new lodger. Well! There's nice.'

She jumped up again immediately, her expression embarrassed.

'Oh, there's rude I am. Anyone would think I didn't know my manners,' she said quickly, holding out a hand to Jenni. 'Pleased to meet you, Jenni. I hope you'll like it here.'

She clasped the hand gratefully.

'I'm sure I will, Renee,' she replied, almost shyly.

She could hardly believe her good fortune. There was love in this house, its warmth was all around her. If only she could be part of it.

'Let's have the tea then, Renee,' Meg prompted.

She immediately pounced on the tea-tray.

'I'll be mother,' she exclaimed cheerfully. 'Now you sit down by there, Jenni, and tell us about yourself. Mam and me are two nosy bodies.'

'Speak for yourself!' Meg laughed heartily.

Jenni felt a tightening in her chest. This mother and daughter were good people. They didn't deserve to be deceived and she hated having to do so.

'Jenni Thomas, I am,' she began, willing her cheeks not to flame with guilt. 'From Cwmgelligors. My mother died of the influenza years ago, and my father . . . was killed in a mining accident at the coal face.'

'Oh *Duw! Duw!*' Meg exclaimed, her face puckering in sympathy. 'Bless you, dear! And you've got no kith and kin like us, then?'

Jenni swallowed hard against the lump of contrition in her throat.

'I lived with my aunt but she died earlier this year. I've no one else.'

Renee's had strayed to her mother's as it rested on the arm of the chair and Jenni saw that her eyes were glistening with unshed tears.

'I'm so sorry, Jenni, kid. It's awful to be alone in the world. At least Mam and me have got each other.'

'Well,' Meg said warmly, 'Jenni can be part of our family now, can't she? Like a sister for you, Renee, love.'

Jenni gasped.

'But you don't know anything about me.'

'I've only got to look at you to know you're a good girl,' Meg said confidently. 'And I know, 'cos I've seen plenty of the opposite in my life. No, I'd wager next month's rent on you, I would, Jenni, love. Bless you, yes!'

Renee had brought home some slices of cooked ham for tea, and Meg insisted Jenni share it with them. In turn, she insisted on paying her share of the cost.

It was clear the Morrises had little money. Jenni thought of the small fortune tucked away in her suitcase, and the money John Davies would send her once Blodwen's house was sold. If Meg and Renee were willing to take her into their cosy home and family then Jenni could, unobtrusively, introduce a few little extras into their lives. She must be careful with her money, though, for who knew what the future held for her? And she *was* still without a livelihood.

Chapter Twelve

After the welcome meal Jenni decided to have an early night, sure Meg and Renee wouldn't mind. The day had been long and eventful. Now she was bone weary.

She was just about to speak up when Renee, removing the chenille tablecloth, replaced it with a sheet of fine canvas and lifted an old sewing machine on to the table. She brought a brown paper parcel from the cupboard, opening it to reveal a garment in the making.

Jenni immediately lost some of her tiredness and jumped up from her chair near the range to look at the handiwork.

'What's this, Renee?' she asked eagerly. 'What are you making?'

Renee bit her lip and looked reticent. Jenni caught the guarded glance that passed between mother and daughter and was puzzled by it. Had she said something wrong?

'I'm sorry, Renee,' she rushed to apologise, though not understanding her mistake. 'I shouldn't pry. A stranger in your house, I am, after all.'

Renee suddenly relaxed and pressed Jenni's arm reassuringly, smiling the cheery smile that was rarely off her lips.

'No, no, kid. It's not you. It's my guilty conscience, isn't it?'

She glanced at her mother as though for confirmation.

'I shouldn't be doing this, see,' Renee went on. 'Moonlighting, I mean. I'll get the sack on the spot if old Samuel finds out.'

'She doesn't mean to be dishonest,' Meg burst out, distress on her face. 'But we really need the extra few shillings it brings in. If old Samuel would pay Renee more we wouldn't have to deceive him, would we?'

'Old Samuel?' Jenni asked, bewildered now by the concern on both their faces.

'Samuel Tregevny,' Renee explained. 'He's my employer. I'm a skirt-hand, see. He keeps that tailor's shop further down the road. You must have noticed it when you got off the tram.'

Jenni nodded, finally understanding.

'Yes, I did, and a fine shop it is, too. A little gold mine, no doubt.'

Renee burst out laughing, giving Jenni a keen glance.

'You're a sharp one, aren't you? It's a gold mine all right, thanks mainly to Richie – or *Mr* Richie as we must call him in the shop. He's Samuel's eldest son. In fine fettle the business is, but the old man won't have any moonlighting. Taking the bread and salt out of his mouth, he reckons. The old tyrant!'

'Oh, come on now, our Renee,' Meg said. 'He's not that bad.'

'No, all right, then!' Renee conceded, but sniffing disparagingly. 'But he thinks he's it, mind. Struts about the shop in his pinstripe trousers and black frock coat like he was the Tsar of Russia. Can't do any tailoring himself now, see, because of the rheumatics in his hands.'

'Tregevny,' Jenni said thoughtfully. 'That's not a Welsh name.'

'Cornish family, they are, love,' Meg said. 'Came to Wales when Swansea was a boom town, no more than seventy odd years ago.'

Meg sat back in her chair, hands resting comfortably across her round stomach, feet on the brass fender.

'Born in the Hafod, *I* was, as were my mam and dad before

me, and their parents before them. Cwm Road was a very poor place but we were respectable, no one can say different. Everybody knew everyone else's business so us girls couldn't get away with nothing, even if we wanted to.'

Renee gave a deep sigh, turning the handle of her sewing machine faster.

'Oh, look out!' she said. 'We're going to take another stroll down Memory Lane.'

Meg took no notice but went on with her reminiscing. Jenni was eager to listen. There was a sense of belonging in listening to Meg talk about the old days. And she needed to learn all she could about her new home and family because family they were, she felt this in her heart.

'As a girl I can just remember old Samuel's father in the tailoring business. There was big money to be made then, and Norman Tregevny made it. He died some five years ago: as old as the hills and as wealthy as sin.'

'And keep it in the family, they do,' Renee remarked. 'Supposed to be getting another skirt-hand to replace Elsie Thomas but old Samuel's too mean to take anyone on. I'm left to do her work as well. Not a penny extra, though. Old skinflint!'

Renee glanced at Jenni.

'Elsie left to get married before Christmas. Sometimes I have to stay on till nine o'clock at night if there's a special job to complete, like Whitsun time, for instance. And they begrudge me a bit of moonlighting.'

'Any chance of me getting a job there?' Jenni ventured. 'I'm a trained dressmaker. Got my indentures as well.'

Renee stopped turning the wheel of the sewing machine, her eyes round as they gazed at Jenni.

'There might be, kid,' she said eagerly. 'I know Mr Richie is urging old Samuel to find another girl. If you was to come to the shop, he might be pursuaded, especially with your indentures, and all.'

Jenni felt her heart swell with hope.

'Well! Bless you, Jenni, dear,' Meg exclaimed happily. 'That'd be the very thing. You speak up for her tomorrow morning, Renee, *bach*.'

'Why not go one better?' Renee jumped up from her chair, excitement lighting her face. 'Come with me to work after the weekend, Jenni. I'll introduce you to old Samuel. Put him on the spot, good and proper. Mr Richie will back you, I know he will.'

'Will he?' Jenni was momentarily doubtful. 'He doesn't even know me.'

Renee nodded her head confidently.

'Mr Richie's got some sense and fairness about him,' she declared. 'Not stuck in the past, like his old man. And when he meets you he'll be all for it. What do you say, Jenni?'

'It's worth a try!' She felt elated again. 'I've got to find a job and it would be wonderful if we could work together — like sisters,' she went on shyly.

She'd been with the Morrises only a few hours, but knew already she'd found a safe haven with loving friends. She wanted desperately to belong to them.

Jenni followed Renee into the shop on Monday morning, well before nine o'clock, nervousness making her breathless, and feeling as if a thousand butterflies swirled madly in her midriff.

This shop was much bigger and grander than the Jukes's. Along either side were long counters of highly polished rich mahogany. Several bentwood chairs stood here and there on the gleaming black and white tiled floor, obviously for the convenience of customers.

Behind the counter on her right, on shelves reaching from floor to high ceiling, lay materials of all kinds, bolt upon bolt and roll upon roll. On the left side glass doors enclosed stacks of merchandise: flannel shirts, men's underwear – obviously every item of clothing a man might require.

Jenni was impressed by it all; more than impressed. She felt intimidated. Would they even consider a young and inexperienced girl from the Rhondda? she wondered, her nervousness increasing. She was almost ready to tell Renee she'd changed her mind but her new friend forestalled her.

'Wait by here, Jenni, love. Old Samuel ... er ...' Renee paused, glancing around quickly to see if she'd been overheard. But there was no one else visible in the long room. 'I mean, Mr Samuel is probably in the workroom. He goes there first thing to oversee work in progress.'

She dropped her voice to a whisper.

'Silly old buffer! He's no more than a figurehead around here but he still holds the purse-strings so the family are careful not to offend him. Especially Mr Jack.'

'Mr Jack?'

'Samuel's younger son and his favourite.' Renee paused again and grinned. 'A real charmer is our Jack. And a war hero, too.' She gave a deep sigh. 'Handsome devil, he is.'

'Renee, I'm frightened,' Jenni exclaimed suddenly. 'This shop's too posh. They won't give *me* a job. I'd better leave before anyone sees me.'

Renee grabbed her arm.

'Don't be silly, mun, Jenni. We want to work together, don't we? We're going to be friends, aren't we?'

'Of course we are,' Jenni responded quickly.

'Well, then, trust me,' Renee said confidently. 'I'll find Mr Samuel and have a quick word with him. Have a sit down while you're waiting.'

She darted away and ran up a steep, narrow staircase at the back of the shop.

Jenni sat gingerly on the nearest chair, breathing in the familiar scents of an outfitter's shop, particularly the smell of cloth which always filled her with excitement as she imagined all the wonderful garments which could be fashioned from it.

Her gaze wandered upwards. Above the counters on either side, wires were stretched, extending towards the back of the shop where they entered what looked like a small office, high up, with a window overlooking the shop floor. Jenni peered into the darkness of the interior, wondering if she were, at that moment, being observed by someone. Perhaps Mr Samuel himself. But all was stillness.

Satisfied, Jenni continued her inspection of the strange wire contraption. Small barrel-shaped objects made of brass were suspended from the wires. She viewed them with puzzlement. What on earth could they be for?

She was tempted to examine some of the bolts of materials, but nervousness and her awareness of the observation window kept her firmly seated on the chair.

Minutes ticked by and the silence deepened. A big clock over the shop door showed it was still a few minutes to nine. Jenni started to count the bolts of material to while away the time and keep her jitters under control.

'Can I assist you, Miss?'

The voice was quiet and well-modulated but the unexpectedness of it made her almost jump out of her skin. She rose hurriedly from her seat.

'I . . . I beg your pardon,' Jenni gasped, staring at the man who stood behind the counter.

He was tall and thin, wearing a high starched collar and a frock coat. His hair, though sparse, was neatly parted in the centre, while a bushy, well-trimmed moustache concealed his mouth. His watery eyes were bright behind gold-rimmed spectacles.

'Miss?'

Jenni gulped with fright, but knew she must take the plunge.

'Are you Mr Samuel Tregevny?'

The moustache quivered. Jenni suspected he was smiling.

'Alas, no,' he said. Jenni thought there might be a touch of irony in his tone. 'Mr Napier, I am, the shop manager. And who might you be, Miss, if you're not a customer?'

Jenni felt her mouth go dry.

'I'm waiting for Renee . . .'

'Oh, yes, Renee,' Mr Napier interrupted in his quiet way. 'Who has gone in search of . . . er . . . old Samuel, I understand. Not exactly the soul of discretion, Renee isn't.'

Jenni caught her breath.

'You were listening!'

Mr Napier took a large handkerchief from his pocket and delicately wiped at his moustache.

'It pays to be quiet and listen, my girl,' he said pompously. 'Knowledge is power. Don't ever forget that. Now, then, why are you asking for Mr Samuel?'

Stung by his somewhat superior tone, it was on the tip of Jenni's tongue to tell him that it was a private matter, and none of his concern, but she checked herself in time. Mr Napier was the shop manager, a very important person. It wouldn't do to get on the wrong side of him.

'I'm looking for work,' she said reluctantly. 'An indentured dressmaker, I am. I understand there may be a vacancy here as a skirt-hand.'

Mr Napier pursed his lips.

'There's a big difference between a skirt-hand and an indentured dressmaker,' he observed. 'If you think there's opportunity for advancement in this establishment, you'll be disappointed.' He sniffed. 'We already have fine tailors in Mr Richie and Mr Jack.'

He looked at her keenly, his gaze skimming her from head to foot.

'And where are you from? What's your name?'

Jenni felt a little tremor of fear go through her, recognising that brightness in his watery eyes as the light of incurable curiosity. The last thing she needed was someone like Mr Napier ferreting out her secret.

She was saved from answering by Renee's footsteps clattering on the tiled shop floor.

'Jenni, come on,' she exclaimed excitedly, ignoring Mr Napier. 'Mr Samuel will see you.' She pointed to the mysterious room above the shop floor. 'Up in the cashier's office.'

Jenni climbed the stairs breathlessly, her mind still on Mr Napier and the sharp appraisal of his keen gaze. She mustn't be so touchy, she told herself sternly. Not everyone was out to unearth her family history. She must learn not to take fright or people would get suspicious.

Mr Samuel was short and a little portly in his pinstripe trousers and frock coat. His greying hair was thick and wiry, and though he'd made an obvious effort to tame it with a lick of brilliantine, a heavy forelock flopped persistently over his brow, while, just as persistently, he tried to brush it away.

A pair of gold-rimmed spectacles were clipped to the bridge of his nose. He kept his head held high, with very conscious dignity.

'Mr Samuel,' Renee began demurely, 'This is Jenni Thomas who I was telling you about. She's got indentures and . . .'

'Very well, very well!' His tone was irritable and he waved a hand dismissively at her. 'That'll be all, girl. Run along! Run along! Haven't you got work to do?'

With a quick glance at Jenni and the ghost of a wink, Renee hurried from the room.

Mr Samuel seated himself in a chair near the window which overlooked the shop below. Jenni glanced through it, too. There were customers in the shop now and Mr Napier was attending to them solicitously, it appeared, by the humble tilt of his head, though a less humble man than Mr Napier Jenni couldn't imagine.

Mr Samuel didn't invite Jenni to sit but stared imperiously at her.

'Now then, young woman,' he began. 'You want to enter my employ as a skirt-hand?'

'Yes, sir,' Jenni answered eagerly, quelling the urge to curtsey. 'Excellent qualifications, I've got.'

Mr Samuel raised his brows and looked down his nose at her. 'Self-recommendation is of little account.'

Abashed and somewhat annoyed, Jenni hurriedly opened her handbag and took out her precious indentures, handing them to him.

'Well, see for yourself, sir,' she said tartly, though struggling to keep her tone even.

He smoothed his moustache as he examined the papers, murmuring a word here and there, but under his breath, so that Jenni couldn't tell whether they were words of approval or not. She waited, her anticipation tinged with apprehension. Surely with her skills he wouldn't refuse her?

Abruptly, he handed the papers back to her.

'I believe I've heard of the sisters Jukes,' he said, his tone a little pompous. 'Their reputation is good.' He looked at her keenly. 'Your qualifications are all you say, young woman. I congratulate you. However, I cannot offer you employment.'

Jenni felt disappointment shower her like cold rain.

'But why, sir?'

'I need a competent skirt-hand, nothing more. Your talents would be wasted.' He stood up abruptly and made a gesture to usher her out. 'Good day to you, young woman. You'll excuse me, I have a business to run.'

'But wait a minute!' Jenni exclaimed desperately, stepping aside quickly and refusing to be steered through the door. 'You could listen to what I have to say.'

She moistened her lips nervously.

'I need a job. I'm quite prepared to do the work of a

skirt-hand, and take the wages, too. I'm not proud, Mr Tregevny. I'm lodging locally and can't afford to travel far for work.'

He looked at her, irritation plain in his expression.

'Please, sir!' she went on.

She almost reached out to grasp his arm, but thought better of it. He'd see that as an impertinence.

'It doesn't make sense,' he blustered, 'your willingness to take less than you're trained for.' He shook his head, the forelock flopping uncontrollably. 'There's no advancement here for the likes of you, you know. We have all the craftsmen we need.'

Jenni nodded.

'Mr Napier explained that,' she said. 'I have many years ahead of me to do what I was trained for. But at this time I just need work. Give me a trial at least. Please, sir?'

He puffed out his cheeks, brushing aside the unruly lock of hair.

'Well, all right,' he agreed reluctantly. 'Against my better judgement, girl. You work hard and keep your place and we'll see how you go. Start tomorrow. Nine on the dot, mind!'

Chapter Thirteen

Renee scrambled up off her knees and wrung out the floor cloth.

'There!' she said, looking down at the gleaming front step with obvious satisfaction. 'That didn't take us long, did it? And we're in plenty of time for work as well.'

Jenni, replacing the mats on the passage floor, couldn't help smiling at the energy in her friend's voice. It was Jenni's first day at Tregevny's and she knew Renee was as excited as she was herself.

Renee grabbed at Jenni's arm as she came out on to the pavement to pick up the bucket of dirty water.

'Jenni, you *are* a good pal, helping me out with the chores like this.'

She laughed as she poured the water into the gutter.

'It's my home, too, Renee,' she said. 'And your mother's so good to me. And so are you. I feel I have a family again.' She shook her head, solemn now. 'You don't know what that means to me.'

'Maybe I do,' Renee answered rather dreamily. 'Don't want to be a skirt-hand all my life, mind. Meet a nice chap, I want to. Get married and have a bunch of kids. I love kids. What about you, Jenni, love? Do you want kids?'

Frowning, Jenni followed Renee along the passage to the living-room.

'I don't know.' She felt silly admitting that when her friend was so positive. 'Haven't thought about it, have I?'

In the living-room Renee looked at her with exaggerated surprise and a grin on her face.

'Don't tell me you're planning to be an old maid, then?' She giggled. 'There's no fun in that, mun.'

'Fun?'

'The fun in getting all those kids I'm talking about,' Renee said, winking.

Jenni felt her face grow warm and knew she was blushing and feeling something like shock. Somehow, Renee's words reminded her unpleasantly of her own mother, and she was disturbed.

'Renee! You haven't? You wouldn't?'

She sighed heavily.

'No! More's the pity. Haven't met a bloke who's looked at me twice yet, let alone anything else. Twenty-one, I am, mind, already. Time's going by, kid. Beginning to feel like an old maid myself.'

At that moment, with the aid of two sticks, Meg hobbled in from the lavatory in the backyard and Renee made eyes at Jenni, warning her to say no more. She was glad. All this racy talk made her uncomfortable and embarrassed.

She didn't have the yearnings Renee seemed to have. Was her indifference unnatural? she wondered. But she never wanted to end up like her mother. Uncontrollable feelings of that kind could only lead to tragedy. And then lives were wrecked.

'You girls are going to be late for work,' Meg said, puffing with exertion. 'Old Samuel will be on you like a ton of bricks.'

'The shop manager, too,' Jenni agreed, suddenly anxious to be going. She didn't want to start her job in the wrong. It meant too much to her.

'Who?' Renee looked puzzled.

'Mr Napier.'

Renee burst out laughing.

'He couldn't manage a rice pudding, kid,' she scoffed,

readjusting hairpins which were barely holding her hair in place. 'Gives himself airs and graces, he does, but he only serves in the shop, that's all, under the beady eye of old Samuel.'

'Thought he must be someone important, the way he dresses,' Jenni said, wondering.

'Old Samuel won't have it any other way. Everyone serving in the shop has to dress like that,' said Renee. 'And if there's a lady customer who needs measuring, one of us girls has to put on a white starched apron before we can see to her.'

'Oh, aye! Everything's prim and proper with Samuel Tregevny,' Meg remarked. 'Deacon of St John's Church, he is. President of the Cheery Boys as well. Finger in every pie. Cunning old devil!'

Jenni listened with growing nervousness. Heaven help her if Samuel Tregevny ever discovered the truth about her family. Maybe she was making a mistake in working for him?

'You've got to watch Napier, mind,' Renee said, as though reading Jenni's thoughts. 'He's a proper old nosy-parker and a gossip, as well. Likes to know everybody's business. Sometimes, I think he spies on us girls for old Samuel.'

Jenni was appalled.

'That's awful!'

'Dan Napier's nobody,' Meg put in. 'Grew up in the Cwm like me. Poor as Job, the Napiers were, but clean-living, I'll give them that. Napier's old mam was staunch chapel and wouldn't have no hanky-panky, thank you very much!'

Renee giggled.

'Maybe that's why he's still a bachelor.'

For some reason Jenni thought of Blodwen and her sense of sin.

'Come on!' Renee urged. 'Let's get out of our aprons and make our way. I bet you're on pins to start, eh, Jenni?'

*

Mr Napier was already in the shop when they arrived at a minute before nine. He took out his pocket watch and glanced at it ostentatiously. Renee stuck her nose in the air and marched past him, clutching at Jenni's arm and pulling her along, too.

She followed Renee up the narrow staircase. They passed the door to the cashier's office on the half-landing, climbing on up to the workroom on the first floor.

On the top landing, Renee pointed to another staircase going down towards the back of the building.

'The lavvy's out the back yard, kid. Don't stay too long out there, 'cos old Samuel times us.'

Jenni swallowed hard, nervousness making her hands perspire. Working for the Tregevnys would be very different from working for the Jukes sisters, and she realised she'd been very lucky in her choice of first employers who'd been kindness itself. They'd known her history but hadn't blamed *her* for it. She realised Samuel Tregevny would not be so charitable.

'Here's the workroom,' Renee said. 'Come on. I'll introduce you to the Tregevny sons. The men who really count around here.'

The room was vast, obviously taking up almost the entire area of the first floor. It was very untidy, too, or at least seemed that way on first impression.

Two large bay windows overlooking the road allowed plenty of light to fall on to an enormous table, which must have been especially made for the purpose. On top were four sewing machines, yet there was still plenty of space to work on material and for garments in the making.

Two men sat on stools at either end of the table, backs arched over their work, fingers expertly manipulating the cloth under the needles. Jenni's confused and nervous mind couldn't take in details of them yet, and when Renee walked forward, she stumbled along in her wake.

'Good morning, Mr Richie,' Renee chimed. ''Morning, Mr Jack.'

'Morning, Renee,' they chorused.

Jenni eyed them with apprehension. Would they be carbon copies of their father, old Samuel? And, if so, how would she like working so closely with them? For the two vacant machines were obviously meant for the skirt-hands.

Renee pulled her forward unceremoniously.

'This is Jenni,' she announced. 'The new skirt-hand, though she's an indentured dressmaker really, aren't you, kid?'

To Jenni's surprise both men rose to their feet.

'This is Mr Richie, Jenni,' Renee said, indicating the elder of the two men.

He held out a hand.

'How do you do, Jenni? I hope you'll be happy in your new job.'

Richie Tregevny was very like his father in looks, though taller and slimmer, and with an unruly forelock of thick dark hair that flopped uncontrollably over eyes of solemn blue.

His grip on her hand was firm, his voice soft and respectful. But he didn't smile, and for all his politeness Jenni felt he was distancing himself from her, and felt a sharp tug at her pride. After all, to him she was only a skirt-hand, the lowest of the low in his profession.

In a moment of pique, Jenni sharply pulled her hand free. She didn't like being looked down on. She'd experienced too much of that in the past. After all, the people of her home village had driven her away with the power of their contempt. She'd not put up with that in future.

Renee swung her round to face the other man.

'And this is Mr Jack, Jenni.'

She heard the admiration in her friend's voice, and when she gazed at Jack Tregevny, she understood why. He *was* very handsome; tall and well-proportioned, and his hair was golden. Not the wiry thatch of his father, but fine and neat, like silk. He was so unlike either his father or brother that one might believe he was not related.

Jack's eyes were blue, too, but there was nothing solemn about them. They glinted with laughter, and something else which Jenni couldn't identify. But she liked it, whatever it was.

The clasp of his hand was warm, and it lingered in a friendly way. Jenni liked that, too.

'Jenni! Lovely!' He smiled broadly down at her. 'At last something beautiful to look at while we work.'

Though pleased at his reaction and welcome, Jenni flushed.

'Well, thanks, Mr Jack!' Renee hooted.

She planted her hands on her narrow hips, as though offended, but Jenni could tell by the twitch at the corners of her mouth that she was joshing him.

'Sit here, Jenni,' Jack said eagerly, indicating the vacant machine facing the windows. 'Your face should always be in light, not shadow. And that hair, my goodness, what a glorious colour . . .'

'Jack!' Richie's voice cut through the moment like a knife, its previous softness and politeness gone.

Jenni glanced at him in astonishment. Disapproval was a cold mask on his face, and there was a warning expression in his eyes as he gave his brother a hard look.

It was obvious he believed Jack shouldn't get familiar with the lower orders. Richie intended she should keep her place, that was certain. He's showing his true colours now, she thought, a touch of anger and resentment surfacing again.

She flashed a look of contempt at him, and was pleased to see his confusion.

As he lowered his gaze to his work, he said, 'Enough time has been wasted this morning. Sit down, Renee. Finish off that pair of trousers from yesterday. The customer will be here later this morning for a fitting.'

He cleared his throat, as though still confused, then pointed to some folded cloth on the table.

'You can start on that skirt . . . er . . . Jenni, if you please.' He waved a hand towards the back of the workroom. 'You'll find thread, scissors, needles – everything you need – on the shelves back there,'

'Yes, Mr Richie,' Jenni answered politely but coldly.

She'd be respectful and reasonable, and wouldn't give him the opportunity to get her the sack, but she wondered about his attitude. Was it just her he'd taken a dislike to? She couldn't understand why. After all, she hadn't been here five minutes. But perhaps he was superior with everyone?

Jenni went to fetch the things she needed, and glancing at Jack, was delighted when he gave her a big, friendly wink.

At least Mr Jack was warm and human. And he was very handsome. It would be a pleasure working for him day after day, and she looked forward to it. She'd ignore Mr Richie, though, just to show him how much she despised his superior air.

Later that morning Mr Napier appeared in the workroom to announce that a customer had arrived for a fitting. Mr Richie immediately rose from his stool, took a man's jacket and waistcoat from a shelf nearby, and also the trousers Renee had just finished, and folded them over his arm. As he moved away from the table, Jenni was surprised to see that he limped noticeably.

She couldn't help staring after him. It was then she saw he wore a special shoe on his left foot, which was twisted inwards so that he walked awkwardly, on the very edge of it.

So, Mr Richie had a clubfoot. She felt a sudden spurt of sympathy, then checked herself. It didn't excuse his haughtiness towards her, though.

She turned her gaze to Jack's ready smile, aware he'd watched her all morning, quick to catch her eye if he could. And although Jenni couldn't resist sneaking glances at him from time to time, she'd been wary of Richie's observation of her. Now he'd left the room she felt relaxed.

'Well, Jenni,' Jack said, speaking to her for the first time since Richie's warning. 'How many young men are chasing after you?'

She blushed.

'None, Mr Jack. I've been in Swansea only a few days.'

'By this time next week, I'm sure you'll have a flock of them after you.' He gave a deep sigh. 'You won't have time to smile at me, then.'

Jenni felt flustered, but pleased and flattered, too.

'Oh, no, Mr Jack. I . . . I could never ignore you.'

Renee giggled, and winked at her from across the table, and Jenni felt even more confused.

She still felt very much the country girl from the mountains, gauche and unfashionable, and couldn't believe that a man as sophisticated and handsome as Jack would even notice her. She knew she wanted him to notice her, really notice her. She'd only just met him, never before known anyone quite like him, but suddenly it seemed very important that he saw her as a pretty young woman, worthy of his attention.

Her hand strayed to her plait. It was such a childish style for a young woman of her age. She decided there and then to have her hair cut, in a fashionable bob perhaps. She had the money for it. And a new dress. Something that would impress Mr Jack. She wanted to impress him; she wanted that very badly.

Jack was making buttonholes in a man's jacket, but his eyes hardly left her face, and Jenni was very aware of him.

He appears to like me, she thought, with rising excitement. He was smiling at her now, his eyes sparkling, and Jenni felt an odd little quiver in the pit of her stomach. The room seemed to grow warmer suddenly, and she felt breathless.

'Do you like going to the pictures, Jenni?'

She smiled vaguely, not understanding what he meant.

'Pictures?'

'Moving pictures, films, cinematograph, you know,' he went on.

Jenni shook her head, embarrassed to admit she'd never seen a moving picture.

'I don't know.'

'Oh, you must let me take you to the Palace,' he offered eagerly. 'Or maybe we could make a trip of it and go to the Tivoli in the Mumbles.'

Abruptly Renee lifted her gaze from her work, her eyes round as saucers as she looked from Jack to Jenni and back again.

Jack gave a little laugh.

'And you, too, Renee, of course,' he said.

Renee gasped with delight.

'Really, Mr Jack?'

'Well, why not?'

Jack was smiling, but there was a touch of chagrin in the curve of his lips, and Jenni had the distinct impression he hadn't meant to include Renee in the trip at all. The certainty of that made her feel quite dizzy, especially the way he was gazing at her now.

'It's time I had a bit of fun,' he said, laughing. 'Time we all had some fun.'

'Fun?'

Richie's cool voice from the doorway seemed to lower the temperature a few degrees.

'What's going on, Jack?'

His tone was hard and somehow accusing.

Jack's face immediately lost its animation and he looked warily at his brother.

'Just making conversation, Richie. What's wrong with that?'

Richie limped back to his machine and sat on the stool.

'You're taking the girls' minds off their work,' he said, his lips tightening. 'Especially Jenni. She's new and needs to concentrate, to learn the ropes.' His expression darkened. 'You're not forgetting your . . . responsibilities, are you, Jack?'

Jack gave Jenni a startled look for some reason.

'Don't know what you're talking about,' he said. 'God! Richie, you're just like an old spinster sometimes. If you'd been through what I went through in the war . . .'

An expression of irritation appeared on Richie's face.

'We all know you're a war hero, Jack,' he answered tightly, a distinct note of contempt in his voice.

Jenni was shocked that he could speak so disrespectfully to a man who'd risked life and limb for his country, and her dislike of Richie increased.

'Father may still be impressed by that,' he went on, his lips thinning. 'But I've heard it too often.'

Jack muttered something under his breath and half rose from his stool, his face reddening. He subsided again, but looked really angry at his brother's unnecessary remarks, and Jenni felt deep sympathy for him.

'You've never suffered, Richie, that's your trouble. You've never had to fight for your very life,' Jack said contemptuously and with unmistakable bitterness. 'While I was wallowing up to my waist in mud in the stinking trenches of Flanders, you were home here, cosy and safe.'

Richie straightened up in anger, his face greying.

'That wasn't my fault, damn you!' he cried out, and Jenni was astonished at the passion in his voice.

Pressing his lips together in a tight line, he bent his head for a moment, obviously trying to regain control of himself, but his fingers shook as he brushed the wayward hair from his eyes.

He looked up, his glance going quickly to Renee and Jenni, deep embarrassment in his eyes. Both of them had stopped working at the outset of the bitter exchange between the brothers, and Renee was staring at Richie in astonishment, as though she'd never seen him in such a state before.

Of course he wasn't to blame for his twisted foot, Jenni conceded, but how could he treat Jack like that? She'd heard the talk of men in the Valley about the hell of France; seen for herself their wrecked lives as they wandered about the streets, broken, forced to beg, unable to work to keep their families. It was the greatest tragedy of all.

Richie's face was still taut as he looked down the length of the table at his brother.

'The war's over, Jack,' he said calmly enough now, though Jenni thought she heard a persistent tremor in his voice. 'It's been over for a long time. It's behind us, and we've got a business to run, and responsibilities to bear in mind.'

Jack grunted and bent his head over his sewing, but she saw his fingers trembled a little, too, as they manipulated the cloth, and her heart went out to him again.

Jenni glanced at Richie's dark head bent over his sewing machine. She could understand his bitterness about the ugliness of his deformed foot and the incapacity it brought, but it wasn't Jacks' fault, either. Richie shouldn't take out his misfortune on his brother like this. It wasn't fair.

He's ashamed now, she thought, continuing to stare at him. His jealousy of his brother was so obvious. But it wasn't only jealousy of Jack, though, was it? Richie felt inferior, too, because Jack was handsome, a hero, and because he was warm and human while Richie's heart was full of resentment thanks to his twisted foot.

He's pompous like his father, she decided, her dislike of Richie Tregevny growing even more. It was very obvious he didn't want Jack becoming too friendly with her. He was treating her as if *she* were inferior, too.

Jenni bent her head over her sewing, feeling the muscles around her mouth tightening in anger. She thought she'd left all that persecution behind in the Rhondda. Well, she'd fight against it now.

She glanced at Jack, sunlight from the windows making his hair glisten like fine threads of gold. She liked him, maybe more than a little. She was attracted to him, that was it. That had never happened to her before, and it was a wonderful, exciting feeling.

If she wasn't mistaken, and her womanly instinct told her she wasn't, Jack was attracted to her, too.

Suddenly, a memory from many years ago popped into her

mind. Dilys's dad had taken them to a funfair, and a gypsy had told Jenni's fortune.

The man you'll love will make his living by needle and thread.

Jenni suppressed a gasp at the clarity of those remembered words, and stole another glance at Jack.

He was the one, she just *knew* he was! Fate had brought her here to meet the man she was to marry.

Chapter Fourteen

The month of May was proving to be warm and Jenni felt the benefit of her new hairstyle. It was cut short, just below her earlobes, with a fringe over her brows. Loosened from its plait and fluffed up, her hair was thick and bouncy, and she was very pleased with the result.

She was sure Jack liked it, too, conscious of his gaze on her often. When they were at the back of the workshop at the same time, amid the shadows, which seemed to happen quite a lot, his hand would stray near hers and he would sigh deeply. Sometimes she'd deliberately go to fetch things she didn't really want, just to see if he would follow. Most often he did.

She liked the warmth of his fingers on hers, the brush of his palm against her arm. These little gestures, the merest whispers of a touch, sent thrills shafting through her. Sometimes she felt so breathless with suppressed excitement she was afraid Richie would notice when she returned to her machine with thread or pins.

But he ignored her for the most part. Everyone had commented favourably on her new appearance. Even Mr Samuel had nodded with approval. But quite obviously to Richie she was invisible.

Jenni was impatient with his arrogance. Anyone would think his family were gentry or something, she thought, fuming. All they had was money. But in these modern times, since the war, perhaps money was all that mattered; to some people, anyway.

The weeks were going by, and Jenni was getting used to the work. It wasn't as interesting and creative as dressmaking itself, but she was happy with it, especially as she was in Jack's company all through the week.

And Mr Samuel, too, had said he was pleased with her, so he wasn't such a bad old buffer really. She wondered when she might find the courage to ask for a rise in wages. She felt she stood a good chance of getting one when the time was right, if Richie didn't put a spoke in her wheel.

Not that she was short of money. When John Davies, the solicitor at Cwmgelligors, succeeded in selling Blodwen's house, he'd sent her quite a substantial sum. She'd gone into Swansea on her half day and opened an account in a bank in Wind Street. That would be her secret nest-egg, to be used only in an emergency or for getting married. She wouldn't touch it until then. Instead, she'd live on her earnings.

Jack had not yet taken them on the promised trip to the Tivoli in the Mumbles, and Jenni waited patiently for him to ask again. Renee talked about the pictures a lot. She made them sound so exciting and fabulous that Jenni longed to experience a visit herself. It would be heaven if she could go with Jack, even with Renee tagging along, too. But the offer remained unspoken, and Jenni wondered, piqued, if Richie had got wind of Jack's plan and had forbidden it.

She'd be patient, though, because in the end love would triumph. And she was in love, she knew that now. What else could it be, feeling the way she did, light-headed and light-hearted? Jack was in her thoughts day and night. She could hardly sleep for thinking of him, and longing for the dawn to come so that she could be with him again.

One morning towards the end of May, Jenni found herself alone in the workroom with Jack. Richie was down in the fitting-room with a customer, and Renee had been asked to take the measurements of a lady who wanted a two-piece suit made.

Never before had she been alone with Jack and for some reason Jenni found her fingers were trembling too much to feed the cloth under the needle properly. She daren't make a mistake with this garment.

On impulse she rose from the stool and went to the back of the workroom on pretext of fetching some thread. Within moments, Jack was beside her. Smiling to herself, pleased with her newfound power over him, she reached up to take thread from a shelf and then felt his hand on her waist.

'Jenni!'

There was a throatiness in his voice that thrilled her. She knew it! He felt the same way she did. With rising excitement, she turned to him. He was looking at her with such earnestness, his eyes sparkling with emotion. His gaze on her face was so strange and intense, Jenni knew it must be love.

'Jenni, listen,' he said urgently, his voice barely above a hoarse whisper. 'We haven't much time. Will you come to the pictures with me tonight? I'll borrow my father's motorcar. We'll go down the Mumbles.'

She didn't really want to ask it but felt she should.

'What about Renee?'

'Oh, Jenni!' he gave a little groan and stepped closer to her. 'We don't need anyone else spoiling things, do we? Just you and me.'

'You and me,' she breathed, closing her eyes and feeling dizzy. 'Oh, yes, Jack.'

She felt his hands on her arms, their warmth radiating through the sleeves of her blouse. He drew her closer to him, so that she could feel his breath on her hair.

'Then, when we come out of the pictures,' he went on huskily, 'we'll stroll on the beach by Brynmill. It'll be a warm night. We can sit in the sand dunes. Would you like that?'

'I just want to be with you, Jack.'

The heartfelt words were said before she even realised it, but she didn't regret showing her feelings. After all, he was the man she would marry some day. There was no need to hide anything from him. They could be honest and open with each other.

When Jack gathered her in his arms she didn't resist, but clung to him. It was her first kiss, and she was eager for it. His lips on hers were warm and soft and persuasive. She felt that funny little quiver in the pit of her stomach again, and other strange and wonderful sensations, all so new to her.

This was love and it was wonderful!

Jack groaned a little as his kiss deepened and held her even closer. Jenni was lost in this new and wonderful world of awakened senses. She was no longer on earth but somewhere else, swirling in the clouds, locked in Jack's arms. This was the way it would always be, she just knew it.

He released her suddenly.

'Someone's on the stairs!' he whispered urgently. He pushed her away and stepped back, and Jenni felt bereft.

'Quickly! Get to your machine.' His voice held a guilty urgency. 'I'll meet you on the corner of Chapel Street at half-six. Say nothing to Renee.'

Within seconds he was across the room and seated on his stool.

But Jenni could only lean against the shelving, her mind still soaring in the clouds, her body still weak yet aglow with her newly discovered feelings.

Renee came bounding into the room, her long legs taking awkward and agitated strides.

'That Mrs Phillipart is the giddy limit,' she burst out irritably. 'She will insist her hip measurements are only thirty-eight when anybody can see she's forty-four. She said the tape measure was wrong!'

Jenni pulled herself together with difficulty, straightening the waistline of her skirt and pushing back her hair, wondering if

Renee had noticed anything different about her. But her friend bounded to the other side of the table and flopped down on her stool.

'You can take the measurements of the next one, Jenni,' she said, obviously still piqued. 'Those silly women get my back up sometimes.'

Forcing down the swell of emotion that still filled her mind and body, Jenni walked back to her machine on shaky legs, afraid to look at Jack.

Did that really happen? she asked herself. Did Jack kiss me or did I dream it?

Jenni couldn't bring herself to deceive Renee about the Tivoli trip. Her friend had been looking forward to it, chattering about it for ages. Jenni wouldn't enjoy herself knowing Renee was left out. There was plenty of time for Jack and her to be alone together in future.

He hadn't looked too pleased, though, when Renee had turned up, too. Still, he seemed to get over it, Jenni remembered, with a smile. She'd really enjoyed the picture, and had cried over the love story.

Jack said the breeze was too cool to stroll on the beach and sit in the dunes, and so he'd brought them home quite early. It had been wonderful, being with him, even if Renee had chattered like a monkey most of the time.

Jenni wanted to get into work extra early the next morning, just to see him again. She'd been dreaming about him kissing her and holding her tightly. In her dream they danced together, like the couple in the picture.

It was wonderful being in love.

Mr Napier was already behind the counter when they arrived. 'You two are sly little birds, aren't you?' he said to them. His inquisitive glance darted from one to the other of them. 'I saw you both getting into Mr Samuel's motorcar last evening, and Mr Jack was driving. A trip in the country, was it?'

'Went to see the picture at the Tivoli.' Renee burst out enthusiastically. 'And Mr Jack bought us tea as well. Oh, he's a good sport, mind.'

Mr Napier gave a slow smile.

'Yes, I'm sure he is.'

Jenni hurried on towards the staircase, making for the workroom, eager to see Jack, Renee at her heels.

'Oh, just a minute,' Mr Napier called after them. 'Mr Richie wants a word with you, Jenni, in the cashier's office.'

Renee grinned at her, and winked.

'What've you been up to, then?'

'Nothing!' Jenni was piqued. 'Mr Richie's got it in for me. I don't know why.'

Nevertheless, she felt a tremor of fear around her heart. Had he somehow found out her secret past? Was she about to get the sack? What about Renee and Meg? Would they demand she leave their home, too? And how would she ever bear being parted from Jack?

Questions filled her head as she climbed towards the cashier's office, panic making her footsteps uncertain and awkward. She paused outside the open door while Renee hovered, neck craning in curiosity.

Richie was sitting at the desk where Samuel had sat the day he'd interviewed Jenni. It must be something serious, she told herself, for her to be summoned like this.

'There's work waiting, Renee,' Richie said bluntly, and Renee hurriedly stumbled up the remaining stairs, her long legs at all angles.

'Come in, Jenni,' he said. He rose from his seat as she entered and indicated the other chair. 'Sit down.'

She lifted her chin defiantly.

'I'd rather stand, thank you,' she answered curtly.

Whatever it was he had to say she'd hear it standing on her two feet. She wouldn't give him the satisfaction of looking down on her.

'Very well.' He gave an impatient sigh and sat down himself. 'I've heard about last evening's escapade,' he said. 'I don't know what Jack was thinking of. It mustn't happen again.'

'*What*?' Jenni was furious. 'I suppose you mean two working-class girls like me and Renee are too common to be seen with!'

She was really angry at his snobbishness, yet there was a measure of relief, too. He obviously hadn't discovered her secret. This was something different entirely. Pride and conceit, that was Richie's trouble! She, a country girl from the Rhondda, wasn't good enough to associate with a Tregevny.

He glanced up sharply, frowning. His blue eyes weren't solemn now. There was a glitter behind them, like cold blue fire.

'No, I don't mean that, miss,' he said testily. 'I mean Jack should know better than to see you, either of you, socially, because . . .'

'How dare you?' cried Jenni, outraged that he was agreeing with her. She wanted to stamp her foot. 'What makes *you* so superior? What makes you believe you can dictate to Jack what . . . friends he has?'

Richie rose from his chair, looking wrathful.

'Now, look here, young woman . . .'

'No, *you* look,' she burst out fiercely. 'I've had enough of you and your lordly attitude! You've got no right to look down on me. As good as you any day, I am.'

She was furious at the injustice of it, but realised she was probably heading for the sack. Still, she had to get it off her chest. She was finished with letting people walk all over her without fighting back.

'I work for your father . . .' she wondered if that was still true '. . . but don't think for one minute that the Tregevny family can run my life. I'll see who I please, when I please, and you can't stop me.'

'You don't understand, you silly little fool!' Richie thundered. 'I'm trying to help you.'

'I understand, all right,' cried Jenni. 'And I know what you're trying to do. You want to come between us — Jack and me.'

'Jack and you?' Richie stepped back, looking stunned. 'What do you mean? What's my brother to you?'

'You mock him because he fought in the war. You're so twisted up with jealousy,' she stormed, oblivious to any possible repercussions, 'you don't want him to have anything. Why are you like that? What's he ever done to you?'

'Jenni, listen . . .' Richie moved forward, hand out as though to take her arm, and she retreated a step, wary of him. He saw her recoil and his lips tightened.

'What's Jack been saying to you?' he demanded wrathfully. 'What's he been promising?'

'It's none of your business!' Jenni exclaimed, enraged.

He glared at her.

'Perhaps I'm wrong about you,' he said slowly, his eyes narrowing speculatively. 'Perhaps you're as much a schemer as . . .'

Jenni tossed her head.

'Can I get back to work now?' she interrupted loudly, not wishing to hear anymore of his insults and wanting the interview to come to an end. 'Or have I got the sack?'

Richie's face was as black as thunder.

'You ought to get the sack,' he said through clenched teeth. 'For your own sake. But it's my father who hires and fires around here, and apparently he's pleased with your work.'

Jenni felt gratified and immediately relieved. She'd have broken her heart if she'd been forced to leave, now that she'd found love with a wonderful man. Though Jack *would* have found a way for them to be together, she knew.

Richie's smile was mocking as he went on: 'You have a gift for charming the Tregevny men, it seems.'

She lifted her chin again, feeling triumphant and much more confident.

'Well, you appear to be immune, Mr Richie,' she answered ungraciously, but feeling he deserved it. 'So *you* have nothing to worry about.'

His face clouded again and he looked angry.

'I can't believe you're so hard-faced,' he said testily. 'You look so innocent. But, then, you can't tell these days.'

Seething, she turned on her heel to leave.

'Jenni, listen!' Richie exclaimed again.

There was a new tone in his voice, but Jenni didn't want to understand it. She'd had more than enough of Richie Tregevny.

'Jack's a man of straw,' he went on urgently. 'Whatever he's promised, he can't keep his word because he's . . .'

Jenni didn't wait to hear anymore but raced up the stairs to the workroom.

Her job was safe, for the moment anyway. She'd find it a strain working alongside Richie but at least Jack would be there and she could bask in the sunshine of his love. That was all she needed to make life bearable.

It was disappointing that Jack didn't appear in the workroom that morning. Meeting Mr Napier on the staircase on the way to the lavatory later, he was quick to tell Jenni, unbidden, that Mr Jack had been in earlier, had seemed disturbed that Mr Napier had observed them the evening before, and had left the shop almost immediately after, destination unknown.

It was getting on for midday. The girls were allowed an hour for dinner. They usually scuttled back to Hafod Row where Renee would make them a hasty meal.

Jenni felt hollow with disappointment at not seeing Jack. Looking at the clock, she saw there was another fifteen minutes to go yet before they could leave their machines.

Richie was with them but hardly uttered two words all morning. Jenni was conscious of a heaviness in the atmosphere since their heated exchange. Renee didn't seem to notice the tension but kept up a cheerful stream of chatter, mostly about their trip to the Tivoli. She went on and on, and Jenni wished with all her heart that her friend would stop.

Suddenly she did, abruptly and in mid-sentence, and Jenni looked up at Renee to find her staring towards the doorway, eyes as round as saucers.

Jenni glanced over her shoulder to see a young woman standing there as though posing, one gloved hand on her hip. She was tall, slender, and wore the most beautifully tailored suit in fine lavender-coloured wool. Hugging her blonde head was a little black hat, trimmed with a puff of veiling, arranged artfully over one eye.

What made Jenni stare the hardest was the cigarette holder, complete with smouldering cigarette, held nonchalantly in her other hand. She had never seen a woman smoke before, and was shocked at the audacity of it.

A cloud of perfume wafted towards Jenni as, fascinated by such elegance and style, she watched the young woman saunter further into the workroom and put her clutch-purse on the table near Jack's machine.

'Where is he?' she asked Richie in an arch tone, ignoring everyone else at the table. 'Said he'd take me to lunch at the Baltic Lounge.'

Richie stood up.

'Your guess is as good as mine,' he answered shortly, a dryness in his tone. 'He hasn't been here all morning.'

'Oh, this is too bad!' The visitor flounced towards the window which overlooked the road. 'What am *I* supposed to do now?'

Her accent was strained and self-conscious, Jenni thought, as though she was trying to speak posh. That and her exaggerated posing made her seem false, and Jenni took an instant dislike to her. Who on earth was she? And what did she want with Jack?

Richie continued to watch her, saying nothing. Jenni stole a quick look at him. His expression was stony and remote.

The young woman turned from the window, the cigarette holder held to her red lips. She barely glanced at Renee, but when her gaze rested on Jenni, she was startled to see a flash of emotion in the smart young woman's eyes; a glint of anger or malice, she couldn't tell which, and was flummoxed.

The dislike appeared to be mutual, Jenni realised with a jolt, but why when they had never met before?

The newcomer's hard gaze rested on Jenni for a moment longer, then was swept away as the young woman snatched up her purse from the table. She stalked towards the door, not turning her head again.

'Tell Jack I'll see him later.'

When she reached the doorway, she called back over her shoulder: 'Oh, and by the way, Richie, tell Violet not to hold supper for me. I may be late.'

Then she was gone.

Richie looked at the clock on the wall opposite before sitting down again.

'You two had better go for your meal now,' he said casually, without looking at either of them, but Jenni thought his tone was as taut as a coiled spring. 'Don't be late back.'

She couldn't wait to get outside. There were so many questions she wanted to ask Renee.

'I don't like *her*!' Jenni exclaimed energetically as they hurried along the pavement towards Hafod Row. 'Who is she? An important client or what?'

'We rarely see anything of her,' Renee answered, racing on. 'Too toffee-nosed for words, she is.'

Jenni was impatient. 'But who is she?'

'Clara, that's her name,' Renee said as they reached the house and clattered down the passage. 'Jack's wife.'

'His what?'

Jenni skidded to a halt, sending the mats awry on the passage linoleum and almost losing her balance altogether. She stared at Renee open-mouthed.

'What did you say?'

'Jack's wife,' she repeated, then stopped and looked keenly at her friend. 'Good God! Jenni, kid, what's the matter? Your face has gone as white as a sheet.'

Jenni was stunned. She couldn't believe it. How could Jack be married when he had kissed and cuddled *her*, been so loving and eager? There must be some mistake.

'Jack *can't* be married,' she cried out, shaking her head in anguish. How could he be married when she loved him so? 'He can't be!'

Renee nodded.

'Well, he is, mun. Two years now. Clara used to be a skirt-hand at Tregevny's. Before my time, mind. But what's the matter, kid? Why are you so upset?'

Jenni's legs felt weak and her body too heavy. She leaned against the passage wall for support, feeling as though the earth had opened up under her and she was about to fall through into – what? The pit of hell?

'Renee,' she wailed, 'I thought you were my friend. Why didn't you tell me? Why didn't you warn me?'

'Warn you?' Renee came to her, looking concerned. Taking hold of her arm, she drew Jenni towards the living-room. 'Jenni, love, what are you on about?'

'You should've told me,' she wailed again. 'Weeks ago. Oh, Renee, what am I going to do?'

Renee clutched at Jenni's arm, her own face suddenly turning white.

'Jenni, kid, you haven't been . . . silly, have you? With Mr Jack, I mean. You haven't let him . . .'

Shocked at the very idea, her eyes widened.

'No, I haven't!' Jenni was aghast.

'Oh, thank God for that, then.' Renee looked immensely relieved. 'You're not in trouble, that's all that matters.'

'Renee, you don't understand,' she cried out miserably. 'I'm so in love with him – and now you tell me he's married!'

She remembered his kiss, so eager and passionate. Surely he hadn't deliberately deceived her? She couldn't believe that of him. No, a man wouldn't kiss a girl that way unless he had real feelings for her.

Clara might be his wife in name – Jenni felt an agonising pain around her heart at the thought of her beloved Jack being married to someone else – but he loved *her*, she just knew it.

'He doesn't love her, Renee,' Jenni cried breathlessly. 'I'm certain of it. I just know he loves me. But what will we do, Jack and me?'

Renee took her by the arm and led her into the warm living-room. Jenni saw with relief that Meg wasn't in her chair. The fewer people who knew she'd made a fool of herself the better.

'Now listen, Jenni, kid,' her friend said earnestly. 'You don't know much about men, do you? When it comes to a pretty face and a figure like yours they have something more on their minds than love. He's no different. Likes to flirt, our Jack does. Can't resist a pretty face.'

Jenni wrung her hands in despair. 'You should've warned me, Renee. I'd never have let myself fall in love otherwise.'

But was that true? It had taken just one look and her heart was captured. It was fate.

'Are you sure?' Renee raised her brows, her tone sceptical as though reading Jenni's mind. 'He lassoed you on your first day, by the looks of things.'

'I can't believe it!'

Renee sighed heavily.

'Look, kid, you can fall out of love as easily as falling in, I shouldn't wonder. You'll get over it, mun. Just as long as you're not in trouble.'

Relenting, she pushed Jenni into a chair.

'Look, love, sit down by there while I make a cuppa and something to eat. You're looking whiter than yesterday's laundry.'

Renee hurried into the kitchen and Jenni was glad of a few moments to herself. She remembered some of the last words her mother had spoken to her.

Men will try to take advantage of you. Never let them.

But Jack wasn't like that, she was certain. He was gentle and tender, and he was falling in love with her, too.

Know what you want in life and in love, and never take less, her mother had said. Well, she wanted Jack desperately. She'd never been in love before.

Renee was wrong. True love didn't just die or fade, it lasted forever. That was the way Jenni loved Jack, and she knew she'd never love any other man like this.

He *did* love her, and she had faith he'd find a way for them to be together.

An image of Clara Tregevny's beautiful but rather hard features came into Jenni's mind's eye then, and for a split second she felt a surge of guilt, realising that perhaps she *was* prepared to take her rival's husband from her.

How ruthless *was* she prepared to be? At that painful moment, when her dreams of a life with Jack seemed hopeless, she knew she was willing to be as ruthless as was needed – to fight tooth and nail for him.

She remembered Clara's strident and careless tones. She didn't seem like a wife who loved her husband, and he certainly didn't love her. Obviously, Clara was selfish and cold while Jack was a hero who deserved so much more. He must love Jenni or he couldn't kiss and hold her so passionately.

She wouldn't lose faith, but would do battle for him, with Clara. It wasn't sinful, she told herself fiercely. She was saving him from a lifetime of unhappiness. Jack was *destined* to be her husband. The gypsy hadn't lied.

Chapter Fifteen

Clara opened the door of Abertawe House and walked into the wide front hall under its glass-domed cupola, her high-heeled shoes clicking on the parquet floor.

The gaslights were turned low. Samuel's penny-pinching again. In irritation, Clara reached out and turned them up, every one of them.

When was the old fool going to get electricity in? Why must they live in the Dark Ages? What was the good of money if it didn't make life more comfortable and pleasant?

Her life *had* been comfortable, though, for the last two years, Clara admitted to herself, since she'd married Jack. She wouldn't let anything change that, either. She was only getting what was due to her, and would let no one take it away from her.

Checking her image in the hall mirror, she pulled off her close-fitting hat and riffled her fingers through the Marcel waves in her blonde hair, turning her head this way and that, admiring the curve of a cheek and the lift of a fine brow. She liked what she saw.

You just wait, my girl, she told her reflection, with a little knowing smile of resolve. Wait until the old fool's popped off and Jack gets his share of the business. We'll live like gentry then; travel, socialise. I'll see to that.

She was only a girl still. There was more than enough time to get all she wanted, all she'd ever dreamed of, all that the world owed her. And the world owed her plenty!

Her mouth tightened at the memory. No young girl should suffer the way she had, used and abused and ill-treated. She deserved better — and she was going to get it or be damned!

Her thoughts went back again, as they had too many times today, to the redheaded young piece in the Tregevny workroom. The new skirt-hand was pretty, seemingly vulnerable and naive. Just the way Jack liked them.

Clara ground her teeth, remembering the way Napier had smiled knowingly when he'd told her about Jack's little trip to the Tivoli. Gone out of his way, Napier had, to let her know. He knew too much altogether, that was the trouble.

How much did he know about *her*?

A little chill went through Clara at the thought, and she clutched convulsively at the string of beads around her neck. Of course he knew her family in the Cwm, but he'd never connect her with them. She'd been careful to conceal her origins so he couldn't know anything.

In the mirror Clara looked at the healthy glow of her skin, the clear brightness of her eyes, the elegant curves of her body. No one would recognise her as that grubby, underfed urchin Clara Price from the Cwm she once was. No one could guess she was Dirty Kitty's illegitimate daughter. No one could know the shame and the pain she'd suffered.

Clara relaxed her grip on the beads, taking a deep breath to calm herself. There was no need to worry. Napier wouldn't discover anything. She'd covered her tracks well, and had cut herself off from her old life.

No, there was no need to worry.

But there *was* something else to think about, she warned herself, and she'd not been able to set aside the anxiety since seeing that red-haired girl in the workroom.

Jack was after her, Clara just knew it in her bones. There'd been others, she acknowledged, but this one looked as though she might be a real threat. Vulnerable the girl might seem, but there was something different about this one. Behind the innocent stare of those green eyes she'd glimpsed something that glistened like stainless steel, and had found it most disturbing.

Clara's fingers deftly pushed a blonde wave back into place as she stared into the reflection of her own blue eyes.

She'd always thought herself a little psychic. There'd been a definite flash of something, a warning perhaps, when she'd first set eyes on that girl today. A feeling of disturbance, upheaval. She felt it now, deep inside her like a black whirlpool. That girl spelt trouble, and Clara had better be ready for it because the rest of her comfortable future depended on it. That's why she was determined to have it out with Jack tonight.

Clara glanced at the hall clock. It was getting late. Where was he anyway? She wouldn't rest until she'd tackled him about his interest in that damned girl, and set her mouth in a hard line in anticipation of the confrontation. She must get the upper hand, and before bedtime, otherwise she'd never be able to sleep.

She turned from the mirror, eager to find her husband, and walked across the hall towards the front sitting-room where she could hear the gramophone playing, the strains of 'The Old Rugged Cross' drifting out clearly to her, even through the oak double-doors.

The old man was home, then. No chapel meeting tonight. The narrow-minded, strait-laced old fool!

But Samuel had the power, and the money, and they must all toe the line; kow-tow to his rigid standards of respectability and decency. Any scandal would be a catastrophe for their trade, he said often enough, and just as often Clara thought bitterly that the comment was directed at her. But she wasn't a fool. She knew which side her bread was buttered.

The music slowed to a drawl then speeded up again to normal

as someone turned the handle, winding up the gramophone.

Clara gave an impatient sigh. If they had electricity they could have one of those new wireless sets. Everybody was talking about them. The new British Broadcasting Company was relaying music now. Why couldn't the old man move with the times?

Oh, where *was* Jack? In the back sitting-room, perhaps, having a drink, she decided.

She hesitated with her hand on the door knobs of the front sitting-room, and sighed with exasperation.

To get to the back room she'd have to pass through the front, and she just couldn't face her father-in-law's high-handedness this evening, or her sister-in-law's mournful stare. That hang-dog expression always got her back up, Clara found. She had no time for women like Violet, with no backbone, except that she'd found they were easy to manipulate.

Turning on her heel, Clara climbed the wide staircase. She'd go up to their bedroom first, change into something more comfortable and tackle Jack when he came upstairs.

When she went into the bedroom her husband was already there, standing before the wardrobe mirror, arranging a necktie. His tweed sports jacket was on the bed. He looked as though he were about to go out, and Clara felt her temper rise. Did he believe she wouldn't guess what he was up to?

'Jack! We've got to talk,' she announced aggressively, throwing her bag on to the bed, followed by her hat and gloves.

'You're late,' he said shortly without glancing at her. 'Violet held up supper for you. The old man was furious.'

To hell with the old man! she thought recklessly. And damn Richie, too, for ignoring her instructions. It was irksome that her brother-in-law still treated her with something like contempt.

But wait until the old man had turned up his toes, she consoled herself. Jack was the favourite, the son who went to war and returned a hero; a son to be proud of. The old man was always saying that, too, and she expected great things because of it. The lion's share, perhaps.

But that was in the future. The fly in the ointment now was that girl.

Clara marched to the dressing table where she found a cigarette holder and a packet of cigarettes, the scented ones she liked. She lit up then stood behind Jack, one arm folded across her breasts, cigarette holder resting lightly between the fingers of her other hand.

'I've been to the workroom and I've seen her,' she said flatly.

'Seen who?' He paused for just a moment then went on adjusting his tie. 'You seem upset, Clara. What's wrong?'

'You know damned well!' she answered through clenched teeth, trying to steady the swell of anger in her breast at his studied indifference. He'd played that game too often, and she wasn't taken in by it.

'Napier told me all about your little joyride. Did you think you'd get away with it? And what if the old man finds out? Are you willing to risk that?'

Slowly and silently, Jack finished adjusting his tie and reached for his jacket on the bed. Infuriated, Clara threw the cigarette holder and the still-lit cigarette on to the glass top of the dressing table.

'Well! Answer me, Jack, damn you!'

His glance was gloating.

'What's all the fuss about?' He gave the reproachful sigh of someone grossly misunderstood. 'I gave the workroom girls a treat. They don't get paid enough to afford little luxuries.' His glance turned sly. 'As you might remember, Clara.'

She felt the skin around her mouth tighten. She hated it when he taunted her with what she'd once been. But, thank God, her husband didn't know the half of it. How long would she last if he ever did find out? she wondered bleakly.

'You might fool the old man, Jack,' she said tightly, 'but not me. It's that redhead, isn't it? I can recognise the pattern. You're after her like a dog with a rabbit, But she's no rabbit, Jack, believe me.'

Clara felt a nervous tremor as she remembered those seemingly innocent green eyes.

'She's playing you like a fish on a line, Jack!'

Her voice was rising dangerously and she checked herself again. Losing her temper completely would be playing right into his hands.

'She made a monkey out of you last night, didn't she? Bringing her friend along, too. Clever! Keeps you panting for more.'

His answering smile was mirthless, cold even.

'Quite a menagerie you have there, Clara,' he said mockingly. 'From dogs to monkeys. What an imagination! Pity it's overstrained.'

She clenched her fists tightly, holding her arms stiffly against her sides. He was belittling her, making her out to be a fool, and she was furious with him.

'It'd better stop, Jack,' She was almost choking in her rising fury. 'I'm warning you . . .'

Realising she was losing control of the quarrel, she took a deep breath, struggling to be calm. He could always make her lose her temper, but he couldn't make her love him. He couldn't break her heart – no man could do that.

'Warning me?'

He stood still for a moment, looking at her. She didn't like that look and to avoid it, reached forward for the cigarette holder, placing it in her mouth and drawing deeply. It was somehow reassuring to see the end of the cigarette glow deeply. When she glanced at her husband, he was checking his appearance in the mirror again.

'Clara, it's all in your imagination,' he said casually, then paused, scowling, and went on: 'I got caught out once. It won't happen again.'

'What do you mean by that!' she blazed, forgetting her resolve to stay calm.

'The baby, Clara – the baby you never had,' he said harshly, features contorted with anger at last. 'The reason why my father *forced* me to marry you to ward off a scandal. Don't say you've forgotten that!'

She swung round, turning her back on him, not wanting him to see her guilty expression which she knew she wouldn't be able to disguise.

'I couldn't help losing it. It wasn't *my* fault,' she answered truculently.

'Not your fault?' he exploded. 'No, maybe it was mine for getting mixed up with you in the first place. You were so willing, so accommodating . . . and I fell for it.'

Clara swung round to stare at him, aghast. What was he saying? Was he calling her a trollop? Deeply insulted, she screeched in anger, unconcerned that her voice might carry outside the privacy of their bedroom.

'How dare you say that?'

He glared at her, eyes narrowed with suspicion, apparently unaffected by her wrath.

'You know what, Clara? I don't believe you ever *were* in the family way.'

Stunned by his sudden insight, she felt a cold shiver pass through her, and knew her voice was strained as she replied: 'Are you implying I tricked you?'

He remained silent, deliberately turning from her to open the top of the chest-of-drawers to take out a silk handkerchief. He folded it and pushed it into the breast pocket of his jacket.

'Don't you turn your back on me, you philandering bastard!' she screeched passionately. 'I'm your wife. If you've anything to accuse me of then say it to my face – or are you too much of a miserable coward?'

He spun round, his expression vitriolic, then his shoulders sagged.

'What's the point? It's water under the bridge now, isn't it?' he said dully. 'I married you. What more do you want?'

He moved towards the door, but Clara grasped at his arm.

'Where are you going, Jack?' she cried shrilly. 'You're meeting her, aren't you?'

He pulled her hand away roughly.

'I tell you, you're imagining things,' he said harshly. 'I've no interest in any girl. How can I? I'm married to you.'

She lifted her chin defiantly.

'And don't you forget it,' she said, voice rising again. 'Don't be stupid, either. If your father gets to hear about your dallying, he might cut you out of the will. We'd lose everything then!'

Taken completely by surprise, Clara gasped in pain and fright as Jack caught at her wrist savagely, twisting it so that her fingers released the cigarette holder and it fell on to the rug.

'Stop it! You're hurting me.'

His face, contorted with fury, was close to hers.

'That's all you care about, isn't it, Clara? Money!' he hissed dangerously. 'You don't give a damn about me. You never did.'

Summoning strength, she pulled her arm free, very much afraid. He'd never laid hands on her in this way before. It was another sign that her future as his wife was in peril. She had to box clever now, beat him at his own game. She knew his weaknesses better than anyone; better than he did himself.

Suddenly relaxing against him, she put one hand against his chest, making soothing motions, and looked at him from under her eyelashes. She knew how to satisfy his appetites, too.

'That's not true, Jack, and you know it,' she murmured softly.

She looked full into his face, then, lips parted, eyes wide and inviting. He might not love her but she knew the way to move him, to excite him. She still had the power to twist him round her little finger when she wanted to.

'Oh, Jack, it's you I'm worried about,' she said gently. 'I want *you* to get what's due to you. You're Samuel's favourite and Richie's only waiting his chance to undermine you, can't you see that?'

Jack shook his head, pushing her away, his tight smile mocking and contemptuous. Clara was shocked at his reaction. Never before had she failed to tempt him with her body. That redhead had a stronger hold on him than she had anticipated.

'Not everyone's a schemer like you, Clara,' he said, his voice still harsh with anger. 'And here's something else for you to think about – Father's insisting we start a family very soon.'

She felt a shaft of defeat go through her at his words, and was suddenly appalled and frightened. Did he suspect that producing a baby was the one thing of which she was incapable?

Jack's searing gaze held hers as though challenging her.

'He wants a grandson. If you don't come up with the goods soon, Clara, perhaps Father *will* start seeing Richie as his favourite son.' He laughed nastily. 'Maybe you can scheme your way out of that!'

Even in her despondency she was stung by his tone. He was disparaging her as if she no longer counted just as other people were starting to respect her; Clara Tregevny, undisputed mistress of Abertawe House.

Violet didn't count. Even her own father dismissed her. Violet was nothing.

But Jack's indifference to her charms and his slighting attitude was the thin end of the wedge, an inner voice warned Clara. Was he planning to oust her? No, Samuel would never stand for a divorce in the family. Unheard of. The scandal would ruin the business. Jack couldn't divorce her, but he could diminish her in other ways; send her packing, perhaps. She had no allies in this house or anywhere else while the Tregevny family had money and could do anything.

Clara's brilliant and comfortable future was in deep jeopardy because of a pair of innocent green eyes. She'd be damned if she'd let that new girl ruin things for her. She wouldn't go back to the gutter. She wouldn't!

She summoned all her determination to defend herself.

'That redhead from the workroom is the only schemer around here, Jack,' she exclaimed hotly. 'We're already quarrelling over her – just what she wants.' She felt her jaw tighten in her growing fury. 'I'm going to see that Samuel gets rid of her. She's a trouble-maker.'

Jack looked at her for a moment and Clara was shocked by the open dislike in his eyes.

'Get rid of her then,' he said dismissively. 'Do as you like. She's just another bit of hot skirt. Means nothing to me.'

'I thought the closing of the copper works would've hit us harder, caused a slump in our trade,' Samuel said. 'But we've recovered from that over this last year. Praise be the Lord for His mercies.'

'It's the nickel works opening up that saved our bacon,' Richie said dryly, dabbing at his mouth with a napkin. 'I think there's worse to come, though, Father. Don't like these vague rumblings about a general strike. It's just rumour now, but it could happen, and strikes mean no money for little luxuries, like a new suit for Whitsun.' His voice took on a sarcastic tone. 'We could all end up in the poorhouse yet.'

Sitting at the breakfast table with the rest of the family, Clara knew his comment was directed at her and lifted her head haughtily, pretending to be unaffected by his sneering.

Damn him! She knew he believed she'd married Jack for money, and he'd never let her forget it. Well, what if she had? She was well entrenched in the Tregevny family now and she'd let nothing oust her, not while she had the power to fight back.

Except that, an inner voice reminded her, not being able to produce a child, an heir, could be her undoing. That problem was insurmountable, and Clara felt a sudden clutch of fear grip her.

The redhead in the workroom could probably shell out babies like peas, damn her to hell!

'There'll be no strike,' Samuel commented with unshakable confidence. 'Government won't allow it. They'll have the troops out.'

Waiting for the breakfast chatter to be over, Clara stirred anxiously, trying to force down her worries. Such discussions bored her, and today she was eager to get her father-in-law on his own.

She noticed Samuel darting glances down the table at his favourite son, unasked questions in his eyes, obviously puzzled by Jack's behaviour. She glanced at her husband impatiently.

Jack hadn't spoken one word to her this morning, and for once had nothing to contribute to the family discussion. He was usually free with his opinions, especially when they coincided with his father's.

He's mooning over that girl, she thought with a stab of anger, and felt an urge to shout at her husband.

Even in her anger, a yawn almost overtook her, but she managed to disguise it. She hadn't slept much last night, mostly because she'd slept alone, Jack taking the bed in the spare room next to theirs; something he'd never done before. But she'd also remained sleepless because she was thinking of ways she could discredit that damned girl . . .

As Doris, the daily maid, came in from the kitchen to clear the breakfast table, Richie rose and limped his way to the dining-room doors.

'I've got an early fitting,' he remarked to no one in particular. 'I want to be in the shop before half-eight this morning.'

Jack rose too, hurriedly. 'I'll walk with you, Richie.'

Normally, he put off making his way to the shop until the last minute, eager to read the sports pages of the papers first.

He was clearly avoiding her, and Clara ground her teeth as she watched him go. Can't wait to see that little slut again, she fumed inwardly. Well, he'd better make the most of it because she'd be gone soon enough.

Samuel put down his napkin and prepared to leave the table.

'Father,' Clara began resolutely, 'can I have a word with you before you leave?'

She followed him out, across the hall and into the front sitting-room.

Doris had arranged the daily newspapers on the table behind the door. Samuel selected the *Financial Times* and, perching a pair of steel-rimmed reading spectacles to the bridge of his nose, seated himself in a chair, his back to the windows.

Violet followed them in and took a seat opposite. Clara glanced impatiently at her sister-in-law, so quiet and unassuming.

Violet was also so frumpish, it was an embarrassment. Mouse-coloured hair caught up in an untidy bun on top of her head did nothing to dispel her drab appearance. And her dress! Where on earth did she get that? It looked as though it might have belonged to her mother, Clara thought with contempt. Violet was just asking to be trodden on.

Nevertheless, it wouldn't do for her sister-in-law to hear what Clara had to say to Samuel. It might be repeated to Jack.

'Violet, would you mind leaving us?' she said haughtily, lifting her chin and looking down her nose at her sister-in-law. 'I want to talk to Father. It's about the business and it *is* confidential.'

Violet rose awkwardly from her chair, twisting her hands nervously.

'Yes, of course, Clara. I . . . I'm sorry.'

When Violet was gone Clara stood in front of her father-in-law, trying not to feel intimidated. Over this last year he appeared to have accepted her, letting her live the life she'd always wanted, the life of a lady, really. Yet she rarely had dealings with Samuel personally, and wondered if he'd take any real notice of her when it concerned the business.

'Father, I want to talk to you about the new girl in the work-room.'

'Yes?' he replied vaguely, not lowering his paper.

Although there was no enthusiasm in his voice, at least he hadn't told her to mind her own business and Clara pressed on quickly, eager to gain an advantage.

'Jack tells me she's very lazy and slipshod in her work. He thinks she ought to be got rid of.'

Frowning, Samuel lowered the newspaper a few inches and peered at her over the top of his spectacles, his expression guarded.

'Why hasn't he spoken to me himself about it?'

'He intended to,' Clara said quickly, perching herself on the edge of a nearby chair. 'But you know how good-natured Jack is, Father. He doesn't want to get anyone into trouble.'

Samuel pursed his lips, nodding in agreement.

'Yes, Jack is a considerate son, but I have to disagree with him about one thing. Jenni Thomas is a good worker. I can't fault her.'

Jenni Thomas! So that was her name.

'But, Father . . .'

'It's nonsense.' Samuel crackled the newspaper impatiently. 'Jenni's meticulous with the tape measure, and the lady clients like her. I've even been complimented on her courtesy.'

'But, Father . . .' Clara repeated, thinking rapidly. 'Jack believes she may be light-fingered, too.'

She was treading on dangerous ground now, and knew it. Jack would never back her up. But once she'd planted the idea in Samuel's mind it might take root. His suspicious and parsimonious nature would take care of the rest.

'Jack's certain thread, other materials, and goodness knows what else have gone missing since she's been there. It's never happened before, Father, so it must be this Jenni Thomas.'

Newspaper pushed to one side, Samuel sat forward, his expression alert.

'Thieving? I won't have that!'

He paused a minute, still frowning furiously, obviously contemplating what she'd said and Clara's heart lightened. She'd be rid of Jenni Thomas yet!

'But it's not Jenni, I'm certain,' Samuel went on confidently, his frown clearing. 'I've suspected Renee of moonlighting for some time now. If there's thieving going on, it's most likely her. I'll warn Richie to keep watch.'

'There's no need for that, Father.'

Clara stood up, grinding her teeth in frustration. She didn't want Richie brought into this. He'd see through her game right away, and might even make trouble.

'I'm sure Jack can handle it,' she went on ingratiatingly, standing over Samuel again. 'And you should rely on him more instead of . . .'

Clara was tempted to say some disparaging words against Mr Napier but thought better of it for the time being. Getting shot of Jenni Thomas was the important issue now.

'Instead of wearing yourself out, Father,' she went on. 'We rely on you too much. Let Jack see to it.'

'Very well, Clara.' Samuel lifted the paper again, settling back in his chair. 'But mark my words, it's that Renee who's the thief,' he said firmly, then shook his head. 'I don't know why Jack's taken a dislike to Jenni. She's pretty and hard-working . . .'

'There's something else, Father,' Clara interrupted hastily, realising she'd have to go much further into the realms of invention than she'd planned.

Old Samuel was no fool, and although it was becoming even more dangerous, she couldn't and wouldn't stop now. She'd go to any lengths to get her husband out of the clutches of that girl.

She sat down again, clasping her hands in front of her and lowering her head in pretence of embarrassment.

'I was hoping I wouldn't have to tell you this about Jenni

Thomas,' she went on, 'because it's rather unwholesome and you'll be disgusted, I know. It's also humiliating for Jack. I think it's why he hasn't spoken to you about his suspicions.'

She looked up. Her father-in-law was sitting forward again and Clara saw she had his full attention. She ran her tongue over her lips, weighing each word as she spoke it.

'Jack's very upset, Father. This Jenni Thomas has been throwing herself at him quite brazenly. Blatantly ogling and making up to him in the most outrageous and loose manner! It's quite obvious to him that . . .'

Clara turned her head away in a show of embarrassment again.

'Well, she's trying to . . . seduce him, perhaps even get money out of him.'

Samuel removed his spectacles and brushed a wayward forelock of greying hair from his eyes. 'I see.'

'She's hardly the sort of girl to be employed by the Tregevnys,' Clara rushed on. 'Jack thinks the sooner she's sacked, the better.' She tilted her head. 'We can't have an employee of that low character in the shop. She's likely to cause a scandal. Don't you agree, Father?'

Looking surprisingly calm, Samuel put his spectacles on the table beside the chair and folded the newspaper. Clara watched him, but not hopefully. She'd expected outrage yet he was acting as though the prospect of a scandal at the shop held no terrors for him.

Things weren't going the way she'd planned at all.

Samuel stood up and looked at his pocket watch, then glanced at her, his face expressionless. Clara rose too, twisting her fingers anxiously.

'It seems I have more faith in your husband than you do, Clara,' he said. 'Jack *was* prone to sowing wild oats when he came back from the war. I didn't approve but I understood – and made him put things right.'

He paused and for a moment there was such a look of

contempt in his eyes as he gazed at her that she quailed and turned her own glance away.

She knew he'd never forget, let alone forgive, the fact that he'd had to force Jack into the marriage to save the family's face. After all, Clara had counted on Samuel's terror of disgrace at the time. Now it was working against her.

He had never openly referred to the matter in her hearing previously. She realised suddenly how tenuous her position might still be. Perhaps only her father-in-law's dread of scandal stood between her and the end of all she'd schemed for.

'Jack's a changed man now,' he went on as he strode towards the sitting-room doors. 'Married, respectable and responsible. He wouldn't be the major beneficiary in my will if he weren't.'

Heartened though she was by this confirmation of her hope that Jack would get the lion's share, Clara shivered at these words. Was that some kind of veiled warning or threat?

'Young Jenni can flirt all she wants,' Samuel continued wryly. 'She'll get nowhere with our Jack, not if he knows what's good for him. You just remind him of that.'

'But, Father . . .'

'You worry too much, Clara.'

Alone in the sitting-room, she sank on to the nearest chair, her heart filled with fear and despair. She could lose everything worthwhile: money, husband, her newfound social position, and she felt sore and wretched at the thought. It was too much to bear.

Clara gritted her teeth and clenched her fists tightly, feeling her nails dig into her palms. That was nothing to the pain of the humiliation that could be facing her if Jack deserted her and she resolved she'd use any means to save herself, any means at all, no matter how low-down and dirty.

Samuel was sure Jack would behave himself rather than risk losing his legacy, but she knew her husband too well. The seduction of Jack Tregevny had been easy for Clara three years ago, and he hadn't changed one iota since. She had to get rid of Jenni Thomas, for both their sakes.

She thought back over her exchange with Samuel. He was incensed by the thought that Renee was moonlighting. Seemed more concerned with that than anything else.

Thoughtfully, Clara ran shaky fingers through her thick blonde hair. Suppose she could get evidence that Jenni was moonlighting? She probably was anyway, but even if she wasn't, evidence could be manufactured against her . . .

Clara rose from the chair, smoothing down the skirt of her dress. She wasn't finished yet. She'd watch Jenni Thomas carefully; learn all she could about her, then catch her unawares. Everyone had something to hide. Jenni Thomas was no different.

Clara remembered again the hidden steel in the other girl's gaze. Yes, there was more to that conniving little redheaded bitch than met the eye — and Clara was determined to find out exactly what it was.

Chapter Sixteen

In the downstairs ladies' fitting-room behind the shop, Jenni helped Mrs Saunders-Jones into her fur coat and handed her her gloves and handbag from the table.

'Excellent, Jenni, my dear,' Mrs Saunders-Jones said. 'Tell Mr Samuel I'm very pleased.'

Jenni bent one knee slightly, feeling a curtsey was looked for by one of the shop's more prominent clients. Mr Samuel had warned her that the lady in question was to be given every courtesy, since it was rumoured Mr Saunders-Jones would be mayor next year.

'And this is for you,' Mrs Saunders-Jones went on magnanimously, pressing a two-shilling piece into Jenni's hand.

Embarrassed, she felt the heat rise in her face. It was gratifying, of course, but was she allowed to take tips? she wondered. Yet she couldn't insult the lady by refusing.

'Thank you, ma'am,' she said.

Mrs Saunders-Jones pulled on her gloves.

'I'll be back for a final fitting a week Wednesday,' she said. 'I want you to attend me, Jenni. I shall remind Mr Samuel myself.'

Jenni nodded, looking at the client's straight back and elevated chin. It must be wonderful to have so much confidence and to be looked up to, she thought wistfully. Would Mrs

Saunders-Jones be so generous if she knew who Jenni really was? She hurriedly pushed that uncomfortable thought aside. She was safe now, and she must remember that.

Jenni opened the fitting-room door, kept locked whilst a lady customer was in a state of undress, and ushered her client out.

Mrs Saunders-Jones swept out like a schooner in full sail while Jenni attended to the garment that was being expertly constructed for her. It was beautifully cut and stitched, and she knew it was the work of Mr Richie.

She didn't like him much. Compared to Jack he seemed dour and distant, but he was a master craftsman, without doubt, and she had to admire that.

She was just gathering up the garment to take it upstairs when Jack came into the fitting-room, closing the door behind him. He turned the key in the lock and leaned against the door, gazing at her.

Jenni felt the breath catch in her throat at the intensity of his gaze and the glint in his eye, and something in her body stirred powerfully in response. But she fought it down. He was a married man, she had no right to feel like this. And he had no right to tempt her.

'Jack, why have you locked the door?' She gazed at him in trepidation, afraid suddenly, not of him but of herself and the powerful feelings that were rising in her like a high tide in a storm.

He moved away from the door, taking a step nearer, but halted just out of arm's reach. Still Jenni trembled at his closeness. She could remember the touch of his lips on hers and ached for it again, although she knew it was wrong, sinful, to feel the way she did.

Was he trying to deceive her; playing the philanderer as Renee suggested? She should be angry with him for it, yet her heart said there was an explanation and she shouldn't condemn him unheard.

'Jenni, I've got to talk to you,' he said thickly. 'You've hardly glanced at me or spoken two words to me all morning. Why? What's wrong?'

Why was he pretending still? Suddenly overcome with emotion, Jenni bit her lip and turned away from him, fussing with the garment on the table to hide her distress. Her hands were trembling uncontrollably, and she didn't want him to see. She'd resisted talking to him more to save him embarrassment than in anger, but also, she had to admit, to avoid these feelings she couldn't control.

'I don't know what you mean, Jack,' she said with difficulty, swallowing hard against the lump rising in her throat. There must be no tears, she warned herself.

'Yes, you do.'

Jenni was momentarily without words to convey her feelings. It would be impossible to tell him how she felt, anyway. The pain in her heart was too powerful to express, her need too great, and she was ashamed of her own weakness. Yet there was resentment, too, she had to admit. How could he continue to dissemble? Did he think her an empty-headed little fool?

She was hurt, her heart still yearning for his touch. It was wicked of her to have such feelings but how could she help it when rendered helpless by their intensity?

Why had he been so friendly and loving towards her, kissing her the way he had and asking her out? Acting as though he had the right to do so.

She *should* be angry with him for deceiving her, but there was no anger in her heart, only love and yearning, and she wondered at herself. Was she weak like her mother where love was concerned? Had she no pride?

'Jenni, when we kissed the other day,' he said softly, 'I thought you had feelings for me.'

'Oh, Jack, I do!'

The words burst out of her. Dismayed at her own unguarded response, she turned and stared at him aghast. What was she thinking of? She was talking like some loose woman, defying the accepted rules of decency, while he was still trying to deceive her, acting as though nothing stood between them. How could she go on bearing it?

'I knew it!' He sounded triumphant. 'Oh, Jenni, darling . . .'

He came to her, grasping her upper arms to draw her near, but she shrugged his hands away.

'No, don't! We mustn't, Jack.' She stared up into his feverish gaze. 'It wouldn't be fair to your wife.'

He stepped back, obviously disconcerted. 'Jenni, I can explain . . .'

Explain away a wife! She stared at him, disappointed that he looked so crestfallen and guilty. She'd been hoping that, by some miracle, it wasn't true. How naive of her. Consternation that he'd been found out was written all over his face.

He stammered, 'How did you . . . ?'

'Find out? She called here yesterday,' Jenni went on miserably, unasked questions throbbing in her brain. 'Renee told me who she was.' Suddenly she was angry with him for fooling her. 'Did you really think I wouldn't find out? Am I so stupid?'

'Jenni, listen . . .' He tried to take her arm but she pushed his hand away.

'How could you kiss me, Jack?' she cried. 'Leading me on, knowing you're not free?'

'But I am free – in my heart.' He tried to embrace her again but Jenni stepped back quickly. He looked at her, a hurt expression on his handsome face.

'Jenni, darling, I can explain everything if you'll only let me! Please?'

He reached out to her. Anticipating the move, Jenni stepped to the other side of the table. How long would he have kept the truth from her? she wondered despairingly.

He stared across the distance between them with such anguish in his eyes that her heart melted. She was being harsh and unfair without hearing him out.

'It's true I have a wife,' Jack said quietly. 'But it's hardly a marriage, Jenni. There's no love lost between Clara and me.'

He glanced towards the locked door.

'We can't talk in here. Someone might disturb us. Will you meet me tonight? I'll tell you everything then.'

She took a deep breath, resolved that she'd let it go no further.

'No, Jack. I won't meet you.'

It hurt to deny him because she wanted to be with him so much. But neither could she betray herself and her own beliefs. He was married and it would be wrong, sinful, to let their relationship develop when there was no hope for them. And there was Jenni's reputation to think of, too. She had to be careful. There must be no talk or scandal. That would finish her.

'While the door is locked no one will try to come in,' she assured him. 'Tell me now, Jack, or let me leave, and we'll never speak of this matter again.'

'All right, Jenni.'

He paused for a moment, as if thinking deeply, then ran his fingers through his hair in an agitated manner.

'Clara used to be a skirt-hand here.' He sat on the very edge of the table, long legs stretched out before him, looking at her solemnly. 'I was just back from the hell of the trenches, hardly able to believe I was still alive, much less unhurt. It you'd seen some of the terrible . . .'

He paused, biting his lip and bowing his head as though in torment. Unable to stop herself, Jenni went to him, putting a hand against his cheek.

'Don't think of those things now, Jack,' she said softly. 'That's all in the past.'

Smiling, he put both his hands on her waist, drawing her nearer.

'You're so tender and loving, Jenni. That's what I adore about you. I'd be so happy with you. If only I'd waited . . .'

Trembling at his words and his touch, she gazed at him, love swelling her heart. He was so handsome, yet inside she felt he was still suffering from those horrendous experiences. He needed love and affection from a wife who'd devote herself to him, and she longed to be that wife.

'I was a fool, Jenni, I admit it,' he went on raggedly. 'Clara was pretty and responsive . . .'

'Like I am?' Jenni said quickly, suddenly hurt again. Did he see her as easy and available, too?

He shook his head.

'No, not like you.' His eyes searched her face. 'There's an innocence about you, Jenni, darling, and a deep warmth.'

One arm encircled her waist. Jenni's heart was beating like a drum. Married or not, she loved him deeply and there was no denying it, to herself or to him. She was as shameless as her mother, but at that moment she didn't care.

'Clara was . . . well, frankly, brazen. She led me on,' he said, his tone harsh. 'And I was foolish. Without saying a word to me, she approached my father directly and told him she was expecting my baby.'

'A baby?' Shocked, Jenni pulled herself from his embrace. She'd had no idea Jack had a child. It made all the difference in the world.

'My father rushed me into marriage for fear of a scandal. The business mustn't suffer no matter how miserable the family is,' Jack said with deep bitterness. 'Clara never loved me. She just wanted money.'

'The child?' Jenni whispered, feeling despair return to her heart.

'There is no child and never was,' he said, lips twisting in anger. 'It was all a trick! As soon as we were married Clara declared she'd had a miscarriage. No one in the family questioned it.' His voice was bitter. 'A delicate subject, not to be talked of or referred to — that's my father's way!'

He hung his head for a moment.

'So what could I do? Clara got away with it.'

Jack stood up quickly and took Jenni in his arms again.

'Listen to me,' he said urgently. 'I stopped caring what happened in my life until you came. I want you, Jenni, desperately. Please believe me, darling.'

'What are you asking me, Jack?' she said in distress. 'How can we ever be together? I have feelings for you, deep feelings, but I also have my self-respect. I can't do anything I feel is wrong.'

A strange expression passed across his face then, so fleeting she had no time to read or understand it. Was it impatience? Anger? She could understand his being angry with Clara for thwarting his plans.

'I wouldn't ask you to do anything wrong, Jenni,' he said softly. 'I want to marry you.'

She was flabbergasted. There it was at last: a sign that the gypsy's prophecy would come true. She *would* be Jack's wife some day.

'Oh, Jack!' She felt heady with happiness.

'I don't care what my father says or does,' he went on boldly. 'He can cut me out of his will if he likes, but I'm going to divorce Clara.'

'Divorce!'

Jenni shrank back a little, deeply shocked.

Divorce! It was a word decent people only whispered, and she was dismayed to hear Jack use it so openly, as though it held little importance. To her the very idea was disgraceful.

But how else could you ever be Jack's wife? the voice of commonsense put in. Wait until Jack becomes a widower? By then she'd be old, dried up, perhaps dead herself. She was young. Must she go through life waiting for love? No, she couldn't. She had to face facts, no matter how unsavoury.

He didn't seem to notice her distress at the notion, however.

'So you see, Jenni, darling,' he went on enthusiastically, gathering her into his arms again, 'there's nothing wrong in loving each other now because we'll be man and wife one day.'

'But what about Clara?'

Jenni was suddenly struck by conscience. Could she really steal another woman's husband? That was wicked, too. But was it more wicked, the inner voice asked her again, than Clara tricking Jack into marriage when he deserved better?

'To hell with her!' Jack exclaimed loudly. 'She's had all she's going to get out of me.'

He held Jenni close against him, his lips touching her cheek, and she was overcome by a feeling so powerful, she wanted to throw caution to the winds and fling her arms around his neck. Yet still she held back.

Mother must have acted like this, she thought, in rising panic. She'd felt these potent sensations, too, and because she'd given in to them, tragedy had overtaken them all.

'Listen, Jenni, darling. I'm going ahead with the divorce. It'll take time, of course.' Jack's lips brushed her cheek, sending tendrils of fire through her. 'But we can't waste our lives waiting. We must be together now, enjoy our love. You can trust me, Jenni.'

'Oh, Jack!' She hid her face against his shirt. 'I'm so ashamed and afraid, too. I want to be with you, yet I know it's wrong while you're still married to Clara.'

He gently lifted her face to his. His lips were warm and firm and tender, and a new fire flared in the depths of her being. It burned so fiercely that she wanted to cry out at the exquisite pain, and only the pressure of Jack's lips prevented it.

'Never be ashamed of love,' he whispered when he released her. 'And never be afraid. If you really love me, Jenni, you won't deny me.'

'I do love you! I do!'

'Then meet me tonight. I'll borrow my father's car. We can go for a run. We'll really be alone. And then I'll show you just how much I want you.'

He looked down at her upturned face. A vein was throbbing in his throat and his eyes were alive with an emotion that made her quiver with anticipation.

'You're so young and innocent, so . . . untouched,' he said thickly. 'There are things, Jenni, things a man and a woman do when they make love that you couldn't imagine. But I'll teach you everything.'

She stared up at him, mesmerised by the feverish glow in his eyes, and felt breathless and light-headed from the rivers of fire that were flowing through her body.

Yet amid the tumultuous madness there was a tiny glimmer of caution, and with it she found the strength to release herself from his embrace.

'Jack, please listen.'

With all her heart she wanted to give in, yet what he asked of her was an irrevocable step. She trusted him without reservation and one day she *would* be his wife, as the gypsy had foretold. But could she betray all she'd ever believed in by giving herself to him now, unconditionally? Not that she wanted anything from him except his love.

'I can't.' She turned her head away, hating to deny him.

'Jenni!' He sounded almost angry. 'I've given you my word we'll be married. What more do you want?'

She felt a flash of resentment. Why wouldn't he understand? She'd been only too willing to understand *his* predicament.

'I'll tell you what I *don't* want, Jack,' she said crisply. 'I don't want to feel ashamed. I'm not like Clara. I'm not brazen.'

'Darling.' His tone was conciliatory as he took both her hands in his. 'I mean no harm. It's just that I want you so badly, it's driving me crazy.'

Jenni pressed her lips together in an effort not to cry. She understood exactly what he meant. Wasn't she suffering, too?

'Do you think *I* don't feel the same way, Jack? I love you and I want your lovemaking, but . . .'

'Jenni! Don't treat me like this!'

'I'm sorry, Jack.' She shook her head miserably. 'I need time to think about it. I don't want some hole-in-the corner love affair.' It wasn't only a matter of pride, it was a question of decency, too. 'We both deserve better than that, don't we? Please be patient with me.'

He turned away with a heavy sigh.

'I suppose I must,' he said in a defeated tone.

She felt suddenly that she'd opened up a gulf between them and was tempted to put her arms around him, to comfort him, draw him back to her, but decided that would be more cruel than comforting.

'Jack, should I give up my job at Tregevny's?' she asked hesitantly.

He turned to look at her in astonishment.

'Good God, no!'

She twisted her hands together. The last thing she wanted to do was give up this job. She was so happy here despite their present difficult situation.

'But if my being here makes you unhappy, Jack, I'll willingly go.'

He shook his head, smiling.

'No, Jenni, my darling, I couldn't bear to be without you. All you have to do is have faith in me,' he said gently. 'I promise you won't regret it.' He drew her close. 'I know you're ready to be mine. Trust me.'

In his arms she longed to give in to his kiss, but in her mind was a shadow: the shadow of the gallows. Her mother had given in unconditionally to her desires, and they had destroyed her.

Aroused though she was, Jenni felt fearful. She was playing with fire, an all-consuming fire, and would the flames of her hunger for Jack, which seared her now, bring about her destruction, too? Was she destined for the same terrible fate as her mother?

Chapter Seventeen

Jenni was thankful it was Thursday half-day. She was still reeling from her encounter with Jack in the fitting-room, and knew it would have been impossible for her to sit in the workroom with him all afternoon without giving the game away. Richie was always watchful and Renee's eyes so sharp.

She'd managed to persuade Jack to wait until Monday for her decision, but was in a quandary, and wanted very much to be on her own to think things through.

What meant more to her: the moral code by which she'd lived her life so far, or Jack and the unknown wonders and delights of his lovemaking? Love was an uncharted ocean to Jenni yet she longed to venture forth.

'Let's go into town this afternoon,' Renee suggested as they finished washing up the dishes after dinner. 'We'll stroll around Ben Evans' and look at the hats.'

'Ben Evans' is too posh for us,' Jenni said dismally, wishing she could just disappear into her room upstairs. 'Never afford a pair of stockings there, we couldn't, let alone a hat.'

'That's the fun of it,' Renee insisted enthusiastically. 'We can swank about the place like a pair of Lady Mucks, and make faces at the shop assistants. Stuck up lot!'

'I'd rather not, Renee.'

Jenni had too much on her mind for fun. At the moment she felt this dark cloud would never lift from her.

Renee put an arm around her shoulders.

'What's the matter, Jen, kid? You seem awfully down today.'

She turned her face away, knowing her eyes must be shiny with unshed tears. If only she could confide in her friend, but she was too ashamed. If Renee and Meg knew she was contemplating giving herself freely to a married man, and her employer at that, they'd be scandalised; so shocked they'd probably ask her to leave their respectable home. And who could blame them? She was shocked at the idea herself. If she were a decent girl, she'd turn Jack down flat.

Oh, but she loved him so!

Thoughts of him filled her mind day and night. Deep in her heart she wanted what he wanted – but not this way, the voice of pride said. Did love really demand that she cheapen herself?

When Jenni didn't speak, Renee sighed in resignation.

'Oh, all right, then, kid.'

She threw the tea-towel in a damp heap on to the draining board, and walked into the living-room. Jenni followed, dragging her feet.

Renee pulled a chair out from under the table.

'Got sewing to do anyway, I have,' she said dejectedly. 'Better get on with it, I suppose.'

'Well, I should hope so!' Meg commented from her chair near the range. 'Betty Roberts will have to go to her daughter's wedding in her birthday suit if you don't finish her two-piece by a week Monday.'

Renee chuckled.

'Now that I'd like to see,' she said. 'She's built like an elephant.'

Meg and Renee started a fit of giggles at the idea, Meg's chins quivering with enjoyment. They were always sharing a joke and laughing a lot, these two, and usually Jenni joined in, feeling very much one of the family. Today, though, nothing seemed to lift her spirits.

If she didn't agree to Jack's request she could lose him altogether, and she couldn't bear that. She'd found the only man she'd ever love, and was letting her scruples come between them. Was she being a fool to herself? There was so much she didn't know about love, but she felt its longings deeply. After all, feelings were her only guide.

Wasn't happiness all that mattered in the long run? Heaven knew she'd had little of that in recent years, and she could all too easily end up like Blodwen, dried up and lonely. It didn't bear thinking about.

Renee got out her sewing machine and fetched the pieces of material, already half constructed into a garment.

'Perhaps I should put a V in the skirt,' she suggested with a mischievous grin at her mother. 'In case Mrs Roberts' bum grows any bigger.'

'Don't make fun, mun,' Meg said, trying to stifle another laugh. 'You wait until you're her age and have had ten kids. You'll be laughing on the other side of your face then, my girl.'

Renee stuck out her lower lip.

'Some hopes I have!' she said. 'Can't get a bloke to tell me the time, let alone give me ten kids.'

'You're a baby yet yourself, our Renee,' Meg said affectionately. 'Plenty of time to find a chap.'

'Give us a hand with this tacking, then, Jen,' Renee suggested quickly, just as Jenni was about to glide out of the room, hopefully forgotten.

With a sigh she settled down to help her friend, but her mind was too preoccupied for her to work very fast.

It was just on half-past two when she heard the sound of a woman's footsteps marching down the passage from the ever-open front door.

Meg was dozing in the warmth of the range and didn't hear,

but Renee and Jenni glanced at each other, startled. There'd been no greeting called first, as neighbours usually did, and suddenly Jenni had a premonition of disaster.

She rose hurriedly to her feet as Clara Tregevny appeared in the living-room doorway.

Jack's wife? Jenni felt her heart contract. What was she doing here in Meg's home?

'What the hell do you want?' exclaimed Renee, jumping up and staring ferociously at their unwelcome visitor.

Clara lifted an accusing finger and pointed at Jenni.

'Catching *her* in the act!' Her eyes gleamed triumphantly. 'And it looks like I'm just in time.'

Renee hurriedly turned her back to the table in an attempt to block Clara's view, but the old sewing machine and the scattered garment sections couldn't be hidden from her gaze.

'Oh, it's no good hiding it,' Clara said nastily. 'I've got the goods on her now.'

There was such malice in her eyes that Jenni felt a shiver go through her, but she straightened her back, determined to bluff it out.

'Touched in the head, you are,' she said loudly, struggling to remain calm. 'Push off before you make a real fool of yourself!'

'You're moonlighting, you little thief,' Clara said, her voice high with jubilation. 'Don't deny it!'

She wore the same little black hat with the puff of veiling and lavender coloured two-piece in fine wool. The suit had all the hallmarks of Richie Tregevny's expert craftsmanship.

'Here, just a minute!' Renee burst out angrily, stepping forward. 'You can't waltz into my home like this and accuse us without so much as a by-your-leave, Missus. We could have you for trespassing.'

Clara's lip curled.

'Samuel Tregevny's your landlord, remember,' she said arrogantly. 'I've got every right. I'm his daughter-in-law.'

'Hey! What?' Meg was roused from her dozing and stared round-eyed and uncomprehending at the three of them. 'What's all the shouting about?'

'It's her, Mam,' Renee said angrily, stabbing a finger at Clara. 'She just marched in by here without even knocking, accusing us of moonlighting. Tell her to get out, Mam. You pays your rent on time – you've got rights.'

Still half asleep, Meg blinked at the newcomer.

'Clear off, you!'

Clara ignored her and stepped further into the room.

'Knew you'd slip up soon, I did,' she said to Jenni with triumph. 'Your sort always does.'

Jenni bridled.

'What do you mean, *my* sort?'

'Oh, now come on, don't pretend with me,' Clara said with a sneer. 'As soon as I set eyes on you, I knew you were a trouble-maker. But I've seen the likes of you come and go. Jack's no angel but he's no pushover either. I see to that.'

Jenni could feel Renee's puzzled gaze on her. Would her friend believe the terrible things Clara was saying? Renee already knew Jenni loved Jack, but Clara was making it sound dirty and sordid, and Jenni couldn't bear the thought of her friend's condemnation.

'What's she on about, Jen?'

Jenni swallowed hard.

'I don't know.'

Clara gave a mocking snigger.

'Oh, mind now, little goody two-shoes!' She lifted her chin disdainfully. 'But I've caught you out good and proper, haven't I?' She pointed to the sewing. 'I don't have to wait for Samuel's verdict on this. I can tell you now, Jenni Thomas, you're sacked on the spot.'

Renee gasped. 'Hey! You can't do that.'

Clara cocked her head on one side, eyes gleaming with spite.

'Oh, can't I? I'm looking after Samuel Tregevny's interests, so I can do anything I like.'

Jenni realised from Renee's expression she was about to confess to the illicit garment-making. But Renee couldn't afford to lose her job, and Jenni was determined to save it for her if she could.

'You're not my employer,' she exploded. 'I don't take orders from you, you spiteful busybody!'

Clara's eyes narrowed and her expression became malevolent, her tone a deep hiss.

'I'll make you sorry you ever set foot in the Hafod, see if I don't!'

Clara's arrogance got Jenni's dander up. She didn't have to take threats like that from anyone.

'Mr Samuel is the only one who can sack me,' she said belligerently. 'I deal with the engine driver, not his oily rag. So push off, before I forget I'm a lady and land you a fourpenny one!'

'Ooh!' Clara's mouth dropped open in utter astonishment and her face turned dark red as Renee burst out laughing.

'Oh, that's a good one, kid,' she hooted. 'She's oily all right! Smarmy, stuck-up cat! Go on! Sling your hook, you!'

Clara collected herself, lips thinning in fury.

'You're still sacked,' she declared truculently. 'Because moonlighting is moonlighting and the old . . . my father-in-law won't stand for it. It's thieving, that's what it is. I've already warned him about your sticky-fingered ways.'

Jenni grew hot with anger.

'How dare you slander me?'

Wronged wife or not, this was going too far.

'Jack's right about you,' Jenni went on loudly. 'No wonder he's so miserable . . . you . . . you lying harpy!'

'And you're a conniving bitch!' Clara screamed, obviously beside herself. 'Putting yourself about like the town tart. But you won't get a penny out of Jack.'

Jenni's blood began to boil with outrage. How could she explain away these mischievous insinuations to Meg and Renee? They'd welcomed and accepted her as part of their family, and now, because of her love for Jack, she was rewarding their kindness with scandal and financial ruin.

'I'll have my solicitor on you for slander,' she warned, almost spluttering with rage. She threw back her shoulders defiantly. 'So be careful what you say.'

'Her solicitor? Hark at her!' Clara laughed mirthlessly. 'You've got some big ideas, you have. Who d'you think you are?'

Jenni looked her up and down, letting contempt show plainly in her expression. There was a touch of the guttersnipe in Clara, for all her fancy clothes.

'Well, I'm not tripe dressed up as veal anyway,' she said cuttingly, tossing her head. 'Still got my self-respect, I have. Can you say the same after the way you tricked Jack?'

Clara's lips drew back in a snarl.

'You'll keep your trap shut if you know what's good for you, you dirty little trollop!' she shrieked belligerently, and Jenni was glad to see her opponent was shaking visibly.

'Oh! Hit the nail on the head, haven't I?' she went on triumphantly.

'Shut up!' Clara looked ready to foam at the mouth. 'I know what your filthy game is . . . trying to get your claws into Jack. But you won't get him, and you won't get a penny out of him, either.'

She raised an arm threateningly.

'I'll see you dead first!'

The hatred in Clara's eyes blazed like a fire out of control. Speechless for a moment, Jenni could only gasp at the intensity of it. She'd made a dangerous enemy here. But backing down, conceding defeat, would be the wrong move.

'I'm not after his money,' Jenni denied angrily. 'But he's told me what a grasping little gold-digger *you* are.'

'Hear, hear!' yelled Renee in delight. She stuck out her tongue at Clara, grimacing like a gargoyle.

Clara's answering glare was venomous.

'You'll both pay for this, I promise you.'

Jenni realised she wasn't doing her friend any good by trading insults with Clara, and had no illusions about whom Samuel would believe. There was no doubt she and Renee were facing instant dismissal. Yet she was so enraged she just had to hit back while the anger was surging in her breast. She wished she could teach Clara Tregevny a good lesson for all the trouble and anguish she was causing.

'Don't you threaten me,' Jenni flared, giving her anger free reign. The damage was already done after all. 'You might get more than you bargained for. I know plenty about *you*.'

Clara still looked nasty, though her face whitened.

'What d'you mean by that? What are you hinting at?'

'That's for me to know and you to find out,' Jenni said obscurely. 'For a start it's obvious you're no lady, despite your ten-guinea suit. Fine feathers . . . but I can see underneath your disguise, don't you worry.'

She had no idea what she was talking about really, but the sudden glint of apprehension she saw in Clara's eyes told her she'd hit a nerve.

'You're talking rubbish,' Clara declared, regaining her composure quickly. 'Trying to wriggle out of trouble. But you can't. You've broken the rules of your employment with Tregevny's,' she went on triumphantly. 'Taking in sewing work is strictly forbidden, on-the-spot sacking, so don't bother to come into work again because I'm telling you – you're done for.'

'Now, look here, Missus,' Renee interrupted. 'You're barking up the wrong tree, see. It's me that's been doing the moonlighting, not Jenni. If anybody should get the sack, it's me.'

'Renee!' Jenni exclaimed in dismay.

'Covering up for her won't work,' snapped Clara, her face

hardening. 'You're lucky I'm not giving you the sack as well. She's finished at Tregevny's. And she can stay well away from my husband from now on.'

Renee planted her fists on her hips and stuck out her chin.

'I don't know what you're blathering on about Mr Jack for, Missus,' she said. 'But we'll see what Mr Samuel has to say on this tomorrow. I'm owning up to the moonlighting, see, so you can keep you nose out of it and push off from by here right now.'

She stepped forward aggressively.

'If you don't, it'll give me great pleasure to kick your backside down the passage and out on the pavement. Right?'

With a look that could have scoured the brass finish off the fender, Clara turned and stalked out. They heard her heels stamp heavily on the passage linoleum and out on to the paving stones outside.

Jenni stood still for a moment, shaking after the encounter. She was in no doubt now that Jack needed to be rescued from the clutches of this awful woman, and she decided there and then not to feel guilty any longer at depriving Clara of her husband.

He really needed her, Jenni decided, and how could she deny him some comfort in his life after all he'd been through in the war? It was ironic, though, she mused, that his wife of all people had helped make up her mind. She and Jack belonged together, so why hesitate any longer?

'Well!' Meg said with a loud exhalation of breath. 'What a spiteful cat! Who is she when she's at home, anyway?'

'Old Samuel's daughter-in-law,' Renee said, looking glum. 'Well, Mam, that's that! I've lost my job.'

She flopped on to a chair, looking really dejected and on the point of shedding tears, and Jenni's heart went out to her.

'What beats me is why she came here out of the blue today,' her friend went on gloomily. 'It was like she was out for revenge. What've we ever done to her?'

Jenni remained silent, feeling dreadful. She'd brought disaster on her two best friends, her only friends. She and Jack had ruined their lives. How on earth could she put things right?

'You should've let me take the blame, Renee,' she said sadly. 'You can't afford to be out of work. Oh, Renee, Meg, I am sorry! It's all my doing.'

Renee looked at her with surprise.

'What have *you* got to be sorry about? It wasn't your fault, Jen, kid. The woman's off her rocker, I think, going on about Mr Jack and all. It must be 'cos he took us to the pictures that time. The jealous cat!'

Jenni bit her lip. Now would be the time to confess her intentions regarding him, but she couldn't bring herself to speak the words. She didn't want to leave Meg's cosy home in Hafod Row, her haven, and she'd have to go if they knew she planned to give herself to Jack; be his mistress. For all Renee's racy talk, she and Meg were respectable people with standards, they wouldn't understand her decision. Neither would they under-stand the depth of her feelings; what she was willing to sacrifice for him.

And having seen Clara's jealous reaction, she'd have to keep her intentions secret for the time being.

'When we go to work tomorrow,' Jenni said, 'let me do the talking. It doesn't matter if they sack me. I'll get a job somewhere else.'

Renee shook her head emphatically.

'You don't know Samuel Tregevny. He'd blacken your name throughout Swansea. You wouldn't get another job, not in the tailoring trade anyway.'

Jenni felt desperate.

'Then I'll work at something else. There're plenty of cafés in town. I can get a job as a waitress.'

'With your qualifications? Don't be daft,' Renee exclaimed. 'What a crying waste that would be. No, Jen, kid, I'm the one who must pay the price.'

Jenni thought again about the money in her Post Office savings account. She'd have to help the Morrises out with that. She could pay the rent at least, so that they'd keep a roof over their heads, but would they be too proud to take it?

'I know that face,' Meg said suddenly. 'I've seen her before somewhere, a long time ago, when I was a girl.'

'Don't be daft, Mam,' Renee said wearily. 'Clara's younger than I am. And you haven't been out and about for years, have you? Anyway, you're hardly likely to see the likes of Clara Tregevny down the local Co-op or up the chip shop, either.'

'Clara?' Meg put chubby fingers thoughtfully to her mouth. 'Now that rings a bell . . .'

Renee smiled fondly at her mother.

'Mam, I don't know what you've got into your noddle but you can't possibly know Clara Tregevny. I mean, once seen never forgotten, eh?'

'Exactly!' Meg said. 'But it's not her, mun. It's her mother. Underneath all that finery she's the image of her mother as she was years ago. I recognise her, all right. Air and graces can't hide the likeness.'

'You're really stretching it now, Mam,' said Renee in exasperation. 'Mr Jack told me not long after they were married that his wife's people live in Carmarthen. They've passed away now.'

'Carmarthen?' Meg's smile was wide. 'No, I don't think so, Renee, love.'

She leaned back in her chair, plump hands resting on the wooden chair arms, eyes gazing into the hot coals in the range.

'As soon as I saw Clara Tregevny standing by here just now, carrying on like a fishwife, I thought of Kitty Price . . . someone from my girlhood in the Cwm,' she said thoughtfully, then shook her head. 'I tell you, I'm right. If Clara isn't Kitty Price's daughter, I'll eat our cat's dinner.'

'It's impossible, Mam.'

'Who was Kitty Price?' Jenni asked curiously.

Meg looked up, eyes refocusing from memories of the past.

'The Prices lived a few doors up from us in the Cwm. Big family they were – seven boys and this one girl, Kitty, a year or two younger than me. Fifteen she was when she started. Any man's for thruppence.'

Rence gasped and so did Jenni.

'On the streets, you mean?' asked Renee, eyes like saucers.

'Incorrigible!' Meg nodded. 'A disgrace to the Cwm. Poor all us girls were, but respectable and decent with it. Bold as brass, Kitty was, and twice as cheap.'

She paused for breath.

'Mind you, I was sorry for old Mrs Price. She'd worked hard all her life, then to end up with a daughter like that . . . It finished her, I'm sure. She couldn't stand the shame of it.'

'But, Mam, what's this got to do with Clara Tregevny?' Renee insisted impatiently.

'Well, give me a chance and I'll tell you,' Meg retorted, then went on. 'There Kitty would be, flaunting herself outside pubs at closing time. Us girls kept well away from her, I can tell you. How any man could fancy her, though, beats me.'

'Was she ugly?'

Meg shook her head.

'No. She was striking to look at, like this Clara, but dirty with it. I don't think she ever washed.'

'Mam, you're exaggerating! Making it up,' Renee said with a knowing smile. 'You're having us on, but we're not falling for it.'

'No, I'm not having you on, mun.' Meg sat forward quickly. 'You ask Mr Napier if you don't believe your old mam. He remembers Dirty Kitty, all right. I bet he's twigged it, just like I have.'

Jenni and Renee glanced at one another, startled. Then Renee jumped up impatiently.

'Mam! I've lost my job and you're prattling on about the old days. This doesn't help at all.'

Meg leaned back in her chair again, resting her arms across her ample middle.

'Renee,' she said severely, 'you can be so dim at times. My old legs might be gone, but there's nothing wrong with my memory or my brain. I can still put two and two together.'

'Oh, aye!' Renee said scornfully. 'And come up with five.'

'Well, pin your ears back and listen to this, then,' her mother retorted sharply. 'It wasn't long before Kitty got herself in the family way. She had a daughter, and if my memory serves me right, she named her Clara.'

Meg sat back, looking at them with a triumphant gleam in her eyes. 'Now, then! What have you got to say about that?'

Renee looked at her mother for a moment, then began to fold up the pieces of material.

'It's a good story, Mam,' she said wearily, 'but I can't give it credit. First off, I can't see Mr Jack marrying the daughter of the local tart. Second, if Mr Napier knew anything he'd have blabbed it all over the Hafod by now. Right, Jen?'

But she was silent, thinking furiously. Clara *had* tricked Jack into marriage. Why would she use subterfuge if her background was really respectable and she had nothing to hide? Although, Jenni realised, she couldn't reveal what she knew. Jack had told her that in confidence.

'Oh, you are thick sometimes, our Renee!' Meg exclaimed peevishly. 'Kitty had three more children after Clara, and never a ring on her finger. And she's still on the game, so I've been told.'

She shook her head impatiently.

'Don't you see? You can tell Clara to go and boil her head because you know all about her illegitimacy. Tell her to keep her mouth shut about the moonlighting, and you'll keep quiet as well.'

'But . . . that's blackmail, Meg!' exclaimed Jenni, aghast. Her expression was grim.

'Maybe you've never been really hard-up, Jenni, love. Cold and hungry all the time. Well, I have, and I'm not going through that again, especially at my time of life. Renee's *got* to keep her job or how will we live?'

Chapter Eighteen

Violet handled the gold locket tenderly. She let it hang just below her throat then admired the reflection of it in the great gilt mirror above the mantelpiece in the front sitting-room, confident no one would barge in and catch her.

It was lovely! Nathan's first gift to her, and he couldn't have chosen better.

She set her thumbnail against the catch and opened the locket, looking eagerly at the tiny photographs inside; hers on one side, Nathan's on the other. His gentle dark eyes smiled at her lovingly, and a great rush of tenderness for him engulfed her.

She held the locket against her lips for a moment. If only they could be married; if only they could be together for the rest of their lives. But Father would never permit it.

Of course, she was old enough to do as she pleased, but Father had controlled her all her life, and she didn't know how to break free, let alone find the courage for it. If only Mother were still alive, she'd have understood.

Violet gazed at Nathan's photograph again, tears starting in her eyes. Father would deny her this chance of happiness as he'd denied her once before when she'd been young and fresh and, yes, beautiful in her own way. Now love had come again, and she was afraid.

Father would say she was too old for marriage at thirty-two. He'd see the eleven-year age difference between herself and Nathan as an insurmountable barrier; and furthermore, he would say, Nathan Joseph was a widower, and what was even worse a pawnbroker. Hardly a trade worthy of the Tregevny daughter.

Father wouldn't see all that mattered was that they were in love, truly, deeply, and it was all the richer and sweeter because they were older.

Violet's fingers clutched at the locket in despair. All Father would see was that in his only daughter he had an unpaid house-keeper for the rest of his life.

If only there were some way she could escape to love. If only she had a friend, someone who would help her.

Violet gazed at Nathan's photograph in bitter hopelessness, tears running down her cheeks, and was startled when a sharp rap sounded at the door and Doris came in, looking agitated.

'Miss Violet, there's a woman at the back door and I'm having a bit of trouble getting rid of her,' she said. 'Could you have a word, if you please, Miss?'

She struggled to compose herself, keeping her back turned while she hastily wiped away the tears with her fingertips.

'What does she want?' Violet asked, trying to steady her voice. An interruption like this was the last thing she wanted at this moment.

'She insists on speaking to Mrs Tregevny, and she just won't take no for an answer. Don't like the look of her at all, I don't, Miss,' Doris persisted, twisting her fingers anxiously. 'She looks, well, common.'

'A gypsy?'

'No, Miss.' Doris's cheeks and ears grew pink. 'What I mean is, not decent, if you get my meaning, Miss.'

Violet slid the locket inside her dress, then turned. She had hoped to slip out and pay a call on Nathan. He never opened for business on Saturday. They could have a few hours together, and she could be back before Father left the shop. Now Doris's silliness threatened to delay her.

'You must learn to deal with these trifling matters yourself, Doris,' she said, speaking firmly.

Always speak firmly to servants, Mother had told her, otherwise they take advantage. And dealing with servants was the only authority she had left since Clara had come.

'Now go and tell her to be off or a policeman will be called.'

'I'm not going anywhere near her!' Doris cried out, taking Violet by surprise. 'I might catch something shameful, and I'm a respectable girl, I am.'

'What on earth are you talking about?'

'I've seen her about the Hafod,' Doris rushed on. 'People say she's . . . she's . . .'

'What?' Violet asked distractedly, glancing at the clock on the mantelpiece. Her precious time with Nathan was trickling away.

'On the game!'

'Doris!' Violet stared, astonished and shocked by the coarse expression.

'I'm only telling you what people say, Miss.' Doris looked defiant.

'And this . . . this person is at our back door?' Violet felt nonplussed.

Doris nodded. 'And asking for Mrs Tregevny. Please, Miss Violet, could you speak to her?'

'Oh, very well.'

Reluctantly, yet with some curiosity, Violet followed Doris through the door at the back of the main hall, along a darkened passage and through another door to what they called the back lobby, an area between the scullery and the wash house where the back door was situated.

A woman was sitting, legs crossed, on an old kitchen chair, smoking a cigarette. She didn't attempt to get up when Violet approached.

'Here!' Doris said sharply. 'I told you to wait by the back door. And put that cigarette out. That's disgusting, that is.'

'Here to see Mrs Tregevny, I am,' the woman said belligerently, clouds of smoke streaming from her mouth and nose, reminding Violet of the breath of a dragon. 'Now where is she? I haven't got all day.'

'It's no good waiting . . .' Violet began haughtily, when the woman interrupted her with a coarse profanity and hunched her shoulders in defiance.

'Well, I'm not shifting from by here till I see her, so there!'

With her face heavily rouged and caked with cheap powder it was difficult to judge her age, which could be anywhere between forty-five to fifty, Violet thought. The woman's blonde shoulder-length hair was lank and greasy-looking.

'As I say, it's no good waiting because my mother has been dead for many years,' Violet said, unable to keep distaste from her tone. 'I'm Miss Tregevny. Now, what is it you really want?'

The woman curled her lip in scorn.

'I know your old mam's gone, you daft cow,' she said irritably. 'I'm not *twp*, mind. It's young Mrs Tregevny I want.'

'You mean Clara?' Violet was surprised.

She could never think of her sister-in-law as Mrs Tregevny. And how could fastidious, fashion-conscious Clara have any connection with such a vulgar creature as this woman?

'Yeah, Clara, that's right,' the woman confirmed, puffing smoke again. 'Like I said, I can't hang about all day. Got business to see to, I have.'

Doris gave a little gasp of shocked sensibility, while Violet wrinkled her nose at the strong odour of unwashed humanity.

The woman looked slovenly, too, wearing a woollen two-piece that was grubby and had seen better days. Her felt hat was perched at a rakish angle, and around the neck of the suit she wore a moth-eaten fur stole. To Violet it looked for all the world like a dead cat slung around her shoulders, and she couldn't suppress a shiver.

'Well, I doubt Clara will want to see you, Mrs . . . er . . .' Violet paused, flummoxed.

'It's Kitty Price, and she'll see *me* all right.'

Violet was puzzled by the woman's confident tone. She was conscious of precious time passing and Nathan waiting in the cosy little sitting-room behind his shop, yet at the same time her curiosity was growing ever stronger.

What was the link between Clara and this woman? For there was a link, Violet felt sure. Kitty Price's assurance seemed to make that a certainty. And there was something else, some vague feeling of familiarity, as though she'd met Kitty Price at some time . . . and yet she knew for certain she'd never set eyes on the woman before today.

'Mrs Tregevny is out,' Violet said firmly. 'And will probably be out all day. Now why do you want to see her, may I ask?'

'Mind your own bleeding business!' Kitty Price exclaimed loudly, rising from the chair. 'It's private and personal, see. I'll only have dealings with her.'

She moved towards the back door. The suit was far too tight on her body which had gone to seed, the skirt straining across her broad beam-end.

'Tell Clara Kitty was here. Tell her, if I don't see her soon, I'll be back.'

It sounded like a threat, and Violet was even more mystified.

'How can she reach you?'

Kitty Price paused in the doorway and threw the stub of her cigarette on the recently scrubbed hall floor, grinding it in with the toe of her shoe. There was a curl to her lip as she looked back at Violet.

'Oh, don't worry. She knows where I'll be.'

*

It was gone five o'clock when Clara arrived home. She laid her package carefully on the hall table while she took off her hat and coat then glanced in the mirror, fluffing up her hair and smiling broadly at her own reflection, suppressing an urge to laugh out loud.

Jenni Thomas was bluffing; Clara knew that now, and relished the thought that she had her rival right where she wanted her!

She sighed with satisfaction, feeling composed and gratified, very different from the way she'd felt on leaving the house on Hafod Row. She'd been frightened after the pointed remarks Jenni had made at first, but later reasoned that the other girl was merely casting empty aspersions in a vain attempt to wriggle out of a bad situation. Well, it hadn't worked.

Clara was elated at having caught Jenni red-handed, but also infuriated that Renee Morris had tried to take the blame. The pair of them had been so insulting about it, too. But they'd both pay for that in full measure.

It didn't matter which girl was guilty, because once she'd finished convincing the old man, Jenni Thomas would be implicated up to her neck. It was the last Tregevny's would see of her! Clara would also make sure Samuel blacklisted both of them, so they'd get no employment anywhere around Swansea.

She picked up the parcel. She'd felt like celebrating and had bought herself a new dress at Ben Evans' as a reward for her own cleverness. She decided she'd go and try it on straight away; perhaps even wear it to supper this evening.

She was about to climb the stairs when Violet came out of the front sitting-room.

'Clara, may I have a word?'

She paused on the first step and turned to look at her sister-in-law impatiently.

There were two little spots of pink in Violet's cheeks, and she was twisting her fingers in a way that suggested anxiety. But then, Violet was always anxious about some trifling thing or other. The bread man was late or the milk had turned sour. God! What a boring life she led.

'I'm busy,' Clara declared. 'Can't it wait?'

'The men will be here later,' Violet said hesitantly. 'I don't want to speak of it in front of them. It's . . . delicate.'

Clara was intrigued despite herself.

'Good heavens, Violet,' she said mockingly. 'What *have* you been up to?'

Violet flushed.

'Come into the back sitting-room,' she suggested. 'Then we won't be overheard.'

Clara sighed languidly.

'Oh, very well! But don't take too long. I want to change my dress for supper, and there isn't much time. I'm starving, too.'

She put the parcel back on the hall table and followed Violet through to the back sitting-room. Clara disliked this particular room because it was so dark; the only light was from two small windows, illogically placed to either side of the fireplace.

She flopped on to one of the armchairs, realising suddenly how tired she was feeling. Well, it had been a busy day, yet a profitable one. Still, she was having trouble summoning the patience to listen to Violet's woes.

'Pour me a sherry, please,' she said offhandedly. 'I might as well have an aperitif while I'm waiting.'

Her sister-in-law brought the drink then perched precariously on the chair opposite, knees pressed tightly together, hands restless in her lap.

'Now what's the trouble, Violet?' Clara couldn't keep her contempt from her voice. Not that she wanted to. Putting Violet in her place was a pastime she enjoyed. 'Although I really don't see how I can help,' she went on airily. 'Housekeeping is hardly my cup of tea, is it?'

Violet fidgeted with the collar of her dress.

'There's no trouble, Clara. Or, at least, I hope not. I just wanted to . . . warn you.'

'Warn me?' Clara was surprised. 'Whatever do you mean?'

She stared at her sister-in-law closely. Had Violet heard something about Jack and that Jenni Thomas? Was gossip already circulating?

'We had a caller asking for you this morning at the back door,' Violet said, her gaze averted. 'An unsavoury kind of person.'

Clara was genuinely amused.

'Unsavoury?' She laughed out loud. 'My friends wouldn't like to hear you call them unsavoury. Oh, really, Violet! Too strait-laced for words, you are.'

Violet's face took on a prissy expression.

'I can't believe this person is a friend of yours, Clara. She smells disgusting and she's so vulgar-looking.'

Clara looked at her sister-in-law with growing scorn. Violet had no idea of the realities of life. She'd never known pain and humiliation; never known fear and degradation. Unsavoury! Vulgar! They were just words to Violet, Clara thought with bitterness. She'd never had to live with them daily, fight them off, as Clara had.

Old and painful memories came flooding back for a moment, but she resolutely smothered them as she had for many years now, schooling herself to forget, to rise up and overcome. And she had won through.

Taking a sip of sherry Clara felt better, although Violet was beginning to bore her. They existed in different worlds.

'Begging, was she?' Clara asked, with a smirk. 'A tinker, perhaps? Threatening to put a curse on you if you didn't cross her palm with silver?'

Clara laughed at the joke. She enjoyed taking a rise out of her sister-in-law whenever she could. It relieved the boredom.

'She asked for you,' Violet insisted. 'Personally. Even knew your first name. Insistent, she was, too, like she had a right.'

Clara laughed again.

'Violet, you're not making any sense.'

She drained her sherry glass dry then rose to her feet, unwilling to waste anymore time listening to this nonsense. There was a new dress to try on, and she couldn't wait to tell Jack his precious Jenni was done for.

'She was begging obviously,' Clara said carelessly. 'She's heard my name somewhere and thought she might get a tanner or two out of me. Fat chance!'

She walked over to the sideboard and put down the empty sherry glass alongside the decanter.

'Some people think if you're a Tregevny there's money to be had out of you,' she went on morosely, thinking briefly of Jenni Thomas again. 'You should've sent her packing with a flea in her ear.'

Violet rose too, and hovered.

'There's more to it, Clara,' she persisted. 'Doris says the woman's well known in the Hafod for . . .'

'What?'

'Well, she says she's . . . a lady of the night.'

Amused again, Clara let out a peal of laughter. 'A what?'

Violet fussed nervously with the collar of her dress.

'A loose woman,' she went on, obviously embarrassed and out of her depth. 'You know what I mean – on the streets.'

Clara was just about to step through the door, but hesitated. The temperature in the room seemed to drop suddenly, and she shivered.

'Don't be absurd!' she said sharply. 'What are you getting at, Violet? Why would such a person come here?'

She spread her hands in a gesture of uncertainty.

'Well, that's just it, isn't it?' she said. 'Why would such a woman be asking for you by name, and with such impertinence, too?'

'What do you mean?'

'She said her name was Kitty, and if she doesn't see you soon, she'll be back. It sounded like a threat. What does it mean, Clara?'

Kitty!

Clara's legs suddenly felt like jelly. There was a high-backed armchair nearby and she took one shaky step towards it, gripping the back and leaning on it for support. For once she was glad the room was dark. She was in shock, and didn't want Violet to glimpse her expression for her face must give too much away.

Kitty!

Clara felt her throat go dry. Kitty had found her! After all this time . . . surely it was all of eight years since she'd set eyes on her mother. And she'd thought herself safe from Kitty at last.

Her heart was beating fast with rising panic, thudding painfully against her ribs. She should never have come back to the Hafod. Never! Why had she been so foolish? Hafod and the Cwm were too close together. She should have known Kitty or one of her cronies might spot her at any time. Clara had counted too much on the fact she now moved in elevated circles. What could she do? She couldn't let her mother ruin her again.

Clara ground her teeth painfully. Well, it was no good running away. She had too much to lose now; everything in the world.

'What else did she say?' Clara asked, straining to control the tremor in her voice.

'Nothing . . . except you'd know where she was.'

Oh, yes, Clara knew all right. That stinking house in the Cwm where Kitty, her own mother, had allowed her to be raped, degraded, almost destroyed because of greed.

And her destruction would have been complete if it hadn't been for her Uncle Billy. He was the only one in her family who'd understood it wasn't Clara's fault; the only one who'd had compassion for her. Now he was gone and no one else cared, not even Jack.

Clara began to tremble uncontrollably as the old, painful

memories began to surface again. Although most times she managed to keep them submerged, they remained always just below the surface, waiting to break through and swamp her.

She struggled with them now. This is not the time to give way, she told herself sternly, looking for that inner strength she knew she had. She was no longer a fifteen-year-old girl at her mother's mercy. She was a married woman now with influence and money.

But, an inner voice whispered tauntingly, one word from Kitty and all that could be snatched away.

'Clara, what is it?' Violet's nervous voice brought her to an awareness of her immediate danger. 'Are you all right?'

Clara pushed herself away from the chair, standing erect, her head held high in her usual haughty manner.

'Of course, Violet, why shouldn't I be?'

The words were snapped out defiantly. She mustn't break down and lose face, she warned herself grimly. There must be no show of weakness in front of her husband's family. She'd left that behind long ago. Her youth and innocence had been stolen, thanks to her mother's callous greed and indifference, but strength and toughness had replaced them. Life had been ruthless with her, and she'd promised herself to be ruthless with life and anyone who got in her way from now on.

'As I said,' Clara went on in a stronger tone, 'the woman was no more than a beggar, looking for a handout. If she calls again, send for a bobby.'

She stalked from the room on legs that were still trembling. Violet came hurrying after her.

'I'll get Doris to serve supper now,' her sister-in-law said fussily. 'Will you be down soon?'

'Don't wait for me,' she replied, anxious to be alone to think and plan what to do next, now that Kitty was back to threaten her. 'I'm not in the least hungry.'

Chapter Nineteen

The shop was empty when they ventured inside next morning. Jenni didn't know whether this was good or bad. She'd expected Mr Napier to be ready to greet them with a knowing smirk, but everything seemed pretty much as usual.

Richie and Jack were already at work when they walked, somewhat apprehensively, into the workroom.

'Good morning, girls,' Jack called cheerfully at the sight of them. He took out his watch from his waistcoat pocket. 'Only just in time, eh?'

'Morning,' they murmured in unison.

As they took off their hats and coats and hung them up, Jenni glanced covertly at Richie. His expression was preoccupied as he stitched an awkward seam in a lady's cashmere jacket. He didn't look angry or upset as she'd expected.

'I think it's all right,' Renee whispered. 'That witch Clara hasn't reported me.'

Not yet, Jenni thought, and sent up a little prayer of hope and thankfulness. She'd been wondering all night what she ought to do. If Renee was given the push, perhaps *she* should give in her notice, too, in support? But what good would that do? the voice of commonsense asked. One of them had to keep her job to pay the rent.

'If we can get through this morning, we may be in the clear,' Jenni whispered back, trying to sound hopeful. But she had little hope that Clara would let them off scot-free.

The girls were hanging around near the coat rack still whispering encouragement to each other when Richie lifted his gaze from his work and glanced sharply their way.

'Come on,' he said tersely. 'It's gone nine o'clock. No more gossiping. You two are as thick as thieves.'

Jenni was immediately nettled by the remark and stepped quickly over to her sewing machine, chin held high.

'Thieves!' she exclaimed sharply, giving him a killing look. 'And what exactly do you mean by that, Mr Richie?'

He looked surprised.

'My word! We are touchy.'

'She's got a nasty head cold coming on,' Renee intervened quickly and soothingly. 'Didn't sleep much last night, did you, Jen, love?'

There was a warning note in her friend's voice and Jenni swallowed down her anger at Richie. It was true she hadn't slept well, so maybe she was touchy.

But what had he meant by that remark? It reminded her too much of what Clara had said. She wouldn't be surprised if Richie and she were in cahoots over Renee's fall from grace. Although, to be honest, Jenni thought, Richie had seemed to treat Clara with something like disdain that day she'd called at the workroom.

On the other hand, looking at his dark, serious face, she judged he wouldn't let personal feelings interfere with protecting the business. He'd side with Clara if it suited his purpose. Did that make Richie her enemy, too?

Jenni tried to settle down to work, and as the morning progressed began to feel more and more at ease. It had just been a storm in a teacup, she decided. Clara was all talk. She hadn't had the nerve to tell Samuel anything of what she'd discovered.

It was well gone eleven o'clock when Jack looked up from his machine and stretched himself.

'I'm parched. I could murder a cup of tea, Renee,' he said. 'Go down and make one, there's a good girl.'

'Hold on!' Richie said tetchily. 'It'll be dinnertime soon. I don't approve of this new idea of taking mid-morning breaks for tea. It runs away with too much working time in a week. if you really want refreshment, Jack, see to it yourself.'

His brother's face was thunderous.

'Renee! Do as you're told.'

She got up from the table and went towards the door, but before she'd reached it Mr Samuel came into the room. There were dull red patches on his lined cheeks and he looked pretty angry about something. Jenni's spirits plummeted. The axe was about to fall.

'Where do you think you're going?' he asked Renee brusquely.

'To the kitchen to make tea, Mr Samuel, sir,' she answered meekly.

'No, you don't my girl!' he exclaimed angrily. 'You get your hat and coat on straight away. You're sacked!'

Renee's face crumpled up as though she would burst into tears and Jenni clapped a hand to her mouth, appalled at her employer's hardhearted manner of dismissal. Renee hadn't even been given a chance to deny anything. Obviously Clara had told on her just for spite. It was so unfair!

Jenni jumped up and ran to her friend. She put an arm around her shoulders as Renee's sobs burst out, tears running down her cheeks.

Richie rose hurriedly, too, and took a few halting steps forward.

'Father! What on earth's going on? Why've you sacked Renee?'

As if he didn't know, Jenni thought angrily.

'Moonlighting!' Samuel boomed. He strutted further into the

room, thumbs jammed importantly into the top pockets of his waistcoat. 'Thieving!' he went on, his voice rising. 'Taken the very bread out of our mouths, she has.'

'Who says so?' Richie asked.

Looking at him closely, Jenni could see he was obviously and genuinely astonished. Well, perhaps she'd been a bit hasty in condemning him this time.

'Never you mind,' Samuel retorted imperiously. 'Caught in the act she was.' He glanced impatiently at the weeping Renee. 'It's no good snivelling, my girl,' he went on harshly. 'You were warned what would happen.'

Afraid to speak a word, Jenni glanced from Samuel to Jack as she continued to comfort Renee, trying to appeal to both men with a look. But Samuel was obviously far too angry to notice her, and Jack merely looked away.

'Father, this is a serious matter,' Richie said, his face darkening. 'It needs looking into before taking such severe action. First we should have the full details.'

Jenni was furious. Oh, trust him to make matters worse, she thought. Perhaps he was hoping she was implicated, too.

'Go on!' Samuel waved a hand at the sobbing Renee. 'Get your coat and leave my premises immediately. You needn't look for any severance pay, either. You've stolen enough trade from us already.'

With a grunt of satisfaction, he strutted from the workroom, Richie following him slowly.

In the doorway he turned and gave Jenni such a penetrating and accusing look she felt uneasy and turned her eyes away. Was he blaming her? Had he guessed something?

'Renee, I'm so sorry,' Jenni said. 'Wouldn't have had this happen for the world, I wouldn't.'

'It's all right, Jen, kid,' Renee said, obviously choking back more sobs. 'It's my own fault, isn't it?' her lips trembled. 'It's just that we needed the extra couple of bob.'

With drooping shoulders she went and fetched her coat and hat and Jenni helped her put them on.

'We can't let it go like this,' Jenni murmured desperately. 'I'll have a word with Mr Jack. Maybe he'll speak up for you.'

Renee put a hand on her arm. She was trying to smile but it wasn't very successful, not with her reddened nose and eyes swollen from crying.

'Keep out of it, Jen, love,' she said. 'It's my problem and I'll have to work it out. See you dinnertime. Okay, kid?'

Jenni reached up and kissed her friend on the cheek. She wouldn't say anymore but she *would* have a word with Jack. After all, in a way it was their fault this had happened.

When Renee had gone, Jenni returned to her sewing machine. She glanced at Jack but he seemed absorbed in his work. He'd been silent throughout the bust-up, and she wondered at it. Had he no idea what his wife was up to?

'What are we going to do, Jack?' she ventured.

His head was turned away as though he was reluctant to look at her.

'Do? What d'you mean?'

Jenni clenched her teeth.

'It was Clara, Jack. She's the one who reported Renee.'

'You're imagining things.' His tone was dismissive.

'I was there!' Jenni said impatiently. 'She stormed into Renee's home yesterday afternoon. Behaved abominably.'

'Renee got what she deserves,' he retorted impatiently.

'Jack!' Jenni was astonished.

'Caught red-handed, she was,' he went on. 'Sewing machine, material, threads, strewn over the table . . . It was blatant.'

Jenni stared.

'So Clara *did* tell you?' she accused. 'You knew all morning, Jack. Why didn't you warn Renee?'

He stood up abruptly and turned away.

'Why should I?'

Jenni jumped up and stepped towards him, putting one hand on his arm and looking into his face. There was a hardness to his features she'd never seen before. It made her uneasy, but she had to make him see the responsibility was theirs.

'You know why as well as I do.'

She felt tears begin to well up in her eyes, remembering how upset and desperate Renee had looked as she'd left. They'd ruined her between them, and all because of their love for each other and Clara's unbridled jealousy.

'You're forgetting,' he said harshly, 'Clara caught Renee moonlighting. She's been going on about it all night, trying to implicate you too, and I'm sick of it.' He frowned at Jenni. 'I warned her not to say anything to Father, though. I didn't want you involved.'

'But don't you see, Jack?' Jenni said earnestly. 'It's me Clara's really out to get.'

'Nonsense!' He looked annoyed. 'Anyway, there's nothing *I* can do. The old man's made up his mind.'

'It just isn't fair!' Jenni exclaimed in distress. '*We're* responsible. Clara wouldn't have come looking for trouble if she hadn't guessed something about us. She's just done this to Renee for spite.'

Jack gave a low scornful laugh and turned back to his sewing machine.

'Us?' he repeated, and there was a touch of mockery in his tone. 'We've only kissed. That's nothing. There is no us, Jenni.'

She sat down again, biting her lip. She had to make the commitment now or she'd lose him.

'Not yet,' she murmured, bowing her head, feeling hot blood rush to her cheeks.

'What?' Suddenly Jack was eager. He grasped her hand as it lay on the table. 'Does that mean what I think it does?'

'Jack, I do love you so,' she said, looking at him earnestly. 'And you're right — why wait to find happiness together? Life's so short and things happen . . .' She paused.

Her thoughts went to her mother. Perhaps Sarah had found some happiness in the arms of Bert Herbert for a short while, but then, suddenly, it had all ended. And she thought of Blodwen, too bound by her scruples to let herself love or be loved, who had died without ever knowing that special joy. Jenni didn't want the same fate.

'After all,' she went on shyly, 'I will be your wife one day soon, won't I, Jack?'

She wouldn't think about Clara now. She and Jack didn't love one another and he'd made it clear enough their marriage was over, if it had ever really been anything but a sham.

'Yes, darling, you will be my wife.' He laughed jubilantly and jumped up again, grasping her hand to pull her to her feet.

'Oh, Jenni, darling!'

He put his arms around her and tried to draw her close, but she put her hands firmly against his chest and held him off.

'Jack, wait! Richie might come in.'

'To hell with Richie,' he said huskily, trying to nuzzle the curve of her throat.

Still Jenni resisted. She couldn't bear it if Richie caught them behaving improperly. She was certain he had a low opinion of her already, for a reason she couldn't understand other than that he thought a skirt-hand far beneath his precious family. If he knew about her and Jack, Richie would separate them, she was certain.

'I want you desperately, Jenni, darling,' Jack said. 'Will you meet me tonight?'

She could hear the need in his voice and quivered at the force of her own rising desire, but shook her head.

'No, Jack. I can't go off and leave Renee and her mother when they're at their lowest. You've got to help her, Jack. Please, for my sake?'

He gave a heavy sigh.

'You're not having me on, are you, Jenni?' he asked, his expression suspicious. 'We are going to be together, aren't we? I don't deserve to be treated shabbily. Clara's done too much of that already.'

She reached up and kissed him quickly.

'Don't rush me, Jack, please.'

Her legs felt weak and trembled so much she thought she might slide to the ground at any moment, but she *had* committed herself now, and wasn't sorry. Perhaps others would condemn her but their love was true, she just knew it in her heart. Jack would make everything right in time.

Jenni worked in a daze for the rest of the day. She hurried home to Hafod Row at dinnertime to find Renee still in tears and Meg looking very grave.

'Never mind,' Jenni said, trying to console them. 'You've still got my lodging money, and I'll pay extra for my keep and a bit of coal. Renee'll find another job. We'll manage Meg, my dear.'

Overcome with emotion, Jenni threw her arms around Meg as she sat hunched in her fireside chair, and kissed her cool cheek.

No one could replace her own mother, of course, and the times they'd had together before the tragedy were sweet in Jenni's memory, but Meg was like a mother to her just the same. And Jenni and Renee were more like sisters every day. They got on so well together, it was really wonderful. And now she'd brought trouble to her dearest friends.

'I've asked Mr Jack to speak up for you,' she said. 'I'm sure he will.'

'He won't do nothing,' Renee murmured miserably between sobs. 'Too scared of old Samuel, he is. I've heard Mr Napier say many a time that Mr Jack'll get the bigger share of the business when old Samuel turns up his toes, so he's not going to upset his father, is he? Not for the likes of me anyway.'

Jenni went back to the workroom after dinner in deep gloom. She was counting on Jack's help. Surely he wouldn't let her down? Maybe he wouldn't do it for Renee, but surely, as he loved Jenni, he'd do it for her?

It was a strange afternoon, Jenni found. She missed Renee's constant chatter which made the hours fly by. Now there was an uncomfortable silence, Richie and Jack hardly saying one word to each other and both speaking to her only in monosyllables.

Jenni wanted to extract another promise to act from Jack but Richie never left them alone long enough, so she prayed instead that Jack would do all he could for her friend.

Jenni was disappointed when he hurried away before their finishing time of six o'clock. Richie was still working as he had a special order on hand, the client to call the next day for a final fitting.

Jenni dawdled over putting on her coat and hat, hanging around, hoping Jack would return with some good news. Knowing she couldn't linger much longer, she fetched her handbag from under the table where her sewing machine stood, and prepared herself to say goodnight to Richie. Not that she wanted to speak to him at all, but under the circumstances she decided it wouldn't be a good idea just to ignore him and walk out.

'Goodnight, Mr Richie,' she murmured mournfully as she walked slowly towards the door.

'Jenni, just a minute.' He stopped sewing and stood up, taking a few uneven steps towards her.

'You understand Renee did something very wrong, don't you?' he said. 'Rules are rules.'

Jenni's lips tightened and she glared at him.

'Rules!' She almost spat out the word. 'What do rules matter when you're living from hand to mouth like Renee and her poor mother?' she cried passionately. 'Do you think they'd take in a lodger if they weren't hard-up? The trouble with the likes of you,

Mr Richie,' she went on with deep scorn, 'is you've no idea what it's like to be short of money.'

The muscles around his mouth stiffened and his expression darkened. She knew she'd been too outspoken. Well! He could sack her if he liked, she thought recklessly.

'I had no hand in Renee losing her job, if that's what you think, Jenni,' he said tersely.

But he'd done nothing to save that job either, and for that she *did* blame him.

'Perhaps not,' she returned with a toss of her head. 'And maybe you'd prefer it if I got the sack instead?'

He frowned. 'Now that's uncalled for, Jenni.'

She said nothing, but lifted her chin, unwilling to give an inch.

'Anyway,' he went on after a moment's icy silence, 'I'm glad to tell you that my father's changed his mind.'

Jenni's mouth dropped open in astonishment, the wind completely taken out of her sails, and for a moment she couldn't speak, couldn't believe the words she'd heard.

'What?'

Richie pushed back an unruly lock of hair that forever flopped into his eyes.

'Renee's been with us nearly two years and has been a good reliable worker until now,' he said. 'So my father's prepared to give her one more chance. She's to be here on time tomorrow morning. But . . .' he lifted his index finger to emphasise the point '. . . she's on probation, mind. Any more moonlighting and that will be the finish. *Kaput!* Do I make myself clear?'

'Oh, Mr Richie, this is wonderful!'

Jenni couldn't help jumping up and down on the spot with joy, and was astonished to see a smile break through his usually serious expression.

'You'd best get off and give her the good news, then,' he suggested.

Jenni nodded eagerly, wanting to dash away home. She'd call

at the chip shop first, get some chips and a fish each for them — no sharing tonight, they were celebrating.

As she hurried home to Hafod Row with her steaming bundle of food, she felt so happy she could hardly contain herself, wanting to burst out singing as she went.

This reprieve was Jack's doing, she had no doubt of it, and he'd done it for her, Jenni thought, a warm glow spreading through her. This showed he really loved her, and she'd been right to promise herself to him.

She longed to be with him, yet in her heart she wished it could be in the conventional way. She wished they could be married first. But still, her heart sang out, he loves you enough to confront his father and win. And when all was said and done, the only thing that really mattered in this world was love, the love she shared with Jack.

Chapter Twenty

Clara sat in the privacy of her bedroom, elbow on the edge of the dressing-table, chin in hand, staring despondently at her own reflection in the mirror.

Everything had gone wrong! She'd failed to get Jenni Thomas sacked, and could kick herself for warning Jack beforehand, unable to resist the urge to crow. She might have known he'd manage to have a word with his father before she could say anything. Cleverly, he'd put his redheaded fancy-piece in the clear.

Clara clenched her fist in anger. A good opportunity spoilt!

With a heavy sigh she relaxed her hand and brushed her fringe from her eyes impatiently. It was no good sitting here mooning. She must find some other way. She hadn't finished with Jenni Thomas yet, not by a long chalk. There was more to that little minx than met the eye. All Clara needed was patience, and time was on her side.

But that isn't true, is it? she told herself. Not now that Kitty is back.

She met her own blue gaze reflected in the mirror and squirmed on her chair, not wanting to face up to the reality of this new situation. Why was she thinking of Jenni Thomas now when something more vital was at stake? It wasn't just her marriage at risk anymore. Her whole way of life was in jeopardy;

her self-respect, and perhaps more importantly the respect of others which she'd come to enjoy these last few years.

Kitty was a threat to all of that, and she was out to make trouble.

News of her mother's unexpected visit had rocked Clara to the core, and now she knew she must do something drastic about it. Kitty could turn up again at any time, and one careless word from her could spell ruin.

Clara twisted her hands together in despair at the thought. It wouldn't do to delay any longer. She'd have to go to her mother, face her down, this very evening.

For eight years she'd stayed away from that house in the Cwm; she'd fought to bury the memory of that terrible night, but could never pretend it hadn't happened. Now she must go there and face it all again. Did she have the courage?

Unclenching hands that were visibly shaking, Clara looked down at the palms. They were glistening with the sweat of unreasoning fear, and she felt an overwhelming apprehension.

She *must* do it, though! Otherwise everything she'd built up over these last eight years would be taken from her.

She left it as late as possible, cursing the lingering light of the late-May evening, hoping there weren't too many people about who'd recognise her.

Supper was over. Jack had gone out, God only knows where. As she came quietly down the staircase she could hear the gramophone playing in the front sitting-room. It wouldn't be wise to slip out without telling anyone, not at this time of evening anyway. She mustn't arouse any suspicion.

Clara opened the sitting-room door and went in. The fire in the grate was built up and the room was overheated. Her father-in-law sat under the gaslight, reading, while Violet was at a small bureau writing a letter. How could her sister-in-law bear the boredom of her life? Clara wondered vaguely.

Richie was nowhere in sight and Clara remembered then that

he always went to a Hafod Brotherhood meeting on a Monday evening. She glanced at the clock on the mantelpiece. She must be careful not to run into him on his way home.

'Father, I'm going out for a while,' she announced with the strong and careful enunciation she always used when dealing with Samuel.

She'd made up her mind from the beginning that she'd never give him a hint of her origins from her way of speaking, or let him dominate her like he did his own children. Her will was as strong as his, and perhaps he guessed that. He'd never challenged her or her actions since she'd joined the family, although, of course, she'd been careful to behave with decorum and dignity as was expected of a member of the Tregevny family. Yet, for all that, she never managed to feel his equal. He was the undisputed head-of-the-house.

Samuel looked up at her, frowning.

'What? At this time of night, Clara?'

'It's only just gone nine o'clock, Father,' she said firmly. 'I'm going to see Mrs Dewhirst in Cwmavon Street. We're organising something for the church bazaar next month.'

'Since when have you been interested in church matters?' her father-in-law asked.

There was a scepticism in his voice which annoyed her. She was well aware he thought her frivolous, but then, Clara knew that was his opinion of most women. Look at Violet, limited and curtailed, her opinions openly scorned; no more than an unpaid housekeeper.

Clara raised her chin, managing to look down her nose at him scornfully.

'I'm always interested in helping charity, Father. My family were noted for it in Carmarthen before they fell on hard times and I had to leave home to seek a living for myself,' she said haughtily.

She'd found since her marriage that ramming home the near-

gentility of her imaginary family in Carmarthen and their fall
from prosperity tended to leave Samuel Tregevny wrong-footed
most times. Perhaps he wasn't so sure of himself, after all? Living
in fear as he did of the failure of his own business.

'Well, it's very good of you, Clara.'

He lost interest immediately and returned to his reading, and
she was relieved.

'I may be late,' she went on casually. 'Mrs Dewhirst is such a
talker.'

In the hall, she reached for her coat from the stand, then hesitated. It was far too fashionable for walking in the Cwm. She'd
stand out like a sore thumb.

On impulse she took down the coat and her smart hat and
walked through the door at the end of the hall and into the dark
passage that led to the back lobby. The lavatory was in this
passage, and next to it a walk-in cupboard where Violet kept the
odd jacket or raincoat.

Clara hung her fashionable coat and hat there, then looked
for something of Violet's to wear. She found a navy wool coat,
probably ten years out of date, and a shabby velour pull-on hat.
No one would recognise her in these things; clothes she normally
wouldn't be seen dead in.

Better dead than disgraced. Clara couldn't help a wry smile at
her own joke as she shrugged into the coat and slipped out of the
house by the back door. Like a thief, she thought.

She walked hurriedly down the Neath Road toward the
bridge, praying she'd meet no one she knew well. The sun had
set, yet the sky was still full of light. People were about so she
kept her head down, but no one seemed to take any notice of her.

At the side of the railway bridge, a narrow dirt path led down
to the Cwm below. Clara paused at the bottom of the path, reluctant to go further until her heart stopped racing.

She was dreading the coming confrontation, dreading seeing
her mother again. She knew she'd have trouble remaining civil to

her, yet she must watch her step where Kitty was concerned. She'd turn nasty in a minute, Clara remembered. She had no reason to believe her mother had changed over the years.

It had always been hard to think of Kitty as her mother. She'd never been kind or understanding or treated her like a daughter. Clara, like the brothers and sister who followed in the same shameful way, was an inconvenience, an occupational hazard, an unwanted mouth to feed. Not that there had ever been much to eat, Clara remembered, as she stepped reluctantly along the cracked pavement towards Copper Row, and only shabby hand-me-downs to wear.

Brought up on scraps. Dragged up, that's what Gran used to say. Poor Gran! So ashamed of a daughter who'd sell herself to any man with the jingle of change in his pockets. She had died of shame, Clara was certain of it.

No, Kitty had never been a mother to her, and wasn't able to tell her who her father was, either. Probably some foreign sailor, Gran had said. Here today, gone tomorrow.

It was a shame no child should have to bear, and Clara ground her teeth painfully at the thought.

Uncle Billy was the only one in the family, except Gran, who'd ever shown Clara any sympathy or compassion; the only one who hadn't blamed *her* for what had happened.

She walked along the narrow pavement past rows of terraced houses. This was the oldest part of the Hafod. The houses were two-up-two-down, narrow and small, the poll-stone blackened by more than a century of industrial grime.

But most people tried to make the best of things. Poor they might be, but they were respectable and proud, too. Threshold stones were still scrubbed white, Clara noticed. Doors sported clean paint; window panes flashed in the last light of the dying day, their net curtains were clean and crisp-looking. Nothing had changed much since she'd run away from here as a girl.

Her steps slowed as she neared her mother's home. Its stark

contrast with the neighbouring houses still had the power to shock. The front-room window was filthy and behind it hung what looked like an old bed sheet. Was it the same one that had hung there eight years ago? The upstairs window had no covering, but it didn't matter because the glass was so dirty hardly anything could be seen through it.

The front door stood open, the bare boards of the passage visible, dirty and unswept. Her mother's nickname of Dirty Kitty was well-earned. Everything looked exactly the same, and a spurt of shame twisted in Clara's breast like a knife.

She paused on the grimy front step, her heart hammering with panic. To step inside would be like stepping into the past, the terrible past of her childhood. But it had to be endured, she told herself firmly. Everything depended on how well she battled her mother over the next hour, and a battle it would be, she had no doubt about that.

The passage and the visible interior of the house were gloomy now that dusk was falling. Kitty relied on candles and rarely used the gaslight, Clara remembered, except to eat by when there was anything to put on the table.

Gathering her courage, she stepped forward and down the passage, the boards sounding hollow under her shoes. The first breath she took almost choked her.

The stench of neglect was overpowering. The stale, sour air drifted into her nostrils and settled on her tongue. It was at once alien and terrifyingly familiar.

Clara staggered to a halt. Putting a hand to the wall at the bottom of the stairs, she leaned against it, her legs weakening in remembered terror.

In the darkness of the passage she was transported in time to the darkness of an upstairs room. She was fifteen again, and *he* was there, his bulk bearing down on her, his hands groping at her body. She could smell the rankness of his breath, fusty with drink and tobacco.

She screamed and writhed, trying to throw him off, and he hit her, the back of his hand lashing at her face, once, twice. Hysterical, she screamed again for her mother – no, she'd screamed to Kitty for help, to come and save her from him. Kitty *was* there beyond the bedroom door. Even in her terror, Clara heard her mother's voice telling her to shut up. She screamed again and again, but Kitty never came.

Kitty allowed him to have his way, allowed her, a child of fifteen to be deflowered and degraded, and all for sheer avarice.

Clara would never forget or forgive her words afterwards.

'Oh, don't make such a bloody fuss, will you? It's what a woman's for. And that's just the beginning, my girl. It's about time you started earning your keep.'

It was then she knew she must get away or end up like her mother. Only later did she know how deeply in trouble she was. A fifteen-year-old girl in the family way might as well throw herself in the river. She might have done too, if it hadn't been for Uncle Billy.

Clara still leaned against the passage wall, trembling from head to foot, her gloved hand over her nose and mouth, trying to protect herself from old and painful memories.

Kitty had a lot to answer for, her debt to Clara beyond price, yet now she was back to extract more from her daughter.

Clara ground her teeth with rising anger at the thought and felt strength flow back into her legs. There had to be a way to defeat her mother once and for all.

Pushing herself away from the wall, She stepped into the back room. It was empty except for a table, a couple of chairs, and a grubby, sagging sofa, pushed against one wall.

She glanced into the dingy scullery. On the draining board lay one dirty plate holding scraps of dried-up chips. Well, that was a step up, Clara thought wryly. Kitty had always eaten her chips straight out of the wrapping paper. No saucepans, of course. She never cooked anything.

Clara stared around at the slovenliness. Did I ever live like this? she asked herself. Where a moment ago she'd been forced to relive that terrible night, now she felt as though that life belonged to someone else. She wasn't Clara Price, illegitimate daughter of Dirty Kitty. Clara Tregevny was someone else altogether.

The quietness of the house struck her for the first time. Where were her two brothers and her sister, Carol? For that matter, where was Kitty? Out touting for trade, perhaps?

Clara felt a shiver go through her. Suppose Kitty were to return now with some man? How humiliating that would be. Should she go? Wait until another time? Leave a note? No! Nothing in writing.

Clara stood for a moment in the dim silence, wondering what to do for the best. She'd heard no sound and wasn't aware she was no longer alone until a man's arm was slipped around her waist and she felt it tighten.

She screamed and whirled away, stumbling several steps backwards and almost falling to the floor in her effort to free herself.

'Hey!' a man's voice said. 'Don't be like that, mun.'

Clara's leg muscles tightened and her first instinct was to flee, to make a dash for the front door, but he stood in the way. His shadowy outline showed a man of medium height, stocky and bulky, and wearing what looked like a trilby. She couldn't see his face in the gloom but she recognised that tone of voice. A man looking for a woman, any woman. How many times had she witnessed such men as this stepping over her mother's threshold in the past?

'Get out of my way,' Clara gasped, fright making her breathless.

'What's your hurry, kid?' he said, taking a step further.

His accent was strong. Not a local man, she decided. From the Valleys, obviously, making the most of a day out in the big town; a tour of the pubs first and then a woman to finish off the night.

'Kitty's not here,' Clara told him desperately, her voice uneven with fright. 'So you can get out as soon as you like.'

He laughed. It was an unpleasant sound and Clara clutched her bag tighter under her arm.

'Well, that's a good one, that is,' he said mockingly. 'Especially since I live here, like.'

'What?'

He stepped closer, trying to peer into her face, and Clara was thankful for the onset of darkness outside and Kitty's meanness with the lighting. The room was too dark for him to see her properly.

'What are you doing in by here anyway?' He sidled closer still. 'Looking for a bit of rough, are you, love?' His tone was insinuating, and his hands went to his belt, loosening the buckle. 'If you are, I can oblige you, kid.'

Clara was appalled.

'Keep away from me!' she screeched, stepping back. 'Kitty'll be back any minute.'

'Naw! She's out on the town. Hey! It's all right, love.' His tone was throaty. 'Got the place to ourselves, we have. Come here, mun. Give us a kiss.'

He moved closer again and Clara cringed away, panic-stricken.

'I can give you a good time, love, and no charge, either,' he said. 'Oh, and Ossie's the name, by the way. Ossie James.'

'Stay away!' Her voice was shrill with hysteria. 'I'm warning you, stay away!'

'Oh, don't be such a bloody silly bitch, will you?' There was a gritty edge to his voice now, as though he were losing patience, and Clara felt a sweat break out all over her body. It couldn't be happening again! It couldn't!

'You come down to Dirty Kitty's for one thing only,' he said nastily. 'Don't like tarts who tease, I don't. What they need is a bloody good hiding to teach 'em a lesson. Now, come here!'

He sprang forward suddenly and Clara screamed mindlessly.

'What the bleeding hell's going on here!'

In the darkness she recognised Kitty's strident voice immediately. That hadn't changed either.

He whirled around and away from her as Kitty spoke, and Clara felt relief wash over her like a spring of cool, clean water.

'I've warned you about bringing your sluts back here, haven't I, Ossie? I won't have it, see. Now, get *her* out.'

'Oh, don't be like that, mun, Kit. We won't be long.'

'Kitty!' Clara cried out desperately. 'It's me!'

There was silence for a moment. No one moved. Then Ossie shifted his weight from one foot to the other.

'What's she mean, Kit? It's her?'

'Shut up, Ossie, and sling your hook.'

'Aw! Now wait a minute, Kit,' he said querulously. 'Come home for a kip, I have. Up all last night, I was, and I'm buggered.'

'I said, push off, Ossie! Get down the pub. You can kip there. Don't come back for a couple of hours.'

'You can't order me about.' His tone was nasty again.

'Would you rather I had a word with Charlie Pendle?' Kitty asked, sarcasm lacing her tones.

With a coarse oath, Ossie moved immediately to the doorway and went out into the passage, a bulky shadow against the lamplight streaming in through the open door. Clara still hadn't seen his face, but he hadn't seen hers either, which was more important.

'There's a candle on the mantelpiece,' Kitty said. 'And a box of matches. Light it while I make sure he's really gone because he's a crafty bugger is Ossie.'

Clara stumbled to the mantelpiece and found the candle and matches. She could hardly strike the match, her hands shook so much, but finally it flared into life and she set it to the blackened wick.

The flame danced in the evening breeze from the open door, sending crazy shadows chasing around the room. She'd spent the first fifteen years of her life living here yet it was as alien to her now as the pit of hell itself.

Kitty came back into the room.

'He's gone all right. I can see him on the corner of Dock Street.' She laughed mirthlessly. 'Only mention Charlie Pendle and Ossie's ready to pee in his pants.'

Clara wasn't surprised. She remembered everyone was scared of Charlie Pendle, one of the biggest crooks around Swansea. A dangerous man to know, everyone said.

'I thought Charlie would be dead by now. What's this Ossie James got to do with him?' asked Clara.

She wasn't really interested in the answer, but was finding it difficult to bring up the subject of her visit. Talking to Kitty was like talking to a stranger. And she couldn't even see her mother clearly in the candlelight.

'Charlie dead!' Kitty laughed. 'They'll have to shoot that old bugger. Somebody probably will one day.'

She moved to the mantelpiece, picked up a packet of cigarettes and a box of matches and lit up. She flopped on to the sofa nearby, and Clara watched the glowing end of the cigarette move about as Kitty took one puff after another.

'Ossie works for Charlie,' she went on. 'Strong-arm stuff, you know, and other things, like housebreaking or a little bit of bone-breaking if a bloke won't pay up what he owes.' The cigarette glowed fiercely as she drew deeply on it. 'Ossie's good at it, apparently.'

'He turns my stomach!' Clara gasped, shivering.

Kitty's voice was thick with scorn.

'You always were a fussy bitch!'

Clara held on to her temper, determined not to let her mother rattle her now when she needed to keep a cool head.

'He lives here?' she asked casually to change the subject, but unable to hide the distaste in her voice.

She wondered what the arrangement was. There'd never been

a steady man in Kitty's life in the past, just an endless stream of furtive strangers.

'Charlie suggested I give him lodgings. No one ignores a suggestion from Charlie, not even me.' The cigarette bobbed. 'Ossie got into trouble in Cardiff. The bobbies were after him, but he managed to get away by the skin of his teeth. Not even sure that's his real name.' Kitty laughed unpleasantly. 'He's a sneaky bastard, all right, but he pays his rent.'

'You move in dangerous circles, Kitty.'

Clara felt uncomfortable. It was like talking to a ghost. She'd been ready for a battle, not chit-chat, and in a battle she needed to see her opponent's face, read the expression in their eyes.

'Oh, I'm well in there, mind,' said Kitty. 'Business has been slower these last few years, and a woman needs a friend some-times.' Her tone became bitter. 'Especially if her family has buggered off and left her to it, without a penny to scratch her arse with.'

Now we're getting to it, thought Clara, the reason why she's suddenly popped up in my life again.

'Can't you light the gas, Kitty?' she asked petulantly. 'I haven't been back here in eight years. It's the least you could do.'

'I haven't got money for gas bills,' Kitty sneered. 'At least, not yet I haven't.' There was slyness in her tone. 'Sit down, Clara, why don't you, while we sort things out?'

'No, thanks,' she answered curtly. 'I won't be here that long.'

'Suit yourself.'

'Light the gas, for heaven's sake, Kitty! It's like the Black Hole of Calcutta in here.'

'Oh, all right!'

Once the gas was lit Clara felt safer somehow. She glanced curiously at Kitty, remembering how her mother had once looked, and felt a jolt of shock. She hardly recognised her. She *was* talking to a stranger. If she'd met Kitty on the street she wouldn't have known her.

Her mother could be no more than forty, but she looked ten years older, hair greying, her figure gone to seed, and lines deepening on her face. The last eight years of loose living had done their work. No wonder plying her trade was getting more difficult and less lucrative.

But Clara could find no sympathy in her heart. Hadn't Kitty let her own daughter be used despicably, for pure greed? And she'd have forced Clara into the vile trade, too, if it hadn't been for Uncle Billy.

Looking at her mother, she could only feel repugnance, and anger, too, that Kitty should try to take advantage of her again.

'How did you find me?' she asked, unable to keep the resentment out of her voice.

Kitty sniffed.

'I knew you was back about three years ago. Saw you in the street. Kept an eye on you, I did.' She smirked. 'You've done all right for yourself, haven't you?'

'No thanks to you!' Clara cried out angrily. 'You didn't give a damn about me. Only Uncle Billy . . .'

'Oh, aye! My brother had money to put *you* right, didn't he?' Kitty replied harshly. 'But he wouldn't give *me* the dregs of his teapot.'

'Why should he?' Clara exclaimed. 'I remember Uncle Billy saying: "Let Kitty wallow in her own filth." That's what he thought of *you*. He was ashamed, like poor Gran. She died of it, she did.'

'You sanctimonious little bitch!' Kitty sprang up from the sofa, flinging her cigarette across the room. 'You ran out on me after I'd brought you up from a kid. I needed you to do a bit of earning, but you buggered off.'

'I was in the family way, for God's sake!' she shouted. 'I was fifteen, still a child. I turned to Uncle Billy, and he gave me money for an operation to get rid of it.'

Clara swallowed a sob of regret. Expecting a child had seemed the end of the world at the time. Well, she was little more than a child herself then, wasn't she? But it had robbed her of any chance of bearing children in the future. Perhaps, if she'd realised that, she'd never have gone through with it. But what would have become of her if she hadn't? She'd have ended up like her mother. Better dead than that!

'I was pretty poorly afterwards, too,' she went on, pushing the repulsive thought from her mind. 'Uncle Billy took me in, nursed me, took care of me.'

Kitty laughed in disbelief.

'What about that prize wife of his? I'm surprised she even let you past the doorstep.'

Clara clenched her teeth. Yes, Uncle Billy's wife had been hostile, but he'd stuck up for Clara. When she was better, he'd got her respectable lodgings in Morriston and a job. It was hard work scrubbing floors, but she'd stuck it out gratefully because it was better than anything she'd ever known before.

'Uncle Billy knew I didn't want to end up like you.'

Clara looked her mother up and down and didn't bother to hide the deep contempt she felt for her.

'He put up part-premium for me to learn my trade as a seamstress. I'd have finished that, too, if he hadn't died suddenly before he could pay it all.'

Clara's voice faltered as she remembered. When she'd lost Uncle Billy she'd lost the only person in the world who'd cared anything for her. When he'd gone she realised she was really alone, and would have to fight for herself, any way she could.

'Huh!' Kitty was scornful. 'He had plenty of dosh to throw about then, didn't he? There must be more money in scrap metal than I thought.' She looked at Clara slyly. 'You were lucky to get a place at Tregevny's, being only half-trained and all.'

Clara raised her chin defiantly, unwilling to answer the jibe. She wouldn't admit to her mother that she'd bluffed her way in, after working as a skirt-hand in less successful establishments. Kitty knew too much about her past already.

'At least Uncle Billy treated me with respect; treated me like his own daughter,' she said miserably. 'To my own mother I was just a piece of young flesh to be sold. You ought to be ashamed of yourself!'

'I'm ashamed of nothing!' Kitty blazed. 'And don't you talk to me like that, you cheap little slut.'

'Oh, no! I'm not the slut,' Clara cried out furiously. 'You are.'

She looked Kitty up and down again, and didn't bother to hide her contempt.

'An old hag, you are, Kitty. A dirty, smelly old woman – used up and finished. No one wants you anymore. You said business was bad – it'll get worse because you're a wreck and you look it. Even a drunken sailor, a year at sea, wouldn't look at you now.'

Kitty looked venomous, her features darkening, making her seem even more like an old witch. Clara remembered how that look had made her cringe in fear as a child.

'Make you pay dear for that, I will, Clara,' she threatened, through clenched yellowing teeth. 'See if I don't.'

'You can't do anything to me,' she said triumphantly. 'I'm Clara Tregevny now. My husband's family are highly respectable, and worth a bob or two.'

Kitty stared at her for a moment, then a sly smile curved her lined and narrow mouth.

'I wonder how old Samuel Tregevny will feel when he learns his son is married to Dirty Kitty's bastard daughter, eh? I wonder how your hubby will like having the local tart as his mother-in-law?' Her smile turned into a sneer. 'They'd be shot of you, my girl, faster than you could say rat-trap!'

Clara was appalled at the venom in her voice.

'Why? Why would you do that to me?' she cried out, distraught. 'What did I ever do to you?'

Kitty stared at her belligerently for a moment, her eyes glittering.

'You were born!' she rasped out at last.

Clara stepped back, reeling a little, feeling the pronouncement like a blow to the heart. There was such bitterness and malice in her mother's expression, it almost took her breath away.

'Don't look so shocked,' Kitty said evenly.

She turned to the sofa again and sat down, reaching for another cigarette.

'You were never wanted. You must have felt it. What the hell did I want with a kid? With any of you kids. More mouths to feed. What good were you?'

'You're unnatural!' Clara gasped. 'And where are the others, anyway? Carol, Pete, Jimmy? What have you done to them?'

Kitty's lips curled back in rage.

'Nothing, more's the pity.'

She put a lighted match to the cigarette between her lips and drew in deeply as though her life depended on it.

'Legged it, they did, the ungrateful little perishers,' she snarled. 'Six months after you left. Don't know where they landed up, and don't give a damn, either. Good riddance, I say!'

Clara was still standing at the centre of the room and Kitty glared up at her, her mouth a tight line.

'Blame you, I do,' she said. 'Just when you could've done me a bit of good, bringing in some extra money, you ran off. That put the idea into *their* heads, didn't it?'

'Well, I'm glad then!' Clara flared. 'I'm glad you're alone. You'll die alone! And you don't deserve anything else. You're scum, you are, Kitty, and I hate you!'

It was a terrible thing to say, she realised, appreciating the wickedness of hating one's mother. But then, she'd never been able to see Kitty in that role. And it was clear Kitty hated her own child. As if to prove that, she sat forward aggressively, her face darkening in fury.

'Oh, right! Scum, am I? Well, the tally's mounting, my girl, and you'll be laughing on the other side of your face when it comes to paying.'

'Paying?' Clara was waiting for this. Her mother had been threatening it all along; from the moment she'd knocked on the back door of Abertawe House. 'You'll get nothing out of me.'

Kitty got up from the sofa.

'Oh, I think I will, though.' She blew smoke towards the ceiling, her whole attitude confident. 'Otherwise I'll be to and from the house till they're sick of me. And I'll do some talking. I'll finish you, my girl, good and proper.'

'You wouldn't dare,' Clara said breathlessly. 'I've told them to put the bobbies on you next time you call, so there!'

Kitty stepped closer suddenly, leaning forward in a threatening stance, and Clara was primed for flight again.

'Listen here!' her mother said nastily. 'You don't threaten me because it won't work, see. I'll tell the Tregevnys you was on the game when you got up the spout. I can paint you as dirty as I like; dig you right deep into the mire. I can make out you was a filthy little trollop all along. Mud sticks, especially with the likes of the Tregevnys. Toffee-nosed buggers!'

She smiled at Clara, triumph glinting in her eyes.

'All I want is a couple of quid now and again, say once a week, like. You can manage that, Clara. You spend enough on clothes, I notice.' Her look was knowing. 'Oh, yes, I watch. I see what goes on.'

'You're mad, you are!' she cried desperately. 'I can't manage a couple of pounds every week. My husband pays for everything. I've no money of my own.'

'Well, you'd better find some then!' Kitty barked angrily. 'Otherwise you'll end up with nothing, my girl. You're warned, all right?'

Clara gave a tremulous laugh, trying not to show how frightened she was.

'I suppose you'll set Charlie Pendle on me if I don't cough up?'

Kitty's lip curled in disdain.

'I don't need the likes of Charlie Pendle because I've got the goods on you. You'll pay or you'll end up back in the gutter.'

Clara stared at her mother helplessly. Of course she'd have to pay. She'd known that all along. Her life so far was one long bluff, but she couldn't bluff Kitty. Her mother was far too shifty herself.

Kitty smiled widely and triumphantly, and Clara knew her expression must be showing capitulation. What else could she do?

'How long will this payment go on for?' she asked listlessly, all hope of defeating Kitty gone.

'I'm your mother,' she said mockingly. 'You ought to be glad to help me out when I'm down on my luck.'

She re-lit the candle then reached up and turned off the gas, plunging the room into a weak light where shadows danced evilly again.

Obviously the meeting was over.

'Bring the money here every Friday night.'

'Oh, no! I'll never set foot in this stinking house again!' Clara cried out defiantly.

'You stuck up little bitch!' Kitty exclaimed, her glance vicious. She made an obvious effort to control her anger. 'All right, where then?'

Clara thought quickly. She wouldn't want to be seen talking to the likes of Dirty Kitty in public. The weekly meeting would have to be somewhere out of the way, far from prying eyes.

'The back lane behind Abertawe Street, top end,' she suggested. The lane was narrow, too narrow even for a cart. Few people would be about there in the late evening. 'Be there by seven sharp Friday evenings or you won't get your money. I won't wait around.'

'Oh, you'll wait, my girl, because I've got you just where I want you.' Kitty's tone of satisfaction changed abruptly to one of scorn. 'Well, Clara, you can bugger off now. Go on, get out! I'm sick of the sight of you already.'

Chapter Twenty-One

Jenni's happiness at Renee's reprieve continued well into the following morning. She worked away as hard as she could to show willing, at the same time revelling in her friend's chatter, thankful that everything was back to normal.

She glanced covertly at Jack from time to time, hoping to catch his eye so they might exchange a loving look. And right under Richie's nose, too.

Jack had worked this miracle and her heart swelled with love for him. Next time he asked her to meet him, she would, Jenni told herself resolutely. He deserved her devotion and she'd deny him no longer. Whatever misgivings she had about what Blodwen would have called sinning, she firmly suppressed. Hadn't she already agreed with her conscience that love was all?

Midmorning, Samuel Tregevny came strutting into the workroom, dapper in his pinstripe trousers, frock coat and stiff collar. He walked around the table once, stopping at each sewing machine, inspecting the work in progress, and Jenni saw Renee shift uncomfortably on her stool. But her work was first class. Mr Samuel would find no fault there.

Finally, he came to Jenni's machine and paused a few minutes longer.

'Very good, young woman,' he approved at last, his tone

edged with self-importance. 'Very good. Yes, I'm pleased with your work, Jenni.'

He moved away and stood at the centre of the room, chin elevated, his thumbs in the top pockets of his waistcoat, as though about to make a speech.

'However,' he began ominously, 'I'm concerned about your character.'

Jenni was stunned by his words. She turned on her stool and stared at him aghast.

'My character, Mr Samuel?'

An icy river of shock ran through her veins. Had he discovered her real identity? Was he about to sack her because her father had been a convicted murderer? Would he expose her and shame her in front of Jack?

'Father!' Richie stood up, a frown marking his dark face. 'What are you accusing Jenni of?'

She was glad someone had asked the question, but wished it had been Jack and not Richie. She glanced at Jack but his eyes were downcast, his expression impassive.

'Accuse!' Samuel thundered. 'I'm not accusing the young woman of anything. However, as I was about to say before I was so rudely interrupted . . .' he glared at Richie '. . . Renee's on probation and could be a bad influence whilst Jenni is lodging with her.'

'Oh, no!' Jenni exclaimed, appalled at the assertion.

Renee jumped up, looking upset.

'Mr Samuel, it'll never happen again. I promise, sir, I swear . . .'

He waved her down with a dismissive gesture.

'Well, that's as may be,' he said superciliously. 'We'll see. I gave you another chance because my son persuaded me to, but I still have grave doubts about you, I'll tell you that now, Renee.'

She wrung her hands in distress.

'But, Mr Samuel, sir . . .'

He held up a hand for silence.

'Enough!' he exclaimed, with an angry shake of his head. 'As I said, only time will prove if you've learned your lesson, Renee. Meanwhile, to be on the safe side, I've decided Jenni must lodge at Abertawe House with my family, out of temptation's way.'

'What?'

She jumped up from her stool, outraged. Samuel Tregevny had no business dictating where she should live and who her friends could be.

'But I don't *want* to leave Mrs Morris and Renee,' she cried out, angry at the idea. 'They're like my family now, and I'm very happy there.'

It was true. She was more than happy. It was as though she'd come home again. Since Sarah's death Jenni had lived without the sustaining warmth of the unselfish love her mother had given her.

Blodwen had given her a home, it was true, but it had been a bleak existence, with only the friendship of the Jukes sisters to comfort her. And with every hand turned against her, she'd despaired of ever being happy again.

Now she'd found Meg and Renee. A big-hearted warmth exuded from Meg, and Jenni had been basking in it for months, the feeling of really belonging growing stronger every day. She felt no guilt at looking on Meg as her second mother and Renee as the sister she'd never had. In Meg's house she was wanted, needed and cherished, she knew beyond doubt. No! A loving family couldn't be snatched from her again. It just wasn't fair!

'I've become very close to Renee and her mother, Mr Samuel, sir. Their ways suit me.'

That was the only way she could express what she felt for the Morrises. She regarded Samuel pleadingly but he stood there, lips pursed, brows knitted, looking deeply annoyed at her outburst.

'Exactly, young woman,' he said cuttingly. 'They're a bad influence! You'll move into Abertawe House Saturday evening, after work.'

'I won't!' Jenni cried out in fury. She almost stamped her foot to emphasise the strength of her feelings. 'You can't make me, either. You employ me, Mr Samuel, but you don't own me.'

His moustache bristled alarmingly.

'Moonlighting is theft,' he thundered, his glance baleful. 'And I won't have it. Now, young woman, either you take up lodgings at Abertawe House, or you can get out and take your cards this minute. What's it to be?'

Jenni opened her mouth to protest again, but before she could say anything, Richie interrupted.

'It's the best thing, Jenni,' he said, giving her a warning look. 'Under the circumstances.'

'Circumstances? What circumstances?' she flared, flashing him a killing glance. 'It's none of your business, is it? How dare you interfere?'

She disregarded a scandalised tut-tut from Samuel.

'This is *your* doing, isn't it?' she went on, glaring at Richie in fury. 'You haven't trusted me from the beginning. This is outrageous, this is! You're like something from the Victorian age, you are.'

'All right! That's it,' Samuel exploded. 'The rot has obviously set in. You're a troublemaker. Good skirt-hands are two a penny so you can pick up your cards immediately, young woman.'

'No! Wait, Father!' Jack rose to his feet. 'There's no need for that, surely? After all, it's understandable Jenni's upset. You've sprung this on her a bit suddenly. Surely she's free to see Renee outside shop hours?'

Samuel strutted about the room, grumbling and huffing and puffing, obviously not wanting to back down and lose face. Jenni watched him wearily. For a small man he made a lot of noise and fuss.

She was grateful that Jack had spoken up for her at last. He understood how she felt. While his brother – she glanced angrily at Richie – was as stuffy and as strait-laced as his father. She wouldn't be at all surprised if he were behind the whole thing.

Of course she didn't want to leave her job here. But she wouldn't let her employer dictate to her either. This was the 1920s after all. Things had changed since the war. But it was obvious Samuel Tregevny, and Richie, too, still clung to the old ways when master craftsmen virtually owned their workers' lives.

'Will you do as my father wishes, Jenni?' Richie asked bluntly. He seemed to have got over his surprise at her outburst. 'After all, it's not a great deal to ask.' He glanced at Samuel. 'I'm sure my father won't expect rent.'

Samuel made some incoherent noises through his moustache, then finally spoke.

'Nothing is scot-free,' he said curtly. 'Jenni can make herself useful in the house. I'm certain Violet can find a few chores for her.'

'I won't scrub floors!' she shouted defiantly, tossing her head. 'I won't be treated like a servant, so there! An indentured dress-maker, I am! My mother didn't sacrifice her . . .'

Jenni stopped abruptly. She'd almost said too much in her anger. She felt goose-pimples rise on the tops of her arms, re-alising how close she'd come to betraying herself in an unguarded moment. She swallowed hard, knowing she must be more careful in future.

Jack stepped forward, a broad smile on his face, and surprised her by putting a hand on her arm, but in a brotherly way.

'Jenni, would it be so bad?'

There was a glint in his eyes as he looked down on her. It spoke volumes to her, and made her want to catch her breath in sudden and unexpected excitement. She'd be living under the same roof as Jack; every evening when she got home from the shop he'd be there with her. It was something she hadn't con-sidered in her anger.

She glanced around quickly at the others, disturbed that they'd seen that telling glance, too, but they seemed unaware.

Jenni considered her new prospects. She would miss Renee

and Meg dreadfully because she loved them, too, but the idea of being closer to Jack made lodging at Abertawe House seem more appealing than it had a moment ago.

There *were* compensations, and she wouldn't be cut off from her new family altogether. She'd be with Renee all day, and could spend her evenings with Meg and her. And she'd be close to Jack day and night. The idea thrilled Jenni. She loved him so very much. One day he'd be part of her family, too, she just knew it in her heart.

But she mustn't be too hasty in agreeing. Renee and Meg's feelings must be considered, and her own need of them.

'No one would stop me seeing my friends on my afternoons off and at weekends?' she asked, glancing suspiciously at Samuel Tregevny.

If he said no she'd have to think again about leaving his employ despite the consequences. There were other jobs.

Living with the Tregevny family was a bleak prospect, except for Jack's presence. She wondered briefly how his wife would take it. Clara could probably make life very uncomfortable for her if she had a mind to, and Jenni wondered if she could stick it. But did she have any alternative?

Her shoulders drooped.

'I don't have much choice, do I, Mr Samuel?'

'Of course you do! You can leave my employ right now,' he said gravely. 'Or give me your solemn promise you'll respect our rules of employment.'

Jenni felt her facial muscles stiffen with annoyance again.

'A promise shouldn't be necessary, Mr Samuel,' she exclaimed heatedly. 'I've never given you cause for complaint yet, have I?'

'Shall we say it's settled, then?' Jack asked, smiling.

It was a dazzling smile and Jenni's heart melted again.

'All right,' she agreed resignedly. There was no other way to turn. 'I suppose so.'

What else could she do?

With a twinge of conscience she turned to look at Renee, who'd been silent all through the exchange. Her friend was looking glum and her eyes were suspiciously shiny. Jenni understood what this meant to her. Renee and Meg counted on her rent for an extra few shillings a week. How would they manage now?

'Sorry, Renee,' she said regretfully. 'You'll find another lodger in no time.'

But a spurt of heartache caught her sharply at the idea of someone else taking her cosy little bedroom at Meg's house, sharing the gossip, jokes and laughter of an evening, greeting the friendly neighbours popping in and out.

She felt guilty, as though Samuel Tregevny had made her betray her dearest friends. Oh, why had he put her in such an impossible position?

'We'll always be friends, won't we, Renee, love?' she asked, trying to reassure herself as much as Renee, and feeling tears sting her eyes. 'Friends for life, isn't it?'

Samuel Tregevny sat back, touching his napkin delicately to his moustache, and Clara watched him with irritation.

Why was the old fool hanging about? She knew from experience that no member of the family would rise from the table until Samuel did. Talk about the Dark Ages!

Clara had no patience with his pomposity, but normally she could keep her feelings in check. This evening, though, she was still nervous and jumpy; still affected by the horrendous meeting with her mother the evening before.

The walk home from the Cwm last night had had her breathless with an unreasoning fear. For some inexplicable reason she'd wanted to keep looking over her shoulder to make sure she wasn't being followed. She'd seen nothing, heard nothing, but the feeling wouldn't go away. She'd approached Abertawe House almost at a run as though demons were at her heels.

She'd not slept a wink, and now the least thing made her irritable. But she must be careful. Jack's future, and hers too, depended on keeping the old man sweet. Damn him!

'Dinner was very satisfactory, Violet,' Samuel said pompously.

He stood and pushed his chair back from the dining table, its legs scraping along the parquet flooring, the high-pitched squeal setting Clara's tender nerves on edge.

'I'll take a glass of port in the sitting-room,' he went on. 'See to it, please, Violet.'

Rising herself, Clara glanced at Violet's meek face and downcast eyes. She was totally under her father's thumb, and Clara felt disdain for her. She felt the irony of it, too. Being nicely brought up had its disadvantages, while being dragged up, as she'd been herself, toughened you. She'd never let anyone dominate her again.

She thought briefly of Kitty and felt a twinge of real panic. Her mother was putting her in a tight spot, but Clara would overcome that, too, and was ready to do whatever it took. No one would take away what she had.

Samuel was striding to the door. He paused and turned back to the family as they were moving away from the table.

'Oh, by the way, Violet,' he announced importantly, 'we're taking in a lodger, starting at the weekend.'

Clara was startled. Taking in lodgers was hardly a thing for the Tregevny family to do, and she wondered for a moment whether Samuel was going into his dotage.

Violet was staring at her father, too, looking completely nonplussed.

'A lodger, Father?' she murmured uncertainly. 'I don't understand . . .'

'You don't *need* to understand, Violet.' Samuel's tone was terse and dismissive. 'It's to do with the business. A young woman, a skirt-hand from the shop, will be lodging here from now on.'

'But who . . .'

'Jenni Thomas her name is,' Samuel called over his shoulder as he strode across the hall towards the front sitting-room. 'Make use of her in the house. See that she has plenty to keep her occupied. I'll leave you to make the necessary domestic arrangements.'

Jenni Thomas? Clara was stunned. She flashed an accusing glance at Jack still seated on the other side of the table, but his gaze slid away from hers.

Richie was following his father across the hall, whilst Violet was fetching the port decanter from the sideboard to take to her father in the sitting-room.

Without looking at her, Jack stood up, throwing his napkin down on to the table, preparing to follow the others, but Clara was determined to corner him before he could do so. She moved quickly to get between him and the door. She had to stop this before it was too late.

'Jack, what's the meaning of this? Did you put Father up to it?'

He still didn't look at her, his face remaining closed and expressionless, but she knew that look. He was hiding something. He might fool his family, but he couldn't fool his wife. She knew him intimately; could read him like a book; knew things others couldn't possibly know. She knew the real man inside. He was weak and wilful. She was the stronger and would master him — in time. If she had time?

'Jack!'

'Not now, Clara. Damn it all, can't a man have some peace?'

'Peace! Don't make me laugh,' she exclaimed, feeling anger sear her throat like a naked flame. 'You're behind this, Jack, aren't you? Contriving to bring your trollop into this house.'

'Don't be disgusting, Clara! It's my father's decision.' His gaze went straight past her shoulder, still unwilling it seemed to look her directly in the eye. 'It's nothing to do with me.'

'Bare-faced liar!' Clara hissed the words, holding on tightly to her self-control, though she felt like giving in to a screaming fit. 'This is the living end, Jack. I won't stand for it.'

'You stupid little fool!' he exclaimed through clenched teeth. 'Your jealousy will be our downfall yet. I'm telling you, it's my father's doing.'

He pushed roughly past her and strode towards the door then paused, turning to look directly at her for the first time. There was defiance in his eyes now.

'Take it up with him, if you must,' he went on. 'But I warn you, Clara, my father won't take kindly to womenfolk interfering in his business. If you know what's good for you, you'll keep your mouth shut.'

She remained in the dining-room for a few minutes, trying to regain control of her feelings, unable to face the others yet.

Jealousy? What a conceited fool Jack was. You had to feel love before you could feel jealousy. She didn't love Jack; doubted she could love any man. They were all the same — only after one thing. He was really no different from the man who'd deflowered her, stolen her girlhood.

She'd made up her mind a long time ago to beat them at their own game, and had prepared herself for it. Where she could, she'd studied the way decent, well-brought up people talked and behaved. She was a good mimic and had the nerve to carry it off, fooling the Tregevnys completely.

Stupid! All of them were stupid.

She'd seen Jack first as a meal ticket, no more than that, then realised he represented a whole new life, one of luxury and power. He'd been easy enough to snare. She should have realised he'd be difficult to hang on to, though, being the weak man that he was. But hang on she would! No one would take this life away from her.

Doris came into the dining-room to clear away and Clara

marched out, her determination to see off Jenni Thomas buoyed up anew.

Samuel was in his usual chair under the gaslight, reading the *Cambrian Leader*, his spectacles perched on the end of his nose.

Violet was sitting opposite engrossed in some needlework, but Clara ignored her. Let her hear what she likes, thought Clara. She's no threat.

'Father?' she began, keeping her tone firm but respectful. 'I am surprised you're willing to allow that Jenni Thomas to come into this respectable house.'

He looked up at her over his spectacles.

'What's that, Clara?' There was irritation in his voice.

'Well, you do remember I told you that this Jenni person has been embarrassing Jack, didn't I? Throwing herself at him in a most shameless way — quite brazen. She's nothing more than a . . . well, frankly, Father, she's loose. I did warn you.'

'Poppycock! I see no evidence of that, and Jack has said nothing to me.'

'He's mortified, Father,' said Clara quickly. 'And ashamed. He's afraid you'll think it's his fault.'

Samuel put down the paper and looked at her keenly, his brows crumpling into a deep frown.

'Clara, we've had this conversation before, if I'm not mistaken, and I'm finding it tiresome. I don't understand why you're so keen to be rid of Jenni Thomas. Do you know something specific against her? Eh?'

Clara shifted nervously from one foot to the other. She *knew* nothing for certain, not yet. But there was something, she *felt* it deep in her bones. The steely yet guarded look she'd glimpsed in Jenni Thomas's eyes that morning in the workroom had been revealing. To Clara, at least.

It takes one to know one, she thought with sudden clarity.

She herself was taking pains to hide a shady past, and if she wasn't completely mistaken, this Jenni Thomas had something to hide, too. She *must* find out what it was.

'Of course there's nothing,' Samuel said confidently at her silence. 'But, Clara, surely you're not implying Jack's not man enough to deal with a chit of a girl? Nonsense, woman!'

'Female instinct, Father,' she retorted desperately. 'Jack is a changed man, I know. And maybe you think less of me because of the way our marriage was . . . well, rushed.'

She knew she was taking a big chance in bringing up the delicate fact that she had supposedly fallen pregnant to Jack before marriage. It had been a gamble, but the only way to force his hand. Two years ago she'd counted on Samuel's pride in his son and his fear of scandal. His pride had worked in her favour then. Now it was working against her.

Jack was weak and would always be easily swayed by a willing woman, though Samuel wouldn't let himself see it. And maybe that was just as well. She wouldn't want her father-in-law to think Jack unworthy and change his will.

'My family were decent and respectable, Father,' Clara went on hastily, endeavouring to put haughty pride into her voice. 'And every womanly instinct tells me this Jenni Thomas is . . . well, not to put too fine a point on it . . . a trollop!'

There was a squeal of shock from Violet.

'Father, is this true?' She stood up abruptly, the needlework falling to the floor. 'Are we to endure a woman of *that* kind in our home? These women are everywhere, it seems. What a sign of the times! Why, only the other day such a woman came to our back door, and Doris said . . .'

'Violet, please keep quiet!' Clara interrupted quickly, terror clawing at her heart, knowing instinctively that her sister-in-law was referring to Kitty. 'Father and I are discussing business matters.'

Samuel whipped off his spectacles, folded the newspaper and rose to his feet.

'The discussion, such as it was, is over, Clara.' He took a watch out of his waistcoat pocket and glanced briefly at it. 'And I trust I'll hear no more of it.'

'But, Father!' She almost clutched at his arm in desperation. 'Jenni Thomas is trying to get money out of Jack, I just know it. She mustn't come here! Think of the scandal!'

'Clara, you're hysterical,' he snapped impatiently. 'Take an aspirin and go to bed. Perhaps we should get Dr McClusky in to look at you.'

She collapsed into a nearby chair, drained, knowing she was beaten.

After Samuel had stalked out, Clara was aware of Violet staring at her, eyes as round as saucers.

'Is she really a trollop?' she asked, her voice barely above a shocked whisper. Yet Clara could see the light of curiosity and fascination in her sister-in-law's eyes, and regarded her with speculation.

There was more than one way to skin a cat. Violet might have her uses yet. If Samuel wouldn't get rid of the girl, perhaps she could be forced out some other, more subtle way.

Clara realised she could make living in this house very difficult for Jenni Thomas if she were clever and put her mind to it. Her spirits rose a little at the new notion. She needed to get Violet on to her side.

'The blatant way she throws herself at my husband is disgusting, Violet, really disgusting.' Clara shook her head and set an expression of deep aversion on her face. 'I don't know what your father is thinking of, bringing that girl into this respectable house, exposing us to her degrading behaviour. We'll be the talk of the Hafod.'

'Ooh!' Violet put her hand to her throat in obvious apprehension. 'What will Nath . . . I mean, what will our friends think?'

'We'll be ostracised, Violet. Think of it!' Clara said vehemently, jumping to her feet as she sensed an opportunity. 'You won't be able to show your face at the Hafod Ladies' Sewing Circle, I promise you.'

Violet flopped down on to her chair again.

'Oh, goodness me! Clara, what are we to do?'

'We'll have to get rid of her ourselves,' Clara responded quickly.

Violet's ringless fingers clutched at her throat again as she stared back. 'What can *we* do?'

Make her life hell! Clara thought with relish.

'Well, she certainly doesn't deserve to be comfortable in this house, does she? Put a bed up in the attic room for her. She deserves no more than that!'

Violet put a finger to her mouth, a doubtful expression on her face.

'It's awfully dusty up there, Clara. It hasn't been used for years. It may be damp, too.'

'Good!' Clara came and stood over her sister-in-law. 'Violet, we've got to stand together against this . . . this viper your father is determined to bring into the very heart of our family. Don't you agree with me?'

'Oh, I certainly do!' Violet sounded breathless with consternation.

'Make her useful in the house, he said,' Clara reminded her. 'So work her hard, Violet. She'll have her food in the kitchen, of course, with the servant.'

Anything else was unthinkable!

'She's never to come into the main part of the house, do you hear? She must use the back stairs,' Clara went on rapidly, realising her sister-in-law was putty in her hands. 'And only the back entrance. She'll use the lavatory in the yard, of course. I mean, God knows what one could catch from such women!'

'Ooh, heavens above!'

'Oh, yes, I know just how you feel, Violet, my dear,' Clara said with a shake of her head. 'It sickens me, too.'

She felt the weight on her heart lift. With Violet's co-operation she could make life at Abertawe House much worse than hell for Jenni Thomas. Then maybe she'd get out of their lives at last.

Chapter Twenty-Two

Saturday evening arrived far too quickly for Jenni. It had been a miserable day in the workroom, with Renee hardly saying a word throughout and Jenni feeling more and more guilty at leaving her best friends in the lurch. On top of the guilt lay a morbid dread of the prospect before her. Again fate was forcing a change to her life, and she doubted it was a change for the better.

Dinnertime at Meg's had been quiet too, until, overcome by misery, Jenni broke down crying, cradling her head on Meg's plump knees, looking for forgiveness and reassurance.

'It's not your fault, *bach*,' Meg said gently, stroking Jenni's hair. 'Manage we will, don't you worry. At least Renee's got her job back, and that's the main thing.'

'I don't *want* to go from you, Meg,' Jenni said, through sobs. 'I'm happy here. I wish now I'd never seen the inside of Tregevny's.'

In her heart, though, she knew that wasn't true. She'd fallen in love with Jack and wouldn't have missed that for the world.

'Listen!' Meg said coaxingly. 'I expect you'll be by here with us most of your time anyway, love, so don't fret.'

Directly after tea Jenni stepped up to the imposing front door of Abertawe House, comforting herself with Meg's loving words. Her heart was pounding and her hand shaking as she lifted the knocker, wondering what her reception would be in the home of her employer.

She'd already made a bitter enemy in Clara Tregevny. How would she like Jenni living in the same house? The whole thing was impossible. Jenni decided the best plan would be to keep out of Clara's way as much as she could, and the rest of the Tregevny family's, too.

She bit her lip at the thought of her isolation. Life promised to be very lonely for her in future. But she'd have to stick it out. She'd been through much worse in Llawr-y-bryn and Trehafod, and wouldn't be browbeaten by the Tregevnys or made a skivvy by them, either.

After all, she wasn't destitute. She had money and could go anywhere. But that meant parting from Jack when they were meant to be together, she just knew it in her heart.

After a nervous wait on the front step, and just as she had an urge to run away, a maid answered her knock.

'Jenni Thomas, I am,' she told the older girl. 'I'm expected.'

'Come in, then,' the maid said.

Jenni stepped into the wide hallway, small suitcase in hand. At least moving home was no physical problem, she thought wryly; she had few possessions in the world.

'Wait by here,' the maid said. 'I'll tell Miss Tregevny. Oh, and I'm Doris by the way. I expect we'll be seeing a lot of each other.'

Jenni smiled gratefully. 'Hello, Doris.'

Before Doris could take a step towards the sitting-room, Clara Tregevny rushed into view, almost skidding on the Chinese rug on the parquet floor in her haste. Jenni had the immediate impression Clara had been awaiting her arrival and bristled at the prospect of further hostility.

They stared at each for a moment. There was a fiery glint in Clara's eyes, and Jenni raised her chin defiantly in response to it. She had no axe to grind. If Clara did, well, that was her problem.

'Look!' Jenni began, deciding it was best to be blunt. 'I don't like you and you don't like me. I didn't ask to come here but let's make the best of it, shall we, Clara?'

'*Mrs* Tregevny to you!' she snapped. 'Know your place!'

Jenni's lips tightened. So it was going to be war. All right! She was ready for it. She opened her mouth to retort but Clara forestalled her.

'And use the *back* door in future.' Her voice was loud and discordant, hardly able to contain her anger. 'Do you hear?'

Jenni felt her hackles rise. She wouldn't be treated like the kitchen drudge.

'Don't you speak to *me* in that tone,' she exclaimed tartly, tossing her head. 'I'm as good as you any day. Probably better, too, from what I've heard.'

'*What?*' Clara flushed deeply, and her eyes flashed a dangerous light. 'What d'you mean by that?'

Jenni held back an answer, realising she'd said too much and knowing instinctively this was not the time to reveal what she knew, or thought she knew, especially not in front of an audience. Meg might have got it wrong and Jenni wouldn't malign anyone, especially without proof. She'd been the hapless victim of that unkindness herself in the past.

'I'm a lodger, not the boot-boy,' she said angrily, side-stepping the question. 'I don't like this arrangement anymore than you do. If you resent me so much, speak to Mr Samuel and do us both a favour.'

'Huh!' Clara put her fists on her hips, looking disdainful. 'Don't act the little innocent. I know why you're here. You've wormed your way into this house but it won't get you anywhere, because I'll be watching you.' Her eyes narrowed. 'There's more to you than meets the eye. I warn you, I'll find out what.'

Jenni felt her face stiffen with shock and fury, aware of Doris standing by, staring from one to the other of them, eyes as round as saucers, as though unable to believe her own ears.

Jenni didn't like that threat; it was a punch too close to her heart. But despite Doris's presence, she couldn't let it pass un-challenged. She was unwilling to let Clara gain an inch.

Lifting her chin, Jenni made her tone deliberately sneering.

'You're making a proper exhibition of yourself, Clara. You'll be the gossip of the chip shop after this performance. Not exactly the manners of a *lady*, is it?'

Clara was visibly fuming, her expression venomous and very revealing of her inner heart. Jenni could well believe everything Meg said about her.

Clara's red lips drew back in a silent snarl.

'You impudent little slut!'

Doris gasped, and Jenni decided she'd had enough.

'Doris! Fetch my employer, Mr Samuel, if you please,' she demanded loudly and firmly. 'I've had enough of these uncalled for insults from this . . . this female by here.'

'Mr . . . Mr Samuel's out,' Doris stammered. 'Miss Violet's in, though.'

'It's . . . it's all right, Doris,' a querulous voice said nearby. 'You can go back to the kitchen now.'

A tall, thin woman with untidy mouse-coloured hair, prob-ably in her thirties, came hesitantly into the hall and stood at Clara's side, staring at Jenni in the oddest way, as though she'd just sprouted horns on her head and had cloven feet.

'I'm Miss Violet Tregevny,' the thin woman said almost timidly, still eyeing Jenni warily. 'This is the family entrance. Please use the back way from now on . . . er . . . Miss Thomas.'

'I've no objection to that, Miss Tregevny,' Jenni said tartly, though striving to be reasonable. 'But I won't be spoken to by *any* member of the family as though I'm a piece of dirt. A respectable, hardworking girl, I am, and I'm being treated shabbily. I'll complain to Mr Samuel.'

Clara hooted derisively.

'Huh! That's rich, that is.'

Jenni held herself in check, remaining silent with difficulty.

She had no wish to bring Jack's sister into her dispute with Clara. The woman looked terrified enough already for some reason. Besides, Doris was still hanging about near a door at the back of the hallway, and she wasn't missing a word.

'Perhaps Doris can see me to my room,' Jenni said, swallowing her defiance. 'Want to settle in, I do. I've been working all day.'

Clara was still belligerent.

'Up the back stairs you go,' she said nastily. 'And remember this: you eat in the kitchen, use the outside lavatory, and you don't come into the main part of the house. Got that?'

Jenni ground her teeth in anger, knowing she had no rebuttal. The Tregevnys could make their own rules; she had no power to kick against them.

Life was going to be miserable from now on, but she'd stick it out, she promised herself, for the sake of her job, and for Jack too. When he finally rid himself of his dreadful wife, things would be different. Jenni comforted herself with the thought of their future happiness together.

Doris came forward again, her plain face alive with interest, glancing quickly at Violet Tregevny who nodded briefly.

'This way, Jenni,' Doris murmured, gesturing towards the door at the back of the hall.

When they were through the door and in a dark passage, Doris paused, pointing to a narrow door nearby.

'The indoor lavvy is by here, look, Jenni.' She wrinkled her nose. 'Supposed to be for family use only. But you use it if you wants to, kid. I do when it's raining. Bugger 'em, I say!'

She moved on, ushering Jenni through another door to a roomy back lobby. She pointed out the kitchen and scullery to the left, and on the other side a big wash-house with two stone sinks, a pair of copper boilers and a couple of mangles.

'Washday every Monday,' Doris announced. 'Mrs Harrigan comes in for that, and it takes her all day, poor old dab.'

Jenni thought of the chores Mr Samuel had mentioned. She'd

kick up a fuss if they tried to make her help with the weekly washing! But she'd probably be given the dirtiest jobs if Clara had anything to do with it.

'Does Mrs Jack Tregevny run the household?' Jenni asked tentatively. 'She seems to have a lot to say.'

'No, Miss Violet runs the house, but it's old man Tregevny what calls the tune.' Doris sniffed begrudgingly. 'Miss Violet's all right, mind, but a proper old maid, if you know what I mean.'

'Mrs Jack . . .'

'Hey! Don't take any notice of that stuck-up piece Clara,' Doris exclaimed dismissively as she started to climb a narrow staircase. '*Duw*! I could tell you some tales about her, I could, but I wants to keep my job, don't I?'

Jenni said nothing. She'd taken a liking to Doris, but she was obviously a gossip. So least said, the better.

'They've put you in the attic room,' the maid went on, sounding scandalised. 'It hasn't been used for donkey's years. What've they got against you, kid?'

Doris led her to a reasonably sized room under the eaves, right at the top of the house. There was a narrow iron bedstead under a small round window that reminded Jenni of a porthole on a ship. Not much light was able to come through the dingy panes.

There was an old chest-of-drawers and a wooden chair, and that was the extent of her comfort. The floorboards were bare, though a small, tatty rug had been put down at the bedside. The room smelled of dust and damp, and Jenni shivered in disappointment. Her room at Meg's had been warm and clean, and she was missing it already.

'Disgraceful, I call it,' Doris commented, looking around the room. 'You said you was a lodger here, Jenni,' she went on, curiosity spiking every word. 'You're not going to pay good money to rent this rat hole, are you, love?'

Jenni put down her suitcase and sat on the bed which creaked loudly under her weight, feeling suddenly drained of all spirit.

Surely Jack didn't know how she was being treated? And what was she doing here at all? she asked herself miserably. She could hardly believe she was letting this happen.

'I think I'm supposed to do chores in lieu of rent,' she said ruefully.

'Tsk! Taking advantage of you, they are,' said Doris in disgust. 'Run you ragged they will if you let them. That's why I goes home every night. That Clara would have me up all hours if I lived in.'

Doris lifted the suitcase on to the bed.

'Put your stuff away, Jenni,' she said, sympathy in her voice. 'Then come down to the kitchen and have a bit of supper. I'll make you welcome if nobody else will.'

Jenni smiled, feeling suddenly emotional.

'Thanks, Doris. I've already had tea with my friends.'

'Well, come and have a cuppa then, and a bit of my fruit cake.'

Later, Jenni ate the cake and drank the tea gratefully, listening to Doris's chatter as she rushed back and forth from the dining-room, clearing up after the family's supper.

She hoped she'd found another friend. Thoughts of Meg and Renee made her heart ache. Suddenly, although she'd left them only a short while before, Jenni needed to see them again.

'It's getting late but I'm going to slip around to Hafod Row,' she said. 'That's where I used to lodge, with Meg Morris.'

'Oh, I know Meg,' Doris exclaimed cheerfully. 'My mam and Meg are big pals. A lovely woman, mind, Meg is. And her Renee's a scream, isn't she?'

'They're my very best friends,' Jenni admitted, unable to keep a sob from her voice. 'And I'm missing them .'

Doris jumped up from the table quickly, touching Jenni's arm and looking earnestly into her face.

'Oh! Never mind, kid,' she said sympathetically. 'You'll be all right. We'll have our supper together every night. We eat whatever the family eats, and that means the very best of food, mind. So there's a bright side as well, love.'

Jenni had to smile at Doris's coaxing tone, which was as though she was speaking to a child though she wasn't many years older than Jenni.

'Doris, I think we're going to get on fine.'

She beamed. 'Good! Supper's at half-six every evening on the dot. I goes home about half-seven after I've cleared up.'

She sighed, looking wistfully at the sink already piled high with used crockery.

'Give you a hand with those before I go, I will,' Jenni volunteered willingly, wanting to repay her kindness.

'Hey, kid, you're a pal!' Doris looked pleased.

Later, Jenni went out into the lobby to fetch her hat and coat and was startled to find Clara standing near the passage door.

She made a pretence of closing it as though she'd only just arrived but Jenni was sure she'd been standing there some time, listening to their conversation as they washed up.

Of all the sly, underhand things!

'Heard enough, did you?' Jenni snapped, glaring.

'Don't know what you mean,' Clara retorted sharply, her nose in the air. 'I'm looking for Doris.'

'Oh, yes? And I'm a Dutchman!'

With a killing glance at Clara, Jenni reached for her coat, hastily shrugged herself into it, and pulled on her hat.

After the warmth of the tea and the friendliness of Doris, Jenni was feeling more settled. She had no choice but to lodge here, at least for the time being, but had made up her mind Clara wouldn't get away with anymore harassment. There was a limit, and Jenni had reached it.

'I'm not stupid, Clara,' she went on disdainfully. 'You were spying on me, and that's despicable.'

'I've told you before, don't be familiar with me,' Clara snapped. 'I'm Mrs Tregevny to you, and don't forget it.'

She stepped closer, her eyes glittering.

'We don't have an audience now so I'll speak plainly. I'm

not giving you a chance to latch on to Jack. He's mine! Got that?'

'He despises you,' Jenni retorted hotly. 'And don't pretend you love him. He's told me everything about you.' She raised her chin. 'Though perhaps I could tell him a few things he doesn't know. Like . . .'

'*What*?' Clara's whole body stiffened and her face became pale.

For a moment a shaft of remorse pierced Jenni's heart. She was behaving like the small-minded people of Llawr-y-Bryn who'd driven her out. Yet she needed to defend herself.

'Don't push me too far, Clara,' she warned. 'Don't make me use what I know.'

'You know nothing!' Clara's breathing was jagged. 'You're bluffing again. God! You're a sly little bitch. Anyone would think *you* had nothing to hide.'

The tension was rising. Jenni felt apprehension prick her skin and was suddenly wary. Clara was too canny by half. Without another word or glance in her direction, Jenni marched towards the back door, unwilling to waste anymore of her evening when she could be in the company of loving friends.

'Going out?' Clara asked rudely,.

'What's it look like?' Jenni snapped. 'And what's it got to do with you anyway? I come and go as I please.'

Clara looked down her nose arrogantly.

'If you're not back by half-past nine, the door will be locked and bolted and you'll be locked out. Don't say I didn't warn you.'

'Well, thanks for nothing!' Jenni called scornfully over her shoulder and went out, slamming the door behind her.

On Sunday, after breakfast, Jenni went round to Hafod Row again, intending to spend the whole day with Renee. They went to chapel in the morning. Jenni guiltily accepted Meg's offer of dinner, then she and Renee caught the Mumbles train to

Oystermouth for the afternoon. Jenni dreaded having to return to Abertawe House.

Meg was still scandalised by Jenni's treatment there.

'I knew old Samuel's wife, Alice. A real lady she was, and shrewd, too. That Clara would never have got anywhere near their Jack if Alice had been alive,' Meg told Jenni. 'Don't you stand for any of Clara's nonsense, Jenni love. Let her know you've got the goods on her, right enough.'

But Jenni had no intention of going any further. If Clara had secrets, so did she, and perhaps more damning than Clara's. With her own shameful background to disguise, she was hardly in a position to throw stones at anyone. She'd have to find another way to deal with her present uncomfortable position.

She was back at Abertawe House by six for supper. Meg and Renee had begged her to eat with them, but she wouldn't impose again. They had a hard enough time providing for themselves on Renee's wages without feeding guests.

Doris served supper to the family at six-thirty sharp. Sitting in the kitchen waiting, Jenni glimpsed the dining-room through the serving hatch and could hear Samuel Tregevny holding forth, his strident tones rising above the others.

Doris then put up two plates of food for them, and handed one to Jenni.

'Here you are, kid. Tuck into that – roast beef and Yorkshire pudding. And there's second helpings, if you want them.'

Jenni stared. There was plenty of roast beef on the plate and all the trimmings – more than enough. What a meal! She thought about Meg and Renee, and wished they could enjoy the same feast.

'Do the family always eat as well as this?'

'Oh, aye!' Doris said, busy with her knife and fork. 'The old man likes his food. And I'm a good cook, even if I say so myself.'

Jenni had to agree. It was all delicious.

They'd hardly started on the food when the bell in the dining-room rang.

'Oh, blast it!' Doris exclaimed testily, throwing down her knife and fork. 'What now? Can't I have my grub in peace?'

She got up reluctantly and went into the dining-room through the service door. Within a few minutes she was back, and with a bemused expression on her plain but pleasant face as she looked at Jenni.

'He wants *you* in there, Jenni. You go on in. I'll bring in your plate. I've already set a chair for you.'

Jenni swallowed convulsively, almost choking on a mouthful of carrots.

'Me? Go in there!' She shook her head vehemently, aghast at the idea. 'Oh, no! Not me!'

'He says you're to have your meals in the dining-room with the family from now on.' Doris giggled. 'Hey! There's shabby posh, isn't it? Sleeping in a rat hole but eating off best Swansea China plates.'

Stunned, Jenni dropped her own knife and fork with a clatter. 'I'm *not* going in there!'

Having to sit at table with Clara, facing her virulent tongue, was unthinkable. Richie would probably try to humiliate her, too. She'd be looked down on by Mr Samuel, and shamed in front of Jack. It was too much to ask.

'I won't, Doris,' Jenni said resolutely. 'So you can go and tell him now.'

'Are you sure, kid?'

'Absolutely! I'm eating out here with you.'

She almost added – where she belonged. And it was true. She had little in common with the Tregevnys, even though she was in love with Jack. Her upbringing was very different from their moneyed ways, and she wouldn't let them demean her even more.

With a shrug Doris returned to the dining-room, and was gone for a few minutes longer.

With a sigh of triumph, Jenni picked up her knife and fork and resumed eating, feeling annoyed that thanks to the unwelcome interruption, her lovely meal was getting cold.

The service door opened and Jenni looked up, a question on her lips, expecting to see Doris. Instead Richie Tregevny limped into the kitchen.

Astonished, she rose to her feet quickly, pushing back her chair. This was the last thing she'd expected.

'Didn't you understand my father's request, Jenni?' Richie asked. There was irritation in his voice, and she bristled at his tone.

'Request!' Jenni threw down her napkin on to the table. 'Sounded more like an order to me, and I won't put up with it.'

She stood defiant and straight-backed yet a tremor began to run through her body, more from anger than nervousness. So, Mr Samuel had sent his son to do his dirty work.

'You refuse? Why? I thought you'd have welcomed it.'

'Like an honour, you mean?' Jenni raised her voice scornfully. 'No, thanks! I'm not about to let you and that . . . that woman make a fool of me.'

Especially not in front of Jack. How would she bear that?

Richie frowned, looking offended yet puzzled, too.

'Woman? You mean my sister?'

'I mean Clara,' Jenni burst out. 'Nothing but insults I've had from her since I arrived earlier.'

'Insults? What d'you mean?'

'Treating me like dirt, she is, and your sister looks at me like I'm something the cat dragged in.' Jenni raised her chin . 'Well, I won't stand for it, so there!'

Jenni was galled to see Richie smile, certain it was dismissively. She should have known she wouldn't get any fair play from *him*.'

'You're exaggerating, Jenni,' he said, shaking his head, and taking a few uneven steps towards her. 'Violet isn't like that. She's as shy as a mouse.'

'That Clara's been telling lies about me,' Jenni flared angrily. 'I know she has. She's got it in for me for . . .' she stammered uncertainly '. . . for some reason.'

If she went in there now Clara's animosity would be obvious to the entire family. Clara hated her and could wound her mortally. Jenni had seen fear in her eyes the day she'd burst uninvited into Meg's house, and it was there again today. Clara was afraid of losing her husband.

Did she have any real feelings for Jack? Suddenly, Jenni felt an uncomfortable spurt of conscience, then remembered Clara's spite. No, she wasn't moved by love – it was plain avarice. She was as hard as nails, Jenni had seen it in her face earlier.

But how hard was Jenni being herself? She felt a quiver of contrition at the idea that she could deliberately and selfishly hurt someone, even someone as loathsome as Clara. Was she turning into the same kind of morally weak woman her mother had been? Was she heading for a fall, too?

But she loved Jack so very much, and how could a love like this be wrong? No, it wasn't wrong. She and Jack were meant for each other. Determined, she looked steadily at Richie, her chin raised defiantly.

'I'm sorry, Mr Richie. I'm staying right here with Doris. Mr Samuel can sack me if he likes, but that's my final word.'

Richie looked down at her for a moment, his gaze intense.

Fleetingly, and incomprehensibly, she thought she saw something of Jack in his face, and felt confused. Two brothers couldn't be more different, and yet . . .

'You're a strange girl, Jenni,' he said slowly. 'Never met anyone quite like you.'

His eyes lingered on her for a moment more, and Jenni felt even more uncomfortable. She still couldn't make up her mind whether she liked him or not. Sometimes he appeared aloof and even arrogant, despite his disability, and other times, as now, he seemed more friendly.

But did she trust him? He was a true Tregevny, cut in his father's pattern. No! He wasn't like Jack at all.

'Very well,' he said after a moment more, and turned to go back into the dining-room. He paused in the doorway to look back at her.

'I understand you're in the attic room. Are you sure you're comfortable there, Jenni?'

Comfortable! Was he being sarcastic? She swallowed down an angry reply. Had he been up there recently? Apparently not! But she was determined not to complain, especially to him. She'd stick things out for Jack's sake.

'I'll manage, thank you,' she answered stiffly.

His gaze was still keen, as though he could see right inside her head, and Jenni shuffled her feet awkwardly. He couldn't know how she felt about Jack, surely? He certainly wouldn't approve, not only because Jack was married, but because in Richie's view the likes of her were beneath the Tregevny family. How had Clara managed to trick them all?

'Well, if there is anything you need,' he said, 'just ask me.'

He was about to disappear when Jenni thought of something and called quickly: 'There *is* something, Mr Richie.'

He waited for her to explain.

'A key,' she went on in a rush. 'A key to the back door. Clara says it will be locked and bolted by half-nine, but that's too early for me, especially with the summer coming and the light nights. I may want to go to the pictures or for a walk with my friends. After all, I *am* a lodger, not a jailbird.' She lifted her chin confidently. 'I have a *right* to a key!'

'So you do!' Richie agreed, surprising her. 'And Violet runs the household, not Clara. Doris must've a spare key somewhere. Ask her. If she can't find it, let me know.'

He smiled again, and the darkness of his usual expression disappeared.

'And you're right, Jenni. Abertawe House isn't your jail. You're as free as a bird.'

When he'd gone, Jenni sat down thoughtfully, only vaguely aware of Doris's excited chatter.

Richie was a mystery. When he smiled he was quite attractive. Pity he didn't do it more often! She wondered why he wasn't married. Perhaps he was too conscious of his twisted foot? But that would be no barrier to any decent woman who loved him, she reflected.

All in all, Richie Tregevny was quite a catch.

Chapter Twenty-Three

Midsummer was proving to be lovely, the late-June evenings scented and balmy. Jenni and Renee made the most of their free time, taking the Mumbles train as far as the Pier or strolling on the promenade. It was all so different from the bleakness of the Rhondda, and Jenni was ready to sit for hours admiring the great sweep of Swansea Bay and the faint mauve hills of Devonshire across the stretch of sea.

She was glad of Renee's amiable company and Meg's friendly and cheerful face, ready to welcome her back into their home. Life at Abertawe House was anything but amiable. She had expected to see more of Jack at the house, but he made no attempt to seek her out. He was being discreet, she decided, wary of Clara's eagle eyes. Jenni didn't know if she were disappointed or not, but still felt lonely.

'You look real down, Jen,' Renee observed as they sat near the Cenotaph commemorating the war dead. 'It's that blinking Clara, isn't it? Has she been giving you hell again?'

Jenni had to smile at Renee's words, but hell described it precisely. Yet she was determined to bear it for Jack's sake.

'She has a go at me every time our paths cross,' she said wearily. 'She was so furious about the key, I thought she'd spit out tin tacks. But since Mr Richie gave me permission there's nothing she can do. She really hates me, though, Renee.'

Sometimes, Clara's undisguised hatred made Jenni's blood run cold.

'You ought to take her down a peg or two,' Renee said with some spirit. 'You know enough about her.'

Jenni shook her head, wary now.

'It's all hearsay, Renee. And, besides, we should be careful what we say about people. There's nothing to be gained from making trouble.'

Many months had passed since she'd left the Rhondda, but the shame and humiliation of her own family scandal still haunted her. She'd hoped she'd escaped it, but one could never tell with fate.

In truth, she couldn't cause that kind of pain to others, not even her rival and most dangerous enemy, Clara Tregevny. There would be no satisfaction in it. Jenni had to believe she'd triumph in the end, and steeled herself not to take Clara's taunts and insults to heart.

'At least Violet is a little more friendly since I started helping out with the chores,' she went on. 'We sorted all the linen closets together last weekend. She even thanked me and insisted I call her Violet! She's all right.'

Renee pulled off her hat and ruffled her hair.

'They're putting on you, they are,' she said with feeling. 'You're too good-natured, that's your trouble.'

She sighed dejectedly.

'I'm fed up, Jen, kid. I wish I had a bloke, you know, with the prospect of getting married. I got you and Mam, I know, but deep down, I'm lonely. God, let's face it, I need a man!'

'Renee!' Jenni was shocked at such candour.

'Well, what *is* there in life for a girl without a man, eh?' Renee asked, looking despondent. 'Rheumatism and a cold bed, that's what.'

Jenni laughed. It was good to have something to laugh about.

'Mr Right will come along, soon, Renee, love, you just wait and see.'

A few weeks later Jenni remembered her prophecy with something like regret, for which she was immediately ashamed.

Heavy velvet drapes and curtains in some of the bedrooms at Abertawe House needed to be taken down for dry cleaning, and Violet had insisted on Jenni's help. Consequently a few evenings went by without the friends meeting to go out together.

On her first free evening in days, Jenni hurried round to Meg's, looking forward to some cheerful company for a few hours before returning to the dreary loneliness of Abertawe House.

Jenni revelled in Meg's warm welcome, then noticed her face was wreathed in more smiles than usual.

'Where's Renee, Meg?'

'Well! I'm glad you asked me that, *bach*.' Meg beamed. 'Our Renee has met a nice young man. She's out with him this evening. Gone to the pictures, I expect.'

Jenni was taken aback for a moment, feeling bereft before realising how selfish that was.

'Well, good for her!' But Jenni was puzzled. 'She never said anything to me in work today. How long has she known him?'

'Only days, I believe.' Meg couldn't seem to stop smiling. 'Renee's shy about it, I think. Didn't know whether he'd turn up or not. Well, she's not come back so he must've.'

Tears suddenly brimmed in her eyes.

'Oh, Jenni, there's glad I am our Renee's found somebody at last. I was worried . . . you know what I mean. After I'm gone, like, I didn't want her to be lonely. Now there's a chance she'll have a family and kids of her own.'

'Bound to happen one day, wasn't it?' Jenni said.

In her heart she was pleased for Renee, but wondered at the

wisdom of banking too much on this being the real thing. Though love could come in a flash, as she knew better than anyone.

'What's his name? Is he local?' Jenni was full of curiosity now.

'His name's Ossie.' Meg beamed happily. 'He's very keen on her, so Renee thinks. And guess what, Jenni, *bach*? Ossie comes from the Valleys, like you, so he's bound to be a tidy bloke, isn't he?'

Jenni leaned forward, giving Meg a warm hug and a kiss on the cheek, overcome by the older woman's obvious delight.

In her heart, though, she couldn't help feeling bleak. With Renee courting – if this was the real thing – she'd have little time for Jenni. She'd miss her friend dreadfully and knew there was a lot of loneliness ahead of her still.

The following morning Jenni couldn't wait to see her friend at work. Renee was already at her machine when Jenni hurried into the workroom.

She knew Jack hadn't come in yet; she'd heard the echo of his voice in the front hall before leaving the house, and had just seen Richie in the shop below, already dealing with an early-bird customer.

This was the ideal time to question Renee about her young man, and wanting to make the most of their precious minutes together, she quickly hung up her coat and hat and took her place at the table.

'Well, Renee?' Jenni smiled at her friend. 'What's he like? Are you really keen? Is he good-looking?'

Renee giggled almost shyly and flushed.

'I'm lucky to have a bloke at all,' she said. 'Never mind a good-looking one. Ossie's okay. I've seen worse.'

Jenni blinked, expecting Renee to be bubbling over with enthusiasm for her new conquest; perhaps a little love-struck, too. Was there some doubt in her mind?

'You're *not* keen, are you, Renee? I can tell,' Jenni said. Or was it wishful thinking on her part, unwilling to lose Renee as a close companion?

'"Course I am!' she exclaimed vehemently. 'He's not Prince Charming, that's all. Just a bloke. He's got plenty of money in his pocket, and he's willing to spend it. What more could a girl want?'

Renee so longed for a bloke of her own. Would she be foolish enough to settle for second-best just for the sake of having someone interested in her? It sounded like a recipe for unhappiness, and Jenni didn't want her best friend to be hurt.

'I dunno, Renee,' she responded uncertainly. 'Love, perhaps?'

'Oh! Give us a chance, will you?' Renee exclaimed. 'I haven't known him five minutes yet.' She paused, then grinned. 'He likes a bit of a kiss and cuddle, though, mind.' She made saucer eyes at Jenni. 'And I'm not averse to that, as you know.'

'Renee!' Jenni was shocked. 'On your first time out together? Oh, Renee!'

Jack had kissed her, Jenni reminded herself, and they weren't even out together. But that was different. Jack loved her and she loved him, so it was understandable. But this Ossie was a stranger. Jenni wanted to know more about him.

'Is he working?'

'Oh, kid!' Renee did enthuse now. 'Ossie's got a job with the Council. I don't know what he does exactly, but it must pay good money. He spent a whole pound on me last night. A whole pound, mind! I told him, my mam and me could live like queens for a week on that. He said there's plenty more where that came from.'

She paused, grinning from ear to ear.

'Hey! Jen, kid, I think I've fallen in lucky by here. Me and Mam could be set up for life if I play my cards right.'

Jenni smiled back, but she still couldn't be so enthusiastic. It sounded too good to be true. Not that Renee couldn't find a decent chap *and* with money, too. And any man who got her for a wife would be the luckiest. She was so good-natured and warm-hearted.

Life wasn't the same anymore, Jenni found, now that Ossie had come into Renee's life. All she could talk about during their hours working together at their machines over the next few weeks was Ossie. Ossie this! Ossie that! Everyone at Tregevny's knew about Renee's young man, the one with plenty of money.

Jenni went round to Hafod Row to sit with Meg each evening for a while, then her visits grew less frequent. She loved Meg dearly, but all she could talk about was Renee and Ossie and what the future would be like when Renee was married.

Jenni spent more time alone at Abertawe House. After supper she spent long hours in her attic room. She bought a few three-penny novels to read, but it was difficult to see. Although she'd cleaned it, little light came in through the high porthole window or from her candle.

They couldn't stop her using the gaslight in the kitchen, she decided defiantly one evening. Sometimes she could even listen to gramophone music drifting in from the sitting-room if she wedged the passage door open.

Renee had been going out nightly with Ossie for over a month, and from what she told Jenni, was hoping for something important to happen soon. By now Jenni was resigned to spending her spare time alone.

One evening she was in the kitchen reading her novel with the passage door open when Violet suddenly appeared in the kitchen doorway. She looked surprised and Jenni jumped up, feeling guilty, and was annoyed with herself.

'I wondered why the gaslight was still on,' Violet said. 'I thought Doris had forgotten.'

'It's too dark to read in my room,' Jenni said defensively. 'I'm a lodger. I'm entitled to a bit of light.'

'Of course you are, Jenni,' Violet said. 'I'm surprised to see you in, that's all.'

Jenni sighed.

'My friend Renee Morris has started courting. Seriously, I think, so I've got no one to go out with now, and it's no fun on your own.'

'Oh, I agree!'

To Jenni's astonishment, Violet pulled out a chair from the scrubbed kitchen table and sat down. Jenni sat, too, wondering.

'So, your friend's getting married, is she?'

'Well, it's early days yet, Miss Tregevny . . .'

'Oh, now, call me Violet, please.'

Jenni bit her lip. Violet had mentioned this several times but Jenni wasn't sure, unable to forget Violet's strange welcome when she'd first arrived.

'Are you sure?' Jenni said quietly. 'You didn't like me when I first came.'

Violet looked shamefaced for a moment.

'Clara said some things about you . . . awful things. Foolishly, I believed her.' She sighed. 'I *am* a foolish woman at times.' She reached across and touched Jenni's arm. 'Now I know what she said isn't true. I'm sorry, Jenni.'

Jenni was sorry too, but not in the least surprised. She'd surmised as much.

'I'm astonished a pretty girl like you doesn't have a young man of her own to love,' Violet went on, her tone almost wistful.

'I am in love!' Jenni exclaimed quickly and without thinking. 'I mean . . . well, yes, I *am*.'

Violet's face brightened.

'Oh, do tell me about him,' she breathed excitedly, her fingers touching a thin gold chain around her throat, just peeping through the collar of her dress. 'Is the young man local? What's his name? Why aren't you out with him this evening?'

Jenni bit her lip. She'd never spoken of her love for Jack to anyone apart from Renee. She could hardly tell Violet, his sister, yet she sensed strongly the other woman had a need to share something herself.

Jenni lowered her gaze.

'We're very much in love, but there's a difficulty . . .'

'It's his family, isn't it?' Violet exclaimed heatedly. There was a strange throb in her voice, and Jenni glanced up at her quickly and with curiosity; surprised by her intensity. Obviously, there were hidden depths to Violet.

She swallowed hard, as though quelling some deep emotion.

'I know exactly how it is,' she said tremulously. 'When I was your age I met a young man, and we were madly in love, but my father . . .'

Her voice faltered, and Jenni was further astonished to see tears glisten on her eyelashes.

'My getting married didn't suit my father.' Violet's tone was heavily laced with bitterness. It sounded like a bitterness that had festered for a long time.

'My mother was an invalid for many years, you see, Jenni,' she went on after a moment's pause. 'And my father needed someone to look after this house, so he forbade it. My young man went away and I never saw him again.'

Violet's shoulders drooped, and she held her head low. Jenni jumped up immediately, overcome by pity. She put an arm around the thin shoulders and gave them a hug.

'Violet, I'm so sorry.'

She could imagine how she'd feel if Jack went away and she never saw him again. Violet had survived that loss somehow, perhaps because she'd had family responsibilities that couldn't be dodged, but Jenni doubted she had the strength to survive alone.

Violet lifted her head valiantly, sniffed back the tears and, pulling a lace handkerchief from her sleeve, dabbed at her nose.

'Thank you, Jenni. You're the only one who understands the pain . . .'

She paused a moment, looking up into Jenni's face, then took her hand.

'I've got a secret,' she murmured, suppressed excitement in her voice. She paused again, looking cautiously towards the open kitchen door then back to Jenni.

'I've found love again. Yes, yes! I have!'

She clutched Jenni's hand even more tightly.

'Promise you won't tell?'

Jenni shook her head, bemused and nonplussed, unsure what to make of Violet's flushed face and sparkling eyes. Suddenly she looked much younger.

'It's Nathan – Nathan Joseph. You know!' she exclaimed when Jenni looked puzzled. 'The pawnbroker next door to our shop on Neath Road.' She nodded excitedly as comprehension dawned on Jenni. 'That's right! Nat and I are in love and we want to get married, but my father . . .'

'He can't stop you, Violet,' Jenni said quickly. 'He can't do anything.'

She wrung her hands, looking so forlorn and desperate Jenni longed to help her.

'Oh, Jenni, I've no money of my own. I have nothing.'

'It doesn't matter,' Jenni reassured her quickly, realising the only help she could give was encouragement to be strong and fight. 'Mr Joseph doesn't give a jot about that. He wants *you*, Violet.'

'Yes, I know! It's wonderful!' she said breathlessly. 'But we have to be practical, too. Getting married costs money.'

'Love is all that matters,' Jenni responded wistfully.

She would see Nathan Joseph most mornings, standing on the doorstep of his pawnbroker's shop; a thin, middle-aged man in a sagging woollen cardigan. But he had a pleasant face, and always gave a wave and a cheery good morning to all who passed by. Jenni liked him.

'My father won't allow it,' Violet whimpered, wringing her

hands again. 'Who'd run the house? Who'd fetch and carry for him?'

'Clara!' Jenni declared firmly. 'Let her earn her keep for once.'

'He'll never agree.'

'Well, he'll have to lump it then!' Jenni said fiercely. 'Violet, you can't let him destroy your happiness again. Everyone's entitled to feel love and be loved in return. You must fight for your chance with Nathan. If you can't be married openly, do it in secret. Get a special licence.'

She touched the older woman's arm.

'Grab this chance, Violet, for heaven's sake!' She didn't add that it might be her last.

Violet jumped up, her agitated expression clearing.

'I'll do it! I will!' She clutched Jenni's hands tightly. 'Oh, thank you, Jenni. You're a real friend. My only friend.'

She ran shaking fingers through her already untidy hair, then looked around as though bewildered by her own decision.

'What shall I do next, Jenni?'

'Tell Mr Joseph your decision,' she urged. 'Make plans together. Don't waste anymore time, Violet. Your father has stolen too much from you already.'

Violet smiled at her.

'Oh, Jenni, you're so young yet so wise. This young man you love – he's very lucky. I hope he knows that.'

Jenni flushed with pleasure.

'I know he loves me, and that's enough.'

Jenni went up early that evening, too restless to read further. She lay in her narrow bed, sleepless and thoughtful. It was getting on towards the longest day of the year, and through the porthole window the mellow evening light was still discernible.

She thought of Violet and Nathan Joseph, Renee and her Ossie, and suddenly wanted to cry. Other lovers were together on this lovely June night while she was alone and lonely, longing for Jack.

She saw plenty of him at the workroom, and when an opportunity came he'd steal a kiss and tell her how much she meant to him. But still he avoided her at Abertawe House.

But Jenni wished he would make a stand now. It was time he told Clara. It was time his family, everyone, knew the truth: that he loved Jenni and they were destined to be together for always. It was time he committed himself.

Jenni turned her face into the pillow, willing herself not to give in to the pain of being alone; the pain of a longing deep in her being that cried out for the touch of her lover's hands.

Perhaps, if she finally committed herself, she thought, gave herself freely to him as he'd begged her to do many times, he'd find the courage to face Clara and his father, and proclaim his love for Jenni.

The creak of a footfall on the back stairs interrupted her wistful reflections. Jenni pushed back the bedclothes and sat up with a sigh on her lips. Must be Violet wanting to talk again. She'd slipped out earlier, secretly, to visit Nathan Joseph. Now she'd come to tell Jenni her news.

A knock sounded at the bedroom door and Jenni called out: 'Come in, Violet.'

The door opened but the outline in the doorway was not that of Violet, and Jenni gasped in astonishment as she recognised the man she loved so deeply.

'Jack!'

'Hush, darling,' he murmured.

He came quietly into the room and closed the door behind him, then approached her bed and sat down on the edge.

'The house is empty, Jenni,' he murmured. 'Everyone's out but us.' He leaned closer, his voice a husky whisper. 'Oh, Jenni, darling. I had to come to you. I can't stand it any longer.'

His arms reached out for her and, with a cry of acute longing,

Jenni went eagerly into his embrace. He didn't kiss her but just held her against his chest, his lips against the curve of her throat, the sensation sending her body into exquisite tumult.

Her mind was in confusion at the suddenness and the power of her feelings. She'd been longing for Jack and now he was here, holding her. It seemed like fate.

The warmth of his body in the deepening gloom brought a tingling sensation to her skin, as though electricity passed from him to her.

She always thrilled at Jack's touch, but now the realisation that they were alone, unobserved, free to demonstrate their true feelings, made her catch her breath as a new exhilaration raced through her veins, firing her blood in a way she'd never known before. Nothing mattered now but her and Jack and the love they shared. Her body spoke to her, telling her this was all she'd ever wanted.

Suddenly, and with startling clarity, she understood her own mother's passion for Bert Herbert. This same overpowering longing and desire had made Sarah throw morals and caution to the winds.

She and her mother *were* alike. They shared the same elemental needs – needs that would not, could not, be denied.

Jack's hand cradled her breast, and in the power of a sudden hunger and indescribable sense of pleasure, her body writhing in need, Jenni cried out: 'Oh, God, Jack! Love me! Love me now!'

It was like a dream, one from which she never wanted to wake. She knew things now, understood things she never had before.

Easing herself gently off the bed, Jenni lit the stub of a candle and placed the candlestick on the old chest of drawers. In the flickering shadows of the room, she lay on the bed once more, elbow on the pillow and resting her head on her hand, watching her sleeping lover.

Jack lay on the bed with her, his handsome blond head on his outflung arm. Jenni smoothed her hand, delicately so as not to disturb him, over the bare flesh of his shoulder and chest.

She felt she was touching a godly being, and gazed at his sleeping face in deep awe. Only a god could take her into the realms of paradise, for paradise was where she'd been for the past hour. She still felt the lingering effects of that heady dream; her body still thrilled at the memory of what she and Jack had done together. They were like husband and wife now. They belonged to each other and it would always be like this, she just knew it. Paradise was hers forever.

Suddenly, she wanted to relive it all again. She felt hunger for him rise like a tidal wave that swept over her, engulfed her, until she was panting in her desire.

On impulse, she seized his sleeping face in her hands and kissed him ardently, demandingly.

He came awake, hands gripping her shoulders, pushing her away.

'What? What?'

'Oh, Jack, darling! I love you so much. Love me again, Jack. I want you to love me again.'

Jenni tried to move her head to kiss him again but he held her off.

'Jenni! What time is it, for heaven's sake?'

He tried to sit up but she pressed him down, running her hands over his chest, the warmth of his skin making her palms burn.

'Love me again, darling,' she cried out passionately. 'The way you did before. I *need* you, Jack, now. Now!'

But he was too strong for her. He sat up, pushing her firmly from him. He swung his legs off the bed and reached for his waist-coat, lying over the back of the chair nearby. He took out a pocket watch and peered at it.

'It's too dark in here to see anything,' he complained, standing up and walking into the candlelight which played over the contours of his body as though caressing him. Jenni was filled with awe again, and a desire so intense she cried out: 'Jack!' She knelt on the bed, lifting her arms to him beseechingly. 'Come by here and love me. I want you, darling.'

'Bloody hell!' Jack swung away from the chest-of-drawers and strode quickly to where his clothes were. 'D'you know what time it is? It's ten-thirty. Clara'll be back, and Father, too.'

'Jack!'

'Why did you let me sleep?' he asked impatiently, struggling into his clothes. 'Get your dress on quickly. You'll have to go down first, make sure the coast's clear for me. I'll nip out the back lane then go round to the front door.'

Jenni knelt there, feeling as if someone had thrown a bucket of icy water over her nakedness.

'But, darling . . .' Her voice faltered with uncertainty. 'It doesn't matter now, does it?' she went on. 'Clara might as well be told tonight as tomorrow.'

Jack was still struggling with his tie.

'Told what? Come on, Jenni, get a move on!'

But she didn't move. A terrible doubt started to gnaw at her. She wanted to shrug it aside as just the workings of her imagination, but it persisted.

Why was Jack being so impatient and distant at a time like this when she felt so warm and passionate? Not long ago they'd both been in seventh heaven. Now he was acting as if they'd done something wrong; as if he felt ashamed and guilty.

'The divorce, Jack,' she reminded him tentatively. 'Clara should be told tonight about the divorce.'

He was shrugging into his jacket but stopped and turned to stare at her. There was no warmth in his gaze, no light of love, and suddenly conscious of her nakedness, Jenni pulled the bed sheet up around herself.

Something was wrong in paradise. It was changing into

something else; something cold and bleak. Jack had changed, too.

'Are you mad?' His tone was abrasive, and Jenni felt the rasp of it as though sandpaper had been applied to her tender skin. 'Do you really think I'm going to throw everything away for just one tumble?'

'Tumble? I don't understand . . .'

'Don't be tiresome, Jenni.' His tone was impatient. 'We've had a great old time, the best I've had for a long while, and we'll do it again, soon.'

He finished putting on his jacket.

'But let's not lose our heads, right?'

He ran his fingers through his hair.

'Get dressed. Quick!'

She began to tremble violently, feeling nauseated with disappointment and disbelief.

'You said you loved me,' she wailed. 'You said we'd be married.'

'Yeah, yeah, we will, Jenni.' He was impatient again. 'When the time's right.'

By his sarcastic tone he might have said they'd be wed when Nelson got his eye back, Jenni thought in horror.

He glanced around in the flickering candlelight.

'This attic room's ideal. Clara did us a favour, eh? A real little love nest. Come on. Get dressed.'

'No!'

'Jenni?'

'What have you made me do?' she cried out in dismay.

Heartache was lodged in her chest, suffocating her.

'*Made* you do?' He gave a scornful laugh. 'That's rich, that is, Jenni. You were begging me – begging! You were all over me. My God! You were a surprise, I can tell you. Talk about hot stuff!'

'How can you speak to me like that?' she cried, raw shame making her cheeks flame and her body quiver with outrage.

His words were sullying all those wonderful new feelings and sensations she'd discovered and experienced with him a little while ago. She'd thought they were heaven-sent by their love; now he was making them seem dirty and sordid. He was speaking to her as though she were any wanton hussy he might pick up off the streets.

'You said you loved me!' she wailed loudly. 'You betrayed me.'

'Be quiet, damn you! Someone will hear us.'

'I don't care if they do,' Jenni cried out wildly. 'You led me on. You've ruined me, you have.'

'Don't be so bloody melodramatic, will you?' Jack snapped. He looked at his pocket watch again. 'I've got to make a move now or I'll be caught.'

He moved towards the door and Jenni scrambled off the bed, clutching the sheet around herself.

'Jack! Jack, don't leave me like this, please. I love you, I really do. Don't treat me like I'm . . . cheap.'

He paused at the door, turning his head to look back at her.

'I didn't say that, Jenni, you did.'

'Jack!'

She clamped one hand over her mouth, whimpering. This couldn't be true. Jack loved her. She loved him. Hadn't she proved it beyond doubt tonight?

'Look, Jenni.' He sounded regretful. 'You really get under my skin and I want you all the time. That's why I talked my father into insisting you lodge here.'

'*What*? It was you and not Richie?' Jenni felt betrayal cut through her like a knife.

He shrugged, looking smug.

'Well, you said you wanted to be with me. This arrangement is ideal for both of us. No sneaking around in back alleys, and it's better than the sand dunes at Brynmill Arch.'

Jenni stared at him in dismay, trying to catch her breath between sobs.

'You don't love me at all! Oh, my God, you've used me!'

Suddenly she felt a great surge of rage and resentment. 'You beast, Jack! How could you?'

'Oh, grow up, Jenni, for God's sake!' His voice was harsh with impatience. 'You're taking it too seriously. You knew what you were doing and there's no harm done. We've had our fun, and there's plenty more to come. Our own little love nest, eh?'

Jenni could only stare, mouth gaping, as he disappeared from view.

Love? The word sounded like an obscenity on Jack's lips. He'd used her cruelly, and the terrible thing was, he couldn't see the wrong in it. What a fool she was! And what was to become of her now?

Chapter Twenty-Four

Jenni steeled herself to find the strength to get up the following morning. With hardly a minute's sleep for the rest of that night, she woke feeling wretched and miserable, unable to quell her tears as she washed herself in the china bowl resting on the chair.

But her wretchedness wasn't only due to lack of sleep and bitter disappointment in Jack. She was miserable because she'd betrayed herself. She felt shame sticking to her, like grease on her skin, and rub and rub as she might with the sponge, she couldn't rid herself of it. Unclean! She knew the full meaning of that word now.

How could she face Jack, Violet, her friends Renee and Meg, after what she'd done – the shameless way she'd behaved in Jack's arms? How could she face the world, bearing this shame in her heart?

Jack had never loved her, that was patently obvious now. And to think she'd given herself to him unrestrainedly . . . Oh, why had she been so gullible?

Because she loved him and still wanted him, that was the awful truth.

Jenni sat on the bed for a moment, face in hands, sobbing. It was humiliating to realise that if he relented and told her he *did* love her, she'd take him back even now. The knowledge made her feel cheap. Had she no spark of self-respect left? Apparently not! Because with Jack's help and her own unbridled yearnings she'd destroyed herself, and now no respectable man would look at her.

Yet life had to go on. She still had to earn her living and that meant facing the Tregevny family, her friends and the world somehow. The pride that had always kept her head high, even in the midst of her greatest adversity, was gone, and there was a terrible void in her heart. She'd given wholehearted love and had been destroyed in return.

The workroom seemed dark and uninviting. Jenni sat at her machine, unwilling and unable to look at Jack. He was very quiet this morning, which was unusual.

But Renee had plenty to say, and for once Jenni wished her friend would quieten down. Renee's chatter, especially about her young man, Ossie, made Jenni's head ache painfully.

'Come back to our house for a bit of something to eat,' her friend suggested to her when dinnertime came.

'I don't want to impose, Renee,' Jenni said unhappily. She felt tainted now and believed she had no right to invade their respectable home, not after what happened and the way she'd behaved.

'Oh, come on, Jen, love,' Renee coaxed. 'You haven't been round for ages. My mam misses your company. So do I.'

'All right, then,' Jenni agreed gratefully, realising Renee wouldn't understand her reticence. 'I'd like that. Thanks a lot.'

Seeing Meg would take her mind off her troubles, but it would only be a temporary reprieve.

The meal was very simple, so different from the meals she was getting used to at Abertawe House, and she felt guilty that Renee and Meg had to manage with so little. If only she could help them.

'Listen, you two, I've got a bit of news,' Renee said with a grin as she pushed the plate of bread and scrape towards Jenni, encouraging her to take another slice. 'Ossie's coming round to tea tomorrow. He wants to meet you, Mam.'

'Oh . . . *Duw! Duw!* That's a good sign, love,' Meg exclaimed. 'Hey! I'll have to have a couple of rag curlers in my hair tonight. Wants to look my best, don't I?'

'He'll take one look at you, Meg,' Jenni said with deep affection, 'and fall in love instantly. Renee will have to watch out!'

Meg giggled happily, her ample frontage quivering, her cheeks pink with pleasure.

Jenni felt suddenly saddened and forlorn. These two women meant the world to her now, but if they learned the truth she'd lose their friendship for good. She felt resentment bubble inside her. Jack Tregevny had a lot to answer for!

'Told him about you, I have, Jenni, you being my best friend,' Renee said, breaking into her dismal thoughts. 'Ossie wants to meet you, too. Oh, kid! I'm so excited. I'm sure something's going to happen.' She rolled her eyes. 'You know, like wedding bells.'

'Oh, I hope so, our Renee,' Meg said, pressing her hands to her bosom. 'Then we'll all live happy ever after.'

Jenni had supper with Doris as usual in the kitchen, then helped wash up. Afterwards, she and Doris took two kitchen chairs and sat just outside the back door, enjoying the late-evening sun for a while longer.

Doris seemed reluctant to go home for once.

'Are you all right, Jenni?' she asked solicitously. 'Looking really pale, you are, mun.'

Jenni gave a weak smile, wondering if Doris suspected anything. The older girl seemed to know everything about the Tregevny family; always hinting that she knew more than she'd tell.

'Been having a go at you again, has she?' She jerked her head towards the house, and Jenni knew she was referring to Clara.

'Now and then,' Jenni said with a sigh.

'Tsk! I don't know who she thinks is,' Doris said, her lips tightening. 'He *had* to marry her, you know, Mr Jack did. Oh, yes! Shotgun wedding, it was. Only it was *his* dad holding the gun!'

She turned her eyes to heaven.

'There was rows here! Barneys you've never heard the like of. And, do you know, the sly little minx never told Mr Jack she was in the family way. Oh, no! She went straight to the old man instead. Now, there's brass neck for you, isn't it?'

Jenni shifted uncomfortably on her chair.

'How do you know all this, Doris?' she asked. 'After all, it's private family business.'

Doris laughed.

'Nothing's private to the hired help, kid. The things I hear when I'm serving meals ... and they forget walls have ears. But I don't talk about it, see. More than my job's worth.'

Jenni shivered. The evening air seemed to have cooled.

'I think I'll go in.'

Doris got up too, but was obviously reluctant to keep a still tongue in her head tonight.

'Funny thing, though,' she went on relentlessly as they carried the chairs indoors. 'There was no baby at the end of it. Nor any sign of one either. So he married her for nothing.'

Doris sniffed disdainfully and looked down her nose.

'But serves him right for his dirty carryings on. Tsk! I dunno. Since the war morals have gone downhill. A girl's got to keep herself respectable, that's what I say. What do you think, Jenni?'

But she could only nod her head, wanting to escape to her room. Was Doris hinting she knew everything about her and Jack?

Jenni made up her mind there and then. If Jack came to her room ever again, she wouldn't let him in. She pined after him still, but wouldn't let him use her from now on.

*

Jenni decided to put her unhappiness aside the next day, ready to meet Renee's young man. Her friend seemed very happy and excited about him, and the prospect of his meeting her family. Jenni didn't want to spoil it by being miserable.

She went round to Meg's early, helping to set the table and put out what food they had. There was jelly and blancmange, a home-made cake, and some delicious-looking Welsh cakes. They'd bought a bit of ham, just enough to impress the young man.

Jenni sat with Meg, waiting for Renee to come in with her bloke. Meg was quivering with excitement, and Jenni felt it too. It would be wonderful for Renee and her mother if she could be settled in marriage with a good, steady man. Ossie sounded as though he fitted the bill, and Jenni was happy for her friend.

She stood up expectantly at the sound of Renee's voice in the passage mingled with the deeper tones of a man.

Her friend bounced into the room, dragging a man by the arm.

'Here he is, Mam. My Ossie.' She turned a beaming face to him. 'This is my mam, and my friend Jenni.'

Renee turned expectant eyes on her friend but Jenni was speechless with dismay and confusion as she stared at the man before her.

Oggie James! She could hardly believe her eyes at first, then was gripped by terror as the awful truth sank into her befuddled brain.

In the past she'd seen him wear only tatty shirts, worn hand-me-down breeches, a cloth cap and muffler. Now he wore a pristine white shirt under a smart three-piece suit, and a trilby perched at a rakish angle. There was even a clean smell about him, as though he'd scrubbed himself all over with scented soap. But neither that nor his smart clothes could hide his rottenness, Jenni thought bitterly. Oggie James didn't have one shred of decency in him, and would never be anything but a thug.

'Well, say hello then, Jen,' Renee prompted, clutching Oggie's arm and leaning against him in an intimate way that made Jenni's blood run cold.

Her tongue felt swollen and dry as she struggled with the words but she found her voice from somewhere. Even to her own ears it sounded hoarse with panic.

'Hello, Oggie.'

'No, no!' Renee giggled. 'It's Ossie, not Oggie, Jen, love. Ossie James.'

He didn't seem at all surprised to see *her*, and Jenni knew immediately that it was no coincidence he was here. He was up to no good.

He advanced a step, offering his hand, grinning widely.

'Hello, Jenni,' he said. 'Haven't we met before? There's a girl I used to know in the Rhondda. Spitting image of you, she is.'

Jenni felt the ground was coming up to meet her, but she clung on to consciousness valiantly. This must be some kind of a nightmare, she thought, as she stared into Oggie's sneering grin.

Suddenly she was overwhelmed by feelings from the past: the terrible pain of her mother's death, the anguish and humiliation of her father's execution. Her life had been shattered then. It was about to happen again, and she could do nothing to stop it. Jack had done a good job of destroying her. Now Oggie would finish her off altogether!

He still offered his hand and Jenni flinched, not only from taking it but also from the cunning gleam in his eyes and the triumphant tone of his voice. He'd planned this, and now had her exactly where he wanted her.

Seeing the way Renee clung to his arm, Jenni was even more fearful for her friend. Oggie was using her like a pawn in his devious game of chess. It was cruel and callous, but so like him.

Jenni was conscious of Renee's beaming face, her eyes fixed on Oggie. She couldn't be in love with him! Jenni felt a shiver of pure horror run through her at the thought of Renee's falling into such a terrible trap. Jenni must do something to save her, but what? How could she ruin Renee's new happiness, even if it was built on a stinking quagmire of lies and deceit? She would be degraded, heartbroken, and it was Jenni's fault.

Renee was still waiting for her response so, swallowing down her own repugnance, Jenni accepted his hand. He squeezed hers harder than was necessary and she winced with pain.

'Renee's been telling me all about you,' he said, his tone oily and laced with scorn. 'Any friend of Renee's is a friend of mine. We'll have to get to know each other better.'

Jenni shivered with repugnance. She knew she was trapped and could only wait in trepidation for Oggie to make his next move against her.

At Meg's urging they sat down at the table to eat. Renee chattered happily and Oggie talked a lot, making jokes and quips, glancing all the time at Jenni, his eyes now taking on an avaricious gleam. And she began to understand how his mind was working. He'd always enjoyed humiliating her. Now he wanted something else as well.

Oggie's sudden appearance in her life again was God's punishment, she thought wretchedly, for the sinful way she'd carried on with Jack.

Under normal circumstances Jenni would have stayed at Meg's as long as possible, savouring the warmth and friendship of her home. But Oggie's presence and his scent even, were rotten to her now; she could hardly breathe for fear of stifling. She must be alone to think of a way to free Renee from his clutches.

After she'd helped Renee wash up, Jenni said she must go.

'Oh, no, kid!' Renee was disappointed.

Jenni smiled faintly, avoiding Oggie's smirking glance.

'Violet wants me to help with carpet cleaning tonight.'

'Hey!' Oggie exclaimed. 'I can get the Tregevnys one of those newfangled vacuum cleaners . . . cheap.' He tapped the side of his nose. 'Just say the word.'

Jenni felt her face stiffen, but she tried to answer civilly for Renee's sake.

'Thank you . . . er . . . Ossie, but there's no electricity in Abertawe House.'

'Behind the times!'

Jenni turned from his bold glance to Renee.

'You enjoy the rest of the evening,' she said, squeezing her friend's arm affectionately. 'I'll see you in work tomorrow. I want to talk to you about something.' She lowered her voice, glancing covertly at Oggie. 'Something private and very important.'

Renee's eyes shone with curiosity.

'What is it, kid?'

'Now now, Renee, love,' Jenni whispered urgently. 'Tomorrow.'

She was thankful to get out of the house into the fresh air. She felt sick with worry, not only for herself but for Renee, too.

How had she got mixed up with Oggie James? Somehow Jenni knew he'd engineered it. He was no good and certainly unworthy of any decent woman's love and affection. It could only end in tears, and Renee would be destroyed!

Jenni remembered his threats the day she'd scratched his face, the day her mother died. He'd uttered them again the day Bert Herbert had saved her from Oggie's assault in the snow. He hated her and wouldn't be satisfied until he'd done her some mischief.

The vital question was how could she tell Renee the truth without exposing the whole sorry story of her family's shame? Would Renee keep her secret, and would she still be Jenni's friend?

Everything was at stake. If Oggie wanted revenge he could decimate her life with a few words. She wouldn't be able to stand the condemnation on people's faces when they knew who she really was: the daughter of a convicted murderer. She'd have to leave the Hafod, find some other place, in some other town. Leave behind friendship and love. Be alone and friendless again.

But wait, commonsense told her; wait to see what Oggie

would do. Running away now would solve nothing. She'd fought him off in the past – could she do it again?

She thought about him, the way he looked and dressed now. He wasn't short of money, that much was clear. His suit was of good quality, and she'd noticed his shoes looked quite expensive. He sounded different, too, in a way. His nature certainly hadn't changed, she could tell that by his words and glances, but he seemed more mature, more experienced – and more dangerous and powerful because of it, Jenni thought, her fear growing. But, no! She wouldn't run like a scared rabbit. She'd wait and see what happened next.

She had to think of Renee first. How could she let her friend go on thinking Oggie was the man for her? He was scum! How could she persuade Renee to give him up? Her friend had been pinning so many hopes on her new bloke. She might even have fallen in love with him, so blinded was she by her longing to be married and settled.

The situation was a potential disaster. Jenni wouldn't let herself think about what else Oggie might have persuaded Renee to do. She hoped it wasn't already too late to save her friend from that kind of ruin.

She was just turning into the back lane behind Abertawe House when quick footsteps behind her made her turn.

Jenni gasped with terror when she saw Oggie James. The muscles in her legs tightened, ready for the sprint to the back gate of the house to escape him.

He must have sensed her intention because he stopped abruptly and lifted a hand, signalling her to wait.

'Thought you'd be glad to see me again,' he said, sneering.

Jenni swallowed her fear with difficulty. If she cried out, would anyone hear her?

'No more than I'd be glad to see Lucifer,' she rasped.

She clamped her lips shut then, realising she mustn't provoke him. His lips twitched but he remained calm.

'And I thought we were friends, Jenni . . . not Goodenough!'

'You can't frighten me, Oggie,' she said resolutely, though she was trembling violently now. 'I know you too well, remember?'

'Not well enough, I think,' he replied, leering.

He eyed her up and down.

'You've filled out all in the right places, I see. Yeah, a nice little bundle of charms.' He put his hand in his trouser pocket and jingled money there.

'Got plenty of mazoomah, Jenni. I could show you a good time.'

'Renee told me you had money.'

'Oh, yeah, her! She was real handy when I wanted to get closer to you. Did the trick nicely, didn't it?' He let out a bellow of laughter. 'You should have seen your face when I waltzed in!'

'You stay away from Renee,' Jenni said thickly, rage and fear making her feel dizzy.

'Maybe I will.' He grinned. 'Getting sick of her, I am, anyway. Clings like a bloody limpet. I likes a change, me.'

'You're disgusting!'

She refused to stand here, listening to him degrade her friend. Throwing him a murderous look, Jenni turned to walk away, but Oggie was behind her in a flash, grasping her arm and swinging her around.

'Take your filthy hands off me!' she screamed, lifting one fist ready to strike him.

'Okay! Okay!' He backed off, just a step, still too close for Jenni's comfort. 'Don't just walk away from me, that's all,' he went on harshly. 'I haven't finished talking to you, and we've got a lot to discuss.'

He jerked a thumb towards the house.

'Can we go inside?'

'No, certainly not!'

He shrugged. 'Just thought it would be cosier. You know, old friends meeting again after a long parting.'

Jenni scowled at the idea, her temper rising.

'Friends? You're my worst enemy, Oggie. I'd rather go through hell's fires than be cosy with you!'

His look was savage. Expecting him to lunge at her again, she tensed her muscles ready to flee. She'd never forget that night in the snow when he'd attacked her. Bert Herbert had saved her then, but no one would come to her aid tonight.

To distract him she went on hastily: 'What exactly do you want from me, Oggie?'

Suddenly he grinned.

'Well, now! That's the question, isn't it?'

'How did you find me?'

'Pure chance. I was following this other piece of skirt and she led me to you. Lucky break, eh?'

Jenni frowned.

'Who are you talking about?'

He shook his head dismissively.

'Never mind that. Let's talk about you and me.'

Jenni clenched her teeth, letting air escape between them like a growl. She'd never imagined she could hate someone this much. Just looking into his leering face made her feel sick to her stomach.

'We've nothing to talk about.'

He laughed unpleasantly.

'Don't kid yourself, Jenni. You had to get out of the Valley because of your father and that tart of a mother of yours. The same thing will happen here unless . . .'

She swallowed down her apprehension.

'What?'

'Reasonable bloke, I am, Jenni. Used to be a *llelo*, but now I'm smart. Knocked about Cardiff for a while, met some interesting blokes. They showed me how to make money.'

He lifted a hand.

'Okay, I did get into a bit of bother with the bobbies, but I dodged 'em and now I'm sitting pretty. Got a bit of clout where it counts and money in my pocket.' He pointed his thumb at his chest. 'Me, I'm a big man now. I work for Charlie Pendle – his right-hand man, like.'

'Who?'

He laughed at her ignorance.

'You don't know nothing.'

'And I don't want to, either,' Jenni cried out furiously. 'Whatever you're mixed up in must be rotten. Now push off, Oggie, before I yell for a bobby.'

His lips drew back from his teeth in a snarl, and his eyes flashed angrily.

'Shurrup!' He stabbed a finger in her direction. 'You don't talk to me like that anymore, see. I'm a big noise around here now.'

He took a deep breath, quickly regaining his composure.

'Look, Jenni, mun. I'm trying to be nice. I've always fancied you, kid. Don't matter to me your old man was topped. And I can keep my mouth shut. All I want, all I've ever wanted, was for you to be nice to me.'

She stared at him in silence, dreading to understand what he meant.

He stepped closer, a leering smile on his lips.

'Be my girl, eh?' His grin widened. 'I know what you women like. We'll have lots of good times. You'll like it, I promise you.'

He was the most loathsome creature she'd ever met, and she felt sick at the thought of Renee being with him.

'I'd rather sleep in a pigsty, Oggie,' said Jenni in deep disgust. 'I'd rather be dead in a ditch.'

His face darkened with fury, and he lifted his arm threateningly.

'I ought to smack you silly, you snobby little bitch! You're no better than me. Nobody'll look at you after I've finished with you.'

'You lay a hand on me,' she screamed loudly, 'and I'll have the police on you.'

Terrified, she struggled not to show it. Panting defiantly, she rushed on: 'You're a wanted man, remember?'

'Don't threaten me, you dirty tart!'

'Then go away and leave me in peace.'

'Got the goods on you, I have, Jenni Goodenough.' His voice was heavy with malice, eyes glaring. 'And since you won't be friendly, you'll have to bloody pay – and through the nose as well.'

'I haven't got any money,' she fenced, her heart jumping painfully.

'Don't lie!' His face twisted in fury, he looked dangerous. 'Blod Thomas left you plenty, everybody knows that. And I want it.' He held out one hand, palm up. 'Now cough up twenty quid. That'll do for starters.'

Jenni was appalled.

'I haven't got that kind of money. I earn only fifteen shillings a week.'

He took another step nearer.

'Do you want me to get rough?' He lifted his hand again. 'I'll belt you if you tell me another lie.'

'All right!' Jenni cried out, recognising defeat. 'But the money is in my Post Office account. I have to give notice before I can draw that much out.'

'How long?'

'A week.'

His eyes shifted uncertainly, then he glared at her again.

'If you're lying . . .' He raised his fist.

'I'm not!' Jenni cried out quickly. 'I'll go to the Post Office tomorrow. I'll meet you again next week to give you the money.'

Maybe she could find a solution before she had to pay him, she thought quickly. There had to be some way.

'Oggie, I'll give you the money freely, and . . . and even more, if you promise to stay away from Renee.'

'Huh! Sick of her already. I'm ditching her anyway.'

Jenni tried not to show her relief. Renee would be heartbroken but she'd get over it, and it was for the best. Jenni couldn't bear the idea of her friend and Oggie together. He was such a vicious swine, he'd ruin Renee's life. She'd find a real man one day.

'When can I have the money?'

Jenni swallowed hard.

'This time next week. But not here.'

It was too near the house. Clara was too watchful, and Jenni didn't want to be seen with the likes of Oggie James.

'I'll be on the corner of Monger Street,' she said quickly. 'Near the chip shop, about half-seven. You'll have your money then.'

'You'd better be there.' He scowled threateningly. 'Because I can call round Abertawe House any time, see. Tell 'em everything I know about you.' His lip curled scornfully. 'You little slut!'

Chapter Twenty-Five

The stairs creaked and Jenni quickly scrambled out of bed. She'd been waiting for that sound, had placed the chair near the door in readiness. Pushing the curved back under the door knob and wedging the legs firmly against the bare floorboards, she stood back, waiting.

She was only just in time. Someone grasped the door knob and turned it, pushing against the door, expecting to walk straight in. When the door wouldn't give, there was silence for a moment and Jenni waited with bated breath. Then a tap came and her name was whispered.

'Jenni!'

It was Jack, of course. She'd known he'd come to her again even though he'd been avoiding her since that night last week when she'd been weak and stupid enough to let him make love to her. Every night she'd been expecting him. Tonight especially since Violet had told her Clara was going to the theatre in town with friends. He'd not miss this opportunity.

She suppressed a little gasp as he pressed hard against the door again, but the chair was strongly made and resisted all his efforts.

'Jenni! It's Jack. Let me in.'

She quivered with emotion but remained silent. After a moment she found the strength to walk back to the bed and get in, pulling the bedclothes up around her chin even though the room was still warm from the day's sunlight on the roof.

Jack remained, tapping and calling softly to her, while Jenni lay with her fingers in her ears, trying to shut out the coaxing and cajoling voice of the man she had believed loved her, the faithless man who would use her again if he could. In truth, there was little to choose between Jack and Oggie, reason told her, so how could she still go on feeling she loved him?

Jenni felt tears sting her eyes as Jack's voice continued to call her name. She wouldn't listen. She'd degraded herself enough. Again, she remembered her mother's last words to her, uttered the day she'd died. The words were as clear in her mind as though her mother spoke to her again.

'Men will try to take advantage of you. Never let them. Know your worth; know what you want in life and in love, and never take less. Always remember you are your own woman. Never be beholden to any man.'

Now she was already soiled goods, and as if Jack's betrayal wasn't enough, Oggie James was after what little money she had in the world. How could she prevent him from taking everything from her? And even if she did pay him, could she trust him not to betray her? He'd do it for spite; she knew his vileness too well.

Maybe she should run away again. But where to? Where would she be safe from him? He'd found her once. He could find her again.

Jenni buried her face in the pillow. What was she to do?

Clara waved goodnight to her friends regretfully and watched enviously as they drove off in one of those new Ford motorcars. She would dearly have loved to ask them in for late drinks. That would have been the sociable and civilised thing to do, but Samuel was probably still up in the sitting-room, so she wouldn't risk it.

Clara ground her teeth. The penny-pinching, sanctimonious old hypocrite!

Bessie and Frank Hennessy, around her own age, were great company, stinking rich, knew all the best people in the town, but she couldn't trust the old man to be civil to them because they were Roman Catholics.

She let herself into the hall, closing the glass door behind her, and at that very moment Jack appeared through the door at the other end of the hall, leading from the back lobby.

Clara paused, staring at him in astonishment. His face was white with fury, his body taut, his fists clenched at his sides. He was obviously in high dudgeon — no, more than that, he was enraged.

He hardly glanced at her but walked stiff-legged to the staircase.

'Jack? Is something wrong?'

'No!'

'Jack? What is it?'

'Nothing, I tell you.'

His voice was rasping; his fingers, resting for a moment on the newel post, were visibly shaking.

Clara stared at him, wondering. She'd not seen him look so wrought up since the day his father had demanded, on pain of Jack's being disinherited, that he marry her. Jack had been beside himself then. Now he looked equally furious.

'Someone's upset you,' Clara persisted. 'What's going on? Have you had words with Richie?'

He shook his head.

'Did Father say something, then?'

'Good God, Clara!' His voice rose almost hysterically. 'When will you let me have any peace?'

With that he rushed up the stairs, disappearing along the gallery which ran around three sides of the hall, heading for their bedroom.

Angered by his attitude, she was tempted to follow him and continue her questions, but paused.

She glanced speculatively towards the back of the hall. Jack had left the door open in his mindless rage. Where had he come from? Who'd upset him and why?

Clara took off her coat and hat and went into the sitting-room where Samuel sat alone, reading.

'Have you seen Jack this evening, Father?'

He looked up from his Bible, glancing at her over the top of his spectacles.

'Haven't seen him at all.' He went back to his reading.

'Where's Violet?'

Samuel gave an impatient grunt at being disturbed.

'She's still out.'

'What? At this time of night?'

Clara glanced at the clock on the mantel. It was just gone ten. Violet never stayed out this late.

What was going on in this house? Had Jack and Richie had another row? It was happening more and more frequently these days. Clara put it down to Richie's jealousy of Jack's favoured position. Soon the old man would be past it, then Jack would take over the business. Richie wouldn't like that!

'And Richie? Where's he?' she asked.

'Questions, questions!' Samuel slammed the Bible shut with a loud snap. 'I'm going to bed where I can have some peace and quiet. When Richie comes in, tell him to lock up securely. Councillor Watkins tells me there's been some nasty burglaries in the Hafod recently. We can't be too careful.'

Samuel rose and marched out of the room. Clara followed more slowly, considering. Father and Jack hadn't spoken to each other and the rest of the family were out. That left only one other person in the house: Jenni Thomas. Jack had been up to *her* room.

A blistering anger rose in Clara's throat at the thought. That redheaded slut and Jack were carrying on, and under the family roof!

A new thought struck her. What if Samuel found out about these goings on? He'd be so outraged and disgusted, he'd cut Jack out of his will. Richie would get everything after all.

Clara felt dizzy with rage, looking round her wildly with an urge to smash something, the way she'd like to smash Jenni's pretty face.

She dashed up the stairs, intending to have it out with Jack right away, but halfway up stopped as a memory struck her: the memory of his white angry face.

Something had happened between them, something Jack didn't like. Jenni was being difficult perhaps? Granting sexual favours then denying them, using her body as a bargaining tool. Clara knew that trick, the oldest in the book. She'd used it herself to entrap him in the first place.

She clenched her fists tightly. Jenni wanted more than a little bit of fun on the side. She wanted what Clara had; she wanted to take everything, and she was setting Jack up for it. Clara knew her husband only too well. He was mad with Jenni now, but in a day or two he'd be putty in that redhead's hands again.

Her legs weakened by anger and a new fear, Clara sat down on the staircase. She must find some way of discrediting Jenni, getting her out of the house and their lives altogether.

Once Jenni was out of sight, Jack would forget her. He didn't love her, Clara was certain. She doubted he could love anyone, not even her. It was lust that had brought them together; lust that drove Jack and had cemented their marriage. But Jenni posed a definite threat to that now.

Clara rose to her feet and climbed the stairs towards their bedroom. She'd say nothing to Jack at present. Instead she'd concentrate on Jenni Thomas, watch her every movement. One of these days the little slut would slip up – and then Clara would have her where she wanted her, good and proper!

*

Clara was diligent in her watchfulness. It was irksome, tedious, and interfered with her social life, but it would pay off, she was certain. She watched Jenni leave the shop most evenings, following her home, keeping well back not to be spotted.

Keeping tabs on her in the evenings after supper was more tricky, but Clara used her ingenuity.

One evening in the week Jenni left the house later than usual. At first Clara thought she was again making her way to the house in Hafod Row where the Morrises lived, but instead she took a turning off the main road, into an area of back streets intersecting with bewildering sameness. It would be a maze to a stranger, but Clara knew the area like the back of her hand.

She walked behind at a distance, keeping an eagle eye on her quarry. There was something in the way Jenni walked tonight, a reluctance in her step, and Clara became curious and excited to see it.

At the corner of Monger Street, Jenni slowed down then stopped. Clara dodged into a nearby doorway as Jenni gazed around, obviously looking for someone. Her stance was furtive and tense, as though afraid of being seen, and Clara's excitement mounted.

After a wait of about five minutes, when Clara's excitement had nearly reached boiling point, a man turned a corner nearby, strolled across the street and approached Jenni. He was of medium height and stockily built, wearing a three-piece suit and a trilby.

Clara frowned, staring hard, as he and Jenni talked together. There was something very familiar in the man's stance and build. It was when he lifted an index finger and tipped back the trilby that Clara got a profound shock.

Ossie James! Her mother's repulsive lodger, and Charlie Pendle's thug. Ossie James and Jenni Thomas! Clara felt her mouth drop open in astonishment at the enormity of what she'd discovered.

Jenni Thomas was an associate of criminals! This was much more than Clara had hoped for. Now surely she had what she needed. But on the other hand, where was the proof?

Jenni and Ossie seemed to be arguing. Clara could hear Jenni's raised voice, but couldn't distinguish her words.

Ossie lifted a hand – threateningly, Clara thought, her astonished gaze fixed on the pair of them. And then Jenni, reluctantly, furtively it appeared, handed him something.

While Jenni fidgeted nervously, Ossie examined it openly, counting the notes from one hand to the other.

Money! Lots of money. Silently, Clara counted with him. Twenty pounds! Where would the likes of Jenni Thomas get such a large sum? Was she on the game? Clara could think of no other way.

Ossie and Jenni talked further and with obvious acrimony, then Jenni whirled away from him, retracing her steps, while Clara quickly ducked down a side street, taking refuge in another doorway.

Jenni passed by on the other side of the street, walking fast now, head down. But Clara was no longer interested in her. She'd gleaned all she could from that source.

Much as she hated the idea, she'd have to turn her attention to the odious Ossie. It was obvious he was blackmailing Jenni. He must know something, something really bad about her for her to part with that kind of money.

Clara was filled with elation that her suspicions were proving correct, but on the other hand, dreaded what she must do now: tackle Ossie James to find out the truth. And there was no time like the present.

She came out of her hiding place and hurried across the street towards where she'd last seen Ossie. She raced around the corner, panting a little, and was relieved to see his bulky figure strolling casually along the pavement. She followed at a discreet distance, her mind churning with various strategies for approaching him.

He was a lecherous creep, and she wouldn't trust him an inch. She certainly wouldn't accost him at her mother's house. She shivered, remembering their last encounter there.

It must be somewhere out in the open, with plenty of people around. She wouldn't feel safe otherwise.

Ossie's pace was slowing and Clara remembered the Copperworks Arms was on the next corner. He was probably heading there.

She hurried her steps. If he went into the pub, her opportunity would be lost. As far as she knew the place was decent enough, but even so a lone woman, if she was at all respectable, wouldn't be seen hanging about outside, let alone actually step over the threshold. If she lost him now she wouldn't find him again without calling at Kitty's, and that she'd never do.

Clara began to run, her high heels clicking loudly on the paving stones. One or two people stared at her unseemly haste, and she felt conspicuous and uncomfortable.

She wouldn't have caught him if he hadn't paused outside the pub, craning his neck to look through the windows, as though checking who was sitting inside. He seemed satisfied and was about to go when Clara halted a few feet away.

'Mr James!'

His reaction was startling. He spun around to face her, his shoulders tense, his face alert and glowering.

'Who're you?'

Clara swallowed hard.

'We met at Kitty's, remember?'

He took a step towards her, peering into her face, and Clara had difficulty in not recoiling.

Relaxing, he treated her to a leering grin.

'Oh, yeah, I remember now. You're the piece who came looking for a bit of rough. Well, I'm all yours, sweetheart. Where do you want to go for it?'

Clara bit her lip, feeling bile rise in her throat. Only once before in her life had she met a man who disgusted her as much as Ossie James, and that other nameless man had almost ruined her life.

'You're mistaken again, Mr James,' she said tensely. 'I just want to talk to you about Jenni Thomas.'

Immediately, the alert expression was back on his unpleasant face, and his eyes narrowed.

'Who?'

'The girl you were just talking to. She gave you twenty pounds.'

'Hey!' He sprang forward, gripping her forearm. 'You know too much, you do.'

She wrenched her arm from his grasp.

'Keep your hands off me!' Clara gasped, as panic made her breathless.

She was thankful they were on the street and it was still light, not in that dark back room at Kitty's.

His lips drew away from his teeth in a snarl.

'What's your bloody game, eh? It's not healthy poking your nose into my business, see. Nasty things could happen to a pretty girl like you. Know what I mean?'

Somehow Clara swallowed down her fear and held her ground.

'Don't worry, I'm not in the least interested in *you*, Mr James,' she said hastily, fear making her voice catch in her throat. 'I want to know all about Jenni Thomas.'

He stepped back, the tension leaving his face.

'You're barmy! I don't know nothing about this Jenni Thomas. So sling your hook, will you?'

He turned to step into the pub.

'I'll pay you!' Clara exclaimed desperately.

He paused and turned slowly back to face her.

'Pay?'

She nodded. 'I'll pay for any information you can give me.'

'How much?'

Fear of him making her unsteady on her feet, Clara opened her handbag with difficulty, her shaking fingers hardly able to manage the clasp. Out of her purse she took a pound note and offered it to him tentatively.

He stared at it for a moment then burst out laughing.

'A bloody quid? You must be joking! I tip more to a bookie's runner.' He laughed again at his own joke. 'You'll have to do better than that, darling.'

'Tell me what you know and I'll give you more,' Clara promised hastily.

He regarded her speculatively for a moment, then jerked his head towards the pub.

'Let's go in by here and talk about it,' he suggested slyly.

Clara stepped back, shaking her head emphatically.

'No! I'm a respectable woman. I don't go into such places, not even with my husband.'

'Oh, aye! Snobby posh. I've seen that big house you live in.'

She drew in a sharp breath of dismay.

'How do you know where I live?'

He grinned widely.

'That night at Kitty's,' he said, 'I followed you home. Been watching the house ever since. That's how I clocked Jenni Thomas. Bit of good luck, that was.'

'You know her well, don't you?'

Clara was clearly fishing. Ossie just smiled and tapped the side of his nose.

'Wouldn't you like to know?'

'Tell me!' Clara couldn't keep her feverish eagerness from her voice.

'Let's get away from by here,' he suggested, looking smug now. 'We can go to Kitty's.'

'If you want my money,' Clara said quickly, walking away down the pavement towards the main road, 'we'll talk in the street. I don't trust you, Mr James.'

'Okay.'

His tone was mild, not in the least offended it seemed. He fell into step beside her but Clara kept her distance from him. His very presence made her skin prickle with abhorrence.

'Well, are you going to tell me or not?'

'Money first, darling,' he said with a low chuckle. 'I wasn't born yesterday, mind. How much have you got in that bag?'

'Five pounds.'

Ossie stopped dead in his tracks, his expression thunderous.

'Wasting my bloody time, you are,' he said harshly. 'I said money, not loose change. I wants a hundred and fifty quid, see.'

Clara stopped, too, appalled.

'That's a small fortune. It's impossible!' she cried. 'I can't get it. I've no money of my own.'

'Get it from your old man, then,' he said impatiently.

'I can't, I tell you! He'll ask questions and . . .'

Clara bit her lip in vexation. She was so close to her goal.

'How do I know the information is worth that much?' she asked, petulantly. 'You could be trying to trick me.'

Ossie laughed.

'Believe you me, what I know about Jenni will make your hair curl. I could destroy her just like that . . .' He snapped his thumb and middle finger together, making a loud clicking sound. 'With just one word.'

His grin widened and he stepped closer.

'Tell you what, darling,' he said. 'Just so you know it's the real McCoy, I'll sell you that one word now for the five pounds in your bag. But I still wants a hundred and fifty for the details.'

Silently, and with her heart pounding in anticipation, Clara took the five notes out of her purse and handed them to him. It was her allowance for the week, but what did that matter now?

He pocketed the five pounds, still grinning at her.

Clara moistened her lips anxiously.

'Well?'

'The one word? *Murder*, darling,' he said with relish. 'Murder!'
Clara felt her jaw drop open. She was totally astounded.

'You mean . . .' she said breathlessly '. . . Jenni was mixed up
in a murder? Oh, my God!'

She'd been expecting scandal, but never something as
monstrous as this. She felt almost overwhelmed by it. Now she
had to know everything, no matter what the cost.

'A hundred and fifty quid.' He rubbed his thumb and fore-
finger together. 'When can I have it? It'll have to be soon because
I'm pushing off from Swansea. Going up the Smoke, I am, see.
Big-time, eh?'

'I'll get it!' Clara hastily assured him, though she had no idea
how she'd do that. 'But I'll need time. Say a month.'

His expression darkened.

'Don't mess me about, you little slut! I haven't finished
milking Jenni Thomas yet,' he said harshly. 'But that'll take just
a couple of weeks more, then I'm off. If you don't cough up by
then, you can forget it.'

'I'll get the money. I will!' Clara cried anxiously. She couldn't
fail now. She had to know the whole story. 'How can I reach you,
Mr James?'

'Kitty's.'

'No!'

'Kitty's! And make it soon.'

Clara rummaged frantically in her trinket box. There were the
diamond earrings old Samuel had given her as a wedding present;
a couple of brooches and some rings, Christmas gifts from Jack.
Her fingers clutched at the necklace she'd worn on her wedding
day. She arranged the jewellery on the dressing table, trying to
gauge how much she'd get for it at the pawnbroker's.

What else could she pawn? Her gaze fell on the photograph
frames on the tallboy; one of their wedding, another of Jack as a

child, and a photograph of his mother. They wouldn't be missed.

Clara handled them eagerly. They were heavy, solid silver. What else was there? There were silver-framed photographs in the back sitting-room, too. The room was so dark no one would notice they were gone. Surely, with all this, she'd have enough?

She reached out to gather them up and saw the engagement ring on her hand. She was tempted to add that to the other things, but paused. No, Jack might notice. Anyway she was reluctant to part with that. It had cost Jack an awful lot and was her most cherished trophy, the symbol of her success.

Clara stepped out of the pawnbroker's, feeling choked with anger. Nathan Joseph had driven a hard bargain. Seventy pounds was all he was prepared to give her.

She'd tried a haughty attitude but it hadn't worked and she was afraid to hang around too long, afraid he'd recognise her as the girl who used to work next door; the girl who'd married Jack Tregevny.

She had no choice but to visit Kitty again, but this time she was only prepared to risk going to the Cwm in the light of day. She was too afraid of Ossie to go at night.

She hurried down the Neath Road towards the bridge, clutching her handbag tightly under her arm. She'd never handled such a large sum of money in her life, and it made her nervous.

Seventy pounds *was* a lot of money, probably more than Ossie had seen in his life, either. It just might be enough. When he saw the cash in hand, she told herself confidently, his greed would be too much for him. He'd settle for that.

Kitty's house looked even dirtier in the bright morning sunshine. The door stood open as usual and reluctantly Clara stepped into the passage, wrinkling her nose at the various smells tainting the air.

In the back room sunlight streamed in through the bare

window, dust motes dancing in the bright beams. You could almost see the smells in those sunbeams, Clara thought, fancifully, feeling tension mount, making her body feel weak and vulnerable as a child's again.

Kitty shuffled out of the scullery on bare feet, wearing a man's moth-eaten dressing gown, the colour long since obliterated by food stains. In her hand she held a thick slice of bread, smeared with jam.

She stopped in her tracks when she saw Clara.

'Good God! Look what the cat's dragged in!'

'I'm looking for Ossie.'

Kitty flopped on to the sofa, taking a hungry bite out of the bread.

'Thought we wasn't going to see you here again,' she said after a moment. 'Thought you was too good for us.'

'I didn't want to come, don't worry,' Clara snapped. 'Ossie insisted. We have business together.'

Kitty laughed.

'You must be hard up.'

'I said, business! Where is he?'

'Right by here, darling.'

Clara jumped and whirled around in fright as Ossie spoke right behind her. She watched him warily.

He was wearing trousers and a singlet; muscles bulging in his shoulders and arms, thick coarse hair covering his chest. Muscles or not, he was no more attractive without his shirt, Clara decided.

Give him his due, the singlet was spotlessly clean, and he looked as though he'd just washed and shaved. She wondered vaguely how he managed to keep clean in these filthy surroundings.

'Have you got the money?'

'What money?' Kitty asked quickly, looking from one to the other.

They both ignored her.

'Yes,' Clara said, opening her bag and taking the bundle of notes out. She unfolded them, spreading them in a fan shape, holding them out to him.

His eyes narrowed.

'That's not a hundred and fifty.'

'It's seventy,' Clara said eagerly. 'It's nearly half. It's all I can get.'

'What's it for?' Kitty wanted to know, struggling up from the sofa.

She came forward quickly, hand outstretched, reaching for the money. Ossie snatched it from Clara's grasp before Kitty was able to touch it.

He'd taken it. She'd known that in his greed he'd not be able to resist. Clara waited expectantly for him to tell her what she wanted, needed, to know so badly.

'Well, Mr James?'

He grinned as he pushed the bundle of folded notes into the back pocket of his trousers.

'It's not enough, darling. I want the rest.'

'I can't get anymore!' Clara wailed, staring at him in disbelief, eyes wild.

Ossie shrugged his bulky shoulders.

'No skin off my rump.'

'You've taken my money!'

'Send for the bobbies then,' he retorted mockingly.

In the doorway he turned to look at her.

'Look, I'll give you a couple of weeks. No more. You want the dirt on Jenni Thomas, you have to pay for it.'

His feet were heavy on the uncovered stairs and she heard his loud footsteps on the bedroom floor overhead.

Kitty was glaring at her, her mouth twisted and ugly with greed and fury.

'What's going on? Where'd you get that money from? What you give it to him for?'

Clara swayed on her feet, unable to believe she'd been swindled out of her money so easily. She had no way of raising anymore.

Her rings, her jewellery, gone! And nothing to show for it.

A sense of outrage began to mount in her breast.

'Kitty!' she began rashly, goaded on by her rising anger. 'You've got to help me.'

'What you on about?'

'Talk to Charlie Pendle. He must force Ossie to give me what he promised.'

'Eh?'

'You said you're a friend of Charlie's, right? Well, I've paid Ossie for information and now he won't tell me what I want to know. Charlie's got to *make* him .'

Kitty looked mockingly amused.

'Oh, you've changed your tune, haven't you? You said Charlie was dangerous scum a couple of months ago. Now you want his help. Don't matter he's a dangerous criminal now, does it?'

Clara was furious.

'You've never done a thing for me in your life, Kitty. And you *are* my mother. I need your help now.'

'All that money you gave Ossie,' Kitty said bitterly. 'And never a tanner for your own mother.'

'What? You get your blood money every Friday,' Clara shouted angrily. 'You're bleeding me dry as it is! I'm at my wit's end to scrape enough together.'

'Oh, poor thing!'

'You owe me something, Kitty,' Clara accused harshly through clenched teeth. 'For ruining my childhood. Now, will you ask Charlie Pendle for help?'

Kitty gave a scornful laugh.

'Take a running jump! I'm not asking Charlie to do nothing 'cos there's nothing in it for me, is there?'

*

Kitty waited for her lodger to come down, and when she heard his shoes on the stairs, hurried into the narrow passage.

'You sneaky little bugger! What you up to?'

'Mind your own business, you old rag-bag.'

Her voice was strident. 'I want a share of that money our Clara gave you.'

He lifted a hand threateningly.

'I'll give you a black eye and a bloody nose in a minute, you stupid old tart.' He jerked his head, face dark with rage. 'Now get out of my way.'

Kitty held her ground, ready to play here trump card.

'I'll have a word with Charlie.'

Oggie's mouth twisted in mockery.

'Oh, aye! He listens to you, all right. I don't think!'

Kitty lifted her chin, a smirk on her thin lips.

'He will when I tell him about the burglaries you've been doing around here.'

'*What?*'

'Charlie don't know about that, does he?' Kitty's smile was wicked. 'He don't like his men working for themselves, especially if he don't get a share of the swag. You could end up floating in the dock with your throat cut.'

Oggie paused, visibly shaken, then rallied, his lips curling in renewed fury.

'You know nothing, and can prove less.'

'But Charlie don't worry about proof, you know that,' Kitty said, enjoying the dismay on his face. 'Charlie strikes first, then thinks later.'

'You dirty old cow!'

Raising an arm, Oggie struck her a vicious blow across the face. Screaming, Kitty sprawled on her back on the bare boards of the passage, blood spurting from her nose and top lip.

'That'll teach you to keep your mouth shut, you old hag,' said Oggie. 'If you talk to Charlie, I'll do you in proper.

And it won't be no loss to anybody, neither.'

With that he stepped across her prone body and out of the door.

Dazed, Kitty lay for a few minutes where she'd fallen, the pain in her face excruciating. After a moment more she managed to scramble on to her hands and knees.

Blood from her nose and lip dripped on to the floorboards, mingling darkly with the grime. She knelt there for a moment, staring at it. It wasn't the first time a man had bloodied her nose. Another occupational hazard.

But this time Oggie was going to pay dearly for it, and Charlie Pendle would do the dirty work for her. He owed her something. After all, he *was* the father of her eldest child and dearest daughter, Clara.

Chapter Twenty-Six

AUGUST

Jenni lay face-down on the narrow iron bedstead, nausea rising again like a tidal wave that threatened to overwhelm and drown her. Hastily she got off the bed, reaching for the enamelled pail she'd brought up from the kitchen the morning before, and retched painfully, feeling she was throwing up her insides along with everything else.

Exhausted, she lay down again, wondering if she was dying. It felt like that. Whatever it was, the vomiting had started the morning before, almost making her late for work. As the day wore on she'd felt somewhat better. But again this morning her stomach felt like the end of the world had come.

Jenni looked at the old alarm clock on the chest of drawers. Quarter to seven and she hadn't even washed herself. She struggled off the bed once more and poured water from the china pitcher into the bowl. She hated washing in cold water but it might refresh her this morning.

Waves of nausea rose and subsided as she valiantly fought against them. She mustn't be late for work. She didn't trust Mr Samuel not to sack her for the least cause, so wouldn't give him a chance to find fault.

If only this sickness would go away! Perhaps she felt like this because her period was late, so upsetting her stomach, she thought, fighting down a new wave of sickness. It had never happened before. But then, her period had never been late before.

What was wrong?

Jenni dressed, feeling worn out already before the workday started. She couldn't touch a thing for breakfast, but might manage a cup of tea.

Doris was fussing around the kitchen like a hen, busy making breakfast which she usually served at eight o'clock on the dot. Jenni sat at the table, feeling wan and listless. How on earth would she get through a day in the workroom, feeling like this?

Doris turned from the range where she had eggs and bacon sizzling in the large iron frying pan. The smell, usually so appetising, made Jenni feel dizzy again.

'Oh, Jenni, love. What's the matter? You look terrible.'

She put her elbows on the table and rested her head in her hands. Doris's sympathetic voice was almost too much for her to bear. Even now she missed the sympathy her mother had always given her.

'Upset stomach,' she murmured wretchedly. 'I feel like death itself.'

'Morning sickness?' Doris's tone was sharp and somewhat shocked.

Jenni looked up.

'What?'

'What have *you* been up to, my girl?' It was an accusation.

'Doris?' Now Jenni was shocked.

'Have you missed your whatsits?'

Jenni nodded, staring at Doris wide-eyed as comprehension slowly dawned.

It couldn't be true! Not after just the once. It was a coincidence, it had to be. Fate couldn't be so cruel. But suddenly, she knew with certainty that it was true, and a deep shame descended on her, more agonising than any wave of sickness.

'Oh, my God! It's true!'

Jenni rose slowly from the table, her face scarlet as she looked into Doris's shocked eyes.

'Hey! I never expected it of you, Jenni.'

She clapped a hand over her mouth. She was ruined! Totally and utterly. She wanted to run away and hide from the expression on Doris's plain face.

She tried to take a step towards the door, but tottered. Doris sprang to her side immediately, drawing her back to the table.

'Now you sit by here,' she said firmly. 'I'll get you a cuppa. See if you can keep it down.'

'Oh, Doris, what am I going to do?' Jenni wailed.

'I dunno, love.' Doris's voice had lost some of its scandalised tone. 'First things first. You've had a shock, I can tell.'

She placed the steaming cup in front of Jenni.

'You sip on that,' she said in a practical tone. 'I've got to serve breakfast then later we can talk. I'll tell old Samuel you're smothering with a head cold, and can't work today.'

Tears sprang into Jenni's eyes.

'Oh, Doris, why are you being so good to me after what I've done?'

The maid sniffed.

'You aren't the first and you won't be the last.' Her glance dropped. 'And *I* know what I'm talking about.' She looked up at Jenni again, two little spots of colour making her cheeks glow. 'I was in the same boat myself once.'

'You, Doris? I can't believe it.'

'Oh, I may be plain, kid, but I've had my moments. Don't you tell a soul, mind!' she said quickly. 'You're the only person in the world who knows my secret.'

The bell in the dining-room rang.

'Tsk! That's the old man wanting his eggs and bacon. You sit quietly by there and we'll talk later.'

After breakfast, although she was still shivering with the shock, Jenni felt strong enough to help Doris with the washing up, anything to take her mind off the awful truth. She felt so grateful to her. Not one word of blame had she uttered.

But others wouldn't be so charitable, Jenni knew. She'd be pilloried, crucified, abandoned by everyone – and what would her friends Meg and Renee say? They wouldn't want to know her, and who could blame them? People would call her terrible names. Tainted, she'd lose friends, job, everything. Then how would she live?

'Yes, I was in the family way, Jenni, love,' Doris told her as she sprinkled soda into the bowl of hot water. 'When I was sixteen. The young lad who lived next door, it was. Naughty children, we were, see. No more than that.'

She handed Jenni a wet plate.

'In a way I was lucky,' she went on rather sadly. 'My parents never got to know 'cos I lost it naturally after three months, which was just as well. He'd never have married me. Hell-bent on university, he was. Like I said, I was lucky.'

Doris glanced at her.

'Will your bloke marry you?' she asked. 'First thing to do is tell him.'

Jenni was silent, bending her head in new humiliation.

'Tsk! He's married, isn't he?' Doris exclaimed, inclining her head and giving Jenni a searching look. 'Anyone I know?'

She dumped the plate she was wiping down on the draining board, not caring if it broke, and flopped on to a kitchen chair, bursting into tears.

She didn't deserve this kindness and understanding. Even though Doris had been in the same position once, this was very different. Jenni and Jack were hardly children. She'd let herself go on loving him when she knew he was married. That was sinful.

And even if that marriage was no good, Jack belonged to another woman.

Well, it was exactly as Auntie Blodwen had said. Jenni's purple sin would be the end of her. It was coming true. She'd wrecked her own life. But it had been with Jack's assistance, and he *must* help her now.

'Mr Jack, it is,' Jenni whispered.

'Oh, the bugger!' Doris exclaimed loudly. 'Up to his tricks again. He ought to be strung up, he did — and not by his toes, either.'

'Only once it was,' Jenni murmured miserably, wiping away tears with the tips of cold fingers. 'I wouldn't let him touch me again.'

Doris sniffed.

'Once can be enough, Jenni, love. Well! You've got to tell him. He's got to help you. Listen, same thing happened with Clara, like I told you, only I'm sure she was swinging the lead, like. Faking it. Never saw *her* with her head in a bucket.'

'Oh, Doris, I'm so ashamed! How will I tell him?'

'Takes two to dance the tango, love, remember that. Men! They get off scot-free. It's the girl what has to face the firing squad. You tell him dinnertime when he comes home for his meal.' Doris chuckled. 'That should spoil his appetite. The lecherous devil!'

Jenni took Doris's advice. Jack had to be told as soon as possible. He didn't love her but with a child coming, he might do the decent thing. If he stood by her they could face the world together. Maybe this child was for the best; maybe it was fate's way of bringing them together as man and wife.

Jack always left the workshop before Samuel and Richie. His brother was always complaining about it. Jenni waited behind the passage door, peeking into the hall now and then to catch him arriving. He came in at last and walked straight into the front sitting-room, waiting for the gong to sound.

Gathering up her courage and taking a deep breath, Jenni left her hiding place in the passage and hurried on shaking legs to the front sitting-room. She rarely came into this part of the house unless accompanied by Violet, undertaking some household chore. Today she felt she was violating the family's privacy.

Tapping the door, she opened it and walked in.

Jack was lounging in an armchair reading a newspaper. He looked up casually, obviously expecting to see Doris. When he saw Jenni he practically shot out of the chair, throwing the newspaper on the floor.

'What the hell are *you* doing in here?'

She clasped her cold hands together nervously, appalled at the hostility in his words.

'I've got to talk to you, Jack.'

'Are you mad? Clara could come in any time. If she finds you here, there'll be hell to pay. Besides . . .' His face darkened. 'You've kept your door locked lately, haven't you? What're you playing at, Jenni?'

'Jack, I'm in trouble . . .'

'*What?*'

His face red, he stood still and stared at her as though she was Medusa. Then he lunged forward suddenly, grabbed her arm and pulled her through the door to the back sitting-room.

It was normally dark in here but today beams of midday sunlight streamed in through the windows to either side of the fireplace, striking the pair of them as if by a spotlight as they stood in the centre of the room.

'*What* did you say?' Jack's voice was rasping, and Jenni quaked with nervousness.

'Jack, I think I'm in the family way,' she said tremulously. 'Everything points to it. What are we going to do?'

He stepped back a pace. In the shaft of bright sunlight, his hair was like burnished gold, but his features were chiselled in stone.

'We?' he said querulously. 'We? What the hell's it got to do with *me*?'

'Jack!'

'Come off it, Jenni!' he exclaimed, really angry now. 'If you've been a naughty girl it's nothing to do with me.'

'What are you saying? Of course it is! You came to my room . . .'

'Oh, no!' He straightened his shoulders, looking down on her with disdain. 'I've been had like that before.' He pointed an accusing index finger at her abdomen. 'You're not passing *that* off as mine. I flatly deny it. Some other man's bastard? Not likely!'

His words were like a slap in the face and Jenni fell back a step, stunned.

'There's no other man, Jack,' she whispered, unwilling to believe he really meant what he was saying. 'You know that.' His denial was unbearable. And she'd loved him so much. He'd promised her so much. 'How can you treat me like this?'

Jack laughed – a mirthless, grating sound in Jenni's ears.

'No other man! Do you think I'd fall for that? You're a barefaced liar, Jenni!' he said through clenched teeth. 'Clara told me about this petty criminal Ossie James you've been knocking about with.'

There was a sneer on his face.

'You've both had your fun and now it's gone wrong, you're trying to pin it on me. Think you'll get money out of me, eh? Well, it won't work.'

'Clara's lying!' Jenni cried out, angry herself now. 'She's been spying on me . . .'

'Oh, so you don't deny you've been seeing this bloke?'

'Yes, I do deny it,' Jenni flared. 'He's Renee's bloke as well you know, Jack. She's been on about him for months.'

'Clara saw you with him in Monger Street some weeks ago.

You gave him money. Don't deny it – Clara *saw* you. He's your lover, isn't he? Or is he your pimp?'

Jenni felt her breath catch in her throat. Clara had witnessed the exchange of the twenty pounds, Oggie's blackmail demand? How much else did she know?

She clasped her hands in front of her as if in prayer.

'Jack, I swear to you, Og . . . Ossie isn't my lover. I hate him, in fact.'

'Then why did you give him money, eh? Why meet him on the sly?'

'I . . . I . . .'

Jenni was so overcome with fear and disappointment she couldn't answer the charge. She'd hoped for his help, never dreaming she'd walk into a trap. How could Jack be persuaded of the truth without her revealing her shameful secret?

But her heart told her that he was making this an excuse to evade responsibility. If he really loved her there'd be no suspicion in his mind. He'd used her cruelly; now he was ready to abandon her to her fate.

Yet surely there must be some spark of decency in him?

'Jack, you took advantage of me, used me,' Jenni uttered miserably. 'You owe me something – some help.'

'Oh, now we're getting to it!' he grated. 'I owe you . . . you cheap little trickster!'

He glared at her nastily, a vein swelling in the side of his throat. The blue eyes that Jenni had once seen glowing with desire for her were now filled with burning hostility.

'I owe you nothing,' he went on, his top lip curling in disdain. 'Not even a job. You're sacked, Jenni, as from this minute. And you can get out of this house, too. Tomorrow morning, first thing.'

'No! You can't do that, Jack,' she cried out, frightened and desperate. 'I must have work. Besides, you can't sack me. I work for your father.'

'You think he'll keep you on after he learns what you've been up to? You'll be lucky if he doesn't have the police on you for blackmail.'

'Please, Jack! Please . . .'

He stepped back quickly.

'Keep away from me,' he shouted harshly. 'Don't touch me, you little whore!'

The beams of sunlight were suddenly dimmed as clouds obscured the sun and the room became shadowy as Jack strode to the door.

'Stay in here until we've had our meal. I don't want anyone to see you in that state. I'll inform my father of your little tricks later today. You can start packing your bags now. Understand?'

With that he went, slamming the door behind him.

Jenni thought her heart would burst with pain at Jack's terrible words, and her mind reeled wildly. She could hardly believe what was happening. She was being thrown out, was without job or a roof over her head at the time of her most urgent need. How would she survive? Where could she go?

But she wasn't without money, reason prompted her to remember. She still had Blodwen's inheritance.

But for how long? Oggie was determined to take every penny of that from her, and if he made public her humiliating background there'd be no place for her anywhere with decent people.

Without a job or a home, she'd end up in the workhouse. Her baby would be born in the workhouse! The shame of that was terrible enough, but it was nothing to the stigma of illegitimacy. Her innocent child would have to bear that cross all its life.

Oh, what a terrible thing she'd done!

Jenni threw herself on to the sofa nearby, and laying her head in her hands, burst into tears of despondency, hot stinging tears that were like acid on her cheeks.

Through her despairing sobs, she murmured a prayer. Oh,

dear God, please forgive me for my sin, and please help me and my innocent child!

The door opened again.

Jenni's first thought was that Jack had come back. He hadn't meant any of it. He was sorry for torturing her like this.

Tears were blinding her. She stretched out her arms to implore him for pity, and cried out: 'Oh, Jack, please! Have a little mercy . . .'

'What the hell's going on here?'

She recoiled in shock, hastily wiping away her tears with cold knuckles.

Richie stood in the doorway, the light from the front sitting-room outlining his tall narrow frame and tousled mass of dark hair.

Jenni was speechless, staring at him in renewed fear as he closed the door behind him and limped towards her.

'Jenni? I thought you were supposed to be ill. What're you doing in here?' He paused, staring at her. 'God, you look awful! Why are you crying?'

She stood up, remaining silent. Richie was the last person she wanted to see or talk to. She had nothing to say, especially not to him. She moved warily, planning to dodge round him, and retreat to the sanctuary of her attic room. It was her sanctuary until tomorrow morning anyway.

She made her move but he was too quick for her, surprisingly agile even though crippled. He grabbed her arm as she tried to slip past, pulling her to stand before him.

'Leave me alone!' Jenni cried out frantically. 'Take your hands off me!'

'Keep quiet!' His tone was harsh. 'Do you want the rest of the family to hear you?'

Struggling wildly, she tried to wrench her arm away, but his grip was too strong.

'Stop fighting me, you little fool. Can't you see I want to help you?'

Jenni gulped back her sobs, trying to gain control of her voice. 'What makes you think I need help?'

'Huh! The state you're in? You look like you've been through a meat grinder.'

'Oh, thanks a lot for nothing!' she cried wrathfully.

'That's better,' Richie said evenly. 'Now you sound more like yourself.' He pulled her towards the sofa. 'Sit down.'

Jenni sat, mainly because, at that moment, there didn't seem much choice but to obey. Richie sat beside her, half turned towards her.

'Now, explain,' he demanded. 'Why were you begging Jack to show mercy? No, it's no good looking towards the door. You won't leave this room until I get the truth out of you.'

Jenni bent her head, lacing her fingers tightly together in her lap. How could she tell him what she'd done?

'It's a private matter . . . between me and Jack,' Jenni answered guardedly. Richie despised her and she had no liking for him, either. 'And none of your business.'

'And I say it is.' His voice had a warning ring to it. 'So tell me!'

Her shame was overwhelming. But it was all her own doing, an inner voice reminded her. No one could help her now, and revealing anything to Richie would only make her shame even harder to bear. He'd be glad to see the back of her tomorrow.

'I said it was private!' Jenni's tone was tart with stubbornness. 'You understand what that means, I suppose?'

He sighed. 'I'll let that impertinence pass because I can see you're not yourself. If you won't tell me, I'll have to ask Jack.'

'No!'

Jack would paint the worst possible picture of her in his present terrible mood, and although none of it was true, Richie would be only too willing to believe the lies.

Jenni felt tears sting her eyes again. But of course Jack would tell Richie everything later today; the whole family would know. It would be better if Richie heard her side first. After all, arrogant he might be yet he was a fair man, she'd give him his due.

'All right, Mr Richie, I'll tell you. I fell in love with Jack . . .'

'Oh, hell's flames!' His fist crashed down on to his knee as though he was enraged by something.

'Are you going to listen, Mr Richie?' Jenni asked angrily. He was blaming her already. 'I didn't know he was married, but then it was too late . . . I mean, I really loved him and couldn't stop. He told me his marriage to Clara was a sham. He said he'd marry me . . .'

She paused as a sob escaped her.

Richie said nothing but listened in heavy silence, his head bent low so she couldn't see his face properly.

'I'm in trouble, Mr Richie,' Jenni went on tentatively. It was no good holding back the truth now. 'I'm expecting Jack's child.'

Richie remained silent, shoulders taut with tension.

After a moment of silence, when Jenni was about to stand up and walk out of the room, he raised his head and the tension was suddenly gone.

'You've just told him?'

Jenni bit her lip, nodding, straining to hold back more tears.

'He's furious. He accused me of terrible things, called me awful names. I'm *not* after his money.' Her tone was so bitter she could hear it herself. 'I'm not a whore like he said. I loved him, totally and utterly.'

She swallowed, hardly daring to look at Richie for fear of what she'd see in his face.

'He's thrown me off, sacked me, told me to get out of this house tomorrow morning.'

Jenni's struggle with tears was in vain, and they burst out.

'Oh, Mr Richie, I'm so desperate and unhappy!'

She put her face in her hands, sobbing, afraid to meet his gaze. What must he think of her? Perhaps he thought the same as Jack, that she was a trickster and a loose woman?

'You naive little fool,' Richie said, a tremor in his voice, and something else – was it pity? 'I warned you Jack was a man of straw, didn't I?'

Jenni lifted her head, surprised at his unexpected show of feeling.

'Yes, I remember,' she confessed. 'And I thought you were just interfering.'

Richie sat quietly for a few moments, one elbow on his knee, chin in hand, obviously thinking. Jenni sat quietly, too.

She was glad she'd told him the truth. It hadn't sounded any less shameful, yet for the moment she felt some slight relief. But she shouldn't be hopeful. There was nothing to be done. Jack would never accept his responsibility, that was now very obvious. Everything was hopeless.

'I wish I were dead,' she murmured miserably.

'Melodrama will get you nowhere,' Richie responded, his tone wry now.

After a moment he straightened and turned to her.

'Jenni, I wonder if you're ready to take a chance?'

She shook her head. 'I don't understand.'

He gazed at her intently.

'Just how far would you be prepared to go to save yourself and your child? Would you go so far as to marry a man you don't love – a man you may even despise?'

She stared at him, uncomprehending.

Richie put his thumb against his chin thoughtfully.

'I'll claim the child is mine . . .'

Jenni couldn't suppress a gasp of utter astonishment.

'You can't do that! Your father would have a fit.'

'Maybe he will at first,' Richie admitted. 'But he might change his attitude when he realises he has a grandchild.'

Jenni stared. Samuel Tregevny, grandfather to *her* child? She hadn't considered that.

'I'll admit to it,' Richie went on. 'And that I'm prepared to marry you to right the terrible wrong I've done you.'

'Are you serious?'

'It'll solve everything.' He spread his hands. 'That is, if you're prepared to marry a man you don't love?'

Jenni was flabbergasted.

'I don't know what to say.' She stared into his face keenly. 'Why would you do this, Mr Richie? You don't even like me.'

'You need help.'

'No, no,' Jenni replied quickly. 'There must be more to it than that. A man doesn't sacrifice his whole life to save the shame of a . . . a fallen woman.'

'I'm sorry for you,' Richie said evenly. 'Why are you so suspicious? For you it's the chance of a lifetime. You'll enter the Tregevny family, have money and a comfortable life for you and your child. My father's first grandchild.'

Jenni's jaw dropped as enlightenment came bursting into her mind.

'That's it, isn't it?' she exclaimed loudly, jumping up from the sofa. 'It's the child. Everyone knows your father favours Jack – married and with the prospect of children. By marrying me *you'll* produce the first heir to the Tregevny money and business.'

She stamped her foot angrily.

'Oh! I should have known there was more to it than pity for me,' she went on, glaring at him. 'You're only doing this to get one up on your brother. You think my child will give you the advantage.'

'All right then, Jenni!' Richie said angrily, rising too. 'It *will* solve my problem. That is part of it. But I want to help *you*, too. You've got to believe that.'

He drove his fist into the palm of his other hand with such force she thought she heard the bones clash.

'I could knock Jack into the middle of next week,' Richie muttered savagely. 'For what he's done to you.'

He reached out and gripped her hand tightly.

'In marrying me you'll teach him a lesson, one he richly deserves. Jenni . . . Jenni, it's the best thing, the right thing, to do!'

'I don't know. I can't see myself marrying for revenge. It doesn't seem right.'

'The child!' Richie leaned towards her persuasively. 'Agree for the sake of the child, Jenni? You owe it that much.'

She turned her face to him, looking keenly into his eyes. They weren't anything like Jack's. They were dark brown. She hadn't noticed the soft light in them before, or the way his lashes curled. Suddenly, she wanted to brush aside the lock of hair that fell over his brow to see his eyes better.

Marry him . . . marry Richie Tregevny? What an astonishing idea. It seemed like an answer to her prayer. But what about Richie's ulterior motives? She didn't want to be mixed up in anything underhand. She and her child could easily become victims of any power struggle between the Tregevny brothers.

And what about love? Jenni asked herself. Did she really want to immure herself in a marriage without love? Could it last? Would she bitterly regret it after a year, when her baby had been born? It would be too late then.

But she was being selfish. Her innocent unborn child deserved every comfort and benefit. As a shamed and condemned un-married mother she couldn't hope to furnish even the least of these, whereas as Richie Tregevny's wife she could provide every-thing a child might need: a comfortable home, an education, security. Did she even have a choice? No, not really.

Marriage to Richie Tregevny — would it be so bad? Worse than what faced her otherwise?

An awful thought struck her. She'd be Jack's sister-in-law! How would she cope with that? Suddenly she wanted to giggle. How would *he* cope with it? And she'd be Clara's equal.

Her rival would be livid! It was almost worth agreeing just to upset Clara.

'Mr Richie . . . I mean, Richie.' Jenni knew she was stammering. She suddenly felt so shy and nervous of him. 'I accept your proposal of marriage. I shall be honoured to be your wife.' She nodded. 'And I mean that, Mr Richie.'

He threw his head back and laughed loudly, clapped his hands then danced a little jig. It was uneven and ungainly, and he looked silly, but Jenni couldn't laugh.

She felt suddenly overwhelmed with gratitude, but also an unreasoning fear. Undoubtedly, Richie was prepared to go to any lengths to defeat Jack.

She watched him now as he jigged, his face alive with some intense emotion. She'd never really liked him, yet thought him fair. Now he was showing a devious side to his nature, and she was uncertain. Could she trust him? She had to, there was no other way to get out of this terrible situation.

'What's going to happen next?' she asked tentatively, still watching him cavort like an excited child on Christmas morning.

He stopped dancing and reached out his hand to her. Obediently, she put her hand in his.

'Now it begins,' he said with obvious relish. 'Now we tell the world.'

Chapter Twenty-Seven

The gong sounded loudly in the hall for dinner and Jenni almost jumped out of her skin, feeling it was the sound of doomsday breaking. Now she'd have to face the family and suddenly she was terrified.

'Are you ready?' Richie asked quietly.

She'd never be ready! Was it too late to turn back? Too overcome to speak, somehow she managed a nod. He still held her hand. She felt his tremble slightly, and was surprised. Was he afraid, too? Well, why not? This was as big a step for him as for herself. This was the rest of his life; the rest of hers, too.

'Now, don't be afraid,' he went on, 'because I'm right beside you. We'll be all right as long as we stick together. There'll be recriminations, shock and possibly condemnation, but we'll weather it, Jenni. You do trust me, don't you?'

'Yes, I do.'

What choice did she have? she thought wryly. She had no control over her life anymore. She'd ruined it and now Richie was picking up the pieces. Her life belonged to him.

'Right! Come on, then. Let's face the music.'

He opened the door and they walked into the front sitting-room. The others were just sauntering towards the hall ready to go into the dining-room.

It was Jack who first turned and saw them. The shock that registered on his face as Richie and Jenni appeared hand in hand was a joy for her to behold. She wanted to laugh out loud, but held herself in check. This was no time for laughing.

'Jenni! What the hell . . .' Jack seemed too stunned to say more.

At his words everyone turned and stared. Richie squeezed her hand reassuringly.

'Listen, everyone,' he began. Jenni thought there was a tremor in his voice again. 'I . . . we . . . Jenni and I have an announcement. She has agreed to marry me.'

'*What?*'

Samuel's shout of disbelief seemed to thud against the ceiling and bounce down again, to vibrate around the walls.

It was followed immediately by a high-pitched scream of rage from Clara.

'Are you crazy, Richie?' she shouted. 'You can't do this!'

'Have you taken leave of your senses, man?' Jack bellowed. 'She's a skirt-hand!'

Jenni could feel Richie's muscles tense and knew he was angry.

'So was Clara,' he retorted loudly. 'Forgotten, have you, Jack?'

'Jenni's a dirty little trollop,' Jack spluttered with rage, glaring at her.

'Funny how history repeats itself, isn't it, Jack?' Richie growled, and Jenni, standing close by him, felt the tension mount in his body.

Jack flashed a startled glance at Clara.

'How dare you?' she screeched, her face turning marble-white. 'Jack, are you going to stand by and let him insult me?'

But the indignation on Jack's face had vanished. In its place came shock, disbelief, and then deep anger. He wouldn't look at his wife but stared at Jenni accusingly.

She turned her gaze away deliberately. Jack had rejected her and slandered her name. He might think she was doing this for revenge but it wasn't true, was it?

Samuel strutted forward, his moustache bristling. He eyed Jenni briefly before his furious gaze turned on Richie.

'I demand an explanation,' he said pompously. 'What's behind this preposterous idea?'

Richie took in a great gulp of air before answering. Jenni sensed his dread and moved closer to him, grasping his arm, showing her support. She was to be his wife, and though it wasn't what she'd hoped for, she was committed to him now.

'Jenni is . . . she's expecting my child, Father.'

There was dead silence for a long moment while everyone stared at them transfixed, and Jenni felt her cheeks burn with shame.

Now everyone knew of her disgrace, they must all think the worst of her; that she was loose and easy. Even when she was married, everyone would remember the circumstances. She'd be gossiped about. Could she ever hold her head up again?

'I don't believe it!' Samuel pronounced after a moment. He turned an accusing glance at Jenni. 'Is this some kind of trick, young woman?'

'No, Mr Samuel, sir,' she uttered meekly.

'Father!' Richie exclaimed, raw anger in his voice. 'Don't speak to my future wife in that tone. Jenni was innocent and naive, and I took advantage of her. I've acted dishonourably, I admit it. Now I'm ready to make amends. I intend to arrange for a special licence tomorrow morning.'

'No, Richie!' Clara screeched.

She took a few short frantic steps towards them, her eyes blazing, and Jenni gathered her courage to repel the vicious attack she knew was coming.

'You can't marry *her*!' Clara wailed, froth gathering at the corners of her mouth. 'You don't know anything about her. Can't you see what she's up to, you bloody fool? She's a little gold-digger — and worse!'

Her face was blotched with fury, and her eyes glittered as they glared at Jenni.

'You don't know who or *what* she is. But I do.'

Her tone was so assured, so positive, Jenni felt a jolt of terror at the prospect of immediate exposure.

Suppose Clara had spoken to Ossie? Jenni shrank from contemplating it. Even though she'd paid him to keep quiet, he'd betray her without a second thought, she knew.

Richie had accepted her transgression with Jack, but if he knew the whole scandalous story concerning her father, would he withdraw his offer of help? She couldn't blame him if he did, and waited breathlessly for Clara to go on.

'She's a slut, and this proves it,' Clara went on, spluttering in her fury. 'She consorts with known criminals. She's probably a criminal herself.'

'That's not true!' Jenni cried out defiantly, lifting her head. 'I warn you, Clara, I won't put up with your vicious lies. Two can play at that game.'

She tried to sound confident, but the venom in Clara's eyes was chilling, and Jenni felt helpless. She had no defence against the ruthlessness of Jack's jealous wife.

'Oh, yes! You'd like to shut my mouth, wouldn't you? You little tramp!' Clara cried out. 'But I know plenty about you and Ossie James.' She pointed a finger at Jenni. 'He's her lover. That's his brat she's carrying.' She turned wild eyes on Richie. 'Ossie James works for Charlie Pendle as a strong-arm thug. Scum, they are!'

Everyone seemed at a loss, and for a moment Clara looked uncertain.

'You must have heard of him?' she went on. 'He's the biggest crook in Swansea.'

'Yes, I've heard of him,' Richie said, raw disdain in his voice. 'He's the kind of man only whispered about in the back rooms of corner pubs, so how do *you* know about him? In the know about criminals, are you?'

Her face fell.

'I . . . I've heard gossip . . .'

'And I've heard enough of your jealous ravings, Clara,' Richie snapped impatiently, giving her a look of utter contempt.

He turned to his father.

'Father, Jenni and I want your blessing.'

'Oh, of course you do, Richie,' Jack said viciously. 'You're afraid Father will cut you out of his will altogether after this sorry episode. You must be out of your mind!'

The malice in his eyes as he glared at Jenni made her cringe. She stared back at his twisted expression, appalled by his hypocrisy. He no longer resembled the man she'd fallen in love with; the man she'd adored for so many months; the man to whom she'd willingly given herself.

Richie was right, Jack was a man of straw. Why hadn't she looked beyond his handsome appearance to where the real man was hiding, weak and worthless?

She'd been so badly mistaken, her judgement and common-sense failing her. What a fool she'd been! Was she being equally foolish in agreeing to marry Richie? Seeing the hostility on the faces around her, Jenni felt as though she'd fallen into quicksand and was sinking fast.

'She threw herself at me first,' Jack said with a sneer. 'When I wouldn't have anything to do with her, she latched on to you. She's a little tart, Richie. That baby could be anybody's, like Clara says.'

'How dare you say such a terrible thing?' Jenni cried out, feeling sick in the face of his terrible lies.

Her reputation was smashed now, whether she married Richie or not. Holding tightly on to his arm, she felt his muscles tense at Jack's words, but he held himself in check.

'Father, your blessing?' he said tightly.

'Blessing!' Samuel's voice shook with suppressed anger, his face turning a dull red as though he'd explode. 'I'm bitterly disappointed in you, Richie,' he said in a hushed tone. 'I thought you a man of honour. I'm ashamed to call you son.'

Richie's face whitened, and Jenni felt compassion for him. She had an impulse to exonerate him, to blurt out that the blame was Jack's. But he would only deny it; call her terrible names again. There was nothing she could do.

'You didn't talk like that when Clara came to you in trouble, did you, Father?' Richie asked, a tremor in his voice as if he was hurting inside. 'Jack's offence was the same, but you spared him this humiliation. His fall from grace was hushed up. Why do you treat me differently? Is it because I'm a cripple? Do you see me as less of a man for that?'

Samuel took a step back, looking confused, as though Richie had struck him. He glanced appealingly at Jack and then at Clara for support, but their faces were closed, lost in their own selfishness.

'That's a monstrous accusation,' Samuel murmured helplessly. 'That I should be accused of favouring one son above the other. I . . . I deny it! I . . . I am deeply hurt.'

'Then give us your blessing, Father,' Richie said, his voice unsteady, too. 'Your blessing rather than your condemnation.'

Samuel seemed to totter slightly, and clutched the high back of an armchair.

'I don't know what to say. This is all such a shock. Your mother must be turning in her grave, God rest her soul.'

'Jenni and I *will* be wed, Father.' Richie's voice rose in anger. 'With or without your blessing.'

'But it's not *your* child, Richie! Why are you lying?' Clara cried out.

She glanced at her husband almost desperately, but he avoided her gaze. She's guessed, Jenni thought. Well, serves him right!

'What are you talking about, Clara?' Richie replied, an ominous note in his voice. 'A man wouldn't admit to something like this if it weren't true.'

'But you don't know what you're doing,' she persisted

desperately, an almost hysterical note in her voice, eyes wild with fury and frustration.

'Jenni's no good, I tell you. I know for a fact that she was mixed up in a . . .'

Clara stopped speaking suddenly and stood with her mouth open, holding her breath. Jenni held hers, too.

With a shock she realised Clara *did* know something, but for some strange reason had changed her mind about speaking out. Why? What had made her hold back when she could have destroyed Jenni there and then?

The stunned silence was broken suddenly by Violet, who'd been silent up to now.

'Well, welcome to the Tregevny family, Jenni, my dear.' She stepped forward and gave her a hug. 'I'm delighted for you both, if no one else is.'

'Violet!' Samuel thundered. 'What are you doing?'

'My duty, Father,' she replied, her cheeks turning pink. 'My Christian duty.'

'You don't know what you're saying, woman,' he shouted. 'This is a serious matter which must be left to the men in the family. You know nothing of the world or the people in it.'

'And whose fault is that?' Violet exclaimed loudly and accusingly, her face growing pinker. She threw back her head defiantly.

'You've kept me under your thumb for years but I won't put up with it any longer . . .'

'This is outrageous!' Samuel stormed. He glared at Jenni. 'Look what you've done, set daughter against father.'

'No!' Violet said. 'Jenni has shown me that I, too, have a right to life and love.'

'Love?' Samuel stared at her, appalled, and seemed to totter again. 'In God's name, what's happening to my family?'

At that moment the sitting-room door burst open suddenly and Doris stood there, looking upset.

'Mr Samuel, sir,' she said, her voice high-pitched with agitation, 'I beat the gong more than fifteen minutes ago. No one's sat down. Is something wrong, sir? Is anyone dead?'

There was silence for a moment. Jack was the first to recover. 'I've lost my bloody appetite!'

He turned on his heel and marched out, pushing roughly past Doris in the doorway who stared at them all perplexed. Jenni heard the front door slam.

Doris's eyes were round. 'Sir?'

'Damn you all!' Clara shouted, and with one last wild look at Richie and Jenni, she flounced out, her shoes clipping the parquet floor of the hall before she raced upstairs.

'It's all right, Doris,' Richie said calmly. 'You can serve the meal now.' He took Samuel's arm. 'Come along, Father. I know this has been a shock. You'll feel better later.'

Samuel was mumbling something inaudible as Richie helped him out of the room, Violet walking in their wake. Usually she would have rushed to her father's aid, pandering to his every need; now she walked behind, sedate and defiant, and Jenni wondered at her new show of independence.

Jenni hung back, intending to follow Doris into the kitchen. But in the doorway Richie turned and looked questioningly at her.

'Jenni, come along.' He frowned. 'What's wrong?'

She moistened her lips, embarrassed by this awkward moment. She could never be a part of this family. The last few minutes had proved that. To Samuel she was unwelcome, to put it mildly, while Clara and Jack hated her.

'I always eat in the kitchen,' she reminded him, unable to explain the real reason for her reluctance – the sudden doubt about the wisdom of agreeing to be Richie's wife. It would never work.

'That was yesterday,' he said, lips twitching. 'Today you're practically Mrs Richard Tregevny. So take your rightful place at the table, Jenni, please.'

His look was meaningful and she could read the message clearly. Start as we mean to go on. In the face of his determination she had no recourse but to follow him into the dining-room, though her heart was filled with trepidation. This was all so wrong, she couldn't go through with it.

Doris was still standing near the door.

'What's going on?' she whispered as Jenni came alongside.

She shook her head in silent warning. She couldn't marry Richie. It would be very wrong — another big mistake. But how would she tell him she'd changed her mind? And without a ring on her finger, how would she and her unborn child survive?

Richie insisted Jenni move immediately from the attic to a bedroom at the top of the main staircase, next to Violet's, and remain there until they were married when, naturally she would occupy his bedroom.

'We'll do it this afternoon,' said Violet, beaming. 'But early.' Her face turned pink. 'Because I have to go out.'

Jenni nodded, smiling even though she felt utterly miserable. She could find little appetite for the meal of fluffy boiled potatoes, salad, and cold cuts of yesterday's honey-roasted ham.

She eyed Samuel warily. He looked white and shaken, and was silent all through the meal. He looked as though he'd experienced a profound shock. Despite her own mental turmoil, Jenni was becoming concerned for him, yet felt she dare not speak to him directly.

He would never accept her, not under these circumstances. He would always see her as a scheming interloper.

She glanced across at Richie. She'd been too hasty in jumping at his offer. She couldn't live like this, constantly parrying Clara's jealous ravings and suffering Jack's vile insults.

Lost in bleak contemplation, she was startled when Samuel straightened up abruptly and spoke to no one in particular.

'The Tregevny Rubies!' he said, and Jenni heard Richie gasp in astonishment.

Samuel slowly turned his gaze on her.

'When your child is born,' he said gravely, a tremor in his voice, 'the Tregevny Rubies will be yours.'

'Father, that's wonderful! Thank you,' Richie exclaimed.

He was smiling broadly, obviously pleased and delighted at his father's pronouncement. But Jenni was perplexed and at a loss, waiting for someone to explain. No one did.

She glanced at Violet and was jolted. Violet's previous look of happiness was gone. Her shoulders drooped and a shadow clouded her face.

The Tregevny Rubies! Whatever they were, by the look on Richie's face they represented the blessing he craved most from his father while to Violet they obviously meant something very different.

Everything had changed in Abertawe House since Jenni had agreed to marry Richie, and she knew she was to blame for allowing herself to fall in love with Jack.

Her thoughts turned to Clara, sulking upstairs, and a cold shiver ran through her. Clara knew something, that was obvious, but perhaps she didn't know it all which was why she'd hesitated. But how long would it be before she decided to speak out?

It would be like living on a knife edge remaining here. Jenni mustn't risk it. Somehow she must explain to Richie that she couldn't marry him after all. Then she must leave. The Hafod was no longer a safe haven. Where she'd go next Jenni had no idea.

The gong sounded again for supper, but Jenni made no attempt to go downstairs. Violet had insisted on helping her move into the bedroom at the top of the staircase immediately after the midday meal and Jenni had gone along with it, saying nothing. Richie must be told of her decision first.

This room was a far cry from the attic and she could have been very comfortable here. But it was impossible for her to stay. She'd spent all afternoon, ravaged by regret and doubt, and now believed she knew what had to be done.

A knock came at her bedroom door some ten minutes after the gong had sounded. Opening it, she wasn't surprised to see Richie.

'Didn't you hear the gong?'

Jenni nodded. 'Yes,' she admitted, turning away.

'What's wrong, Jenni?' He came further into the room. 'Look, I know you're nervous, but we have to make it look good. Make a stand.'

She took a deep breath before turning to face him. The sooner she told him of her decision, the better.

'Richie, I'm going away.'

'What?'

'I can't marry you.'

'Jenni!'

Suddenly his expression turned grim.

'Is is because I'm a cripple?' he asked harshly, and she was appalled that he should ask her that. She shook her head vehemently. Before she could answer the charge, he went on: 'Does my twisted foot repel you that much?'

'My decision has nothing to do with that, Richie,' she cried out. 'I'm hurt you should think me so shallow and unfeeling.'

'Then what is it, Jenni?' His voice was still tense. 'What other obstacle could there be?'

'It's wrong!' she said. 'Marrying for all the wrong reasons, we'd never be happy together.'

She twisted her hands, feeling wretched at the look of consternation and disappointment on his face. But he'd get over it. After all, he didn't love her so he couldn't really be hurt.

'You're expecting a child,' he said quickly. 'That's reason enough.'

Jenni shook her head.

'Not your child, Richie.'

A spasm of pain flashed across his face and Jenni was immediately sorry she'd said that. Hurting him was the last thing she wanted.

'Your family is in turmoil because of our decision to marry.'

'To hell with the family!'

'You don't mean that.' Jenni was shocked at his tone and expression.

'Yes, I do!'

Jenni shook her head in despair. Why was he making it so difficult?

'Richie, I don't love you and you don't love me. Besides, there'll never be anything but disharmony in this house. I can't live like that. I won't bring up my child in such a dismal atmosphere.'

'But, Jenni, listen. We can live elsewhere. I'll find us a house . . .'

'No!' She shook her head and waved her arm vehemently, not wanting to hear his arguments. Her mind was already made up. Nothing he could say would change that.

'Within a year we'd regret it,' she said quickly. 'We'd end up hating one another. I know what I'm talking about. It happened to my parents. They . . . destroyed each other.'

'But, Jenni, think!' he said earnestly. 'What the hell will you do? An unmarried mother. How will you live?'

'I'm not without funds,' she replied proudly. 'I have a little money, a small inheritance. I won't starve.'

If Oggie didn't take it all. She had to meet him again tomorrow as he was demanding a further twenty pounds. She'd pay him that then disappear. It was the only thing to do. She should have realised that as soon as Oggie reappeared in her life, her time in the Hafod was ended.

'How long will that last?' Richie asked. 'You don't know the prejudice you'll face out there. You won't survive.'

'Oh, I know all about prejudice.' Jenni nodded sagely. 'I've dealt with it before.'

Yes, she'd run away from it then as she was doing now, an inner voice mocked her.

'What Jack and I did was very wrong,' she went on sorrowfully. 'Now I must pay the price.'

'But you don't have to,' Richie said, anger colouring his voice. 'Damn it, Jenni! You can't *do* this to me now. My father's beginning to come round. You're ruining everything!'

She was suddenly furious.

'Oh, I know it spoils your plans, Richie!' she blurted out. 'But I can't help that.' Couldn't he appreciate her side of things? 'Getting the upper hand with your brother is important to you, I know, but I won't let you use me or my child to do it.'

Richie's face paled and his lips tightened.

'That's unfair!' he said, his tone hard. 'I offer you and your child comfort and security for the rest of your lives.'

'I believe I'll need more than that,' Jenni retorted sharply. 'Maybe I don't deserve it but I need love, too. And there's little love at Abertawe House. No, Richie, it won't work for us.'

'But I've told everyone,' he said, a savage note in his voice. 'Everyone at the shop, and some of the clients, too.'

'You had no right to do that!' she flared.

'I thought I had every right. We had an agreement.'

An agreement? That was the way he saw it. A business arrangement. Well, of course, he was right. That's what it was, all it ever could be. She was right to withdraw.

'I suppose you told them the real reason, too, did you?' she asked tremulously.

'No, of course not!'

Jenni was thankful for that. She'd go away, far away, to

another town, perhaps, then Renee and Meg need never know of her shame. Hopefully, they'd always think of her fondly and with respect.

'I'll go where no one knows me, buy a second-hand wedding ring,' Jenni told him. 'I'll call myself Mrs Thomas, a widow. I'll manage.'

He stared at her for a long moment, his expression strained.

'You won't reconsider, then?'

'My mind's made up. I can't stay here with Clara and Jack hating the very sight of me . . . your father thinking I'm dirt beneath his feet.'

He took a step forward.

'Jenni! Would it make a difference if I said I didn't want you to leave . . . that you mean something to me?'

'No, Richie, because we both know it's not true.' She shook her head, saddened. 'No more promises. No more lies.'

She turned her back on him and walked quickly to the window. There was no more to say. Whatever her future was, she was certain now it did not include Richie Tregevny.

So much for the gypsy's prophecy!

Jenni felt like a coward, hiding in her bedroom.

She expected Violet to come and see her after hearing Richie's news, but she saw no one. Perhaps he hadn't found the opportunity or the courage to tell the family that the marriage was off. Well, that was up to him.

Tomorrow, after paying off Oggie, she'd spend the day looking for lodgings on the other side of Swansea. One thing was certain: she'd shake off the dust of Abertawe House before the coming weekend, and would be glad to see the last of the Tregevny family.

Doris came up just before she went home to tell Jenni that Renee Morris had called to see her. Jenni ventured downstairs and found Renee sitting in the kitchen. She sprang up when Jenni came in, her face alive with curiosity.

'Hey!' she exclaimed immediately. 'What's this I hear about you marrying Mr Richie? You're a dark horse, aren't you?'

Jenni felt embarrassed in front of Doris, who was obviously all ears.

'Come up to my room,' she suggested to Renee. 'We can talk there.'

Upstairs, Renee looked around her with open admiration.

'*Duw!* There's posh! You've fallen on your feet by here, kid.' She flopped down on the bed. 'Come on now,' she urged, grinning widely. 'Tell me all about this big romance. Every last detail, mind.'

'There's no romance,' Jenni said, swallowing the lump in her throat.

She hated deceiving her friend, telling barefaced lies, but the truth was far too shameful.

'Richie did ask me to marry him,' Jenni went on listlessly, 'but I turned him down.'

Renee looked astounded.

'What? But he's telling everyone you're going to be wed, and by special licence, too. What's going on, Jenni, love?'

'Richie jumped to conclusions so it's his own fault if he's made a fool of himself.'

'What's behind this?' Renee asked slowly, a shrewd expression on her plain face. 'I got the impression you were sweet on Mr Jack.'

'Certainly not, Renee.' Jenni tried to sound indignant. 'He's married, after all.'

She lifted her chin, struggling for composure.

'It's simply a misunderstanding,' she went on, knowing the explanation sounded paper thin. 'The fact is, I'm going away, Renee. I can't stay here any longer. I'm certainly not going back to the shop.'

Renee jumped off the bed and came to her, putting an arm around her shoulders, giving her a warm hug.

'But why? What's all the mystery?'

'There's no mystery,' Jenni said quickly. 'It's time I moved on. I'm thinking of going to Cardiff to work.'

'Oh, no, Jen! You can't leave now, kid. Not now . . .'

Renee sat down again, pulling Jenni down beside her.

'Listen, love,' she began. 'I've got some news too. I'll probably be getting married myself very soon.' Her glance at Jenni was almost shy. 'The thing is . . .' She moistened her lips, hesitating a moment. 'Well, kid, I'm in the family way.'

Jenni stared at her, her mouth dropping open.

'What? Oh, my God! Renee! No, no!'

She couldn't keep the consternation from her face or voice and Renee's smile was suddenly wiped away.

'Oh, don't look like that, Jen, mun,' she said. 'I'm practically engaged, aren't I? You're the first one I've told. I'm telling Ossie tonight. So, you see, I'll be getting wed myself.'

Jenni felt as though icy water was running through her veins instead of warm blood. Her own problems were forgotten in the face of this new disaster.

'Oh, Renee, my dear girl, this is terrible,' she wailed, clutching fiercely at her friend's hand. 'You don't know how terrible. And it's all my fault. I should've warned you but I was too much of a coward . . .'

Renee gave an uncertain giggle.

'What are you on about, kid?'

'He'll never marry you, Renee,' Jenni burst out. 'He's no good, never was. His family are a pack of thieves and jailbirds.'

Renee stood up, looking angry, and pulled her hand away from Jenni's grasp.

'What's the matter with you, Jen? Why are you saying these awful things about Ossie?'

'His name isn't Ossie. It's Ogmore James. He's from my

home village, Trehafod. I've known him for years.'

'You knew him before?' Renee stared at her. 'Why didn't you tell me, then? Why all the secrecy?' She tossed her head. 'I don't believe it! You're fibbing for some reason – and I thought we were friends.'

'Yes, we are friends, and I've let you down.' Jenni wrung her hands in despair. 'Oh, God, what are we going to do?'

Why hadn't she found the courage to speak out against Oggie sooner, denounce him for the swine he was? Now her best friend was ruined for life, and it was all her fault. She'd never be able to forgive herself.

Renee's predicament was even worse than her own. At least Jenni had a little money behind her, but Renee had nothing, and there was Meg to think of. She'd be so ashamed. It would be the end of her.

'I'm not staying to listen to this!' Renee exclaimed angrily, stepping towards the door.

'Wait, Renee!' Jenni exclaimed urgently, jumping to her feet. She'd have to reveal the truth, or at least part of it.

'I'm not lying. Oggie is a bully and . . . and a blackmailer. He knows something about me, about my family, and I'm paying him to keep quiet.'

Renee stared at her in disbelief.

'You're lying! You're jealous, that's what it is. Jenni, I thought you were my friend.'

'I am! Listen!' she went on quickly. 'Don't tell Oggie about the baby. Just finish with him. I'll help you out with some money when the time comes, but say nothing to him.'

'Are you *twp* or what?' asked Renee, staring at her as if she thought Jenni had lost her senses. 'He *will* marry me. We've already talked about it. I made sure of that before I ever let him touch me.'

'But you can't trust him!' Jenni cried out. 'Oh, Renee! Renee, I'm *so* sorry!'

Renee stared at her a moment, her face pale.

'And I'm sorry I ever called you friend, Jenni,' she said angrily. 'Your romance with Richie has gone sour so you want to spoil mine as well. Jealousy, it is! After all Mam and I did for you.'

Renee marched to the door then looked back, her gaze cold.

'Don't come round to Hafod Row anymore because you're not welcome. I'll never speak to you again, Jenni Thomas!'

Chapter Twenty-Eight

Jenni had known she wouldn't be able to sleep after hearing Renee's devastating news. She didn't. Not until dawn began to lighten the bedroom did she drift off fitfully for a few hours.

She woke knowing exactly what to do to help her friend: marry Richie Tregevny after all. As his wife, a Tregevny, she'd be in the ideal position to help and protect Renee, not only in the difficult months ahead but later when she was struggling to bring up her child as an unmarried mother.

Jenni's marriage might well bring her a lifetime of unhappiness, but that was a price she'd have to pay. She'd caused this tragedy. If it hadn't been for Jenni, Oggie James would never have attached himself to her friend.

But how would Richie react to her change of mind? He'd be angry for sure, and suspicious of her motives, but she'd be honest with him; explain her reasons openly. The sooner she talked to him the better.

She washed and dressed at speed, thankful that this morning the sickness was in abeyance. As she ate breakfast with Doris in the kitchen she could faintly hear the voices of the family in the dining-room, but Richie's wasn't among them.

'Mr Richie had his earlier,' Doris volunteered, as if reading her mind. 'He's gone off to the shop.'

Maybe it was just as well, Jenni thought. What she had to say must be spoken in private. It wouldn't do if the family suspected their unity.

It was a minute to nine when she stepped over the shop's threshold. Mr Napier greeted her with a lopsided smile, a knowing expression in his watery eyes.

'Well!' he began, his tone bordering on sarcasm. 'You're a deep one and no mistake.'

Jenni was immediately nettled.

'I beg your pardon?'

'Snaring Mr Richie for a husband. Very neatly done, my girl. Got the family pretty stirred up, so I've heard.'

'How dare you, Mr Napier?' Jenni was indignant at his familiar manner and the notion that she was being gossiped about. 'Mind your own business!'

He shook his head, looking smug.

'Oh, I never do that, as I've told you before. To know all is to gain all.' He fingered his moustache, preening. 'Besides, you may have done me a bit of good, too.'

'How?'

'Apparently Mr Samuel's not well enough to come in.' Expanding his narrow chest, he hooked his thumbs into the armholes of his waistcoat, looking extremely pleased with himself. 'So I'm in charge of the shop today and perhaps even longer. Weeks, months . . . who knows?'

A gleam came into his eyes, and Jenni was confused to recognise it as admiration.

'I've worked here thirty years, man and boy,' he went on, wonder in his tone. 'Mr Samuel never missed a day's work before. Unheard of. You're a blooming catalyst, young Jenni, that's what you are.'

She had no idea what a catalyst was, but didn't like the sound of it and wondered if, despite that gleam, she was being insulted in a roundabout way.

'I'll thank you to watch your language in front of me, Mr Napier,' snapped Jenni, lifting her chin proudly. 'I'm a respectable girl.'

Well, she *used* to be respectable, she thought sadly, making a dash for the stairs.

There was already a heavy silence in the workroom, the atmosphere oppressive with bad feeling. Jenni called 'Good morning' as she entered, but no one replied.

Renee sat, head bent over her work, shoulders hunched. Jack's face was a mask of bad temper, while Richie looked sullen and wretched as though a storm cloud had just rained on him.

Jenni hung up her coat and hat and sat at her machine, hesitating to speak again. She stared hard at Renee's bent head, willing her to look up. It was heartbreaking being out of favour with the girl who was like a sister to her.

'Renee, how's Meg? Are her legs any worse?'

Renee gave a loud, disdainful sniff, and said nothing.

Richie flashed an impatient glance at Jenni.

'Why are you here?' he asked, an edge to his voice.

'I still have to earn a living,' she replied tautly, annoyed at his unfriendly tone.

'Really?' He raised his eyebrows, mouth twisted in scorn. 'I thought you were preparing to leave us?'

Renee's head shot up at these words, and so did Jack's. They were both staring at Jenni in curiosity and she shifted uncomfortably on her stool, not liking the speculative glitter in Jack's eyes. The sooner she told Richie of her changed plans the better.

'I need to talk to you – in private, Richie.'

'What's left to say?'

Jenni bit her lip in vexation. Must he be so irascible when she was trying to make amends? It didn't augur well for their future together. If it weren't for Renee she wouldn't dream of marrying him, and she cursed Oggie for forcing this on her.

'Please?'

'Oh, very well.' He got up from his stool. 'We can talk in the cashier's office.'

In the office, Richie sat and indicated a chair for Jenni. She took it thankfully. Now the moment had come she didn't know how to start, and was embarrassed and nervous, unable to shake off the notion that she was about to take the most disastrous step of her life.

It was sheer madness tying herself to a man she didn't even like, let alone love; a man who certainly didn't love her but probably despised her. Only guilt about Renee's plight kept her steadfast. She wouldn't let her friend down no matter what it cost her personally.

Richie waited for her to begin, looking idly out of the window at the shop floor beneath where Mr Napier bowed and scraped to a few early-bird customers.

'It's about your marriage proposal,' started Jenni, tentatively. 'Is it still . . . on offer?'

He turned his head slowly to stare at her, eyes glinting dangerously. As if that bleak stare wasn't enough, his continued silence unsettled her, too, and she twisted her hands together hard, feeling and hearing the joints crack.

'I've thought it over, Richie,' she went on with difficulty, the moisture in her mouth drying up, making her tongue stumble over the words. 'And . . . and I accept your proposal.'

'What d'you think you're playing at?'

Jenni bridled at the rawness of his tone.

'You mean, you don't want to marry me now?' she asked loudly. She hadn't considered that.

His expression was dark.

'I mean, what's your game?'

Nervously, Jenni flicked a strand of hair behind her ear. The glint in his eyes had changed to open hostility, and she quailed.

If Richie withdrew his proposal, how could she aid Renee in her trouble?

She was prepared to face the shame and humiliation of unwed motherhood, she'd fended off prejudice before, but Renee and Meg would be at the mercy of general scorn and condemnation and she doubted they'd survive. Her joining the miserable Tregevny clan was the only way.

Jenni took a deep breath and lifted her chin.

'All right, Richie, I'll tell you the truth.' Or at least part of it, she thought guardedly. 'Let's be honest with each other. You believe that if Jack gets the major share of the business, he'll force you out. Am I right?'

Richie stared at her in silence, his jaw rigid. Jenni passed her tongue across her lips, hesitating at the sight of his closed expression but forcing herself to press on.

'But with a wife and baby you'll gain favour in your father's will, and the business will be virtually yours. You want this desperately.'

He still didn't answer but continued to glower. Clearly, he wasn't going to make it easy, and Jenni bit her lip in vexation.

'For my part,' she went on doggedly, her wary gaze on his face, 'with a ring on my finger I'd be saved from shame and probably poverty. Our marriage would be of mutual benefit, I do see that now.'

'Honesty you said, Jenni, remember?' Richie growled at last. 'We'd never be happy, you said, so why change your mind?'

'I haven't!' she exclaimed without thinking.

His answering glare was one of fury, and she hastily went on: 'What I mean is — you'd get what you want, and my happiness, my need for love . . . well, that doesn't matter any longer. I owe a debt to Renee, and I can help her best as a member of the Tregevny family.'

She thought he looked shocked. When he opened his mouth

to speak, Jenni forestalled him, crying: 'Yes! All right, Richie, perhaps I *am* being mercenary about it. But it's all for Renee.'

His frown deepened, puzzlement creasing his brow.

'What the hell has she to do with our marriage?'

Jenni swallowed hard. Now she'd have to reveal a confidence. Renee was already angry with her, and would probably see this as a new betrayal.

'Renee's in trouble,' Jenni mumbled. She lowered her gaze, feeling ashamed for her friend. 'The worst kind of trouble, and it's all my fault.'

To do him justice, Richie looked concerned.

'I'm sorry,' he said. 'But what's it got to do with you?'

'Oggie James, the man responsible, is blackmailing me.'

Richie shot out of his chair.

'What's that?' His puzzlement turned in a moment to thunderous anger. '*Why*, in God's name? And why didn't you tell me before?'

Jenni rose, too, holding her back straight and her head high.

'I will *not* tell you why, Richie, so please don't ask.'

She sat down again, suddenly weak with apprehension.

'Oggie's from my home town in the Rhondda,' she admitted hesitantly. 'He knows something about . . . my family. That's all I'll say.'

Richie began to pace about the small office with ungainly strides. Jenni watched him, her unease growing. He was probably scheming how he could wriggle out of the proposal now he knew a scandal hung over her.

Suddenly he stopped pacing.

'You've given him money? How much?'

'Twenty pounds,' Jenni admitted, surprised he wasn't making excuses to bring their discussion to an end. 'But he wants more — much more.'

Richie crashed one fist into the palm of his other hand, a habit of his when he was enraged.

'You should've come to me.' His lips curled in a snarl. 'I'd have dealt with *him*.'

Jenni shook her head.

'Oggie's a dangerous man, Richie. You don't know him like I do. He's violent and unscrupulous. He latched on to Renee to get close to me again, and now she's paying the price. I *must* help her, and you've got to help me.'

His gaze was on her, but this time there was a new look in his eyes; perhaps seeing a side of her he didn't recognise and didn't like the look of. She'd seen it often on the faces of the people of Trehafod.

'I swear to you, Richie,' Jenni cried out, concerned that he thought the worst of her, 'before I came to Swansea, I'd done nothing to be ashamed of.'

His expression revealed disappointment.

'You don't trust me, Jenni,' he said quietly. 'If we're to be married, don't you think I should know everything about you?'

She felt breathless with near panic.

'If you knew my real name . . .' she faltered, gathering courage to go on '. . . you might change your mind. If you haven't already.' She lifted her chin. 'I'm asking you to trust me, Richie.'

They looked deep into each other's eyes for a long moment, and Jenni felt a tremor go through her body. Was the gypsy's prophecy about to come true? If so, it was in a way she'd never dreamed of.

'Very well. We shall be married.'

His reply was cold, detached, but he reached out a hand to her and, grasping it, Jenni rose to her feet, her heart pounding with renewed hope.

'That special licence,' he said blandly and with no warmth, 'I'll apply for it today. We'll be married early next week. Do you need money for a trousseau?'

Jenni shook her head, lifting one hand to her throat, suddenly overcome with relief and gratitude.

'No, thank you, Richie.' She paused, wondering if she'd made her conditions clear to him. 'You understand my obligation to Renee, don't you? You will support me?'

'Of course,' he said dismissively. 'You'll be my wife. I'll need your support, too, in persuading my father this marriage is a good idea.' He looked at her steadily, his gaze piercing. 'In love or not, we have to make it a success.'

'I'll do my best.' She touched his arm. 'Oh, and Richie, please don't let Renee know I've told you about her problem. Things are going to be difficult enough for her as it is.'

He stared at her for a moment, unsmiling.

'I may be a cripple, Jenni, but I'm not a callous, bigoted fool.'

Violet's uncharacteristic chirpiness at breakfast gave Clara a splitting headache.

Samuel, usually a hearty eater, scraped his knife and fork round his plate as though he'd forgotten what they were for, leaving his food untouched. The skin around his jowls looked loose and grey and the lines on his face had deepened overnight.

When he announced, rather pathetically, that he wouldn't go into the shop that day, Clara was startled. And so was Jack, by the astonished expression on his face. She saw this quickly turn to speculation, and knew intuitively what her husband was thinking. *The old man is finally past it; finished; he's letting go of the reins. Time to step in and take over.*

If only Jack *could* take over before Richie made the mistake of marrying Jenni Thomas. Jack's mistress, his trollop, married to the eldest Tregevny son? It was unthinkable. Nothing would ever be the same for Clara again when Jenni's bastard child was born.

She felt her blood turn to ice-water at the thought, and gritted her teeth at the shiver that went through her. She wouldn't let it happen. There were ways and means of getting rid of Jenni for good, and she'd do whatever was necessary.

When the so-called breakfast was over, Jack hurried off to the shop, probably anxious to see what Richie was up to there. Violet, dressed up for once, went out too, leaving Clara wondering vaguely where she was going that early in the morning. Violet was out so much these days, and staying out so late. The hitherto smooth running of the household was beginning to falter, and Clara was disturbed by the changes.

Samuel slouched, eyes closed, in a chair in the front sitting-room, not even interested in the daily papers. Avoiding him, Clara went to her bedroom.

She felt that cold apprehension run throughout her body again, but in her mind anger burned brightly and resentment smouldered like embers unable to die. Her hands shook uncontrollably. She knew it was from desperation.

She *had* to stop that marriage, and the only way to do that was to discover the full story behind Jenni Thomas. But where could she get the eighty pounds she still needed for Ossie James?

Of course! Take the Tregevny Rubies and pawn them. The idea had been at the back of her mind for days in a vague way, but had seemed too dangerous, too outrageous, even for her.

Alice, Samuel's wife, had been the last Tregevny woman to wear the jewels and at her death they were stored away, awaiting the first Tregevny wife of the next generation to give birth to a son. That would never be Clara, but she'd be damned if it were Jenni Thomas, either.

Clara had never laid eyes on the rubies, but knew where they were kept. In the top of the chest-of-drawers in Samuel's bedroom, so she'd been told by Jack, lay a red velvet box, and inside was the ruby necklace.

If the necklace was missed there'd be a hue and cry, but she could blame Jenni for the disappearance. One more black mark against her to turn Richie' mind from such an ignominious union.

Still in dread of what she was about to do, Clara went out on to the gallery and leaned over the banister to look down into the hall, listening. Doris was still in the kitchen washing up, no doubt, and as long as Samuel remained where he was, Clara was safe.

Without wasting anymore time, she tiptoed along to the master bedroom. The chest-of-drawers stood against the wall opposite the bed. Clara opened the top drawer and lifted the folded underwear lying there, being careful not to disturb it too much.

Her heart gave a great lurch as the red velvet box was revealed. She'd leave the box still in place, she thought cunningly. That way no one would realise the gems were gone, and she could expose Jenni as the thief in her own time.

With clammy fingers she opened the box and lifted out the necklace. It was surprisingly heavy, its ornate design reminding Clara of a candelabra. It was ugly, she decided at once, and she'd never have worn it. Well, perhaps she would, just to show off the stones. But anyway, she'd never have the chance.

Clara hurried back to her bedroom, wrapped the necklace in one of Jack's linen handkerchiefs and put it in her bag. She donned a shabby jacket from the cupboard in the passage downstairs and tied a scarf around her head. It was too warm in this weather and wasn't much of a disguise, but it would have to do.

Quietly, she left the house and made her way to Neath Road to catch a tram. There were several respectable pawnbrokers in town. Surely one of them would give her the eighty pounds she needed?

Clara was in a mood of desperation when she returned to the Hafod some time later, the rubies still in her bag. She was angry, too, at the looks of deep suspicion she'd received from most of the pawnbrokers she'd approached. Those who were prepared to take the gems had offered her a paltry amount. If she hadn't felt so despondent she'd have laughed in their faces.

The tram passed the row of shops on Neath Road, and

looking idly out of the window her glance fell on the pawn-broker's next door to Tregevny's shop. She had dismissed Nathan Joseph previously as being unlikely to afford such a vast sum as eighty pounds. But now she was at her wits' end.

There was no reason to suppose he would be anymore accommodating than the others. Yet what had she to lose?

Clara clutched at her bag as she rose to get off the tram at the next stop. The rubies were no good to her in themselves. She needed cash. Nothing ventured, nothing gained.

'Are you sure you want to part with this, madam?' Nathan Joseph asked. 'It looks old. Has it been in your family long?'

Clara felt exasperation rise, fuelling her nervousness.

'Are we going to do business or not?' she demanded tartly. 'I can go elsewhere, you know. You're not the only pawnbroker hereabouts.'

Perhaps she shouldn't have risked coming in here, she thought, her unease rising. This *was* too close to home.

'No, no. I assure you, madam, I'm willing to deal.' Nathan smiled ingratiatingly. 'But it's better to know the history of a piece, I find, especially jewellery. It makes it easier to sell later . . . that is, if the customer doesn't redeem.'

Clara put her nose in the air.

'Of course I'll redeem.' It was ridiculous, of course, but she couldn't bear for his sort to think she was badly off. 'This is merely a temporary measure.'

'What sum did madam have in mind?'

Clara moistened her lips. This was the crunch. If he refused, she was done for.

'I want eighty pounds, not a penny less.'

He raised his heavy eyebrows.

'Eighty!'

Clara grabbed at the necklace lying on the counter.

'I'll go elsewhere!'

'No, madam, please!' Nathan Joseph lifted both hands in protest. 'I'm agreeable to the sum. I have it here.'

To her astonishment and relief, he reached into a drawer nearby and, taking out a bundle of large white notes, counted them out one by one on to the counter.

'Eighty pounds in fivers, madam. I trust that's satisfactory?'

Clara's cold fingers relinquished their hold on the necklace, and clutched at the money.

'Yes, that'll do.'

Hastily, she gathered up the notes and pushed them into her bag, then turned to leave.

'Just a moment, madam. Aren't you forgetting something?'

Clara turned, eyes wide.

'What?'

'Your ticket.' Nathan held the pawn ticket out to her. 'You won't be able to redeem the necklace without this.'

Clara gave him a haughty look and snatched the ticket from his fingers. As she did so a brilliant idea came to her. Planting the pawn ticket in Jenni's bedroom was an ideal way to implicate her. Once Clara discovered the truth about Jenni and denounced her, to blame the theft of the rubies on her, too, would be an extra nail in her coffin. She might even go to prison, she and her bastard child!

Clara hurried away from the pawnbroker's, feeling tension vibrate in her from head to toe; even her vision seemed blurred. At the same time she felt elated. She'd got away with it! She'd fooled Nathan Joseph completely.

Now she needed to see Ossie James as soon as possible, but felt too weak at the moment to face both him and Kitty. She decided to return to Abertawe House instead, have a cup of tea, settle down and compose herself before her next ordeal in the Cwm.

When she stepped over the threshold Doris was hovering in the hall, an anxious look on her face.

'Oh, Mrs Tregevny, there's glad I am to see you back.'

'Pardon!'

Clara looked down her nose with disdain, a look she reserved for servants, especially those who got above themselves as Doris often did.

Doris nodded her head towards the front sitting-room.

'There's a *person* waiting in by there to see you.'

Clara felt the hairs on the back of her neck rise painfully. Kitty! Oh, my God!

'Barged in, he did,' Doris went on, her lips thinning in annoyance. 'Wouldn't leave when I told him you was out.' She gave a loud sniff. 'Count the silver, I'm going to.'

She gave a meaningful glance towards a new-looking suitcase standing at the foot of the stairs.

'Whose is that?'

'It's his,' Doris replied with disdain. 'It's heavy. He's already got stolen stuff in it, I shouldn't wonder.' She tossed her head. 'But I knows every little trinket and gewgaw in there, 'cos I dusts 'em every day. I'll know if anything's missing. There's some silver photo frames already gone from upstairs, and elsewhere too. It's disgusting!'

Clara swallowed hard.

'That'll be all, Doris, if you please!'

Clara watched the maid disappear through the door at the back of the hall before entering the front sitting-room.

Oggie James was fingering a fine china figurine on the mantelpiece. He turned with a ferocious frown, probably expecting to see Doris. When he saw Clara, he grinned impudently.

'Well, hello, darling! Didn't expect to see me, did you?'

She was almost breathless with fright and indignation.

'Why did you come here? Are you mad?'

He stood in front of the fireplace, hands in pockets, his overcoat and trilby flung on to a chair nearby.

'I'm buggering off from Swansea today,' he said. 'Thought I'd give you another chance to buy what I know about Jenni.'

Getting over her fright, Clara looked more carefully at him. His face was battered; a black eye, a split lip, and there were bruises on one cheek bone.

'Did Charlie Pendle do that?' she asked with sudden insight.

Oggie looked nasty.

'You're too clever for your own good, you are.' He touched his bruised cheek. 'Your bleeding mother grassed me up!' he went on savagely. 'Now Charlie's out to get me. His boys had one go last night but I did for 'em both so now the bobbies will be after me as well. That's why I've got to get out today.'

Clara held up her hands in horror.

'I don't want to know anything about it!' she cried, appalled. 'I don't want to be involved. Besides, Kitty's *not* my mother. She's not!'

'Ought to have done her in, too,' he growled. 'The dirty old bag.'

Clara suddenly wished with all her heart that he had done for Kitty, then she'd be rid of the shame for good. With a sudden rush of heat to the face, she wished fervently he'd do for Jenni, too. If she were dead everything would return to normal. If only Jenni would die!

Startled, yet exhilarated by the direction of her own thoughts, she opened her bag and took out the money, her tongue trembling on the question she longed to ask. Would this man kill Jenni for eighty pounds?

Suddenly cold caution made her bite the words back. Perhaps he would, but then she'd be in his power for the rest of her life. It would be like putting an invisible noose around her own neck. No, she'd have to settle with Jenni herself.

At the sight of the money Oggie's murderous expression cleared instantly.

'Well, that's better!' He held out his hand. 'How much?'

Clara pressed the money protectively against her chest. He'd tricked her once before. Now she'd make sure she got her money's worth.

'No! I want the information first.'

He shrugged.

'Okay, darling. I'll give you a name. That should tell you everything. Jenni's father was George Goodenough of Trehafod in the Rhondda.'

Clara looked puzzled.

'This means nothing to me.'

Oggie looked impatient.

'Goodenough, the murderer. Did his wife in, didn't he? About four years ago. She was whoring around, the dirty tart. Strung him up, didn't they? It was in all the papers from Carmarthen to London. You must have heard about it, mun. The trial and hanging were the sensations of the year.'

Clara opened her mouth wide as memory clicked into place.

'Goodenough . . . of course!'

'That's why she changed her name,' Oggie went on. 'Had to get out of the Rhondda, see. Nobody'd give her the time of day – well, tarred with the same brush as her mother, isn't she?'

Clara handed the money to him then sat on the arm of a chair nearby, relief and excitement making her dizzy. The truth was well worth everything she'd paid. Now she had all she needed to destroy Jenni. When Samuel knew about it, he'd cut Richie out of his will completely should he still insist on marrying her. But Richie wasn't a fool. He wouldn't let himself be dragged down by the likes of her.

Oggie was still standing there, lighting up a cigarette, looking perfectly at home. Clara was anxious to see the last of him now. He'd served his purpose and was dangerous to have around. The police were surely looking for him even now. It would be disastrous if they tracked him to Abertawe House, thereby involving her and the family.

She stood up resolutely, straightening her back, determined to take control of the situation.

'You'd better go now, Mr James. Our business is done.'

His smile was sly as he carelessly tapped cigarette ash on to the immaculate hearth.

'Not quite, darling!'

Clara jolted.

'What do you mean?' she asked, her heart in her mouth.

He was totally treacherous. She should have realised she wouldn't get rid of him so easily.

Cautiously, she edged closer to the bell-pull at the side of the fireplace. Even Doris's presence might make a difference.

'I wouldn't do that, darling,' he jeered. 'You won't want a witness to what I've got to say.'

Clara paused in her cautious manoeuvre, fear of him making her mouth dry and her heart jump like a frightened frog in her breast.

'I know something else,' he went on, his smile insolent. 'It's worth a bit.'

'I've no more money to give you.'

He grinned.

'That fancy ring you're wearing will do nicely. Give it here!'

Clara's fingers closed over her engagement ring protectively.

'Don't be absurd. I've already given you eighty pounds, and besides, I know all I need to about Jenni Goodenough.'

He grinned, obviously enjoying himself.

'This secret's not about her – it's about you.'

'About me? You're lying!'

Fear was sending tremors like forked lightning up her spine and into her neck and temples. The room began to spin alarmingly.

'Get out of this house before I call the police,' Clara cried. 'Get out!'

He laughed.

'Not yet, darling. This is another little titbit your mother told me when she was stinking, falling-down drunk.' His eyes were iridescent with cunning. 'You'd better cough up. It won't do you no good if I spread it around.'

'You're leaving Swansea,' Clara gasped, struggling to quell the weakness in her knees. 'Charlie Pendle's after you, remember? Not to mention the police.'

He sniggered.

'They haven't caught me yet, and I can write, darling. Your old man would be very interested in what I have to sell.'

'You're trying to trick me,' she said, her voice rising as renewed panic set her heart throbbing anew, and she wondered if Doris would hear her if she screamed.

He gazed at her for a moment as a stoat mesmerises a rabbit. She could feel a scream rise in her throat. Then, abruptly, he threw his cigarette into the hearth and turned away, reaching for his hat and coat.

'Okay,' he said, too casually, putting on his hat. 'I just thought you'd like to know who your father really is.'

'My . . . my father?' Clara took a few tottering steps towards him. 'What do you know about my father?'

He held out a hand.

'The ring, darling.'

Her heart pounding and with the sound of blood rushing in her ears, Clara eased the ring off her finger and reluctantly handed it to him.

'Well?'

She wanted the truth yet feared it for the light in his eyes told her the news would be a crushing blow and he'd get pleasure from delivering it.

'Your father's a big man around here. Or thinks he is,' Oggie said, stark hatred replacing mockery in his shifty eyes. 'But he's just a scabby crook who'll get what he's owed when the time comes.' His lips drew back from his discoloured teeth in a savage snarl. 'And I might be the one to let him have it, too. Right between the eyes!'

Clara shook her head in disbelief.

'No! No!'

'Oh, yes, darling. Charlie Pendle's your old man, all right. And he knows about you – Kitty saw to that. Knows all about his bastard brat who's done well for herself, and you can bet he'll want a piece of that.' Oggie laughed unpleasantly. 'Maybe he'll come calling one day, eh? Nice family get-together. I'd like to be a fly on the wall then! What a laugh.'

'No! No! It isn't true!' Beside herself with rage and humiliation, Clara flew at him, her fingers clawed, nails aimed at his grinning face.

'You're a dirty liar!' she screamed hysterically. 'Liar! Get out! Get out!'

Oggie quickly side-stepped the clawing hands and, putting the palm of his hand against her chest, pushed her, sending her sprawling on to the sofa nearby where she lay, her face in a cushion, her body convulsed with sobs.

'You're lucky I don't smash your face in,' he growled viciously. 'You dirty little slut! You're all the same, you women. Sluts all of you.'

It felt so wicked, so daring, being in bed this time of day with Nathan beside her. Violet turned her head on the pillow, watching his sleeping face, and smiled, feeling the warm glow of happiness. It was a wonderful sensation, this loving and being loved.

She caught a glimpse of the alarm clock on the bedside table beyond Nathan's head. Half-past twelve! She'd be late for dinner.

She sat up and swung her legs over the side of the bed, gently so as not to wake him.

'Where are you going, Violet, my love?'

Nathan's hand was on her back, smoothing the skin along her spine, sending ripples of delight coursing through her.

'I must get back to the house,' she said, wanting to giggle like a young girl but holding it in check. 'And you should be opening up the shop again. Customers will be wondering why you're closed.'

Reluctantly, she stood up and reached for her clothes on the bedside chair.

'Get back into bed, my love,' he said persuasively. 'I've got a surprise for you.'

Giggles bursting out uncontrollably, Violet scrambled back into the bed, gazing at Nathan expectantly, her heart beating fast, eyes gleaming with excitement.

He laughed, pulling her closer and kissing her cheek.

'No, not that, my love!'

Violet tried not to show her disappointment. She was shameless, she had to admit, but this new life she was leading was so exciting and wonderful she didn't care, as long as Nathan loved her.

He reached into the drawer of the bedside table and, taking out something bundled in a man's handkerchief, handed it to her.

'What is it?'

With curiosity Violet let the contents of the bundle fall on to the counterpane, then stared in disbelief.

The Tregevny Rubies! Countless times she'd seen them adorn her mother's throat, knowing she'd never possess them. The gems twinkled in their ornate gold setting and Violet's hands shook as she picked up the necklace, letting the stones cascade through her fingers.

'Mother's rubies! Nathan, I don't understand. How did you get them?'

'Your sister-in-law pawned them. She must have taken them.'

'Clara!' Violet's mouth dropped open at the enormity of it. 'Clara stole them? She must be mad! I can't believe it.'

'She came into the shop earlier, as bold as brass,' he confirmed. 'Demanded eighty pounds for them.'

'But they're worth ten times as much, if not more.' Violet was aghast at this turn of events.

'I know.' He put an arm around her shoulders. 'And I know how much they mean to you, my love. So, I give them to you. It's up to you what you do with them.'

'Oh, Nathan!'

Her mother's cherished rubies! How she'd always longed for them to be hers one day. But it was impossible. The rubies were meant for daughters-in-law; the women who would produce the next generation of Tregevnys. It was so unfair!

Violet's fingers clutched convulsively at the necklace. Now they *were* in her possession she wouldn't part with them. It dawned on her that she had considerable power over her sister-in-law. Clara had always treated her with belittling arrogance. Now, with one word, Violet could cut her down to size. But, she thought with misgiving, if she revealed the theft of the rubies, her father would force her to give them up. No, she wouldn't!

'Thank you, Nathan,' she murmured gratefully. 'You've made my happiness complete. But put them back in the drawer, my darling, for the moment. Now I must go.'

She began to dress quickly.

Nathan sat on the bed, his arms wrapped around his bent knees.

'Violet, when are you going to tell your father we're married?'

She paused for a moment, thinking. An hour ago she'd have made another vague and cowardly excuse, but with the rubies now in her possession she realised the situation was completely altered, and for good.

'I think it'll be soon, Nathan, very soon. I sense a big show-down coming that'll shake the family to its foundations.'

'I want you here with me, Violet, all the time. It isn't right a man and wife should be apart.'

'I know, my darling,' she said gently. 'And it won't be long now. Jenni's coming into the house has changed everything irrevocably. She's marrying Richie, and I'm glad for him. She's a very special young woman who helped me take the plunge in marrying you.'

'Well, thank God for Jenni,' Nathan said with a smile. 'Remind me to pick out a good wedding present for her.'

'Yes,' Violet said thoughtfully. 'Make it a generous one because she will never have the Tregevny Rubies.'

Chapter Twenty-Nine

Jenni was thankful when dinnertime came. The oppressive atmosphere in the workroom weighed heavily on her. It was daunting to realise this would be her future, now that she was marrying Richie. She could learn to live with Jack's enmity and Clara's hatred, but she missed Renee's friendship sorely, and felt she'd suffered a bereavement.

At one o'clock Jack dashed off. So did Renee, to Jenni's disappointment. She hung around a moment longer, wondering whether she should wait for Richie and walk back with him now that they had a firm understanding. But, ignoring her, he went down to the cashier's office, busying himself there, and Jenni felt slighted to think he was avoiding her. She knew she couldn't look forward to love, but at the same time his surly attitude didn't promise much companionship in their future, either. In fact her future looked pretty bleak, she reflected peevishly.

Annoyed by his remoteness, she returned to Abertawe House alone. As always, she came in through the back entrance, called a hello to Doris in the kitchen, then went out into the front hall, deciding she'd go to her bedroom first to take off her hat and coat.

She was climbing the stairs when she saw Clara standing furtively near the bedroom door. Jenni had a sudden and clear impression she'd caught Clara just coming out of the room, and indignation rose anew in her breast.

Pounding up the remaining stairs to challenge her, Jenni reached the landing as Clara turned around, and Jenni could tell by the other girl's guilty start that she *had* been inside Jenni's room, and probably up to no good, too.

'What were you doing in my room, I'd like to know?' Jenni challenged, feeling the muscles around her mouth go stiff with anger. 'You've got no business in there.'

But Clara didn't look contrite. Her scarlet lips narrowed into a thin line, and her eyes gleamed spitefully.

'You've got the cheek of hell showing your face here,' she snapped. 'Your friend Mr James told me everything. Father a convicted murderer and mother the town tart! You shouldn't be under the same roof as respectable people.'

'What?'

Jenni felt shock wash over her like the icy water of a mountain stream. She'd known Oggie couldn't be trusted, had expected his betrayal even, but this sudden exposure was like a blow to her heart and she could only stare open-mouthed at her opponent.

'Oh, I know all about it,' Clara rushed on, her face glowing with triumph. 'The people of the Rhondda drove you out. And so they should! No one's safe in their beds with you around. Bad blood will out, that's what I say!'

Bad blood! Jenni reeled at the words. How many times had they been thrown at her in the past? How far she had run to get away from them, and now the past had caught up with her again.

But there'd be no running this time. She squared her shoulders, determined to make a stand. After all, so much now depended on her marriage to Richie, Renee's future as well as her own.

'You jealous, treacherous cat!' Jenni shrieked in boiling fury. 'You're no better than Oggie James. But it won't do you any good, spreading lies about me. I'll marry Richie next week and nothing you do can stop me.'

'That's what you think!' Clara's lips twisted in a sneer. 'When I tell Richie and Samuel about your notorious family they'll throw you out like the rubbish you are. Jenni Goodenough — daughter of a murdering swine!'

Clara tried to push past her to go downstairs.

'They're in the sitting-room,' she went on elatedly. 'I'll tell them right now.'

Quickly, Jenni blocked her way, holding out her arms to either side to prevent Clara getting past.

'Don't do it,' she warned, her voice catching in her throat as panic gripped her. 'You'll regret it if you do.'

'And don't you threaten me!' Clara spat out the words. 'You tried to steal my husband. Don't deny it! Your mother was a slut and so are you. Like mother, like daughter!'

Clara was pushing forward again, the line of her mouth vicious, and Jenni's temper began to fray, realising how weak her position was standing at the top of the stairs with nothing to do but retreat, and she'd never do that.

'You're making a big mistake,' she said desperately, still holding her ground. 'If you want to stay married to Jack you'll listen to reason.'

Clara's laugh was brittle, bordering on hysterical.

'Is that supposed to frighten me? You're bluffing, you cheap little trickster. I've got you just where I want you. Now get out of my way!'

She caught at Jenni's outstretched arm, trying to push her aside, but Jenni resisted doggedly.

'When Jack learns . . .' she began, but Clara's furious cry dried up her words.

'Jack? He never loved you — never!'

Clara paused in her struggle, eyes glittering with deep malice and something else. Jenni shivered involuntarily.

'You were no more to him than a dirty little tart he could pick up off any street,' Clara hissed, her eyes burning. 'Not the first, either. You thought you could get him for yourself. Well, no one takes what's mine. I'll see you in hell first!'

Jenni felt the bitter words like a blow to her heart but still she held her ground. It was time to fight back, reveal what she knew; hit Clara where it hurt the most – her unfounded pride.

Jenni pushed back boldly against Clara's clutching hand, setting her jaw in a hard line.

'No! You listen to me, Clara. If I've got something to hide, so have you,' she said breathlessly. 'At least *my* parents were married.'

Clara took a step back, her mouth dropping open, and seeing the consternation in her face, Jenni rushed on.

'You're illegitimate, Clara. No decent family; squalid background. I know all about it. How will your smart friends like that? They'll give you the cold shoulder. You'll be finished around here.'

Clara's face was the colour of putty. Her mouth opened, but she seemed unable to speak. Jenni didn't wait for her to recover.

'My mother made one unhappy mistake in taking up with another man,' she admitted loudly. 'But *your* mother made a career of it. Anybody's for a tanner! That's Kitty Price – your mother.'

Clara's eyes were staring, brightly lit with panic, but Jenni wasn't finished with her.

'People – your so-called friends – will tar you with the same brush, Clara,' she went on. 'A laughing stock, you'll be. And what about the Tregevny family you're so proud of joining? You'll be nothing but dirt under their feet.'

Clara staggered sideways, hand clutched to her chest as though she'd been struck a physical blow, and Jenni thought for a moment that her opponent would fall.

'My father was executed for murder,' she said, the terrible truth bitter on her tongue. 'But at least I know his name. You don't even know who your father was. Do you want to explain that to Jack and Samuel?'

Clara was visibly shaking, in the grip of some deep

uncontrollable emotion. Jenni couldn't tell whether it was fear or rage that took the pallor from her face and left it suffuse with blood.

'You bitch!' Spittle foaming at the corners of her scarlet mouth, Clara shrieked the words so loudly the family in the sitting-room couldn't fail to hear. 'Richie thinks he can get it all by marrying you. Well, I won't have it, damn you!'

She stood there still frothing at the mouth, her body convulsed by tremors. She appeared to have difficulty in moving her jaw and her next words seemed to tear themselves raggedly from her throat.

'If I can't have Jack's child then neither will you!'

Jenni saw the murderous flash in Clara's eyes a split second too late, and felt the powerful thrust of a fist striking her breast-bone.

She staggered back, arms flailing, feet scrabbling madly to keep their balance on the edge of the top stair. She was saving herself when Clara's clawed hands grasped her shoulders and pushed forcefully.

'Die, you slut! Die and be damned to hell!'

Jenni screamed in terror as the heels of her shoes slid over the edge of the stair, then she was falling, tumbling over and over, crashing against each stair as she went.

Scream after scream was torn from her throat.

'My baby! My baby!'

At tremendous speed, the cold, hard parquet of the hall floor came rushing to meet her. She hit it with a sickening thud, and a great spasm of pain, like death itself, engulfed her. Just before the blackness took her, she saw faces bending over her as she lay there. She had no idea who they were.

Jenni felt the heaviness of her lids and struggled to open her eyes. It took such an effort she didn't have enough strength to raise her head but stared up at the ceiling. It was so high, much higher than in her bedroom, and she wondered where she was.

Her wandering gaze saw tall narrow windows bereft of curtains; there were strange, alien sounds; someone cried out in pain, and brisk footsteps hurried past. She, too, wanted to call out, but her mouth felt so dry.

In confusion and fear Jenni tried to sit up, but a sharp pain in her side made her gasp with anguish and she lay back.

What was this place? And why was she here?

Suddenly a figure appeared in her line of vision at the end of the bed; a middle-aged woman in a dark blue dress and starched apron, with a triangle of white cloth on her head, the points set in sharp rigid angles.

'I'm Sister Williams,' said the woman.

'Where am I?'

'You're in hospital.'

Jenni's confusion grew.

'Why am I here? What's wrong with me?'

Sister Williams came round the bed, looking down at her.

'Don't you remember?'

'No.'

'You fell down the stairs, my dear. You've been very poorly for two days.'

'Fell?'

Jenni struggled to remember. There must be something to recall. Suddenly she remembered a face, a woman's face filled with evil hatred. Clara! The memory filled her with fear. Clara had deliberately pushed her down the staircase. Clara had tried to kill her!

'Oh, my God! My baby!'

Jenni tried to struggle up despite the pain, but Sister Williams pressed her gently back on to the pillow.

'You must rest another week or more.'

'But my baby? Is my baby all right?'

Sister Williams took Jenni's hand and held it tightly.

'I'm so sorry, my dear.'

'No! No! It can't be true!' She felt a scream of grief rise in her throat. 'My baby!'

Sister Williams squeezed her hand again.

'Maybe it's for the best, Jenni,' she said. 'After all, you have no ring on your finger.'

'For the best?' Jenni snatched her hand away and struggled up. 'You stupid, heartless woman!' she cried out in anguish. 'Don't you understand? I've lost my baby . . . my precious baby!'

Sister Williams straightened up, her back rigid.

'You're upset, I understand that.'

'Leave me alone!' cried Jenni, falling back and turning her face into the pillow, feeling hot tears fill her eyes. 'Oh, why didn't I die, too?'

'Now stop that melodramatic nonsense,' Sister Williams said sharply. 'There's no permanent damage. There'll be other babies for you – when you're married.'

But Jenni could only sob bitterly. Despite Jack's rejection and his treachery, their baby had been conceived in love, for she had loved Jack so much; enough for both of them.

And although she'd known a life of shame might well have lain ahead of her, another part of her had longed for the baby – someone of her very own to love, and who would love her un-conditionally; her own family. Now jealous, murderous Clara had taken that away from her. Even in the depth of her grief, Jenni felt anger and resentment rise up in her like a volcano, and her grieving heart cried out for revenge.

She must get well, regain her strength before confronting her most bitter and dangerous enemy. Clara would pay for what she'd done, and pay dearly.

But killing Jenni's baby was not her only crime. Jenni was in no doubt that by now Clara would have told everyone the truth about her and her past – Jenni Goodenough, the daughter of a convicted murderer. Her life in the Hafod was finished. She'd have to move on again. But not before she'd taken her revenge. She felt the need for it like brine on her tongue.

In the early evening visitors poured in and Jenni wished with all her heart that Renee would come to see her, although she didn't hold out much hope.

However, she was astonished to see Violet hurrying down the long ward, a bunch of flowers in her hand. She pulled up a chair and sat close to the bed, concern in her eyes.

'Jenni, my dear, how are you?' she asked kindly.

Tears flooded Jenni's eyes immediately.

'My baby, Violet. It's dead!'

Violet took her hand, her eyes shiny with tears, too.

'I know, my dear, and I'm so sorry. How dreadful. Richie is very upset.'

Jenni couldn't help feeling resentment. Of course he was upset. He'd learned the truth about her from Clara, and if that wasn't enough to put him off, her losing the baby meant their marriage was out of the question now. So all his plans were in ruins. He was probably very angry, too, but he could blame Clara for that.

'Clara tried to kill me, Violet,' Jenni said. It sounded fantastic saying that, but it was true.

'She's told everyone your real name,' Violet confirmed. 'My father's appalled and Clara's building on this. She says that being the daughter of a murderer, you're not to be trusted. You'll lie about everything.'

'You all saw what she did!' cried Jenni wrathfully.

She remembered their faces now, and knew the whole family had witnessed Clara's evildoing.

'She claims you tripped over the hem of your coat,' Violet said, looking shamefaced.

Jenni was furious, her mouth set in a hard line of disbelief. Surely they wouldn't still support Clara after this?

'She wanted my baby dead, and me, too.' Jenni's voice was rising on a hysterical note, she couldn't control it. 'But I'm not dead, and I know exactly what happened. And she'll pay for this, I swear it!'

'That's what my father's terrified of.' Violet nodded. 'He's afraid you'll bring charges against her. The scandal!'

Trying to calm down, Jenni looked closely at Violet, detecting excitement in her voice, as if the prospect of scandal for Samuel pleased her no end. Did she resent her father that much?

It was on the tip of Jenni's tongue to tell her about Kitty Price. That would really be something for Samuel to chew on. But she thought better of it. She'd give nothing away yet, but would confront the whole family with her knowledge in her own time. All the better to savour Clara's disgrace, Jenni thought, knowing she was being vindictive but not caring.

'I suppose Jack's worried about the scandal, too?' she asked bitterly.

It was strange. The love for him that had swelled and glowed in her heart so powerfully had died; not immediately but gradually, and now, like her child, it was gone, as though her baby's death had cut the last link between them. She could even hate him now; hate him with a vengeance.

Violet's lips tightened.

'Not in the least,' she said, an edge of disapproval in her voice. 'He thinks he's free of all blame now. After all, although you never said so, we all knew Jack was responsible. My father knew it, too, deep down. He's bitterly disappointed.'

'I couldn't care less how your father feels!' cried Jenni. 'I've lost my baby and all I can feel is despair and grief. I'll never get over it, Violet. Your family has treated me shabbily from the start.'

Violet fidgeted on her chair.

'I hope that doesn't include me?' she asked, a tremor in her voice.

Jenni relented, reining in her emotions, knowing she should consider Violet's feelings too.

'No, you've been nice to me. Even now when you know who I am.'

Violet reached out a hand to grasp hers.

'None of us can be responsible for our families, Jenni. What happened to your parents was a tragedy, but it has nothing to do with you. You've done nothing wrong.'

'Thank you, Violet. I'm glad we're still friends. How's Nathan?'

For reply Violet held up her left hand and Jenni saw the shiny new wedding ring on her finger.

'My husband's wonderful! I told Father I was married to Nat the same day you were rushed into hospital,' she said. 'Hit a tyrant when he's down, I say!'

Jenni was shocked, yet couldn't help smiling at the look of satisfaction on Violet's face.

'He was absolutely floored.' She giggled, obviously enjoying the memory. 'I packed my bags that same night and moved in with Nat. Oh, Jenni, my dear, it's all your doing. I'd never have found the courage alone. I'm so happy!'

'And I'm glad for you.' Jenni smiled. It was good to know fortune smiled on someone.

Violet ran her tongue over her lips.

'Richie would like to visit you, Jenni,' she said hesitantly. 'He really is distressed by what's happened.'

Jenni was angry and suspicious. Why would he wish to see her, knowing what he did about her now? Probably, like Samuel, Richie feared she'd cause humiliation for the family, and his only purpose in coming to see her was to ensure her silence. Well, she wouldn't give him the chance to talk down to her. Nothing could avert the retribution that was coming to Clara.

'No! I won't see him,' she said firmly. 'I've nothing to say to your brother.'

'He went with you in the ambulance, you know,' Violet coaxed her. 'I've never seen him so upset. He was almost in tears.'

Jenni didn't believe it. Newly married, Violet's perception was tinted with a rosy glow.

'He needn't have bothered. No one asked him to,' said Jenni truculently. 'I won't see him. There's no point. I know the marriage is off after all that's happened. He doesn't have to explain.'

'Where will you go when you're discharged?' asked Violet. 'Nat and I would love to have you with us. I'm sure we can find room.'

Jenni shook her head, sorry for her bad temper. Violet didn't deserve it.

'I won't intrude on you both,' she said with a smile. 'This is your honeymoon after all.'

The following day Jenni was feeling stronger and sat in her bedside chair most of the time. When visiting hour came she was in bed again, not expecting anyone to come to see her.

Glancing up, she was disconcerted to find Richie standing at the foot of the bed, holding a brown paper bag. Drawing in a deep breath of resentment, Jenni turned her head to look anywhere but at him.

'I've brought you some grapes,' he said. He put the bag on the locker next to her. 'Jenni, I'm so sorry for your loss.'

'I bet you are!'

'How are you?'

'I'm improving. No thanks to Clara. She tried to kill me.'

'Jenni, are you sure . . .'

'How dare you!' cried Jenni, realising that her voice was rising and that other visitors were staring at them in curiosity. But she didn't care.

'How dare you doubt my word?' The words exploded from her. 'How dare you look down on me? I know why you're here, but you're wasting your time. Clara will be punished for what she's done, I shall see to that.'

Richie's face flushed darkly.

'Jenni, listen to me . . .'

'No! You're only here to do Samuel's dirty work. Get out!' she screamed, her tone bordering on hysteria. 'Nurse! Nurse! Make this man leave. He's upsetting me.'

Sister Williams and a nurse came hurrying up the ward towards Jenni's bedside. Richie, obviously seething, didn't wait to be ordered out but marched off with his ungainly, lopsided stride, shoulders stiff with indignation.

Jenni was very upset by the encounter and lay with her eyes closed as her fluttering heart slowed to normal.

Despite her anger with Richie, she couldn't help wondering what might have been. Had she and Richie married, would they ever have found happiness? Now she'd never know. She'd always thought him a fair man. But how fair was he being, trying to protect Clara? she thought tetchily.

On the other hand, he worked hard at his trade and would make a good provider and husband for any other woman. But not her. Yes, he was a far better man than Jack could ever hope to be, but nevertheless Richie was a Tregevny and she was finished with that family for good.

She deeply regretted not being able to help Renee in the way she'd intended. But her friend had turned her back and Jenni was alone again. She must find a new place now, and new people, hopefully friends.

But would she ever escape the tragedy of her parents' fate?

Her eyes closed, deep in thought, Jenni heard the chair next to the bed being pulled up closer and her eyes snapped open, half expecting to see Richie back again.

She sat up with a jerk, overjoyed, unable to believe she was actually seeing Renee sitting there instead, looking a bit shamefaced.

'Renee! Oh, there's lovely to see you!'

'Hello, Jen, love. How are you?'

To Jenni's delight Renee impulsively reached forward and kissed her cheek. Clinging tightly to her friend, Jenni strove not to burst into tears.

'All the better for seeing you, thanks.' Tears welled in her eyes anyway despite her best efforts. 'I've lost my baby, Renee. I'm heartbroken.'

'I'm so sorry, kid.' Renee looked saddened. 'I didn't even know you were in the family way.'

Despite her obvious sympathy, there was an edge to her voice, too, as though she was resentful of being kept in the dark over such an important matter.

'I am your best friend, Jenni, if not your sister.'

Jenni felt sorry, too.

'I was going to tell you that day you came to see me, but . . .'

Renee's eyes filled with tears and she took Jenni's hand, squeezing it hard.

'Oh, Jen, love, please forgive me for being so nasty to you then. I didn't mean it, and I wouldn't have had this terrible thing happen to you for the world.'

'I know and there's nothing to forgive, Renee, love,' Jenni said warmly. 'We're the best of friends and always will be, I hope. But . . .'

She hesitated. Renee may not yet have heard the story that Clara was spreading about her, and she knew the time had come to explain.

'I have a confession, Renee.' Jenni felt a sob rise in her throat. 'My real name is . . .'

'Listen, Jenni, kid,' Renee interrupted quickly, 'I know all about it. Mr Jack has talked of nothing else in the shop, and Mr Richie's been wild with him over it.'

Jenni wasn't surprised. After all, the Tregevnys wouldn't want it generally known that the daughter of the infamous murderer George Goodenough had worked for them; lived in their home; had even agreed to wed their eldest son. Yes, Samuel and Richie would want that kept very quiet indeed.

Renee smiled and patted her arm.

'Nobody blames you, Jen. You can't help who your father was anymore than Clara can help who her mother is, right? And as my mam says, we know our Jenni's a good, honest girl who's been led astray by those who should know better.'

Jenni smiled through her tears.

'I'm not an angel or a saint, mind, Renee. I was foolish and strong-headed, too, in my feelings for Jack.'

Renee shrugged her shoulders, a sad expression on her face.

'Well, we both learned something about men, didn't we?' she said. 'You were quite right about Oss . . . Oggie. He pushed off the same day you had your accident.'

Jenni sat up, looking alert.

'He's gone?'

Renee nodded miserably.

'He asked if he could lodge at our house last week, some problem with his landlady. I thought it sounded ideal. He had my bedroom and I slept in your old room. I thought when he knew about the baby he'd get a special licence or something.' Renee put a hand to her throat, her expression tight with pain. 'What a fool I was.'

'What happened?' Jenni was half afraid to ask.

Renee gulped, her lips trembling.

'It was that morning, the day you fell . . .'

'I was pushed!' Jenni exclaimed.

'Oggie was so nasty about the baby,' Renee went on. 'Called

me filthy names and hit me . . .' Her eyes were as big as saucers. 'I was so frightened of him, Jen. I'm glad he's gone.'

'Did you . . . did you love him, Renee?'

Her friend smiled, looking shamefaced again.

'No. Didn't even like him, really. But he seemed so keen on me and he had money, I was flattered. And now I'm up the spout. Serves me right!'

For a moment Renee looked as though she didn't know whether she should laugh or cry, then her sunny nature shone through.

'Tsk! I'm a silly cow, aren't I?'

Jenni clutched at her friend's hand.

'It's going to be all right, Renee. I've got a little money put by – from a legacy – and I'm going to help you; make things right. And I'll get another job, you'll see.'

'Listen, Jen, kid.' Renee sat forward eagerly. 'Don't worry about that. Things'll work out somehow. Mam's forgiven me, that's the main thing. I don't know what I'd do if she turned her back on me, but she's going to stand by me.'

She squeezed Jenni's hand.

'We both want you to come back to Hafod Row to live when you're discharged. Make your home with us. We're still your family, mind.'

Jenni burst into tears; she just couldn't help it in the face of such kindness.

'There, there, Jen, love,' Renee crooned, patting her shoulder. 'Don't upset yourself. You've got to build your strength up. You've had a nasty fall.'

Jenni curbed her sobbing with difficulty. Renee was right. She had to face Clara and the Tregevnys soon, and wreak her revenge. That would take all her courage and fortitude, but she was determined.

Renee went after promising to visit regularly, and Jenni was feeling much happier now that the rift between them was mended.

The knowledge that friends supported her made all the difference in the world.

After three or four days, Jenni felt ready to be discharged and sure enough, on his morning round, the young doctor told her she could go home the following day. Jenni was ecstatic. She could hardly wait to see Meg again, and beg her forgiveness, too.

She waited eagerly for visiting time, but when the visitors poured in that evening, Renee wasn't amongst them and Jenni's excitement was dampened. Well, she thought dejectedly, she shouldn't expect her friend to come every day.

She was watching the ward door wistfully when a figure she recognised came in and looked around, obviously searching for her. Jenni stared in total astonishment. Surely he wasn't coming to visit her! But he was. He made his way briskly to her bedside and pulled the chair forward.

'Mr Napier!'

Although her flannel nightdress had a high neckline and long sleeves, Jenni pulled the bedclothes up around her chest in embarrassment, and stared at her visitor, dumbfounded.

'Ah, Jenni!' he began.

'Why are you here, Mr Napier?'

'Thought you'd like some company, young woman.'

Jenni set her lips in a firm line.

'Your nosiness is leading you too far this time, Mr Napier,' she said severely. 'We've never been anything like friends, and only friends may visit me.'

'Not here to pry, I'm not,' he said complacently, touching his moustache delicately with a gloved index finger. 'I know all there is to know about you. Clara took great pleasure in giving me all the details. And I've been to the library to search out old newspaper accounts of the trial.'

'You've done what?' Jenni exploded. 'You've got a blooming cheek! And now you've come here to quiz me, too.'

She tossed her head angrily.

'You'd better leave, Mr Napier, before I call the nurse and have you thrown out.'

He quickly lifted his gloved hand.

'Now don't be hasty, Jenni. I've come to give you a bit of information – something you can use against Clara.' His tone was lofty. 'It's time that stuck-up young madam got her come-uppance. She's been trying to get rid of me for years. I know too much, see.'

Jenni sniffed.

'I know all about Kitty Price.'

Mr Napier chuckled darkly, a note of underlying satisfaction in it.

'Oh, it's much more juicy than that.'

Jenni was uncertain. She hated gossip and its purveyors. Gossip had caused her much pain in the past – should she stoop to listen to it now? But Clara was a powerful and dangerous enemy, and too evil to deserve any consideration. In the name of her dead child, Jenni was prepared to use any weapon against her foe.

'What is it?'

Mr Napier edged his chair closer to the bed then glanced around the ward, as though to be certain they were not overheard. Obviously satisfied they had privacy, he asked: 'Have you heard of a man named Charlie Pendle?'

Jenni nodded.

'Oggie James worked for him. I don't think it was respectable employment, though.'

'That's an understatement if ever I've heard one!' Mr Napier chuckled again. 'Charlie's a big-time crook in this town, a powerful and dangerous man – probably a murderer many times over. There's nothing evil he hasn't got a hand in. Gambling, house-breaking and . . . er . . . prostitution, if you'll excuse the expression.'

Jenni felt her cheeks flame with embarrassment and looked askance at her visitor.

'I don't want to know, Mr Napier.'

'Yes, you do, Jenni.' He nodded sagely. 'Clara tried to kill you, remember?'

She stared in surprise.

'How do you know that?'

He smiled, preening his moustache again.

'Doris tells me everything that goes on in Abertawe House. We have an understanding. Well, at least, Doris *thinks* we have an understanding. It's very useful.'

Jenni sat up straight, forgetting her embarrassment.

'Doris is my friend, Mr Napier, and a good woman,' she exclaimed hotly. 'Don't you *dare* deceive her.'

He raised his eyebrows, obviously surprised at the heat in her voice.

'Wouldn't dream of it,' he replied blandly. 'Doris is quite safe, I assure you. I'm no womaniser like Mr Jack.'

Jenni plucked absentmindedly at the bed cover, wishing he would leave.

'If that's all you've come to say, you'd better go.'

Mr Napier gave an impatient snort.

'Don't you understand, girl?' he snapped, moustache twitching furiously. 'Charlie Pendle is Clara's father!'

Jenni gaped in horror. Was he making this up to mock her? he was a strange man and she wasn't even sure she trusted him.

Mr Napier nodded at her shocked expression.

'Oh, yes, my girl. It's true. *Now* you have something to fight her with.'

Jenni swallowed hard.

'How do you know all this, Mr Napier?'

He looked smug again.

'Although I'm teetotal, I visit various pubs in the town of an evening, listen to the gossip in bars and back parlours. It's my hobby.'

The smugness went from his face suddenly and he lowered his voice, looking grave.

'I tell you, Jenni, there's many a poor dab found floating in the Tawe river with his throat cut — *that's* Charlie's style. But he's too smart for the police.' He looked over his shoulder furtively. 'You never know who's about. I'm taking a chance even talking about him to you.'

Jenni felt a shiver go through her.

'Then don't! Not another word, Mr Napier. Please go!' She wriggled down into the bed, pulling the clothes up over her chin and staring up at him fearfully. 'Go now!'

'Well! Would you believe it?' Mr Napier exclaimed abruptly, standing up, his expression showing disappointment and irritation. 'Clara killed your unborn child, Jenni, and I've come here this evening to give you all the ammunition you need to destroy her — and *you* tell me to go.'

His moustache twitched fiercely again.

'Tsk! Is this all the thanks I get?'

Chapter Thirty

It was so good to be back in Meg's cosy home in Hafod Row. Jenni, helping to lay the table for tea, said a little prayer of thanks. Her friends were still there for her, even knowing the truth. That was real friendship. Despite all her pain and grief she knew she had a lot to be thankful for.

Yet still she ached for the child she'd lost; the child she'd never know, who would always be in her thoughts and prayers. Perhaps there would be other children for her in the years to come, but in her heart she knew her first child could never be replaced.

Wistfully, she glanced into the scullery at Renee who was singing away happily as she cut thin bread to butter and eat with the Penclawdd cockles she'd brought home from the market.

Renee's child was what mattered now. Jenni was determined to help her friend all she could when the baby was born. She'd work her fingers to the bone for them all.

But first Clara had to be dealt with; justice of some kind had to be done.

Jenni poured the tea when it was ready, handing a cup to Meg first.

'Been thinking, I have, Jenni, *bach*, about Clara,' she said as she took the cup and saucer. 'And what you're going to do.'

'I'm seeing a solicitor first thing tomorrow,' Jenni announced firmly. 'Her days of freedom are numbered, believe me! She'll pay for the wicked thing she did.'

'Solicitors are no good for that,' Renee said, taking a hearty bite out of a folded piece of bread and butter. 'It's the police you need. Tell them how she tried to kill you. Get them to arrest her. I'd like to see her in prison, murdering devil that she is!'

'No, no, girls,' said Meg, shaking her head and pursing her lips doubtfully. 'The scandal would be too much.'

'Well, that's what we want, isn't it, Mam?' Renee said pertly.

'I'm thinking of Jenni,' she said quietly. 'It'd all come out about her father. Name in the papers and her photograph. People pointing a finger in the street. A proper circus, it'd be.'

Renee looked concerned.

'Mam's got a point there, Jen, kid. Clara would drag you down with her for spite, the vindictive cat! She's got no conscience, that one.'

'And then there's work,' Meg went on. 'Jenni wouldn't get a job for love nor money after the uproar. Notorious she'd be, like.' She shook her head again. 'No, Jenni, love. You're fired up with wanting to get your own back, but the game's not worth the candle.'

'I can't let her get away with killing my baby!' she cried.

'God will punish her for that,' Meg said sagely. 'No, love, you get on with your life and try to be happy, because it's short enough. You'll meet a decent chap soon and settle down. There'll be lots of babbies then.'

Jenni saw the sense in what Meg was saying. Having her family's tragic past dredged up again would be too much to bear. Yet Clara should be punished for all the pain and heartache she'd caused; for a life taken before it had begun.

'I'll think some more about it, Meg,' Jenni agreed reluctantly.

'I'm going round to the Tregevnys' tomorrow to fetch my things – my clothes and family mementoes.'

Her world in a suitcase.

Standing on the front doorstep of Abertawe House at dinnertime the following day, Jenni remembered the first time she'd stood here, afraid and uncertain. She felt very different now; grieving and weary perhaps, but confident and determined, too. No going round to the back entrance today like a beggar.

She slammed the knocker down with a sharp rat-tat and waited impatiently until the door was opened by Doris.

The older girl stared for a moment, then grinned gleefully.

'Hello, Jenni, kid. There's nice to see you better.' Her face clouded for a moment. 'I'm sorry about the baby.'

'So am I,' said Jenni grimly as she stepped over the threshold. 'And Clara will be even sorrier, believe me.'

'It's about time she got what's coming to her,' Doris said in a hoarse whisper. 'It's a long time overdue.'

'I've come for my things,' Jenni went on. 'It's all right, Doris, you can tell the family what I'm doing. I don't want to get you into trouble. You were good to me while I was here.'

'Don't you worry about me,' Doris assured her. She turned towards the back lobby, then paused. 'Clara's upstairs. You're not going to do anything . . . silly, are you, kid?'

'I could kill her for what she's done,' Jenni admitted tensely. 'But I'll be sensible, Doris. Natural justice will take care of Clara, I'm certain.'

As Jenni crossed the hall towards the staircase Jack came out of the front sitting-room. He stared at her, a startled expression in his eyes for a moment; obviously, she was the last person he'd expected to see in Abertawe House. Did he think she'd be too afraid to come here again? He scowled darkly at her and Jenni felt she was looking into the eyes of a stranger.

'What the hell are you doing here?' he asked harshly.

She lifted her chin boldly, and didn't bother to hide the disdain she felt for him now. Had the man she'd loved ever existed? Looking at Jack's scowling expression, she knew it had all been a mirage, conjured up by her deep longing to find the warmth of love once again.

'I've come for my belongings,' she declared steadfastly, marvelling at the steadiness of her own voice. 'I've every right!'

He stared at her belligerently for a moment.

'Well, get them and then get out!' he said brutally. 'The likes of you aren't wanted around here.'

'Pity you didn't show those sentiments the night you came barging into my room uninvited,' she flared heatedly. 'You'd have saved me so much grief and pain.'

He didn't answer, but with a furious glare whirled round on his heel and returned to the sitting-room, closing the double doors behind him.

Jenni stared after him, feeling her blood rise within her and boil with anger. The callous beast! Had he nothing to say to her about the loss of her baby?

Enraged, she ran across the hall after him and burst into the sitting-room, flinging the doors open with such force they banged against the furniture.

Jack was standing by the fireplace, lighting a cigarette. He looked up, startled, as she burst in unceremoniously. His father, in his chair near the window, tried to struggle to his feet at the sight of her, muttering a feeble protest.

Jenni ignored him, her mind on Jack and the cold-blooded way he'd spoken to her.

'Don't you care that your wife murdered *your* child?' she cried out passionately. 'Because the baby was yours as well as mine.'

'You're a liar,' Jack bellowed, his face reddening with fury.

He flung the lit cigarette into the fireplace and came towards her, his expression ugly.

'I told you to get out, you cunning little cheat! I curse the day I ever set eyes on you. You've brought me nothing but trouble. Now get out before I throw you out!'

'You heartless swine!' shrieked Jenni, standing her ground despite his threatening attitude. 'Clara killed my baby and she'll pay, I swear it!'

Samuel managed to push himself up from his chair finally, and held out a hand to her.

'Jenni, please! I beg you,' he said. His voice, once so strident, was now weak and tremulous. 'Don't drag the family through the courts.'

She was shocked by his appearance and manner. He'd aged since she last saw him; his shoulders stooped, eyes were sunken in a grey face. He looked so pathetic, she felt almost sorry for him.

'The business will never survive the scandal,' he went on. 'Show a little mercy.'

'Mercy!' she repeated furiously, his words wiping away all her pity. 'What mercy did Clara show me and my baby? Is she to be excused murder because she's a Tregevny?'

Samuel swayed on his feet.

'It's all a misunderstanding . . .'

'I never believed in the expression bad blood,' Jenni interrupted shrilly. 'But I do now! Clara has no human decency at all. She's a cold-blooded killer – it was born into her. She comes from the very pit of degradation, I tell you.'

'Oh, my God!' Samuel collapsed on to his chair, crumpled and old. 'She means to destroy us. We'll end up in the workhouse. It's all finished!'

'Father, pull yourself together and calm down,' Jack exclaimed sharply, looking impatient. 'She has no proof. It's Clara's word against hers, and who do you think the authorities will believe, eh?'

He laughed mirthlessly, his expression scornful as he looked at Jenni.

'Certainly not the daughter of a convicted murderer.'

'Perhaps you're right, Jack,' Jenni answered tightly, reining in her feelings of anger, knowing they would do her no good. 'Bringing charges against your wife isn't the answer — I don't want any scandal myself.'

Jack sneered with self-satisfaction.

'Very wise. Now get out, and don't come back.'

His belittling tone set her teeth on edge again, and she wanted to scream at him that she *would* take them all through hell and back anyway, scandal or not, but staunchly held herself in check.

'I'll go when I'm ready,' she responded acidly. 'After justice has been done. Perhaps you won't feel so uppity when you learn Clara's true origins. For a start, her mother is just a common . . .'

Before Jenni could say another word Clara herself came rushing into the sitting-room, eyes wild with triumph.

'I thought I heard your voice, Jenni Goodenough!' she exclaimed, then glanced quickly at her husband, her features alive with vindictiveness. 'Jack! Don't let her get away. She's a thief! She's stolen my diamond earrings and engagement ring.'

Jenni's heart turned over. Clara was obviously prepared to concoct any malicious story to blacken her character.

'This is outrageous!' Jenni burst out furiously. 'I've stolen nothing. Clara's making it up, Jack.'

But his gaze was stony, his eyes cold and empty except for the merest shimmer of consternation. Jenni felt deep loathing for him. He wasn't man enough to go against his wife, even though he knew she was doing wrong.

Clara lifted one hand and waved it about excitedly.

'Look! I found this in her room,' she said, malice simmering in her eyes. 'A pawn ticket. That proves she's a thief. Doris told me things were missing — silver photo-frames and now my jewellery.'

'If you found anything in my room, you put it there yourself,' Jenni declared hotly. 'You were in there the day you pushed me down the stairs. I've been in hospital for nearly two weeks, remember? You ought to remember – you put me there. So how could I be the thief?'

'This pawn ticket is dated before you went into hospital,' Clara went on. 'You're guilty all right!'

'I've done nothing wrong, you conniving witch!' Jenni cried out.

'You stole the jewellery for your lover, Ossie James,' Clara persisted, her vicious gaze fastened on Jenni, the flames of hatred in her eyes. 'You planned this all along. Heaven knows what else you've taken.'

'Murderer!' Jenni screamed, beside herself. 'Haven't you done enough harm in taking my baby from me? Is there no end to your mad jealousy?'

'Send Doris for a policeman, Jack,' Clara urged, her mouth twisting with scorn. 'She must be charged with theft immediately. Then no one will believe anything she says.'

'You killed my innocent baby, Clara!' Jenni sobbed in despair, the bitter pain of her loss swelling in her breast, almost overwhelming her. 'But I won't let you get away with it. I'll make you suffer!'

The mad urge to rush at Clara and claw her eyes out was almost overwhelming, but Jenni held herself back with difficulty. She wouldn't play into their hands by adding assault to the charges they were trying to build against her. She must keep her head and think clearly.

Clara's smile was mocking.

'Not from a prison cell, you won't. Jack! Send for a policeman now, before Richie gets back. He might try to interfere for his own ends.'

Jenni turned an anguished gaze on him.

'She's up to no good, Jack. Are you prepared to have this on your conscience all your life?' Her lips felt stiff and cold with dread and she could hardly pronounce the words. 'You *know* I'm not a thief.'

'You tried to foist your bastard brat on me,' he said sullenly, his eyes bleak. 'Clara's right. You're capable of anything. I can see that now.'

'Of course she is, Jack,' his wife agreed triumphantly. 'She's a common criminal, like her father.'

Running to Samuel's chair, Clara waved the pawn ticket under his nose.

'Quickly, Father!' she cried. 'The Tregevny Rubies! She could've taken them, too. You must look!'

'No! Not the rubies!'

Samuel rose unsteadily from his chair, the greyness of his skin accentuated by the panic in his eyes. He tottered across the room and out into the hall. No one tried to help him although he appeared ready to collapse at any moment.

Despite her own predicament, Jenni couldn't get over the change in Samuel over this last few weeks. Gone was his habitual strut and self-satisfied air. He looked a pathetic, bewildered old man, without wit enough to see through Clara's connivance.

Yet Jenni couldn't waste her feelings on him, even though the gloating light in Clara's eyes told her the rubies *would* prove to be missing, and Samuel would be devastated.

With a sudden blinding insight Jenni realised that Clara was behind this treachery, too. After all, she must have needed money to pay Oggie for information. Clara was using Jenni as a scapegoat, but since there was no way to prove it, nothing could be done. She could only protest her innocence to the last, but who would believe her with the whole Tregevny clan out to destroy her?

Desperately, Jenni turned to Jack again. Had he no spark of human decency? There must be something left of the man she'd fallen in love with; to whom she'd given her body and her trust so eagerly?

'You can't let this happen, Jack,' she murmured in quiet desperation. 'I'm entirely innocent and you know it. Clara's jealousy has unhinged her mind. Not content with taking the life of my baby, she wants to see me in prison. It's pure revenge.'

'You brought this on yourself, Jenni,' he rasped. 'I can do nothing.'

'That's not fair!' she cried, feeling tears burn behind her eyelids. But she mustn't break down now. 'All I did was love you. Am I to be punished for that?'

He was silent, a morose expression on his face, and Jenni suddenly saw how morally weak he really was; weak and incapable of loving anyone but himself.

'You're a snivelling coward, Jack Tregevny,' she cried disdainfully. 'You'll never be happy as long as you live because you're an empty shell with nothing to give anyone. You and Clara are well matched.'

Without a word he turned his back, leaning one arm on the mantelpiece, and Clara laughed, a hysterical pitch to the sound.

'You'll go to prison, all right, Jenni Goodenough, and it's where you belong, you dirty little tart!' she cried in exultation. 'I'll teach you to covet what's mine. Prison will finish you. You'll be an old hag when you come out. No man will give you the time of day.'

Uncertain what to do, Jenni looked towards the hall, instinct telling her to run while she could; before Samuel returned; before it was too late to get away.

Clara seemed to read her mind.

'Go on, then! Run! But the police will find you,' she taunted. 'They'll drag you off to the police station in front of everyone. It'll be in all the papers. Murderer's daughter rots in prison.'

At these words Jenni had a sudden vision of a terrible moment from years ago: her father being led away in handcuffs, the gawking crowd taking in every word and gesture. Her blood ran cold at the resurrection of the buried memory.

Like her father she had nowhere to run. She couldn't return to Hafod Row. She'd done enough damage to Renee and Meg. No, she must stay and fight this out. She had to believe that right would prevail and somehow she'd be saved.

She had weapons, she reminded herself, her courage reviving. Clara had her own murky history to conceal. It was time to speak out; fight back the only way she could.

Moving quickly to where Jack was standing silently by the mantelpiece, Jenni pulled at his arm, forcing him to face her.

'Listen, Jack!' she demanded. 'There's something you should know about your wife – something discreditable. She's been hiding the truth from you for years.'

She pointed an accusing finger at her tormentor.

'Clara's not the refined lady she makes herself out to be. She's the illegitimate daughter of a woman called Kitty Price, a common prostitute from the Cwm. If you don't believe me, ask Mr Napier.'

Jack's stare was stony. Deliberately he took a cigarette from a box on the mantelpiece and lit it. Jenni watched his expressionless face in consternation.

'Didn't you hear what I said?' she cried, puzzled and concerned by his calmness. 'Her family are the scum of the earth. Your mother-in-law sells herself to any man for the price of a brown ale. And her father . . .'

'Be quiet!' Jack thundered. 'I know about Kitty Price already. Clara has told me everything.'

Jenni could only gasp, and Clara laughed spitefully.

'Spoiled your little surprise, eh?'

'No one knows her history but us, and Napier will keep his mouth shut if he knows what's good for him,' Jack went on. 'Clara has no connection with her mother at all.'

'Oh, really?' Jenni shouted angrily. 'Then why does Kitty come round here every Friday to be paid off? I've seen her myself.'

Jack whirled round, sending a furious look in his wife's

direction, but Clara laughed scornfully in response, obviously confident that she had the upper hand.

'She's lying in her teeth, Jack. After all, she lied about your being the father of her bastard child. Her kind will say and do anything to stay out of prison.'

'You're a fool, Jack!' Jenni rapped out impatiently. 'Ask her about her father. She hasn't told you about him, I'll bet . . .'

'The rubies have gone!' It was a cry of despair from Samuel as he came staggering through the sitting-room door. 'They've been in the Tregevny family for three generations. Oh, God! It's an omen. The end of us all!'

Jenni rushed to his side as he tottered, taking his arm, trying to guide him to a chair. He stared at her, eyes wide, then shrugged her away violently.

'Viper! Take your hands off me, you thief! Call the police, Jack. Do something! We must get the rubies back. She must tell us where they are.'

'The pawnshop, Father,' Clara said eagerly. 'That's where she took them, I'm certain.'

At that moment the front door opened and Richie came into the hall. Clara's look of dismay at his arrival was quickly concealed. Instead she rushed out to meet him, as though welcoming him.

'Richie! Thank heavens you've come home,' she panted, excitement vibrating in her voice. 'Jenni Goodenough is a thief. She's stolen my diamonds and, worse still, the Tregevny Rubies. I found a pawn ticket in her room. We're sending Doris to fetch a policeman.'

Richie limped into the sitting-room, taking off his trilby and unbuttoning his coat. He stared around at them all without speaking, his expression grave and stony. Light flickered in his eyes like flames of cold fire and Jenni was afraid. She'd ruined his plan to usurp Jack so now he'd be against her, too. She felt all hope seeping out of her heart.

Everyone else, staring at Richie's calm reception of the news, seemed to be struck dumb, too. Unable to bear the dreadful silence any longer, a silence that seemed to hold her future in the balance, Jenni cried out despondently: 'I didn't do it, Richie! It's all lies!'

'I've been waiting for this,' he said grimly. 'I've known the rubies were missing for over a week.'

'What? Why the hell didn't you say something?' Jack shouted at him wrathfully. 'We could've had her behind bars sooner.'

'I said nothing because I've been waiting for the thief to make a move. Now she has.'

Jenni felt the hand of fate close around her heart, squeezing out the last dregs of hope. Since her mother's death she'd been the victim of spite and prejudice. Jack had betrayed her and made her a fallen woman. Now Clara, with Richie's help, would send her to prison for no other reason than that she had loved unwisely. Was there no justice?

'Richie, I swear I'm innocent,' she uttered shrilly, despair settling on her like a shroud. 'I'm not a criminal. Please help me.'

But he ignored her plea as if she'd not spoken.

'The rubies are safe, Father,' he went on without a change of expression. 'Nathan Joseph remembers the young woman who brought them in; Clara's diamond earrings and the photograph frames, too.'

Samuel seemed to rally at the good news.

'We must retrieve the rubies. Jack! Take the ticket. Go now, immediately.'

'No!' Richie thundered, moving to the fireplace, his stance authoritative. 'Nathan's given the rubies to Violet and *I* say she keeps them,' he went on firmly. 'They last belonged to Mother, and it's only right her daughter should inherit them.'

'But the family tradition of the Tregevny Rubies must go on, Richie,' Samuel blustered, struggling to his feet again. 'I demand Jack fetches them now.'

'Family tradition, my backside!' Richie exclaimed furiously. 'We're done with all that hypocrisy, Father. What've *we* got to be proud of as a family, eh?'

He gave his brother a scornful glance.

'Jack's a feeble, unprincipled philanderer . . .'

'Damn you, Richie!' Jack exploded. 'I'm a war hero.'

'You're a pathetic weakling who can't keep his flies buttoned!'

'Richie!' Samuel's grey face turned pink for a moment before he subsided.

'I won't beat about the bush, Father,' Richie snapped. 'I've kept the business going throughout the war and since. It would've gone to the dogs otherwise, and if you leave the shop to Jack, then it surely will.'

'You're a bloody hypocrite yourself!' Jack shouted. 'I'm not standing for this.'

'No, it isn't the time or the place, Richie,' his father quavered. 'The Tregevny Rubies were taken from this house.' He lifted a shaking hand and pointed at Jenni. 'And she's stolen them.'

'Never mind the bloody rubies!' Richie stormed, his eyes flashing with anger. 'Things are coming to a head in this house. It's my future I'm thinking of now. I haven't worked the skin off my fingers all these years to take a back seat when you're gone.'

'This is betrayal,' wailed Samuel, sprawling in his chair. 'I can't stand much more. I'm an old man . . .'

'Yes, you are, Father,' Richie said sadly, his shoulders sagging. 'You should've left the business years ago, and divided it equally between Jack and me. That would've been the fair way, but instead you took pleasure in playing your sons off against each other. Well, I've had enough!'

He glanced around at them all, a sardonic smile on his lips, yet Jenni thought it was self-mocking, too.

'Tregevny tradition be buggered! This family hasn't much to crow about – a self-centred wilful old man clinging blindly to the past; a whining womaniser with no guts; and me, a cripple . . .'

His voice caught. 'What woman will look at me as a husband? What chance have I of a family of my own?'

Jenni was touched by the despair and longing in his voice, and felt a sudden sympathy for him. They'd never got on very well but now she realised, perhaps too late, that he was worth twenty of his brother. At least he had integrity and wasn't two-faced and selfish like Jack. If only he'd help her now.

'Richie,' Jenni began pleadingly. 'Please believe me . . .'

'Be quiet!' he retorted harshly, his previous anger returning. 'I'll get to *you* soon enough.'

She stepped back, shocked, chiding herself for giving him a moment's sympathy. Of course she wouldn't get any help from him. For all his criticisms of his family, he still believed the Tregevnys were a cut above and she no more than the daughter of an infamous murderer.

She glared at him, disappointment fuelling her anger, but with an impatient shake of his head he turned away to look at Clara who bridled immediately, hand clutching at the string of pearls at her throat.

'And as for my dear sister-in-law,' he said, raw scorn in his voice, 'Clara believes money and the Trevegny name can make here into a lady despite having the town tart for a mother. Yes, I know about that, too.'

Clara glowered at him in fury for a moment, then after a swift glance at Jack visibly relaxed, letting go her tight hold on the pearl necklace, obviously relieved Richie had nothing worse to say of her.

'I can't help having Kitty for a mother,' she said, her chin rising in a belligerent tilt. 'And I've risen above it. I've kept myself respectable and cultivated influential friends. I'm a Tregevny through and through.'

'You're a liar, a thief and a murderer!' yelled Richie wrathfully, his face turning dull red with anger. 'I knew you for trash from the start.'

'No!' Clara screamed a furious protest, lips drawn back in a snarl, looking like a cornered alley cat.

'You stole the rubies and you deliberately pushed Jenni down the stairs,' he continued passionately. 'Not out of jealousy over Jack, because you wouldn't give two tin cans for him. No, it was from plain greed and base pride. If Jenni had married me, her child would have put you in the back seat as regards Father's damned will. So you decided you'd be better off if Jenni and her child were dead.'

Clara rushed to Samuel's chair, falling on her knees and taking hold of his hand. The old man seemed dazed, looking from one to the other of them in utter bewilderment. For a moment Jenni wondered if his mind had gone completely.

'Don't listen to him, Father,' Clara cried out, panic in her voice. 'Nothing he says is true. He's out for his own ends – trying to discredit Jack and me. He pretends he wants equal shares but really he wants it all. He condemns Jack when with that game foot he's only half a man himself.'

Jenni could only gape with astonishment at this sudden turn-about and the spectacle they made, a family in turmoil.

No one was taking any notice of her and she was tempted to slip away. She took a few tentative steps towards the door, then hesitated as Richie spoke again.

'Clara's guilty and I have the proof,' he said flatly. 'Nathan Joseph recognised her when she brought the rubies to his shop. She seemed desperate for money and he gave her eighty pounds. So, if anyone goes to prison, it should be her.'

Samuel moaned and muttered incoherently while Jack took a few steps towards his brother, expression tight with anger, fists clenched as though about to square up. He thrust his head forward belligerently.

'It won't work, Richie, because I'll stop you.'

He looked scornfully at Jack's clenched fists then glanced up at his scowling face.

'Don't be a bloody fool, Jack,' he said contemptuously. 'She's not worth it, never was, and you've always known that. Now you're going to rue the day you married her.'

'Jack, you're a fool!' Clara shrilled hysterically, rising to her feet. 'You're letting him ruin us both. Do something! Stop him!'

But Jack's face turned pale as he stood for a moment eye to eye with his brother then stepped back.

'Damn you, Jack!' Clara's piercing scream was one of hysteria. 'Stop being such a weak, lily-livered coward.' Her eyes were glittering with naked malice. 'Act like a man for once. Shut him up. Kill him if you have to!'

There was a shocked silence in which even Jack stared at his wife in dismay while she stood there, hatred and contempt for each of them on her face. Her expression was so raw and revealing that Jenni had to turn her gaze away, feeling she was witnessing something obscene.

'Well, there you have it, Father,' Richie said scornfully, breaking the awful silence that gripped them all. 'Your blue-eyed boy and his lady wife. Condemned from her own lips.'

'You stupid, greedy bitch!' Jack howled in fury at Clara. 'Now you've really done for us. I knew you'd go too far one day.'

'Jenni, do you want to bring charges against Clara?'

Mesmerised by the drama of it all, she jumped at the sound of Richie's question and hesitated, staring at the undiluted malice and hatred still shining in Clara's eyes. Her tormentor should be punished, but it would only mean Jenni's exposing herself to more ridicule and she didn't have the strength to face public humiliation again. All she wanted now was to be left alone to get on with her life as best she could and finish grieving for her child.

'No,' she answered quietly. 'But that's not for the sake of the Tregevny name. After being deceived, betrayed and losing my baby, I've been through enough pain and persecution already. I can't take anymore.'

A slow smile of relief was spreading over Clara's face. Seeing it, a great rage swelled in Jenni's breast and she turned her furious gaze on Jack.

'You've turned a blind eye to having a common tart for a mother-in-law, Jack, but can you stomach a big-time gangster for a father-in-law?' asked Jenni in ringing tones. 'Mr Napier knows all about that, too.'

'What?'

'Didn't Clara tell you about her father – Charlie Pendle?' Jenni's smile was bitter. 'I'll bet she didn't! He's the most feared criminal in this town. An evil man who'll stop at nothing, not even brutal cold-blooded murder. Well, like father, like daughter!'

Clara's face paled and her jaw dropped at the mention of that name. Jack threw his wife an uncertain glance.

'What's she talking about?'

'It's true, Jack,' Jenni assured him loudly and with satisfaction. 'It's only a matter of time before Charlie Pendle decides blackmailing his daughter and well-to-do in-laws is a profitable little sideline. After all, Kitty Price has been doing it for months.'

'She's lying, Jack!' Clara cried out, taking quick steps towards him. 'I swear!'

'You're the liar!' he shouted, his face twisted with rage. 'Well, I've had enough of you and your scheming and conniving. Look what you've done, you bitch! You've ruined me.'

He turned and strode towards the door. Clara raced after him, tearing at his sleeve as he reached the doorway.

'Jack! Where are you going? Don't leave me here to face things alone. You've got to stand by me, I'm your wife . . . I'm a Tregevny!'

He pushed her from him violently.

'No! Stay away from me, Clara!'

'But I did it all for you, Jack, for our future,' she wailed like a banshee. 'That cheap little tramp was after you but I stopped her. The baby was a real threat. I . . . I can never have children, Jack, and Father would've favoured Richie with a wife and child. I *had* to do it! It was for us.'

'Liar!' Jack spat out the word, his face chalky white. 'You did it for yourself. I had no part in it.'

His gaze on her was icy cold and Clara's face paled, eyes widening with panic.

'We're finished,' he said, his voice hard and unforgiving. 'As from this minute you're no longer my wife; no longer a Tregevny. You're nothing and no one. And remember this . . .' he stabbed an index finger in her direction '. . . you had bugger all when I married you, you take bugger all when you go. No clothes, no jewellery. Nothing. Understand me?'

'You can't do this to me!' Clara shrieked, dread in her voice. She tore desperately at his sleeve again as he tried to stride away. 'What will I do? I have no money. Where will I go?'

'What the hell do I care?' he thundered, shrugging her away. 'You're poisoned meat! Go to your filthy mother in the Cwm. Get back to the gutter where you belong!'

'Jack!'

Wrenching himself free of her clutching hands at last, he strode out into the hall. A moment later Jenni heard the front door slam behind him.

Clara turned slowly in the doorway to stare at them, her white face stricken with horror and disbelief. She took a few hesitant steps forward, entreaty in her eyes as she looked at Samuel.

'Father?'

But with a strangled cry he struggled up from his chair and shuffled to the door, edging round her into the hall as though she were a gibbering monster from the depths of hell.

Clara turned back to the room and seemed to sway on her feet, arms hanging loosely at her sides, jaw slack, eyes vacant.

Jenni had never seen a person so utterly crushed and distraught as Clara was at that moment. It was hardly surprising, though. Everything she'd acquired for herself, everything she'd schemed and plotted for, had been taken from her. Her whole hard-won way of life was gone, past and future wiped out by her own avarice and jealousy.

Looking at Clara, destroyed by her own base nature, Jenni couldn't feel one smidgen of pity. Natural justice *had* prevailed. Her baby was revenged.

Jenni's one thought now was to get out of Abertawe House and never return. She didn't want anything from here, not even her own meagre possessions; they were tainted somehow.

She moved towards the door and no one tried to stop her. She paused as she came level with Clara.

'You did this to yourself,' Jenni said to her with deep contempt. 'And I wouldn't be you for the world.'

Chapter Thirty-One

Jenni's step was light as she jumped off the tram in Neath Road and hurried quickly towards Hafod Row, eager to tell Renee and Meg her good news.

She hardly glanced at Tregevny's shop as she went by. Ten days had passed since that terrible showdown with Clara, and though Jenni still wept at night for her lost child, she'd pushed everything else into a dark corner of her mind, hoping it would all be lost and forgotten.

She stepped eagerly over the threshold of Meg's house, running down the passage to the back room, shouting gleefully.

'Renee! Meg! I've found a job!'

Renee bobbed her head out of the scullery as Jenni burst into the room.

'Oh! Jen, kid, glad you're back. Listen, there's . . .'

'Did you hear what I said, Renee?' Jenni exclaimed with a laugh, snatching off her hat. 'I've got a job. A very nice ladies' and gents' outfitters in Oxford Street, opposite the market. Very handy, isn't it?'

'Jen, love, listen . . .'

She shrugged out of her coat and threw it over the back of a nearby chair. She was so pleased about this job, especially since Renee had given up hers at Tregevny's, unwilling to work for the people who'd treated Jenni so badly. Things had been tight for a week or two, but now she could start repaying her friends all she owed to them.

'You'd like the manager, Renee,' she went on, bubbling with excitement. 'Mr Bennett's very nice, a real gentleman. I'll be doing alterations first, but Mr Bennett says there's plenty of scope for a girl with my qualifications.'

Renee came quickly out of the scullery and clutched at her arm.

'Jenni! Listen, will you?'

She glanced round at her mother sitting silent in her chair at the range, and then Jenni noticed Meg's round eyes and flushed face, and knew something had disturbed both of them.

'What's the matter?'

'You've got a visitor waiting in the parlour.'

'Who?'

'Mr Richie.'

Jenni's feeling of euphoria disappeared immediately as though washed away by a shower of cold water. The muscles in her chest tightened spasmodically and suddenly she was short of breath.

'I won't see him, Renee! Tell him to go.'

Her friend squeezed her hand reassuringly, tilting her head and smiling coaxingly.

'Don't be hasty, kid,' she said gently. 'He's been waiting over an hour. He looks a bit – well – upset.'

'Upset?' Jenni blurted. 'Well, that's rich, that is! After what his family did to me.'

'Now, Jen!' Renee said, reproach in her voice. 'No one can be held responsible for their families, can they? Mr Richie never did anything to you personally.'

Jenni bit her lip in vexation, unable to refute that argument. He'd tried to help her when she was expecting, and he'd exposed Clara, saving her from prison, perhaps. But he'd helped himself, too!

Renee was right, though, Jenni conceded, and her shoulders drooped. She knew she'd have to give in and see him.

'Only for a minute, mind, Renee,' she said grudgingly. 'What does he want anyway?'

Renee shrugged, glancing at her mother again, and Jenni hoped with all her heart no further trouble was in store for them. Suppose old Samuel wanted to evict them? She wouldn't put it past him.

Bristling with indignation, she flung open the parlour door and Richie rose awkwardly to his feet. They stared at each other for a moment before Jenni marched in, hands on hips, chin high.

'What do you want, Richie? Why are you here?'

In summertime the sun shone through the parlour window for most of the afternoon and so it was very warm. Richie put his fingers to the knot in his tie and made an attempt to loosen it, a film of sweat on his upper lip.

'I wanted to talk to you . . .'

'Talk!' Jenni responded waspishly. 'After all that's happened? Huh! I'm surprised you've got the nerve to look me in the eye!'

'I thought you'd want to know what's happened since Clara . . .'

'She can go to hell as far as I'm concerned!' Jenni exclaimed in exasperation.

'She probably has,' said Richie. 'Jack kicked her out that same night. It was very late. I don't know where she went. I thought he might've left it till morning but Jack's as unforgiving as granite, as you well know.'

'So am I,' Jenni said quickly. 'I'm not interested in Clara or any Tregevny for that matter. I'd hoped never to set eyes on any of you again.'

A trace of emotion passed across his face. It was so fleeting Jenni had no time to recognise it.

'If you've come to tell us we're evicted,' she went on, a bitter edge to her voice, 'think again! Meg's rent book is up to date so Samuel's got no legal reason.'

'My father's past reason,' Richie said with a tremor in his voice. 'He can do no more now than sit in the front room, bemoaning the imminent collapse of the business.'

Jenni was startled and stared at him aghast.

'The business is in trouble?' For all the harm the family had done her she wouldn't want that.

'Of course not,' Richie assured her quickly. 'His mind has gone. The business is doing well and Jack's much subdued. Pulling his weight at last.'

'Well, if it's not to evict us then what has brought you here? What more does your family want from me?'

'I couldn't help overhearing you mention a job in town,' he said cautiously. 'I wanted to tell you there's still a job for you at our shop. You and Renee, too.'

Jenni stared at him in disbelief.

'Is this some kind of a joke?'

'You need work . . .'

'I've found work. What I *need*,' replied Jenni between clenched teeth, 'is plenty of distance between me and anyone named Tregevny. Do you imagine I could ever work alongside Jack again?'

'We could work something out . . .'

Jenni turned to the parlour door and held it wide open.

'You'd better go, Richie.'

'I know you've been through a lot . . .'

'I've been through hell, Richie!' She clasped her hands to her head, suddenly overcome with anger and grief. 'God! I wish I'd never set eyes on the shop, or you, or Jack. Look what you've done to me.'

'Not me personally, Jenni,' he retorted sharply. 'I tried to help, remember? I asked you to marry me and you accepted. That offer still stands.'

She stared at him for a moment in utter astonishment, then expelled her breath noisily, her exasperation growing.

'When I said I'd marry you, Richie, that was in another life – another time. I was desperate, wasn't I? Hardly in my right mind.'

He scowled, his face darkening.

'You mean, in your right mind you wouldn't dream of marrying a cripple. Is that it?'

'You're twisting my words!' she exclaimed in consternation. 'That's not what I meant at all! I agreed because I was in trouble, and you wanted a ready-made family to influence your father. It was convenient for both of us, wasn't it?'

He was silent, and she took a deep breath before going on.

'There's no reason for us to marry now. My baby's gone, and you've toppled Jack already. There's nothing to be gained.'

'People marry for reasons other than gain,' he said quietly. 'Like love, for instance.'

'Love?' Jenni was scornful. 'I loved and look where it got me! No, I've had enough of love for a while.'

'You don't mean that.'

She set her mouth angrily.

'Stop telling me what I do and don't mean, Richie,' she cried loudly. 'You're not welcome here. Please get out of this house.'

She tried to shepherd him towards the door, but without warning he caught at her arms and shook her.

'Shut up and listen to me, you little spitfire!' he yelled.

Jenni struggled furiously against his grip.

'Take your hands off me! How dare you? This is outrageous!'

'Be quiet then and listen,' he gasped, his face reddening. 'I'm trying to tell you that I love you.'

Jenni stopped struggling and stared up at him.

'What?'

'I've loved you from the beginning, but I could see you had eyes only for Jack.'

'Richie, you don't know what you're saying . . .'

'I know what I'm saying only too well. And I've known heart-break, watching you fall under Jack's spell; knowing what a philandering swine he is; knowing you were heading for disaster.'

Jenni's mouth tightened.

'Then why didn't you tell . . .'

'I tried to warn you he was married, Jenni, but you wouldn't listen. You were pigheaded then, and you're pigheaded now.'

He released her and she stepped back, her head tilted to one side, regarding him closely.

Yes, that day in the cashier's office, Richie had said Jack was a man of straw, but she wouldn't wait to hear one word against the man she adored. She could have saved herself so much torment if only she'd listened. She'd paid too much heed to a gypsy's prophecy. Real life wasn't like that. So much foolishness!

'Yes, I remember, Richie,' she said quietly. 'I thought you were warning me off because I wasn't good enough for a Tregevny.'

'Not good enough?' He gave a gentle laugh. 'I wanted you for myself. I was besotted, and jealous as hell of Jack. I thought showing him up for a fraud would give me a chance.'

He stepped closer to her and his voice was throaty as he went on: 'I want you, Jenni, desperately. All along I wanted to marry you for love, not gain. I still do.'

'Richie, please don't say anymore . . .'

'Look, Jenni, can't we put the past behind us? Forget all that's happened. Start again. I love you, I really do. Please say you'll be my wife?'

She stared up into his face for a moment, seeing the light in his eyes, a light she'd glimpsed briefly before. It half convinced her he was speaking from his heart, but the idea was still too fanciful.

She turned to stare out of the parlour window, weighing up her words, searching for the right ones. An old dray horse, pulling a wagon piled high with sacks of coal, clumped past on the road outside. It reminded her of the first day she'd arrived in Swansea, so full of hopes and dreams. How badly wrong she'd gone, but she'd not rush into another mistake. Perhaps Richie did love her, and then again, perhaps not.

She turned to him, her answer clear in her mind.

'I suppose I should say I'm honoured,' she began. 'But too much water has passed under the bridge for that.'

A spasm crossed his face.

'Jenni, please wait . . .'

'I won't marry you, Richie, for a number of reasons. I couldn't live in Abertawe House if you paid me. It's where my baby died, and I hate each and every brick, every damned slate on the roof. I never want to set eyes on Jack or your father again .'

He took a step forward as though to seize her again.

'Jenni, I'll give up my interest in my father's shop. Jack can have it all, and welcome. I'm a damn' good tailor. I'll start my own business some other place. I'll buy a house somewhere – anywhere you say. All I want is you, Jenni.'

'You can't give up your birthright. It wouldn't be right.' She shook her head, impressed by his words despite herself, but she wouldn't be swayed. 'Besides, it wouldn't work.'

'Why not?'

Jenni bit her lip, knowing that what she had to say would sound brutal.

'Because I don't love you, Richie, and I won't marry a man I don't love.'

He looked stricken, and his voice was thick with emotion when he replied.

'You can't dismiss me so quickly. I love you, Jenni, and I've waited so long . . . I can't go on without you. Please don't turn me away out of hand.'

She was upset.

'Please don't make this anymore difficult, Richie . . .'

'I'll go down on my knees.'

To her utter astonishment, he went down on one knee, his

poor crippled foot twisted at a painful angle on the rug behind him, and she was immediately and deeply touched by the sight.

'Look! I'm begging.' His eyes were glowing with feelings so intense she was in no doubt of his sincerity. 'Please, Jenni, please marry me.'

'Get up, Richie, for goodness' sake!' Deeply embarrassed, as much for him as for herself, Jenni tugged at his arm, helping him to his feet.

'The answer's still no, I don't love you.'

He turned away in despair, clutching his hands to his head.

'Oh, God! What do I have to do?'

He sounded so lost Jenni's heart was wrenched by pity and guilt. Causing him pain was the last thing she'd intended yet she needed to be wary. She'd suffered too much to be impulsive now.

Richie did love her, of that she was certain at last, and real love, true love, was too precious to be kicked aside as Jack had done to hers. It was only right that she should give Richie his chance, but without making any rash promises. There'd be no rushing headlong into a relationship. What she needed, what they both needed, was time. Perhaps given that she could learn to love him.

'What are your feelings about courtship, Richie?'

He turned to stare at her, apparently so astonished his hands remained resting on his head.

'What?'

Jenni was nettled by his astonishment and lifted her nose in the air.

'I'd want to be courted like any other girl.'

He lowered his hands slowly, gazing intently at her, his expression one of incredulity.

'You want me to court you?'

'Yes, why not? Couples court, see if they're suited and often fall in love.' Half smiling, she gave him a pert look.

'Perhaps I'll even fall in love with you, Richie – in time.'

Something lit up in his eyes and Jenni rushed on hastily, 'I'm not promising anything, mind.'

He smiled, his expression more relaxed.

'What a splendid idea! I'm just surprised I didn't think of it myself.'

Jenni looked down her nose at him.

'Oh, of course!' she said sarcastically. 'How can a simple girl from the Rhondda have any original ideas? A good way to begin a courtship, I'm sure!'

He lifted his hands in apology.

'All right! I'm sorry.' He ran a finger around the inside of his collar. 'When do we begin this courtship?'

Jenni considered. She'd started something now and had to follow it through. It might be interesting at that!

'Next Sunday?' she suggested. 'You can take me for a stroll on the promenade in the afternoon.'

He glanced down at his feet and Jenni knew immediately what was on his mind.

'You're sure you won't mind being seen . . .'

'Richie, forget your foot!'

'All right.' He looked relieved. 'The prom it is. And then?'

'Then we can have tea here with Meg and Renee.'

'Here?'

'I live here, Richie. This is my home. Renee and Meg are my family.' She shrugged. 'Love me, love my family, right?'

'Right!' He nodded. She thought he looked a little bewildered. 'Tea with your family,' he repeated. 'What then?'

Jenni's mind raced. What did courting couples do of a Sunday evening?

'Then chapel – the one you usually go to,' she said confidently. 'We'll be like any other couple, taking time to get to know each other – understand each other.'

'I see.' He rubbed his thumb along his jawline thoughtfully.

'How long will this courtship last? I mean, how long before you know whether you can love me or not?'

Jenni pursed her lips, shaking her head, looking vague.

'Years and years, probably.'

'Oh!'

His crestfallen expression was comical and she had difficulty in controlling an impulse to laugh. He wouldn't understand the sudden lift in her spirits.

'Of course,' she said with studied indifference, 'if my idea of courtship doesn't appeal to you, if it sounds too commonplace and ordinary — well! That's just the way I am, isn't it?'

'Commonplace? Ordinary?' He laughed out loud, tenderness sparkling in his eyes. 'Oh, no, not you, Jenni!'

He lifted his hand and gently stroked her cheek. Jenni was surprised to feel a quiver of pleasure at his touch.

'You're the most beautiful, wonderful girl in the world.' He gave a deep sigh. 'I do love you, Jenni, and I'll wait, no matter how long it takes, just so long as we're together.'

She realised she'd been holding her breath and let it out slowly, feeling a glow of something — was it happiness?

'Well, then,' she said breathlessly, 'I expect my family are dying to know what we're talking about in here, and they'll want to quiz my new young man.'

She took his arm, drawing him towards the parlour door.

'Come on, Richie,' she urged eagerly. 'Come and have a cup of tea while we tell them our good news.'